Limbus, Inc.
Book I

A Shared World Experience

Jonathan Maberry
Joseph Nassise
Benjamin Kane Ethridge
Anne C. Petty
Brett J. Talley

JournalStone
San Francisco

JOURNALSTONE
YOUR LINK TO ARTISTIC TALENT

JournalStone books may be ordered through booksellers or by contacting:

JournalStone
www.journal-store.com
www.journalstone.com

ISBN: 978-1-936564-52-1   (sc)
ISBN: 978-1-936564-74-3   (hc)
ISBN: 978-1-936564-75-0   (ebook)

Library of Congress Control Number: 2012956364

Printed in the United States of America
JournalStone rev. date: April 26, 2013

Cover Design: Rob Grom
Cover Photograph © Shutterstock.com

Edited by: Anne C. Petty
Epilogue and Prologue: Brett J. Talley

Dedication

For Constance L. Payne, my daughters, Emily and Cassidy, and my unborn son, Domenic

—Christopher C. Payne

Acknowledgements

Special thanks to Anne C. Petty for coming up with the incredible idea, pulling the stories together and for her patience with me throughout this process; also thanks to Brett J. Talley, Jonathan Maberry, Benjamin Kane Ethridge, and Joseph Nassise for working with JournalStone and taking a chance on us.

—Christopher C. Payne

Endorsements

"This shared-world anthology about a mysterious metaphysical employment agency is pleasingly consistent in tone. The execution and intriguing theme leave the reader wanting more." —Publishers Weekly

"In this initial volume of a shared-world anthology, five authors provide their takes on one-of-a kind jobs that are not always survivable. **VERDICT:** Though the employment agency frame might not seem compelling, the stories cut to the heart of sf, fantasy, and horror." — Library Journal

"*Limbus, Inc.* is a brilliant concept that lets writers share a world while allowing their imaginations free rein. Ethridge, Mayberry, Nassise, Petty, and Talley take full advantage of all that creative elbow room and serve up some tasty stories. Do not miss this." —F. Paul Wilson

"Listen up, fans. *Limbus, Inc.* is a delight. Remember all those alternate universes suggested by classics such as The *Outer Limits* and *The Twilight Zone*? Turns out they're for real. Only one sinister corporation controls all of the entrances—and there are no exits." — Harry Shannon, Stoker nominated author of *Dead and Gone* and *The Hungry*

"*Limbus, Inc.* is one of the strangest, creepiest things I've read in a long time. Guaranteed to send all you conspiracy theorists out there into paroxysms of paranoid delight! Well, you did warn us." —Brian Knight, author of *The Phoenix Girls, Book 1: The Conjuring Glass*

"Get street level in crazy town. *Limbus, Inc.* finds a new kind of noir."
—Weston Ochse, author of *Seal Team 666*

"The five novellas in *Limbus, Inc.* are the kind of horror fiction I love most: Smart, scary, funny, edgy, melancholy, and set in a world I recognize all too well. The most frightening elements here aren't alien princesses with insatiable appetites, ancient murder cults, or shapeshifting assassins, but desperation, hunger, neverending wars, and a wealthy class all too eager to prey on the rest of us. *Limbus, Inc.* isn't just kickass—it's five kinds of kickass." —Lisa Morton, four-time Bram Stoker Award-winning author of *The Castle of Los Angeles*

"*Limbus, Inc.* is the best shared world anthology I've come across in the last twenty years. It was absolutely outstanding—five perfect stories from five of the top names in the business. Editor Anne C. Petty has put together such a flexible, yet finely realized world here that the five voices she's brought together sound like a choir warmed up in hell. This book is going to set the bar for shared world anthologies for a long time to come. Mark my words." —Joe McKinney, Bram Stoker Award-winning author of *Flesh Eaters* and *Inheritance*

"It's an inventive piece of *fiction* that will haunt your dreams forever." And remember, always read the fine print." - Betsy A. Riley, HorrorZine

"I can honestly say that all of the stories in *Limbus, Inc.* were riveting – to the point of being mesmerizing. If you are looking for an anthology that is truly different from the run of the mill, and one that takes itself seriously enough to commission the best tales from its first class authors, then I highly recommend you pick *up Limbus, Inc.*" - TT Zuma – HorrorWorld.com

"An infinity of Earths and an infinity of possibilities…all connected by a single shadowy entity—*Limbus, Inc.* Too large for a single volume, the tales of *Limbus, Inc.*, explore worlds of the imagination. And far beyond. But beware! Like so many good things, the stories of *Limbus, Inc.*, can be addicting. One is just not enough. For those of us who welcome the obsession to excellent storytelling, there is an entire volume…and more to come." – Dr. Michael R. Collings

"Five excellent authors. Five wonderful stories. Slaughterers and robot emissaries. Slave traders and monsters. Welcome to the amazing multiverse of *Limbus, Inc.*" – Allyson Bird, Author

What Is Limbus?

Limbus is Latin for "edge" or "boundary," but that's not the whole story.

Welcome to the world of Limbus, Inc., a shadow organization at the edge of reality whose recruitment methods are low-rent, sketchy, even haphazard to the ordinary eye: a tattered flyer taped to a bus-stop shed or tacked to the bulletin board of a neighborhood laundromat, a dropped business card, a popup ad on the Internet. Limbus's employees are as suspicious and ephemeral as the company, if indeed it could be called a company in the normal sense of the word.

Recruiters offer contracts for employment tailored exactly to the job seeker in question. But a word to the wise... it's always a good idea to read the fine print.

Table of Contents

Prologue

Ichabod Templeton hid in shadow, for the ones he feared walked in the light. He clutched a leather-bound book to his chest, eyeing the early evening revelers as they passed. They didn't notice him, crouching in darkness. Or maybe that was all part of their plan. Lure him into a sense of ease. Make him think that he had finally escaped their gazes. And then strike. No, Ichabod thought, shaking his head against the idea. He had come so far. He would not fail now.

He crept through the alleys and back ways of Boston, hiding himself in the maze of the city. But he was not lost. He knew where he was going, even if he had never been there, even with no map to lead the way. Something inside, some preternatural sense, guided his footsteps.

He found himself in the North End of the great city, not that he would have known the name of that place. He cut through the old burying ground at Copp's Hill, past the ancient, crumbling tomb of Cotton Mather, into the labyrinth of narrow corridors and side streets north of Prince. He stopped at the mouth of one and stared with sudden recognition at a ramshackle storefront. He had reached his destination. He pulled the old book closer, rubbing his hands along the coarse leather while the setting sun cast longer and deeper shadows than even the one in which he stood. Yes, this was the place. This was his destiny.

* * *

The antique grandfather clock—the one he had inherited from his father's father—struck seven, but Matthew Sellers didn't hear it. He stared at the blinking cursor on his computer screen, as if willing it to type some good news. It was well past closing time, and Matthew should have been home, tucked away in the garret that sufficed for a living space. But he always found himself staying late on the days he reviewed the budget, as if working harder would result in more income. But as his eyes scanned the black and red numbers in the ledger—the latter in greater quantity and size than the former—he knew that such was wishful thinking at best.

The used book store had always been a dream of his, as had the small-press publishing company he had started along with it. He'd created Unbound with money his parents had left him in their will, and at first, the store had been something of a cultural phenomenon in Boston's increasingly bourgeois North End. Unfortunately, like all such phenomena, Matthew's star had burned out as quickly as it had ignited. The elite moved on to the next distraction, and Matthew often wished he had opened the store in the Back Bay or on Newbury Street, even if he knew he could never have afforded it.

It had been bad for a while, but the last month had been particularly unsuccessful.

"Well," he mumbled to himself, "I guess it's time to get a real job."

The door to the shop opened, and the antique bell Matthew had installed above it announced his visitor with an enthusiastic jingle. Even though he needed the business, Matthew looked up with every intention of turning the customer away. His mouth hung open, the words died in his throat when he saw the man standing before him.

He didn't know whether to pity or fear him. The man was one part professor, another part homeless derelict. His tan trench coat hung limp from his skeletal frame, splattered with mud along its edges. His soiled clothing and unkempt beard said he hadn't bathed in days or perhaps weeks even. But it was his eyes that held Matthew. Blue as the ocean on a summer's day, yet trembling in what Matthew could only assume was fear behind the wire-rimmed glasses of an artist.

"Can I help you?" Matthew stammered. It was only then he noticed the leather-bound tome the man hugged, clinging to it as if it were the most important item he had ever possessed. As if he feared that at any moment, someone would try to take it from him.

"Yes," the man croaked. "Yes, I think you are the only person who can."

For a long moment the two men assessed one another across the swirling dust that filled the space between them. Then something in the stranger's mind clicked, and he took a step into the center of the room. He held the book in his hands, reaching it out to Matthew as he stumbled toward him.

"This is for you." He placed the book on the desk, but it still did not leave his hands. Matthew saw a storm of conflicting emotions in his eyes. Finally he withdrew, and as he did, a wave of relief poured over his face.

"Please," Matthew said, "take a seat."

The man glanced down at the chair, and just as Matthew began to doubt he would accept the offer, down he sat.

"So I didn't get your name."

"Ichabod. Ichabod Templeton."

Matthew tried not to smile. He was sure it wasn't an alias. No one would be so creative.

"Matthew Sellers."

He opened the leather cover of the book and immediately frowned. It wasn't an antique book as he'd originally thought. Instead, it was some sort of diary, one that someone— Ichabod, likely—had filled with his own ramblings. Some pages were nothing but handwritten scrawl, barely legible in parts. Others were poorly typed, while yet more had computer printouts glued or stapled on top of them.

"Mr. Templeton . . ."

"I wrote it in three days," Templeton said. His hands shook and his voice was feverish. "I didn't eat or bathe, nor did I sleep. It was my obsession. It is my masterpiece."

"Mr. Templeton, I am sure you worked very hard on this, but I only purchase published books for the store. I am afraid I . . ."

"Oh, no no, you misunderstand, Mr. Sellers. I don't want to sell the book to you. I am giving it to you. I want you to publish it. The story I have to tell is far too important to be confined within the meager leather bindings of a single manuscript. No, the world must read it. The world must know what I know."

Matthew leaned forward and shook his head. "I don't think you understand, Mr. Templeton. There's a whole process to selling a book. I have to read it and like it. There are legal considerations, contracts to sign. Then we have to think about artists and titles and distribution strategy. And besides, I run a small press here. If you want the world to read your book, you'll probably want to take it somewhere else."

Templeton smiled for the first time, revealing yellow-encrusted teeth. "None of that will be necessary, Mr. Sellers. The book is yours now. I have no doubt that after you read it, you will want to publish it. And then, the world will see. They won't have a choice."

Matthew flipped through pages, suddenly convinced that it was better to play along with Templeton than anger him. He was a man on the edge, and at any moment, he could fall in completely.

"Writing the book wasn't easy," Templeton continued. "Sometimes I had to write by hand. Other times I used my old Olympia Deluxe typewriter. When I was lucky, I wrote on a computer."

"I guess I don't understand," Matthew said. "Why couldn't you just use your computer to write the book?"

"Oh, well, I was on the run most of the time. They were after me, of course."

Matthew closed the book and looked up at Templeton. "Now Mr. Templeton," he said as calmly as he could, very afraid of his guest, "why would anyone be after you?"

"Because I know things," he said. "I know things that are now in that book."

"So this is nonfiction?"

"It is truth," Templeton answered without addressing the question, "distilled down to its finest essence. The line between fiction and nonfiction is a fine one, after all."

"But how did you come upon this story then? Do you have sources? Research?"

Templeton laughed. "Come now, Mr. Sellers. Don't you understand? I didn't ask for this assignment. It was given to me. By God, perhaps, though the origin is irrelevant. I was fated to complete this task. It is my job to reveal them, for what they are. I am the only one who can."

"Them?"

The man smiled again, and this time Matthew saw pity.

"Mr. Sellers, the world is a machine, and like all machines, it requires someone to run it. Otherwise, it would spin out of control. Things must be done, adjustments must be made, the system must be tweaked."

"You're talking about the Illuminati? Free Masons? Conspiracies and secret societies?"

"No, no Mr. Sellers. Nothing so quaint. And nothing so secret. They walk in the light, not the shadows. Secrets breed questions, and questions sometimes have inconvenient answers. No, they are all around you. Working every day. They are neither good nor evil, as such notions are normally counted by mankind. They stand on the edge of the pit, and stare down into its depths. They do what they must. They do what we cannot."

Matthew grinned, shaking head, no longer able or willing to contain his doubt. "I'm sorry Mr. Templeton, but I don't think I buy any of this."

Templeton rose from his seat and adjusted his glasses. "Read the book, Mr. Sellers. Read it, and then you will know. Belief will follow, as thunder follows the lightning."

Before Matthew could object, Templeton had turned and strode to the door. He didn't stop when Matthew called out his name. The antique bell rang again, and he was gone.

Matthew leaned back in his chair and looked down at the book that sat before him. He rubbed his hands along the leather, opened the cover, and started to read.

The Slaughter Man

By

Benjamin Kane Ethridge

Time stood still, as it always did in this moment, and he felt neither dead, nor alive. As far as his life went, everything important existed only in this sad moment. Nothing before. Nothing after. He couldn't decide if he hated that truth, loved it, or just needed it that way. Living in this instant was who he was, and yet, he'd never really been acquainted with that person. Not really.

Who am I?
What do I want?

As the Sticker punched through the jugular vein and dark red flooded over his apron, he saw a minor commotion up the chain. The first bolt hadn't penetrated the cow's solid cranium. The shackler, Jackson Turner, jogged over and exchanged glances with the stunner, Carl Cabers. The two men spoke something inaudible over the driving noise of the process line. Carl lowered the captive bolt pistol and fired into the cow's skull again. Jackson gave a little electrified hop and returned to the side, taking up the shackles for the animal.

Blood flowed from the drains up the Sticker's ankles and he responded by stepping on a pedal for the hidden sump pump. Further consideration told him this was a bad idea. The abandoned thirty thousand gallon underground tank had been filled to its limit just yesterday. He could no longer use it as a shortcut. The tank had plumbing issues when *Sunshine State Natural Meat Processors* first built the facility, and so it was capped off but never properly backfilled with gravel per city requirements.

The main drain was hidden from view, under the work table where the Sticker's gory equipment usually sat. He ran the pump only when work got moving fiercely. The grade in the floor sloped toward that particular drain anyway, so using it enabled him to go faster than the other stickers (who weren't privy to its whereabouts).

Last week the blood flow started rising under the table. Rather than throw the pump in reverse and send the nasty smelling stuff out to the appropriate drains, he got caught in the workday rush and put it off.

Today, the Sticker just let it be. He would have to be a mortal employee now like everybody else and work at a normal pace. No more super killer, processing twice as many animals as his peers.

A month ago, when Annette had still been in his life, he might have plotted how to empty that tank so he could retain his star quality, and possibly get called up for a management position. That might have made Annette proud of his return to the stockyards. Might have made her see his potential still existed.

Might have made her stay with him.

That wasn't the reality anymore. Annette was gone and he was free to be as mediocre as the rest of the people working in this land of shit and blood.

Jackson brought the shackle up to the cow's dangling hoof. It happened with such suddenness the Sticker only saw Jackson falling, arms out like a messiah, and then he was prone on the corrugated metal floor. The cow's free hoof continued to fling wildly.

The Sticker ran to the thrashing beast, its labored calls louder than the process line. Carl arrived with his bolt gun. He'd already been working on another cow and knew this had to be done quickly. *The chain will not stop* was the company mantra and nobody took it for granted.

Carl aimed at the cow's head. The animal shifted its weight, fell off the processing bar and struck him bodily against the side wall.

The Sticker dropped his knife and threw all his weight into the cow's midsection. Carl broke free; he held his head and blinked spastically before rising on one knee. Jackson still rested on the floor, palm pressed to a spot between his eyes. The Sticker took the bolt gun, put the cow in a side headlock and discharged a bolt into its temple. The bolt retracted and the animal's body jerked. It swung forward and sent the Sticker into the wall, knocking all the air from him. He pushed off the wall and hurried away from any other attack.

As he turned, he caught a glimpse of Jackson staggering over to the cow's inert body. He'd already taken up the shackles again. Someone touched the Sticker's shoulder and he jumped. Carl extended his hand for the bolt gun. The Sticker handed it to him, and then took his knife off the ground and returned to the bleeding floor.

By the time he was set back up, the renegade cow, hanging upside-down in the air by both its ankles now, slid toward him. He stuck the knife just under the jaw and swept across. *You didn't quit*, he thought as he watched the scarlet cascade over his mesh gloves and arm guards. *I used to value the good fight, sir, but now… look at you. Look where the fight ended.*

He pressed the button and the process line buzzed on, the next cow immediately upon him. The Sticker slit another throat and then kicked some accumulated blood toward the other drain. He was surprised the USDA rep hadn't had more to say about his workspace. Oh well, cleanliness wasn't his business. He was just here to do a job and get paid. To live out his wonderful life.

Divorce papers waited for him at home. He wasn't going to be dramatic; he'd sign what had to be signed. He never thought he'd deserved Annette, and over time he guessed she'd discovered this truth as well.

From the time he was seventeen until he was twenty-seven, he'd worked as a sticker. Then he got married and knew that had to change. He got a management job at the frozen onion factory, worked there until he was thirty-one. Five years ago he'd had a plan. He would become a treatment plant operator at Fabulous Onion Foods and take management courses, work up that chain, save money, open a blood sausage facility someday, since there was a surprising demand in the industry. After a paperwork mishap though, the CEO of Fabulous Onion, Trevor Milstead, was the asteroid that destroyed that prospective world and others.

The unemployment wasn't enough to sustain his household. The Sticker refused to let their underwater mortgage go into default for the sake of some out-of-state jobs Annette found online. Leaving his trusted territory in the Inland Empire made him uncomfortable, but he didn't appreciate how much Annette despised that discomfort until it was already too late.

He went back to his old line of work at a new slaughterhouse, which was a pay cut of twenty-five grand—but he knew this kind of work and he trusted this kind of work. Even if he could hardly afford his dumpy apartment.

There was nothing else for Annette to admire in a man so quickly neutered. Her husband was a failure, and an ugly failure at that. The Sticker's crooked teeth were not only unsightly for their angles, but coffee stained. He had bad skin begging for skin cancer, courtesy of his Irish father. And just last week he noticed a small barren spot forming in his otherwise thick blond hair. He'd always called it a cowlick before, but now, no such delusions could be made in earnest. So this was how the hill looked, just as you went down the other side. So much of his life had already passed and yet he'd never felt like it had begun.

The Sticker's gaze drifted outside to the long, winding corral where the cows marched. The bends in the line were so they wouldn't see what they were directly headed for, to keep them tranquil. It was probably the first time the Sticker felt envious of the poor animals.

* * *

Lunchtime wasn't a refreshing occasion. Despite the sterile interior and air conditioning of the admin building, the walls hummed with the odor of cattle and dirt. The Sticker sat at the plastic table in a daze. He tried to will himself to open his brown sack lunch; he knew he'd be hungry later if he skipped, but with Annette lounging over his brain, always in his thoughts, forever and ever there, *with him*, it was impossible to think about eating. He could only glance around at the various groups of workers: the steamers, the singers, shavers, the splitters, shacklers, stunners... it was like a conspiracy of language used to reinforce the idea that all jobs here were created equal. And that wasn't the case. Just ask the shavers and splitters about that.

Personally, he had always been happiest as a sticker (the term bleeder was frowned upon by the management), because his job involved no heavy machinery or lifting. His body was torn up by now anyway, but more from shoveling waste chambers at the onion plant. The rest of these guys, these younger men, they were popping

Advils and Tylenols (Vicodin secretly) and some had bandages chronically appearing on different parts of their body. No way of denying it; the crew was a gruesome lot by day's end.

The Sticker noticed an employment agency's flyer hanging from the cork board. Limbus, Inc. read the top banner, and beneath it, a picture of a globe glowed with needles of light. None of the phone number tags had been ripped from the bottom.

Funny thing to see in this place. Could have used them when I got canned.

Jackson and Carl rambled on about the immortal cow from earlier. Every now and then they would involve the Sticker in the conversation and he would nod with their assessments. Jackson, right as rain now, had a gash in his forehead like a miniature crimson hockey stick. He was lucky he'd backed up when that hoof lashed out, or he'd probably be on permanent break-time right about now.

The room went silent suddenly. Gerald Bailey, facility manager, came through the door. The man never visited unless he wanted to ream someone out. Despite not having a manual job, he was always oily. He lived an air-conditioned existence but kept his blue collared shirt open at the top, where puffs of hoary chest hair sprung free. Seeing as everybody had to wear a hairnet and beard-nets, it was a disconcerting sight to say the least.

"Anybody know why there's a product with three bolt holes in its brain?" he demanded of the entire room. His eyes roved to Jackson. "How'd you get that forehead smile, Action Jackson?"

Jackson stammered. "Shackles struck me in the face... on accident. Got it documented."

"Be the hell more careful." Gerald seemed to grow less agitated and his posture slackened. "So nobody knows about the bolts? Any stunners in here?"

Carl began to stand.

"Sit son, you're still on break. I'm just getting details here."

Carl lowered back down but his eyes didn't move from Bailey. "The first two didn't do the trick, boss."

"Didn't *do the trick*? Is that your excuse?"

Carl frowned. "You counseling me in front of everyone, boss?"

Bailey turned away, muttering something tired and vicious, and his tremendous gut bumped into the Sticker. "Oh pardon—hey you're the new hot shot that upped productivity that one week."

"Two weeks," the Sticker replied.

Bailey's mangy brown eyebrows hauled his weasel eyes up with them. "I know you, don't I? Yeah. You used to work at the Fabulous Onion, on the cutting floor."

"Small world."

"It is. You know Trevor Milstead? Hell of a guy."

"I know him."

Bailey, noticing the conversation's one-sided tilt, went to leave. He halted at the sight of the Limbus flyer and promptly ripped it off the board. "I don't know who keeps putting these up, but they'll likely need to apply at this Limbus place if they keep at it. Any ideas?"

Nobody said anything. After a moment Bailey marched off like a crestfallen general going to war alone.

Somebody whispered, "Why does it matter, one bolt, two or three?"

"Some of the meat is ruint," another replied.

"Inhumane," another guy added.

Leaving his lunch unopened, the Sticker slid out from the table and tapped Carl's shoulder. "You still smoke?"

"Like a chimney."

"Good, I want one."

"Since when?"

The Sticker left the break room and a moment later heard Carl push out his chair.

* * *

He admittedly didn't like the taste, but the lightheaded sensation was welcome right now. In the time it took the Sticker to finish one, Carl had smoked two cigarettes and mistook this as a chance to catch up. The Sticker just wanted to stare off into the trees that lined the parking lot outside the processing plant. Just watch their leaves shake with the occasionally breeze... drift... forget this place... forget her.

Carl ground the butt of his second smoke like he was doing some 50s dance move. "All right then, Mister Talkative, I'll see you on the floor."

He didn't notice as Carl left. These days he didn't notice anybody around him. People were just like those brain-dead cows that came swinging up to him. Substantial only that they took up space and had to be addressed in the moment.

Why? Why was he alone now?

Well, it was simple to explain but impossible to accept. Annette had wanted a life that began and ended in victory, and he'd always hoped she was patient enough for him to accomplish big things. As good as his intentions were to put away money, she saw the writing on the wall after the onion plant. You couldn't save what you didn't have, and when a guy only knew the boundaries of his bubble, finding the wisdom to drop every cent into the right tech stocks was a pretty hard feat to pull off.

Still, his heart wanted him to find a way. That's why he'd gone on Facebook this morning and sent her a message: *Can you just tell me what to do? Come home and I'll do whatever you want. I'll be whatever you want. Right away. This minute. This second. Please. I love you so much. I don't care that you were with Milstead. If you want to come home, none of that matters. I'll be a different person. I'll go anywhere. I'll show you. I'll show you that I'll go far away from here. Another state. Another country. Goddamn, another planet! I don't give a shit anymore. I just need you back.*

Looking back, the message was painfully embarrassing, but he couldn't wait to get home and go online. See if she'd responded.

The warning whistle blew then.

Time to work.

* * *

After a restless night stalking Facebook and staring at his bedroom ceiling, the Sticker shambled from his pickup truck. He closed the door and took a long drink from his coffee thermos. Noticing his shadowy face in the reflection of his window, he leaned forward and started scraping at his bent front tooth. *Love coffee, but goddamn.* Another face floated into the reflection and he turned quickly around.

A black girl, perhaps ten or eleven, stood there. Her hair was straightened and fell down her shoulders like a nighttime rainstorm. She had the peculiar, yet smart, outfit of a business woman. The Sticker had never seen such a small pantsuit in his life. To fit her overall stature, her charcoal coat was also stylish. On the lapel the morning sunlight played off a platinum pin that looked like a miniature globe.

She stuck out her petite dark hand. Her emerald gaze cut into him with intelligence and her smile bent gracefully, powerful with charisma, like a politician's dream. "Tasha Willing."

"You lost from private school, kid?"

Her smile faded only a bit. "I thought we might talk about a job offering. I work for an employment agency."

"That right?" The Sticker took a deeper sip from his thermos. He looked to the processing plant. "Got a job, as you can see."

"You can do better than this."

"Where are your parents, kid? Your old man work here?"

"Perhaps we can set up a meeting after work today?" She expertly retrieved a business card from a side pocket in her coat.

He took it, rather unconsciously and quickly glanced at it. The text on back said: *Take a shot and you'll go far. We employ.*

"Limbus, eh? Well done, kid. Guess you're the one who's pissing off Bailey."

"Bailey?"

"The guy who's gonna be upset if I don't get in there soon."

"Don't let me keep you any longer, sir. Just give me a call when you decide you're ready for something better than this."

The Sticker chuckled. "You're a nut, kid. Have a good day."

He walked past her.

"You too, sir," she said, watching him go.

He must have completely misread the back of the business card before.

Your new job is written in the stars. We employ.

* * *

This wasn't good.

It was only a half an hour until lunch break, so it was very strange that Bailey would call anybody to his office. He normally waited until break and then pretended he "didn't want to interrupt." Reporting to the operational manager's office wasn't as bad for the Sticker as it was for other workers though. He didn't have to walk clear across the plant. Bailey's office was only twenty feet from the bleed floor, right near the mostly shuttered USDA office. Just a hop over the spill containment berm and he was at the door.

The Sticker stood in the surprisingly clean, cinnamon smelling office, taking in the glossy wood paneling, the glass paper weight with a scorpion trapped in it, the photo of a boating event on the Colorado River, the framed newspaper of some quad-bike racing event, the recessed lit painting of a country cottage. Everything was lovingly in its own place, and the greasy man with his disgusting public display of chest hair did not fit the rest of the room.

"Have a seat, man," said Bailey. His eyes were fixed on a Yahoo news article that featured an unflattering photo of President Obama yelling. He closed the web browser and swiveled around in his seat. He noticed the Sticker still stood. "I said sit."

"Hurts my back."

"Fine, shit, fine." Bailey offered a weary look of lifelong annoyance. "So do you know why I called you in here?"

"No clue."

"Really?"

The Sticker shrugged.

Bailey blew out a sigh between his rubbery lips and picked up a stack of papers from his in-basket. He dropped them at the other end of his desk. "What are those?"

"My paycheck stubs, looks like."

"*Looks like* because they are, smart-alec."

"I don't get it."

"Come on, man, don't play dumb. What's all this overtime here?"

"I logged it," replied the Sticker. "HR didn't say anything."

"You don't get to make your own hours, buddy. I ask you to work over and you accept or decline."

"This went on for a month. You saw me here, you never—"

"This is abuse. Other people here are entitled to an eight-hour day."

"First I'm hearing about it."

"No, actually it isn't. Look down at the comment section on the stub."

The Sticker read the note, which looked to be in a different font. *Overtime shall be approved per arrangement by management. See supervisor.*

"When did you add that?"

"Excuse me?"

"That wasn't there before."

"See, that's the problem with you direct-deposit folks. Always forgetting your stubs." Bailey took out what looked to be about a month's worth of paycheck stubs, sealed in envelopes, a rubber band holding them together. All the envelopes looked crisp and new.

The Sticker felt his blood catch fire, but he refused to show the man anything. "You and Trevor Milstead must be good friends, for you to go to all this trouble."

Bailey's face went robotically placid. "Finish your day out there and I'll give your full two weeks pay. Otherwise, you can leave right the hell now and get nothing. Go and have a ball."

Regardless of all he wanted to say, and subsequently do, the Sticker walked out of the sanitary confines of the office and back into the plant, to finish his last day in the blood and filth.

* * *

The Sticker leaned against the moist railing of the production line and wondered if Bailey was still in his office. At this point he was of two minds: he could threaten with wrongful termination, or he could just beat the ever-loving shit out of the guy. As he pondered these options, he found himself strolling the walkway, heading for the office.

No anger, no fear, he arrived at Bailey's door and pushed it open. The man sat in his chair, head back, snoring, that pubic mound of chest hair rising and falling. The Sticker watched him for a couple moments and then shut the door quietly.

Security hadn't come by yet. Those guys were still having their last beers in shipping and receiving probably, but the Sticker didn't want to chance a diversion from their routine, so he moved fast. It was almost laughingly perfect, as though a plan set weeks ago had now come to fruition.

He stopped up the drains and set the hidden sump pump in reverse. The tank was so overloaded, the pump wouldn't make any real noise until the level hit bottom. Curdled, septic, black blood wormed through the grates under his work table and fanned out over the floor. He fought a dry-heave and plugged his mouth with his fist. Stepping around the sludge, he took another moment to admire its grotesquery and happily cringed at the rotten reek. The containment around the bleed floor would not suffice for long. With the pump going full bore, this biological gruel would cascade over the berm in about ten minutes.

The Sticker hoped it flooded Bailey's pristine office before the jackass even woke from his nap. It would be a downright crime not to witness that, but he'd stuck around here long enough and getting going was a better idea.

* * *

From the bed of his pickup, the Sticker watched a blood soaked Gerald Bailey trudge out to the parking lot. The Sticker laughed and unfortunately some Scotch went down the wrong pipe. He coughed out through his watering eyes and tried to clear his sinuses. After cursing a bit, he regained himself and scanned the parking lot for another trace of any of the misery he might have caused. Bailey's headlights went on and he wheeled his truck around in the darkness.

So much for my fun. Wish I could see the full cleanup effort tomorrow.

"Well done," said a voice.

The Sticker almost dropped his bottle of Black Velvet. "Jesus kid, what in the hell are you doing here? Holy shit!"

Tasha Willing stood at the very threshold of dusk. Her green eyes shone. "I heard about what happened and I just wanted to drop by to express how angry I am, on your behalf."

"Heard? How?"

Tasha wound her hand in circles. "All sorts of ways out there to reap information. That's not why I'm here, though. Now that you're free, I'd like to present an opportunity. May I sit?"

The Sticker pressed his lips together and shook his head. Little kids made him uneasy, but calling this girl different from most kids was a colossal understatement. He sidled over. "Sit, but park it way over there. I'm not gonna be framed as a pervert."

Tasha hopped up and smoothed her suit pants down. "May I have a tug on that?"

Looking down at his Scotch whiskey, the Sticker simpered. "So you're determined to get me arrested?"

"That's pretty cheap stuff and it would be better with a little water, but I've had a longer day than you can imagine."

The Sticker glanced around. "Well I didn't see you take it..." He handed over the bottle.

Tasha tipped the Scotch back, swallowed and ran her tongue over her teeth. "Rough stuff, but it's better than the air around here."

He quickly took the bottle back. "Yes, one big cow pie."

"Indeed. Now sir, I'd like to talk about that job—"

"Just cut out the game, kid."

"Tasha."

"Just cut it out, *Tasha*. I'm not in the mood for talking or playing pretend."

"I can find you any job you like, any*thing* you like."

The Sticker glanced up to the sky, gradually dissolving of all light except for a few stars. "Unbelievable," he whispered. How had he managed to lose his job and take on a midget-sized stalker all in one day?

"I'm not lying. Dead serious here."

"Okay," he said, lifting the bottle, then dropping it back down on his knee. "Doesn't matter what the job is, but how about something far the hell away from here? How 'bout that for starters, little girl?"

"You've lived in Azusa your whole life."

"How did you . . . ? Oh forget it. Yeah I have, and I ruined my marriage by staying, so . . . shit why am I saying this stuff to you?"

"I'm the Master Recruiter. I can find you a job somewhere else. That's a non-issue. What do you believe you're good at? I already know your abilities from reading your file, but what you believe is more important."

He opened his mouth and snapped it shut.

"You aren't going to scare me if you say *killing*," Tasha noted.

The Sticker hopped off the tailgate. "Please get down."

"We're just talking here."

"Get down, now. I need to go home."

Tasha slid off the truck and folded her arms. "But really. What now, Slaughter Man?"

That was a good question, but not one with a simple answer.

"I'll be okay. Thanks for caring. Really. It was nice meeting you. Never met a whiz-kid before."

"Me neither."

He laughed dryly and shut the tailgate with Scotch still in hand.

"I'll check in with you tomorrow," she said.

"No, don't."

"Hey, I think you can appreciate keeping a boss happy."

"Might be able to appreciate it, but I'm not very good at it lately."

"Yes, well, I still don't know what you think you're good at."

"Well, I wasn't just going to say *killing* before," he told her and rounded his truck. He opened his door and looked back at the indistinct slaughterhouse. "It's the being numb part that I'm really good at."

Tasha gave him a tiny smile as she fell away, into the night.

*   *   *

He slowly stirred at her touch. The Sticker had been drunk the past three days. He vaguely remembered a call last night from a representative of *Sunshine State Natural Meat Products* inquiring about the discharge of hazardous waste in his work area. The call was intense and legally intimidating (to say the least) and it wouldn't have been a surprise to open his eyes to a fresh-eyed young cop bent over him with a wakey-wakey grin.

But instead, the Sticker saw the one and only person he wished it to be.

Annette fell away from him and sat at the worn swivel chair in front of the computer. Her dark hair was shorter, more styled, and she wore a flowered blouse that revealed enough cleavage to quicken his pulse. He knew though. By her darting eyes and sullen face, it was obvious. She wasn't here to take him back. So he couldn't work himself up to any peak, only to plummet off the side when she left.

"You come over for the last of your clothes?"

She nodded.

"Did you get my email?"

"I haven't been online for a few days," she said.

"Doesn't matter," he replied.

"What did it say?"

He propped up on the couch with one quivering arm. His head felt like a site of constant underwater demolitions. It would have been painless to vomit right now. A morbid part of him fancied puking all over Annette's beautiful blouse and those tits she flashed so cruelly in his face.

"What'd it say?" she repeated.

"Nothing."

"Why did I know you'd answer like that?"

"Probably because we were married…"

She kneaded a knot in her neck. She got those when she was tense. Other than her apparent awkwardness in the moment, she looked great. Her skin was a richer, bronzer color. Natural though.

She'd been to the beach or somewhere outdoors recently. He wanted to tell her but silenced himself before the words formed.

Like some sort of social martyr, her eyes politely drifted away from the table where all his empty beer cans and obliterated bottles of booze congregated. "I just wanted to say, before I go—"

He sat up straight. It felt like someone shot him through the temple with a poisoned arrow. "Yeah?"

"Anyway, I just wanted to say, and this isn't to over-salt your wounds—"

"Hey, I'm not wounded," he snapped.

Her eyes handled him like a mother with a child. "I haven't stopped caring about you, just so you know. I always care. That hasn't changed."

This was an altogether different arrow to the head. "*What?* What does that even mean? I mean, *what the fuck?*"

"Just because we can't work in a marriage doesn't mean we can't work as friends."

The laugh crawling from his throat was nearly sinister. "You walked out because of some bullshit lack-of-ambition reason, when you damn well know I've worked my ass off in everything I've ever done. Now, after all this, you have the nerve to pretend to care about me? I don't believe you. How can you care about this loser, this guy who hasn't amounted to dick? You aren't going to be my friend. You don't need my friendship. You've got a wealthy guy now."

"I don't care about money. I just don't want a hamster in a wheel anymore."

"Well, that Trevor fucker's a rat in a maze."

Annette shrugged. "I wanted a partner. After five years, I'm tired of all the desperation. I'm tired of spinning these wheels. But just because I am, doesn't mean I want you thinking I'm some cruel bitch that never had feelings for you."

The Sticker studied the blue paisley pattern on his boxer shorts. He was silent, unsure of her, unsure of himself. "This is like a bad dream."

Annette looked far more uncomfortable than before. She picked up her purse from the floor and struggled to put its strap over her arm. "I need to go. You'll be late for work."

"I quit."

Her eyebrows knitted. "Really? What, you got something else?"

"Sure did. Met somebody, too."

Annette sharply laughed. "Who?"

"Wouldn't know her. Name's Tasha."

"Ah, I see." She looked up in fake jealousy. "Well, ok, I'll be in touch."

He jumped up, ignoring the shifting world around him. "Don't leave yet. We can have coffee at least, can't we?"

Annette went through the door before he could get there. Chasing her outside would be too much.

But what if this is my last chance?

The Sticker put his hand on the doorknob but couldn't beckon the will power to turn it. He dropped his head against the wood frame and closed his eyes.

When he opened them, he noticed the Limbus card had fallen on the carpet.

The back of it read: *What are you waiting for?*

* * *

By the time he found parking in downtown Los Angeles, the Sticker was close to gassing up and heading back home. It'd been a long, traffic-filled afternoon, and once off the freeways, his web directions led him on several inane detours before reaching the office building. Had he more to go home to, he certainly would have, but with another lawyerly voicemail this morning that added animal cruelty on top of illicit hazardous waste dumping, he supposed there were worse things than being in L.A. with a full bladder and nowhere to park.

He grumpily paid the lot fee and after a brief stop in a gas station bathroom, the Sticker headed toward his destination. A number of businesses shared the office building, mostly real estate and insurance entities. The sparsely decorated lobby was unremarkable in its avocado vinyl chairs and teak and aluminum tables. He was happy with the powerful air conditioning though as he searched the wall chart for Limbus' room number. It was a little nutty, he thought anyway, that he'd come to accept Tasha as a legitimate job contact, but he supposed he was at that point in his life now. Nothing was too crazy. He couldn't stay in his bubble. That damned thing had lost him a good woman. That damned thing had to be popped.

Office #A10.

It bugged him to see a number sign before a letter. He knew it shouldn't, but it always did. Hopefully that wasn't a bad omen from the get-go.

By the door the Sticker noticed an intercom with a silver globe adorned on its side. A helpful bronze plate had PRESS FOR ENTRY engraved in it.

He pushed the plate and an intercom bell trilled.

"Limbus Incorporated, do you have an appointment?" said an androgynous voice through the speaker.

"I'm here to meet with Tasha Willing."

"Wonderful, and what government do you represent?"

"I… uh… am here for a job."

"Does the Master Recruiter expect you today?"

"I guess so."

There was a pause. "And what location are you calling from?"

The Sticker opened his mouth and caught himself. "I'm right outside."

"Yes sir, but at what office location?"

"Los Angeles." He laughed nervously, thinking he'd failed to understand the question.

"Thank you, sir. Come in."

The door knob pulsed and unlocked. He twisted it and walked inside. Something frosty swept through him for a split second and everything behind fell away, pulled back, into nothing.

The Sticker stood in the center of a lobby the size of an airport now. His hand was still poised in the air from opening the door, but there was no door anymore….

He glanced around to make sure. The hallway he'd just come from was nowhere to be found. Twenty yards away, a giant globe spun before him, spears of light extruding and retracting in different locations over its surface, dazzling the floor, its every tile inlaid with what looked like cut diamonds in a flower petal pattern surrounded by a mother of pearl circle.

Tasha walked this luxurious floor with the same confidence she had at the oil-stained stockyard parking lot. A smile glued itself to her face. Today she was in a smart-looking red dress with matching hair clip that posted her straightened black hair to the side.

"You should see your expression," she said, stopping before him. "Was that fun, or what?"

"I'll go with *or what*." He rubbed his arms to confirm he was still part of reality, that this wasn't a drunken dream.

"If you think that small vapor convey blew your mind, just wait. I haven't received the full employment report yet, but you'll be going through a membrane transport and that's like several hundred cosmic slaps to the face." She laughed. It was a strange, ancient sounding laugh, but something about it calmed him. He liked Tasha. Maybe that was essential to her duty in bringing people into this weird place though. Maybe he shouldn't trust her, but he did. Had he not, the Sticker would have been running to get out of this place right about now.

"I don't know what to say..."

"That's because the vapor convey integrates with our visitor's panic synapses. We've altered your reactions to receive these new ideas in a measured fashion, invoking a less hostile animal response."

"Come again?"

"It's like valium, only permanent."

"I still feel like me."

"It doesn't change who you are, just how you'll perceive concepts normally catastrophic to the human psyche. We don't want to spend months rebuilding your grip on reality. This is quicker. Painless. And especially since you're going to another star system, it's imperative. Your body will have to adjust to membrane travel, life in space, and all that comes with it. Despite your ability to be numb, as you said, it's probably a good idea if you bring every precaution with you."

"Space?"

"You said *far away* and I listen to my applicants. Come on, Slaughter Man, follow me to my office."

He trailed her around the globe over to a hallway that ran with bright white marble rather than the intricate lobby tiles. After passing a few shadowy offices, she stepped into a small room and flipped on the light.

She sat down behind a slate colored desk. "Have a seat."

"Feels better on my back if I stand."

"*Nessun problema*," she replied. A wide screen monitor rested before her, but it was astonishingly simple looking. In fact, Gerald

Bailey actually had a fancier model in his office. Tasha typed a few things on a concealed keyboard and concentrated her dazzling green eyes on the screen. "I'll just be one moment... the report should be... yeah, there it is." She clicked her mouse a few times and softly snorted.

"How'd you get this job, Tasha? If you don't mind me asking."

She smirked. "My father runs this company."

"Ah. I never could have worked for my old man. Bet that's hard."

Tasha was distracted by something on the screen. "Not really," she replied, "haven't seen him in seventy-two years."

The Sticker laughed at this but Tasha's look of concern deepened. She picked up a slim red cell phone from under the desk and held it next to her ear. After a moment, a miniature voice answered. "You've sent my guy to the Princess's ship. Just what do you think you're doing?"

She waited, her green eyes absorbing an answer she didn't like.

The Sticker glanced up at the wall and his mouth fell open. He hadn't noticed before, and this was a testament to how truly unobservant he was, but thirty or more framed photos stared back at him: there he was with a bat over his shoulder in little league, another in front of burgundy satin curtains with his prom date Ruth Pietro, another in his blue overalls standing next to a water tank at Fabulous Onion Foods, and another, there with Annette on the strip in Las Vegas, the weekend of their marriage and subsequent honeymoon. There was even a photo of him around twelve or thirteen, not too much older than Tasha, and he was in a canoe with a young woman. He wore a smile. His mom wore one too, though less sincere. The photo had to have been taken only a year or two before she ran off with that other man. Since then, he'd only heard from her on birthdays and once last New Year's when she was drunk off her ass.

The Sticker's eyes fluxed from her photo back to Annette's. *No,* he thought, *they were different people. That was a different situation.*

"This is the exact same crap the directors pulled on me last time," Tasha told the phone angrily. "Yeah, yeah, I'm listening." She looked at the Sticker and made a gabby hand-puppet.

The Sticker's eyes came back to rest on Annette, hand on the lacy white hip of her wedding gown, the MGM Grand, an omnipresent green behind her. How could she consume him still? Here, in this strange place he'd happened upon, a whole new world, and all that twisted inside his bitter mind was his wife's shadow. He'd stepped way outside of his bubble, more than he ever bargained for, but evidently his heart and mind hadn't come along for the ride.

"You miss her, don't you?"

He looked at Tasha. Her conversation had ended without him noticing, the cell phone resting quiet on the desk.

"I really don't want to talk about that."

"I'm good with that."

"Why do you have so many pictures of me?"

Tasha batted her eyelashes. "I adore studying you."

"Funny."

"So, okay then, I'm going to do everything I can to transfer you from this assignment. You might have to spend a couple months there, but—"

"I don't care. Is the pay good?"

She tilted her head. "How's four hundred and fifty thousand a year sound?"

"Much better."

"Marginally," she said with a giggle that trailed off. "Really though, ordinarily I wouldn't assign you to something so dangerous. I'll check in on you though."

"Sounds fine, except the part with me doubting whether I'm schizophrenic now. That aside, I'm used to dangerous jobs."

"Yes, I know. That's why you're Super Slaughter Man."

He blew out and rolled his eyes.

Tasha's face furrowed with concern. "But you haven't worked in one of the Princess's ships before, and few have lived to say so. You'll be asked to do more than stick a knife in a brain-dead animal's throat. Depending on the Princess's appetite, you may have to make hundreds upon hundreds of kills on any given day. It will all be challenging."

"Could be."

"It will be," Tasha reinforced and stood from her chair, only coming to his waist. From a drawer, she took out a single sheet of paper and a pen and put it before him. "You will have three or four other workers helping to spread the work out. So, is this something you think you can do? If it is, go ahead and sign and we'll get started."

"I can't really say if I can do this, not until I know what these animals are."

"I'd love to tell you, but what the food source is can change on a whim with the Princess's tastes."

"The meat is only for her, eh?"

Tasha nodded solemnly.

The Sticker read the contract. It was the simplest, shortest legal document he'd ever seen. He had to read it three times to make sure he wasn't missing something. Afterward, he signed on for the job.

"Did you need to return home? Or are you ready to start today? You won't be taking anything with you. All your needs will be met there."

"Where do my wages go?" the Sticker asked, eyes again on Annette in the honeymoon photo, frozen in laughter, lost in Las Vegas sepia tones.

"Special account," she replied. "No taxes. The IRS is not an issue for us, if you're wondering."

"Sounds stupendous."

"Great, I'll show you to the membrane station then. You'll like it. It's not completely cutting edge travel—really more of a bastardized human version of Gultranz patch gating. It has improved quite a bit though and is probably more secure than the alien technology."

"*Alien...* sounds weird to hear that word used seriously."

"It won't be weird for long." Tasha sauntered around him and made for the hall.

"Wait."

She turned. "Yes?"

"Will I able to check Facebook over there?"

* * *

The membrane station was a rectangular chamber with a smoked glass observation window from beginning to end. Those on the other side of the window looked out to a blue ramp hanging with long glassine flaps, which reminded the Sticker of some kind of science fiction car wash.

Tasha sat him down on a short stool, the only piece of furniture in the room. Just in his boxer shorts, it was weird enough being there with a kid, but he blushed a little when a young Japanese woman in medical scrubs entered to take his vitals.

Tasha stood behind the technician, hawking maternally over the process. "You'll receive a one-time injection of DNRM-33," she explained.

"And that does what?"

"It sounds scarier than it is, but it will modify your DNA and RNA to accept instructions from the membranes, so your reassembled structure doesn't take on abnormalities."

"That's a mouthful. Does the drug work for everybody?"

"You have a seventy percent chance of success."

"What?"

Tasha laughed. "I'm kidding. This is a reliable molecular alteration. I've never heard of a problem, *ever*."

The technician held up the syringe. The fluid inside was clear, benign. "Ready?" she asked.

The Sticker nodded and received the injection. He wasn't too fond of needles, but as long as he looked away and focused on his breathing, he could handle it.

"Will I feel anything... from this?"

He noticed her phone was at her ear now. "Yes, this is Willing," she said. "He's received DNRM-33 therapy. You can fire them up. What? Oh, are you kidding me? Why the hell is he doing that?"

The door opened and Trevor Milstead walked in.

The Sticker could not accept this. The man, his old boss, in that moment, had become the most unbelievable thing in the room. Trevor looked more tanned, just as Annette had. He wore a silk Hawaiian shirt and khaki pants. Some expensive sunglasses nestled in his thick movie star hair.

"What are *you* doing here?"

"Me?" asked Trevor. "Shit man, you wouldn't have this job without me. A good crowbar couldn't have pried your ass out of that cow factory."

"Mr. Milstead," Tasha said. "Now isn't the time, in my opinion."

"Nobody's asking your opinion, Willing." Trevor hunkered down, coming eye level to the Sticker. "I thought Annette would stop talking about you... but even after visiting every damn island in Hawaii, she's guilty over your ass drying up in some cut rate slaughter house, no offense to my good ole boy Gerald Bailey."

The Sticker narrowed his eyes. "You got me fired."

"You got yourself fired, from what Bailey tells me. And now you've got some regulators looking for you—something about toxic waste and torturing a cow with a stun gun. I don't even care if all that stuff's real. With that kind of heat, I can't hire you back at the onion plant, not even to appease Annette. I have to get you out of the picture and hope she forgets your dumb ass."

"Sir," said Tasha diplomatically, "but is working the Princess's ship really the answer to that?"

"It's a slaughter ship, isn't it? That's what he does, *isn't it*? You told the committee he wanted to go far away, didn't you?"

Tasha looked down from his gaze and shook her head unhappily.

"Everybody on the committee signed off on it. Your father even endorsed the idea."

"Father is only getting his information from you, and he won't answer my calls."

"A wise man." Trevor stood and his knees crackled. The Sticker found comfort in that, made the asshole mortal, if only a little bit. They locked eyes for a moment. "I'd offer my hand," said Trevor, "as your old boss, or as your new one, but I know that's a waste."

"You're not as dopey as I thought."

Trevor gave him a crooked smile. "Have a safe trip. Don't get yourself killed out there too soon. That drug therapy is an expensive investment. Meanwhile, your wife will never go wanting."

Trevor patted Tasha on the shoulder before leaving.   The Sticker slid off the stool and nodded to the blue ramp. "Is that where I go? Can I just move on? Right now? *Far away*, please?"

Tasha regarded him stoically. "Milstead shouldn't have come down here. I'm sorry for the harassment. I was hoping you'd never even know he was my supervisor."

"It's okay. That's par for my life, and I have nowhere else to go now, do I?"

Tasha gestured to a pair of feet in a dashed outline on the ramp. "Stand there. That's all you have to do. I will try to visit tomorrow. You'll be greeted by some of our other employees once you settle."

The Sticker pointed at the outline for further confirmation.

Tasha nodded.

He stepped into the dashed feet.

"I'm going to leave the room," said Tasha. "You can go ahead and take off your underwear then."

He cleared his throat. "'K."

The transparent membrane flaps pulsed before him.

A moment later the door shut and she was gone.

The Sticker dropped his boxer shorts and kicked them to the wall. His face heated as he speculated on how many people were on the other side of the observation window. He'd never been a shy person, but the idea that Trevor might be looking on was more than unnerving.

The crystal kelp looking things waved faster before him.

Guess there's more important things to worry about than nudity . . .

A cold, plastic kiss touched his neck. He turned.

Layers of those flaps stretched behind him. It went into infinity. *But how—?*

"Keep forward please," said a voice piped into the room. Pieces of the command distorted and repeated in his brain and his ears. "Please forward keep." "Keep keep keep forward forward forward please please please." "Peep Korward Flease." "Kuh-kuh-kuh, fuh-fuh-fuh, kee-kee-kee." "Ease, Orward, Eep."

He saw people before him, stretching forever. But it was him. Trillions, (zillions?) of the Stickers. He saw the back of his head, the long scar down his right flank, his bare ass, legs. He shifted and all the copies shifted. It wasn't a reflection. They were there! They were all there, all alive. This wasn't happening like this, right?

The membrane flaps smacked past his body, jarring him left and right. Just as he began to question whether more were coming, the process quickened tenfold. His body stung as the membranes continued their assault. It'd become so fast, they didn't seem physical now, like the flaps moved through him, a mist, a poison, an aggressive spirit that possessed him and exorcised itself at the speed of light.

When it all stopped, the Sticker heard himself screaming incoherent things that conflicted with the thousand ill thoughts in his mind.

Three men lingered before him in a freezing cold metal room. They were younger than the Sticker, probably early twenties. Two were African American and the other Caucasian. The lighter skinned

African American grinned. He had a stack of clothing under his right arm. "Yup, that's about how I remember my trip, too."

The other two men evenly smiled and nodded.

"That's Harper and Timothy," he said.

"And who are you?" asked the Sticker.

"Razz," he replied. "Welcome aboard."

* * *

The Sticker changed into his new clothes, which appeared to be a thin cream colored bodysuit made of long-john material. It did the trick though. This place was freezing and the inner lining of the suit sent comforting, if foreign-feeling, waves of warmth into his skin. He guessed he was onboard a spaceship, but he couldn't see any windows showing space outside. There was a strange back-and-forth feeling in the core of his stomach, as though an imaginary fish hook tugged at his intestines; he assumed this had to do with some kind of artificial gravity imposed by the ship. He could only guess. The Sticker was more of a western type of fellow and hadn't even sat through *Star Wars*.

His shoes were closer to apparel to which he was accustomed: work boots with hard, difficult to tie shoelaces and reinforced steel in the toes. He got the first on and was busy tugging on the second when the manually operated cabin door slid open.

The man named Timothy entered the room, his skin as pale as a ghost. Sporting a bald head, he indeed could have passed for one of the Casper variety.

"Yeah?" asked the Sticker.

"You have to come right away. She's hungry again."

"Who?"

Timothy tossed him what looked like a small firearm. It didn't resemble a ray gun, more like a starter pistol with a bronze comb on top of it.

The Sticker followed Timothy into the hall. "Is this about the Princess?"

The other man walked so fast, the Sticker had to jog alongside him. "Sorry, you usually get a few days to acclimatize to the environment, but we are shorthanded, and didn't expect the Princess to acquire another Fanjlion ship today. She's already had three hundred processed today. Her appetite is getting worse."

"What's this weapon you gave me?"

"It's called a Fixer Gun. It will fire bursts of fifty staple-darts and that clip holds twenty-five hundred. Target only the head. The Princess will not eat brains."

"I'm not used to this... kind of work. Guns. I don't do guns."

"We were all new to this once. Don't worry, the Fanjlions are only a passing taste. The Princess will get bored of them eventually."

Timothy took another corner and the two other men, Razz and Harper, waited in an area where the hall expanded into a docking chamber. "Come on," they both said, waving frantically.

The Sticker and Timothy sidled up against the wall with the other men.

"Thought you weren't going to make it," Razz said critically.

"It's a long hallway, man," Timothy snapped.

"Shut up, guys." Harper's brown eyes narrowed as he focused. Sweat had formed up on the hotdog shaped rolls of ebony skin on his neck, making them glisten. "The inner chamber is unsealed. Should be coming in here any minute."

"We're doing this in the hall?" the Sticker asked.

Razz checked his gun. "What'd you expect?"

A hiss of air released and a single blast of a horn sounded.

"Ready," breathed Razz.

Everybody put their guns up.

The bodies rushing into the hall could have been a rolling wave of tree branches and knives. The Sticker couldn't get a bead on what was what at first, not until Harper and Timothy fired their Fixer guns. These alien creatures, the Fanjlion, were humanoid, around five feet tall, rods of muscle over a small bone structure, skin with a mottled tree bark texture, like twig-men from some haunted forest. Each wore a tight white membranous material over their small heads. In the center of the latex-like mask, a square had been cut so a singular eye could stare outward, a radioactive pineapple slice.

"Don't gawk, shoot!" yelled Razz. He kicked one of the aliens as it leapt for him. Before it hit the ground he fired into its face, the Fixer gun letting out a metallic cough. Golden blood burst like a water balloon from the pineapple eye.

The Sticker raised his weapon as a threesome of the Fanjlions sped toward him. He didn't want to kill these things. He hated guns. Hated their sole purpose. Hated seeing kids under bloody sheets on the news. Hated... how after his mother left, his father went on a week-long hunger strike that he finally broke by eating a bullet from his Beretta.

The tallest creature of the lot charged out in front. The shiny black webbed hands that extended from the bundle of sticks that was its arm suddenly became blobs that elongated into blades. It flung the lethal points forward—the Sticker jumped back and opened fire on the group. The gun's coughing sound played hell with his eardrums and the hardware grew colder in his hands with every shot. Taking the lead creature down dead in the chest, the other two aliens ended in a series of misplaced shots in the arms, legs and torso.

But they're dead, is the point.

"The hell you doing?" shouted Harper, close to his side. "You're wasting food. The heads, the heads, dummy!"

Or not.

"Well sorry!" he said, just as another group fell upon them.

Harper finished them: one and two and three and four, and number five's head buckled back and it fell sideways on the pile of his companions.

"Shit," the Sticker whispered.

"That's how it's done, buddy." Harper flashed a deviant smile. "Come on, let's back up Tim and Razz."

The Sticker kept behind the broad shouldered man and rounded the corner where the two other Limbus employees waged a two-man war against a seething mass of Fanjlions. Harper took aim and began squeezing off shots into the crowd. The Sticker lifted his gun, but only for show. Harper must have had hawk eyes to make headshots from this distance.

Unconsciously Harper moved forward and the Sticker followed his lead. Over the sight of the gun, he attempted to track those red glowing pineapples—perfect bulls eyes when you considered them—but the alien gathering coalesced like a confused forest growing into itself and it was a tableau of chaos. The Sticker stuck out his gun, as though getting it marginally closer would help as well.

Then something warm and wet struck his elbow and his gun jumped out of his hand. The Sticker stepped back and realized that the warm and wet was him: he was bleeding from a deep slash down his elbow to the base of his pinkie, the material of his jumpsuit torn clean in half.

Harper took a few more shots and looked satisfied by them. He spared a glance at the Sticker. "What the shit? Did you lose your gun?"

"I—"

The next moment Harper's head broke apart, first in a clump that took his right eye, then another that destroyed his jaw, the rest of the meat cascading gruesomely to the side and falling off. A single, thin jet of scarlet erupted from the neck just before the man's body fell to the floor.

"Fuck!" the Sticker shouted.

The alien who had taken the Sticker's gun took two steps closer, dipping its head as it walked. Its gloved hand around the gun mimicked a human hand, just as surely as it had mimicked a blade earlier. The gun discharged and the Sticker ducked and ran. He had no clue where, but he was running. The creature bounded after him. He could hear Timothy and Razz yelling, but he knew it would be deadly to look back.

The paneling of the ship changed suddenly. It was darker, with glowing red circuitry underneath. The Sticker took a left, charged up into the shadows and wheeled right. He could hear the Fanjlion thankfully fall for the trick and scamper into the opposite side of the room. In the dim light of this new hall, he saw his pursuer gallop up to the threshold. It touched a wall panel, made a circular motion with its hand, and a thick door slid over and locked with a hiss. It turned around and made an aggravated clicking sound, the Fixer gun poised over its head. *No wonder it didn't shoot me. It's not coordinated enough to hit a moving target. Had Harper only known a few moments earlier...*

The faces of Razz and Timothy filled the port hole in the door. They were speaking to each other, hopefully planning how to get him out. The Sticker's body trembled. He was on the Fanjlion ship.

A bass trilling filled his skull as Fixer darts released right over his head. The Sticker swept down and ran, his every step only inches ahead of ensuing shots. The attack trailed him all the way across the room, where he was able to drop behind a narrow support structure.

Twenty-five hundred darts. Fifty unloading every second, likely. How many were left in the Fixer? At least three hundred outside... but after that last spread?

There was only one way to find out.

Benjamin Kane Ethridge

The Sticker shook his head once, *idiot*, and then hauled ass across the hallway. This time he counted, and hoped, god did he hope, that it wouldn't be the last thing he did. Shots coughed after him, again, again, again. He made it to the other side and shielded himself around another support. Seven seconds. Another couple times and that should do it.

He made another run for it and immediately a dart grazed his hip. The Sticker slammed to the floor on one hand and groaned. Blood poured from his leg and filled up his work boot. Made him woozy. The Fanjlion's feet scratched against the floor, somewhere in the shadows. The Sticker looked up and saw Timothy and Razz, mouths moving in silent shouts. They pointed to the wall. To the panel.

"Oh," said the Sticker. He tried to stand. Hobbling left and right, he heard more shots ring out and impact sparks flung off a nearby support. He reached the panel and swiped his hand in a circle as he'd seen the alien do. A droning sound emitted and a light glowed behind it. Then died.

The alien lunged after him, firing what was left in the clip. The Sticker dropped to his knee from the pain in his hip, but it was good that he had—there was a clear path to that pineapple eye. The Sticker grabbed the eye and crushed it between his fingers. Oily blood ruptured over his knuckles and the Fanjlion made several husky burping sounds before collapsing on the floor, a column of gold running from its head down the dark paneled floor.

A minute later, the door opened and Timothy proclaimed, "That's what I thought, override is always on the seventh panel."

Razz immediately went down on a knee to help the Sticker. "You okay?"

"Yup."

"Fucked up your new clothes, man."

The jumpsuit was shredded, painted in glittering blood, of both red and gold variety. "Guess I did... that guy, Harper..."

"We saw."

"It was my gun they used."

"Not your fault. There were more of them than usual," said Razz solemnly.

"Will Limbus send Harper back to his family somehow?"

Timothy pursed his lips. "No," he said after a moment.

The Sticker looked at Razz, who looked away. "Work's done today. The Princess's clean crew will take care of the rest here."

The Sticker growled in pain as he stood. "So what happens to Harper? No mysteries, guys. I ain't in the mood."

Razz sighed. "He'll be taken down to be rendered and prepped for consumption with the rest of these bodies."

"Along with the aliens? You said the Princess had particular tastes though."

"Yes, but she won't turn down getting one of us."

"Not ever," Timothy added.

* * *

Razz and Timothy were in a funk for a couple weeks after losing Harper. Especially Razz, being the youngest of all the men there. The Sticker wagered he'd never seen anyone he cared about die. Both men would often tell the Sticker stories about Harper while preparing for the day's work. Some of the stories were funny, some serious, but all equally endearing, and to hear them speak about their friend this way proved them decent guys, which made the Sticker feel more at peace with the company he was now in.

As much as they liked to go on about Harper, neither Razz nor Timothy wanted to share too much about how Limbus talked them into this job on the Princess's slaughter ship. The Sticker knew how they felt and kept that particular course of events from their conversations. He figured they would all end up sharing everything eventually. After a month of killing Fanjlions, Bezdebos, Horta Sa-inj, and Grettish Friars, they were more like comrades in a war, rather than employees working a job.

And just when life on the Princess's ship got predictable, her tastes would change. They would learn from her robot emissaries that Fixer guns gave the meat a "smell" or that the bludgeons she next instructed them to use had splintered some of the spines and bone shrapnel had spoiled the meat. Now, a full two months later, the Sticker and his two fellow slaughterers were using short-hafted spears, not much different than the long knife the Sticker was accustomed to in the stockyards.

After their kills, a fleet of peculiar robots would sanitize the floors and transport the bodies to the rendering facilities. Their gelatin-red bodies reminded the Sticker of the cinnamon bears he used to eat with abandon, which led to several root canals. These robots had no visible power supplies or hinged iron limbs like those he'd seen in movies. The eyes were the only mechanical looking component to them, alarming yellow diodes that blinked as they processed information. Efficient at their tasks though, the robots kept things moving in an orderly fashion, especially the emissary models that conveyed messages in unstilted American English.

The Sticker would watch them move around like furious gummy children, pushing mops heaped in gore, moving puddles of thick alien blood with squeegees, picking up corpses and flinging them into the small dump trucks. It was amazing to behold mechanical devices moving around so fluid and unerring.

Which was why the Sticker couldn't understand the sorry-ass lag-time and glitchiness of the personal computer in his dorm room. Tasha had the computer sent over a couple days after he arrived. The laptop was modern, nothing special, save for the fact that the self-sustaining battery never lost a charge. So again, why all the lagging? Why all the glitches? He was grateful to have some sort of connection to Earth, but this was weak.

The Sticker didn't post much to any social sites, but he was an avid lurker that read about his friends and sometimes distant family members. One person held his attention the most, however.

He sent Annette another message the day he set up the computer: *Did you ever read my email?*

The answer came back a few days later. *Tell me where you've gone. I've received phone calls from the Regional Water Quality Control Board, the EPA, and the police department. Your boss, Gerald Bailey, was put in the hospital with a life-threatening infection. They are blaming you.*

He typed back: *Sorry to hear that. I'm out of state. I don't think I'll be back in a long time.*

A week passed and another email came through: *You need to get back to me soon about this. Are you in town still? I've called your uncle Pete, and he hasn't heard from you.*

He replied: *Did you get my last email? I said I'm out of state.*

Her response: *Do you want to go the Freeman's BBQ this Saturday?*

The Sticker sat there, scratching at a burning claw wound from a Grettish Friar on his cheek. Annette had sent this email years ago... why was it coming through again?

Huh? he returned to her.

Then a follow-up email came in: *So what state are you in then?????* *This is serious. You need to contact me.*

He didn't bother to respond.

The next morning the Sticker quickly got dressed. Aside from warmth, the jumpsuits nourished and hydrated them as well. The small amount of body fat he'd had before was nearly gone. He would have felt great had his body not been constantly abused by outside factors. As he suited up, feeling nice and full, *satisfied*, he heard a knock at his door. He slid it open and found one of the cherry red emissaries standing there.

At first he got a bad feeling that spears were no longer acceptable and the Princess would now like them to strangle her various forms of cattle, but the robot relayed a message from Tasha, in her own voice.

"I'm sorry that I will be unable to visit the ship. The chain of command in our division has insisted I remain on Earth. I'm sorry for this. I hope the lap-top with internet access will bring you some repose. I'm working on getting you transferred, or at least your contract altered so you don't have to be locked into five years. Take care of yourself and I'll contact you soon."

The robot backed away and gracefully strode down the hallway.

The Sticker felt so far away from anything real, but that guidepost for reality wasn't the Earth, but Annette. Before he slept every night, he wondered if she missed him. With each day that passed, did she realize her mistake? He knew her dreams, saw them grow up from a modest beginning and blossom out. She wanted to become an accountant, but hated school. He coached her through the lectures, tests and all the dreariness that came with it, and then just last year she became a CPA. She thanked him. Profusely. Did she forget the man who did that for her? Would there be a moment when she reflected back to the time she'd felt so small and he made her feel like a giant?

He didn't want praise. He just wanted some credit.

If she really was going to leave him forever, he at least deserved that.

He attempted to email her several times that night.

Six months passed after those attempts.

No other email came through.

Not even those of the panicked legal sort.

Nothing.

The same day he vowed to stop using the computer was the first time he heard the Princess's voice. He was loading Fanjlion bodies onto the conveyor and while one of the actuators momentarily powered down, there was a brief course of silence through the rendering facility. The Princess's scream was pained and infant-like in its misery, and the Sticker thought, without much further reflection, *that's the voice of the thing that will chew me up someday. My body will be mush in her mouth. She'll swallow me down.*

And Annette would never know the difference.

* * *

"Hey Slaughter Man, you okay?" asked Razz.

The Sticker opened his eyes. They felt thick and greasy. The sides of his face stung. His nose wasn't much better. Probably broken in twenty places, or at least it felt that way. He couldn't breathe through it, so he had to suck in a big breath through his mouth. The slight whistling between his missing front tooth sent a reminder to him of that Joxle beast, how it had picked him up by the neck and slammed him to the floor like some exotic pro-wrestler from beyond the stars. The Sticker had got him good in the end. The creature was smart, but he got it to fall into a hatch for a service tunnel. He bled it out right there. Joxles bled red, just like cows. That was a bit of a nostalgic moment for the Sticker, though it was hard to enjoy after having his ass kicked by something roughly twice the size of a sumo.

"You can just rest there. Timothy and I got this one today."

"Nah," said the Sticker. He pushed up on his arm and it felt bruised from shoulder to knuckles. Bruised to the bone.

Razz's broad African features could hardly be seen in the room. The cabin lights had not powered up yet. "You gotta know something…"

The Sticker lied back down. "Yeah?"

"We were given new orders last night."

"Don't tell me it's the Friars again. If it is… shit, I might have to sit this one out after all. Let you younger guys handle it."

Razz let go a trembling breath and shook his head. "You got cut up pretty bad yesterday."

"Thing had sharp claws. Maybe worse than a Friar. Hell, it was just so goddamn strong."

For a moment Razz didn't say anything, just sat there, looking numb and featureless.

"What was the order?" the Sticker prompted.

"You bled all over that thing. The Princess got a taste for you…"

The Sticker pushed all the way up in bed now and edged himself painfully against the freezing metal wall. "Grossed her out, eh?"

Razz sadly snorted.

"So, okay, I get it. Now what? You guys gonna fall in line?"

"I don't know… my contract for this job ends in a year. I hear that some people end up working for Limbus itself. Recruiters, scouts, that stuff. They might even promote me when I get back. I was banking on my luck to bring me there."

It was a joke they'd both said to each other before. Razz and the Sticker played backgammon every evening and shared the same self-deprecating nature. Neither was that competitive; no shit talking ever came about. They just liked playing games. Timothy wasn't much for games and chose to read instead, and for that, the Sticker was closer to Razz, which was likely why he was the one to bring this bad news.

They had arrived at a point where neither could take a move.

"You know…" Razz took a while to form the words. "It's not just the job. You know Tim and I wouldn't… *not for that.*"

"Nice to hear."

"One of the guys before Harper, his crew's first day of work was getting rid of the last crew. If we refuse her anything, the Princess will demand new people. They'll take us all out then."

"Yeah." The Sticker cleared his throat and swallowed a bad taste in his mouth. "So when does she want you guys to deliver me to her?"

"After you're completely healed," Razz replied.

"Makes sense."

Razz stood and grunted. "No, it fucking doesn't. But that's where we are."

"Why did Limbus send you here anyway?"

"Screwed up my Army job. Too much to go into. Let's just say Saigon will never be the same."

"Really? We still have forces over there?"

"Sure do. Don't believe everything you read. But what about you? Why'd Limbus send you here?"

"Same friggin thing. Screwed up my last job."

Razz laughed and then trailed off, eyes hazy. "I don't know what to do, man. I just... *don't.*"

The lights in the room came on then, illuminating them both.

"Now do you?" asked the Sticker.

Razz's mouth peeled back into a grin. "You asshole."

"Go on now. I need to think about this."

"We could keep beating the shit out of you, I guess."

Now the Sticker laughed. "As much as that sounds really fun, I think the Princess will take notice."

Razz's face went grim. "She would at that."

"You've seen her then?"

"Just been outside the audience chamber, to deliver a pallet of her digestive enzymes. Heard her eating... smells like a boneyard in there."

"I know that smell."

"Not like this, man." Razz went to the door, all his good humor drained from him. "Take it easy, and Tim and I will come here for our break."

"Sounds like a plan."

"Oh," Razz added. "Don't put on your jumpsuit. It'll heal you faster."

"Good to know."

* * *

The robots came by every morning to check the Sticker's injuries. By the fourth day his cuts had crusted over and his bruises had shrunk from purple clouds to jaundice strata. He was getting better and the robot's vital scanners were taking note.

Every night the Princess's hungry screech rattled the walls of the ship. *Dying for food. More.* It hurt his insides to even listen to the sound. He'd gone back to using his computer and tracked down some classical music by composers he'd never heard of, enjoying both the brooding kind Annette had taught him to like and the more energetic symphonies that lifted his spirits despite everything else.

Razz and Timothy visited him several times a day, but never had much to say. It was becoming obvious that Razz had resigned himself to the worst outcome, while Timothy still held out hope they would think of something.

Around that fourth day, they did think of something, although the plan didn't summon much excitement from the Sticker.

Robots were in and out of the medical supply cache throughout the day to deliver various digestive supplements to the Princess, including those enzymes she required to process some of the different alien tissues she consumed. But there weren't only gastrological medications in the cache. In a few instances in the past, the Princess experienced a form of pain that only cybernetic organisms could acquire; *steel-shock* was the layman's term, and as the Sticker understood it, this kind of pain involved the inflammation of organic nerves, while the blood took on a high metal content; essentially the whole body experienced something akin to being struck by lightning, continually, for hours. Therefore, in the medical cache, copious drums of a preferred anesthesia called Lethardohl 90/30 could be found. The drug worked successfully on a wide spectrum of life forms, humans included.

Razz's plan would be to sneak in during the day and hide behind the garbage compactor in the back of the medical cache. The delivery robots had tunnel vision and never did any security sweeps of the room. He would hole up in there for a few hours after they stopped coming for supplies, since they still did a patrol of the halls until all lights went out. It was risky, but worth it for the Sticker. After they had the Lethardohl, he only needed to take a teaspoon orally of the syrup. He would fall into a stupor and he would not feel their knives, nor would he know his final moment.

Brain-dead… and then they'll cut my throat. How nostalgic.

The Sticker agreed to the plan more for his friends' sake than his own. If the roles had been reversed, he wouldn't have wanted to cause them pain either, or see the look in their eyes as he slashed through their jugular.

But you wouldn't take their way out; you'd fight for them. Right? The Sticker shook his head. *Not if Annette was waiting for me. I would do what I had to, to get back to her.*

At least, he used to think he would have. Now, he wasn't so sure. Being far away from her had made him realize that he could breathe fine on his own. He still loved her, but he didn't think about her every waking moment like he used to.

The night of their medical cache raid, he waited in the hallway, feeling comfortable and less hungry now that he wore his jumpsuit again. This hall was one of the few with a window to space. With the lights out, standing there was standing in nothingness. Only a dim, peach glow came from underneath the door. They could hear Razz slowly breaking the door's seal from within.

"I don't want to do this," said Timothy. "We *shouldn't* do this."

The Sticker said nothing. He was not going to insist on their plans to kill him, not by any stretch.

The padding sound of a robot's footsteps came from down the hall. The two men froze. With a sucking sound the door to the medical cache opened and Razz poked his head out. The Sticker put his finger to his lips.

The robot's footsteps faded and they retreated inside the room. Litter and assorted junk spread out over the floor like a small cyclone had gone through the room. Several drums had been knocked over amidst the mess. The Sticker stepped on a pile of thin aluminum and cringed at the crumpling sound he'd made.

"What the hell has gone on in here?"

"Oh, too much to explain, boys, but I've been having some fun." Razz looked excited, out of breath and like he hardly knew where to start. "Tim," he finally said, "Remember what Harper said about membrane transport?"

"That DNRM-33 stuff?"

"Yeah, the transport stores all biological profiles using that stuff to translate our DNA, blabbety-blab."

"Ok."

"He said that in times where astrodynamic computers were down, he knew people who took double doses of the stuff, stepped in and it kicked them back to their original location."

Timothy nodded, though his face was dubious. "It might be an urban legend, but yeah, Harper thought the membrane's internal memory cannot possess identical biological data. Another couple doses of DNRM-33 will instruct it to code something previously coded, not once, but twice. This is registered as an anomaly error, a safety measure is supposedly then taken by the system and a forced return occurs."

"Is there enough of that stuff here for us all to go back?" asked the Sticker.

"There's a drum of it." Razz smiled. "We're good."

The Sticker ran his hands through his shaggy hair and entwined his fingers at the back of his head. "Holy shit."

"Hold on though." Timothy's face took that ghostly look as he turned from them in the dark. "We can't fool ourselves. Only one of the robots has a physical key to the membrane station door. If it was a code or a keycard, I could probably work it out, but it's an old school iron key, as primitive as primitive comes. We don't know which robot holds it either. They aren't going to tell us, and if you hadn't noticed, the robots all look identical. Believe me, I like your idea, but I'm just sayin'…"

Razz glanced at the Sticker. "No worries. I'm not banking on my luck this time."

"No?"

From his pocket, Razz pulled out what looked like a piece of black trash bag. It curled as he took it out, a living, moving thing.

"You stole one?" Timothy asked.

The Sticker tried to adjust his eyes in the dark. "Stole what?"

The black material bent around Razz's hand and formed like a glove. His hand grew four more fingers, turned into a ball with spikes, and then into a foot-long machete. After a moment, it dissolved down to a bar shape with a key at the end.

"How did you steal one of the Fanjlion's gloves?"

"I didn't," explained Razz. "These robots aren't much for discerning treasure from trash. But as you can see from my mess, I am."

After a moment, Timothy forced a smile. "I really hope this works. I don't want to be right."

"Don't trust your gut. You have that irritable bowel syndrome thing anyway."

The Sticker laughed.

"*Ha-ha-ha.* Fuck you." Timothy scowled. "So what do we do then?"

"Take that bag of syringes there on that drum of DNRM-33 and fill them at the port on the side. We'll need two each, so fill six. The stuff looks like water but it's as thick as tar, probably will take some time."

"Piece of cake." Timothy picked up the sealed bag of syringes.

Razz looked to the Sticker. "Back me up while I get the Membrane station open. I need eyes in the main hall."

"Wait!" Timothy went stiff. "What about eyes out in this hall?"

"Hide behind the compactor; believe me, they don't look there."
Razz flashed a grin.

* * *

With the aid of the Fanjlion glove, the membrane station lock
turned over so easily that Razz and the Sticker stood, gaping, for a
couple minutes. Timothy arrived soon after and they helped each
other take their doses of DNRM-33. Razz turned on the membranes
and let them warm, then disconnected the terminal, just in case the
thing had some strange origin plugged in, which hopefully wouldn't
alter the course of Harper's theory.

Or myth.

"How much longer do they have to warm up?" asked Timothy.

"Probably fifteen minutes." The translucent flaps patterned
unnatural light over Razz's face and sloped down his nose.

"I gotta *go.*"

"You're kidding me, right? This is no time for your irritable
bowels."

"Membranes aren't going anywhere. They're just warming up.
The lav is just across the hall."

"Good God, just go on, hurry up, damn." Razz waved Timothy
away.

Timothy took off into the dark hallway, the sounds of his huffing
breaths soon vanishing.

The Sticker leaned against the wall and shut his eyes a moment.
It was unreal. The past week he'd thought only about his impending
death sentence. Now this. *Escape.* Even after all he'd been through, he
didn't feel he'd earned this. He was lucky to have been put on board
with someone as clever as Razz.

The Sticker picked up the Fanjlion glove and put it on. Razz had
let him fool with it a little earlier, changing his hand into different
shapes.

"What's on your mind?" asked his friend, who admired the
membranes, head cocked curiously to one side.

"Wondering what you'll go back to. You were almost through
with your contract."

"Well, there are more important things."

"Yeah, but… this is one hell of a job. You've earned your money.
What if they say you're in breach and don't pay anything?"

Razz shrugged. "We're alive. That's all that matters."

"I guess." He stopped playing and let his hand resolve back into four fingers and a thumb.

"So what are *you* going to do? With all that shit waiting for you back home?"

The Sticker had forgotten he'd told Razz about Annette and Trevor and how he'd left his last job. It was just as well, but still embarrassing to be worrying over those things in the face of all they'd seen. "I haven't got it sorted out. Maybe Limbus will find me another job. Forgive and forget?"

Razz shook his head. "I don't know. I cannot predict that company's motivations. I will say this: I always have a contingency plan, and nobody gets to know about it but me."

"Pretty slick dude, you."

"Like buttered Vaseline, baby."

They laughed and then waited in silence for ten minutes. Razz started pacing over to the door to search outside for Timothy.

After another five minutes, his voice edged with panic. "What the hell is he doing taking so long? This isn't some casual trip we're taking. Shit!"

"I'm going to go get him." The Sticker started off and Razz took his arm. "The membranes are warmed up. We can go. Maybe you shouldn't risk it."

"With all you guys did for me, I couldn't do that."

"I was afraid you'd say that." Razz nodded. "I'll wait until you get here, though I'm not looking forward to seeing any of you guys butt naked."

"The feeling's mutual. And don't worry, Tim's probably fine. We would have heard something if he wasn't."

"Probably fell in, the dummy."

The Sticker took off into the hall, darkness immediately folding around him. The lavatory was only a dozen yards or so from the Membrane Station, around a corner. It was surprising that Timothy even had problems with his bowels. The food delivery gleaned from their jumpsuits did cause their bodies to produce stool, but it was runny and thin and only a couple ounces every other day. It took less than a minute to be done with your business, so it was concerning that so much time had passed. He got to the lav door and pushed it open.

The door shut behind him and the blackness was absolute.

"Tim, are you okay? We're waiting."

The Sticker took a few steps and strained his ears. If only he had a flashlight—

He let out of shout of pain. Something had pierced through his neck and a terrible sensation flooded down his chest and into his heart. The Sticker stumbled back through the door, knocking it open. Timothy came rushing out like a bald wraith.

The Sticker tried to speak but his lips were numb, his throat passage thickened. Every inch of his skin warmed and then froze.

"I'm sorry," said Timothy into his ear. "That fool thing Harper said won't work. They'll come for us anyway. They'll find us. She'll eat everybody here. I have to do the right thing."

The Sticker tried to get the man off his chest, but his muscles had turned to water.

"You won't feel it. I could have done it in the bathroom. Just cut out your throat. I didn't. I could have let you suffer. I didn't. You don't deserve that. You're a good man. We're all good men." Timothy picked up his knife spear. "We just have a really *bad* fucking job."

With the only energy he still possessed, the Sticker brought up his hand, Fanjlion glove turning it to a blade.

The point came out the top of Timothy's skull. The man's eyes went hazy. His lips tried a few words, but they came out gummy nonsense. He fell off the Sticker, blood rushing from his mouth like a river at last free from a lifetime obstacle.

The Sticker got up to his knees, looking around dizzily.

The lights in the hall blinked on.

All the commotion had signaled the Princess. Hundreds of padded feet fell in the hall, coming from all directions.

He crawled around the corner. Razz stood in the threshold of the membrane station. Another river of red, this one, an army of like-minded slaves came blasting down the hall from both sides. Razz spotted the Sticker and emerged. The robots were almost upon him.

"Come on!"

The Sticker shook his head. "Go!" he hollered over the noise. "Go!"

Razz fell back inside the room, terror in his face. The door to the membrane station shut.

Good, thought the Sticker. *That's good.*

And then he stopped thinking; his presence of mind ripped away and shoved itself into a colorless place.

* * *

He didn't know how long he'd been asleep but the Sticker awoke gagging. The death smell around him was palpable. In his early twenties, working a stockyard in northern California, he'd been assigned the atrocious duty of cleaning out a dumpster that held spoiled beef livers. That was vile.

This was worse.

His eyelids sagged as he fought to open them. The half-moon shaped room took on the ominous look of a mechanical dragon—thin metal plates on floor, ceiling and walls. Several dozen robots scrubbed blood off the eastern wall, and a few scattered throughout the room worked the floors. More huddled behind him, blocking the exit.

The Sticker stood, against all warnings from his body to do otherwise. He faced a large platform that took up most of the room. On it sat, generators, supercomputers, machines tumbling drums of the digestive enzyme, steel cables flexing from dark locations; seeing it all took his eyes for a dizzy ride that landed on the most horrible part of all. Above the mass of unified machinery, an immense head stretched forth, connected to the cables by sinew and taut reams of leathery red muscle. The head had a canine shape, though there was no fur or even skin to speak of, just muscle and bone with two eyes like globes of jet.

The Princess shook from side to side and let forth a spiteful choking sound.

A robot approached the Sticker and said in a bland female voice. *"Sit down."*

He looked back at the snarling head, which was large enough to snap him up whole in its jaws. "I'd love to," he said, and did as asked, his lower back at once exploding with its normal achiness. Exhaustion rolled throughout him and he jerked his head back to keep awake.

The Princess clicked a large bloody tongue against her pink fangs, long as fence posts.

"Your friend escaped through the transport," the robot translated. *"Are you happy?"*

"Yes," the Sticker replied.

The robot clucked and snickered in the Princess's language.

"That is fine. One friend did not get away."

A steel caged cart pushed through the gathering of robots at the door, two other robots laboring at its weight. Pieces of Timothy were piled inside. His face looked up at the ceiling, mouth open, chin painted in brown blood.

The Sticker looked on, numbly, thankful for the surrealistic lens imparted on him by the sedative. It took him a moment to remember what had happened. A man who he thought was his friend, so desperate he'd made the wrong choice. The Sticker thought he should be more repulsed by the sight, even under the influence. Maybe it was all the death he'd seen. Maybe because he would never see Annette again. Or maybe he'd always envisioned an awful end to his life and this confirmation held him in morbid awe.

When the robots started tossing Timothy into the Princess's mouth though, it was gratifying to the Sticker to feel his gorge rise a little. He hadn't lost his humanity through all this.

As the Princess's teeth slammed together and ground up Timothy, drums of enzymes twisted and twirled, lights on the computer displays dazzled like a toxic Christmas display, holograms of the food source molecular breakdowns pulsed in the air. Blood sprayed down from the Princess's jaws and pooled on the floor near the stage. Toward the end of the meal, she made a sickening yummy sound that turned into one of her infant hunger screams.

"More," said the robot. *"Fresh,"* it added.

A steel collar clicked around the Sticker's neck and a force pitched him forward. He twisted his face back and saw several robots handling a large boom connected to his collar. They drove his body across the slippery floor until he slammed into the stage. He thrashed around to break their grip, but his muscles seized at their rock steady resistance. They pulled and he hitched back on his rear.

The Sticker threw an arm behind his neck to see if he could reach the boom. He grasped air, nothing more. As he brought his arm back something tremendous dropped over his bicep. In silent terror he watched as the Princess severed his arm just under the shoulder, ripped it away from his body and greedily chewed it up in the left side of her mouth.

The pain felt like a distant horror waiting to visit upon him. He could smell the meaty odor of the Princess's breath. Her glassy black eyes rolled back in ecstasy as she ate.

Robots seized him by the legs and lifted the Sticker in the air for presentation.

"Too good," an unseen robot translated. *"More,"* another said. *"My destiny."*

The Sticker kicked to get free; the Princess caught that leg in her mouth and took it off at the kneecap. Heart racing, blood pumping free of his leg and shoulder, the Sticker closed his eyes and tried to think of Annette, the good times, only the good times. It was difficult to concentrate though, listening to his body parts being sloppily consumed. Another roar of hunger filled the room and shock overtook him.

* * *

The Sticker passed out hearing the tremendous, insatiable wailings of the Princess, and this horrific, soul-rattling sound was the same thing that woke him.

But he was in a different place now. He'd been here once before to get bandaged up by robots, after he took that beating on the last job. The medical bay...

Why was he here now?

The Sticker glanced down at the frayed veins and bone protruding down from his shoulder. A thin blue coating of some medicinal chemical sealed everything off, almost like plastic wrap around a chicken drumstick. He couldn't see his leg stump from this prone position, but it had the same tight feeling down there.

Oddly, but not so oddly, his good leg rested in a rectangular pan of brine, and his good arm soaked in another concoction that smelled of vinegar and spices.

Variety, he thought with a sickening inward twinge.

He tried to move but found his body strapped to the exam table like Frankenstein's monster. *Only they aren't giving me body parts; they're taking them.*

The Princess's screams heightened to eardrum piercing levels. He'd never heard her so worked up. The maddening repetition of screeches and tantrum sobs worked at the Sticker's shredded mind. He wanted to scream with her. He almost began to sympathize with her pain. He almost wanted to end it as much as he figured she did.

But he wanted to live, too.

Live? What life do you have now? You're going back with less than you came with. Hell... you'll be like one of those sad, sorry fucks begging near the freeway. LOST JOB, LEG AND ARM. GOT A DOLLAR?

"Shit," he laughed.

A calm robot voice came over the ship intercom. "Additional hands required to assist with enzyme blending and conveyance. Immediate need. Code 78-9 directive."

That didn't sound good. The announcement wasn't exactly the same as others the Sticker had heard in previous months, but usually more enzymes meant more eating. Just how long had she planned on marinating him here? And why? She'd never done such a thing with her other meals. Certainly not Harper or Timothy.

She likes your taste.

Invisible knives sunk into the core of both his stumps and the Sticker shouted out, blinded by white hot pain. Whatever that blue plastic seal stuff was, it didn't have anything to take the edge off. The sedative Timothy had pumped into him wore off sometime during his blackout. This next go round with the Princess would be *au natural.* Would she leave him alive again? Slowly take him apart piece by piece? Or would this next time be the end to all of this?

"Critical need. Code 98-9 directive," the overhead droned.

Good, maybe I upset her stomach. Maybe she'll die.

The Princess answered this by suddenly going quiet. The screaming stopped.

The Sticker lay there, staring at the dim canned lights in the ceiling of the med bay. New thoughts raced through his head. If she did die, what would the robots do? Let him rot here, more than likely.

After twenty minutes had passed, those sorted fantasies faded. The Princess began to groan and call again, more fervently than ever.

From down the hall, padded robot feet sounded in parade. The Sticker twisted once in his bindings, just to reassure himself there wasn't a weakness he hadn't exploited. The bindings held firmly.

The med bay door opened and the red gelatin bodies of the ship's robots quickly filled the room, seeming eager to complete their tasks.

Losing no time, they stuck a boom into the side of the collar still snug around his throat. They untied the two straps around his body and pushed him into a sitting position. The Sticker yelped as barbed strings of agony pulled through his chest and groin. The robots disengaged the wheel locks on the exam table, and pushed him out of the med bay. He wanted to grab one of them or grab the boom, but that would mean letting go of the table, and thereby choking himself.

The calls from the Princess intensified as they neared the audience chamber. At the urgency of her tone, the robots pushed the exam table faster.

Here we go.

As they turned the corner and he caught sight of the room, the Sticker straightened and cold resolve shot through his gut out to his extremities, real and ghost alike.

Fuck this.

He swung his leg hard and smashed a robot in the face with his heel. The gummy substance of its face was nothing like the candy, however. Bones bruised and fractured in his foot on impact. He would have yelled out but the air was taken from his lungs as his weight pitched the table sideways.

The robots moved with merciless grace and righted the table.

The Sticker pushed up on his only arm. A robot came around the table, red arms extended to capture him, diode eyes oscillating wildly.

His fingers brushed something. The boom! It'd disconnected from his collar. He wrapped his fingers gladly around it, picked it up and slammed it into the robot's red skull. Hard vibrations shook his arm but he did it twice more, bending the metal end of the boom's length. The robot, unhindered, continued toward him.

"*All hands report to enzyme catalyst station,*" the overhead blurted. "*Repeat, all hands.*"

The robot stopped, lowered its arms. It turned quickly on one heel and headed off with the others.

The Princess gurgled something in her own language from beyond the door.

The Sticker remembered the translation. *More.*

He grabbed the edge of the exam table and using the boom like a ski pole, got to a standing position. He headed for the membrane station. Several robots charged past him, no longer concerned with him.

Razz must have fouled the enzymes, he thought. *His contingency plan.*

The Sticker prayed the membrane station wasn't locked again. If the Princess wasn't dead, this happy little escape would be all for nothing.

His pace was dreadfully slow and unbalanced. He fell more times than he wished to count, but thankfully, not only was the door to the membrane station not locked, it wasn't even attached anymore. The robots must have knocked it off its hinges attempting to stop Razz.

The Sticker activated the membranes like he'd remembered seeing. He painstakingly removed his collar as he waited for them to heat up. Returning to Limbus Los Angeles was still a hope-filled concept. Just because Razz went through this thing, didn't mean he got sent back to the offices there.

Whatever happened was better than this, the Sticker decided.

When the time came for him to enter the membranes, he had to kneel, making him wonder about unintended consequences.

After enduring the insanity that was membrane transport, the Sticker realized he hadn't returned exactly to the same place he'd left.

He was back at Limbus, but he wasn't in the same station. Instead he was in the lobby, near the rotating globe, wailing gibberish at the top of his lungs. He fell sideways, having reformed in a standing position on one leg. As he collapsed on his face, several people in business attire rushed over to help him.

* * *

The Sticker glided his tongue over his teeth to re-taste the Frosted Flakes from the Limbus cafeteria earlier that morning. He'd forgotten how wonderful food could taste, having relied on his bio-suit for almost a year now.

Tasha was still depressed. Him showing up missing body parts and smelling of alien meat tenderizer, she took all responsibility for. At breakfast despite all his memories of her intelligent, snarky demeanor, she broke down crying. Though secretly anxious to get back to his third bowl of sugary corn flakes, he put down his spoon and touched her hand.

"At least I made it back. My friend Razz can't say the same, right? I don't blame you, so it doesn't make sense to blame yourself. Got it?"

Tasha shook her head and wiped away jeweled tears from her intense green eyes. "I could have insisted on my visiting. I shouldn't have bowed so easily. You didn't deserve a job like that. I should have fought harder for your reassignment."

Anything else he'd said hadn't made a dent. She sat next to him in Trevor's office, her small arms folded tight over her chest, her face pensive.

Trevor strolled in, after keeping them waiting for nearly an hour. The Sticker's heart jumped in his chest.

Annette was with him. She gave him a leery, but sympathetic smile, then patted his shoulder, just above his missing arm. Trevor sat and she rounded his desk to stand at his side.

"Annette? You... know about this place?" he stammered.

"As of last week," Trevor answered, moving a stack of papers off his keyboard. "When you left for your job. Annette was getting an ulcer from all those calls from the water board and the authorities. I had to protect her, and I wanted to be honest with her, since we're in love."

The Sticker flinched. "*Last* week? I've been gone almost a year."

"Actually," Tasha said, leaning over, "your unorthodox way of returning was the only reason why you didn't return at exactly the same moment you left."

"Technically, Trevor tells me that you went back in time," said Annette, her tone filled with romantic mystery. "Fifty years ago!"

"In respect to the multiverses, things happen simultaneously throughout history," Tasha said. "Time really doesn't matter. Every moment is happening all at once... think about it that way."

"No thanks," the Sticker commented. He shook away the disturbing idea. "So wait, that's why I kept getting old Facebook posts and news articles?"

"I tried to send you current database information for those websites, but it took about five Earth years to send it, which complicated the gesture."

"Are you girls done chatting about space and time?" Trevor asked, blond eyebrows lifted impatiently. "There's some serious shit that needs attending."

"Go then already," said the Sticker. He'd have loved to stand and clock the guy, but with this broken body, from now on, fantasizing would be the only way he could ever seek vengeance.

"We need to negotiate a deal with the Princess of Ganymede. Since she's refused other slaughterers, we can no longer keep her armada out of striking reach of this circle of clientele. We will sustain a serious loss of partnerships if we allow her to attack this planet. She's hungry, and she doesn't bluff. There is one bargaining chip we still have, though."

"Me."

"You. Let me read something our people translated. This is from the Princess herself."

With his good arm, the Sticker propped himself up straighter. It wasn't every day you got to hear a missive from a thing that would rather see you on a platter than alive.

"*I have found the One,*" Trevor read. "*This man you sent to me, I've tasted. I savor his taste like nectar from the Five spirits of Blyne. I know he does not want to cooperate with any terms I shall set, especially after how he was treated last we met, but Mr. Milstead, you must find it in your bland human heart to understand how I can no longer live without his taste. I've found perfection in his texture, richness, and I lust after his strong, fragrant blood. If I cannot have him forever, then I see no more sense in rotting away in one of my ships. I will no longer seek employees from your agency and I will encroach upon your territory. You will not stop me. I will eat. I will be full. I will, however, admittedly not be content. You could give contentedness to me and prevent all of this.*

You see, I'm in love with this man. If he worries about death, tell him not to fear, because I will accept any food he grows through mechanical synthesis. I will NOT accept cloned tissues or organs. All meat must be grown from his hallowed body. If you give me this… my fleet stays in this system. This is my promise. –PoG"

Trevor folded up the printout. "Fairly steamy stuff there."

Tasha and Annette both frowned, likely for completely different reasons. After a moment, they all looked at the Sticker, who bent forward as their eyes probed, a little self-conscious of being made to sound important.

"So... I don't really understand."

"We have a cellular regeneration corridor at this location," said Trevor. His handsome face seemed to be the only thing in the room covered in shadow, until he moved his chair forward. "I've got to say though, it's a painful process, especially when you rush it. The Princess will need us sending shipments of your... parts, almost on a daily basis."

"How bad is it?"

"Worse than giving birth is the most common reaction I get from females. Men are normally at a loss for words to describe it. But come on, you're being maimed of all your limbs, maybe some of your organs eventually and then you're forcing your body to regrow itself in a day's time. It's hardcore, buddy."

"Sounds like it," said the Sticker.

"No!" Trevor smacked his desk and nearly came out of his seat. "This isn't an occasion to be flip, you bucktoothed fool! This is NOT the occasion. Believe me. Look man, you might not like how things have gone between us, but I respect you enough to at least get the same in return. This is our fucking world we're talking about here. As I see it, you're responsible."

"How?"

"You're the one she wants so friggin' bad. Shit. Regenerating your tissues will cost a fortune. Until you went out there, we only needed to send a handful of able bodies willing to bring home a decent paycheck. Now, we'll probably have to devote one of our molecular chambers just to you."

"No you won't," said the Sticker. "Because I'm not doing it. Jail is better than this deal." He glanced at Tasha. "Can you get me out of here?"

Tasha looked down and shut her eyes.

"Hey, Tasha..."

"She knows," said Trevor with a smile.

"Knows what?"

"Knows you're fucked. If you leave, law enforcement is waiting for your crippled ass outside, waiting for my signal. They'll have you before you can even hop once to your truck. Not that you could even drive, *lefty*."

The Sticker, though unnerved that Trevor knew he drove a truck, just stared blankly at him.

"What's more, I'm going to take down your entire crew at *Sunshine State.*"

"What?"

"Pablo, Jackson, Carl and any other folks around you that day. They'll all be implicated. Because of *you.*"

The Sticker looked at Annette, who couldn't meet his eyes. "What happens if I say yes?"

"Superb." Trevor breathed out a sigh of relief. "I like where you're going with this... so if you say yes, a few things will happen. For one, you will have total freedom. We will get rid of your outstanding issues with Gerald Bailey and *Sunshine State Meat Products* and you'll be free. You'll be able to leave the offices here, whenever you want, find a place to live, preferably near Los Angeles, so you can come back every day to *donate* and *heal.*"

"How much will I get from this?"

"After you help pay for the cost of the cellular synthesis—"

"What?"

"Remember, this is your fault."

The Sticker wanted to find something heavy and hurl it at the man, but pieces of paper were the only things he saw on the desk.

"What will my pay be then?"

"You'll make a little more than you did at the stock yards. If there's any new technology that comes about that makes this more affordable, of course, your salary will be adjusted less that cost."

"Cocksucker," Tasha muttered.

"What?" Trevor snapped.

Tasha folded her arms tighter and glared at him.

"I guess you have me where you want me," said the Sticker.

Trevor eyed him closely, uncertain. "So we have a deal? I'll get a contract."

"Can I have the afternoon to think about this?"

"There's nothing to consider, but sure, you can have a couple hours," said Trevor. "The Princess hasn't responded to us in a few days. I think she's trying to scare us a bit with her silence, but, I'll send a correspondence you've been handed the terms."

The Sticker looked at Tasha. "Can you help me into the hall?"

"Of course I can." She put her arm around his mid-section.

As they left, the Sticker glanced back to Annette. He was both startled and overjoyed to see her following them outside. For an instant he thought she may have come to be with him—it'd been so long, but for her, only a few days had passed since they'd last seen each other.

Tasha helped him over to a chair and Annette sat in the other seat next to him. He wanted her to look more worried than she did, but the woman he'd married seemed to have turned a corner and he'd been left on some side street, alone, with no sense of direction to find her again.

Tasha left, probably sensing he wanted to be alone with Annette. Despite what he faced, he was glad to know that somebody here at Limbus was on his side.

"I think you're being very brave by taking this deal," said Annette.

"Really?"

"Yes."

"Not sure I have much of a choice... unless you want to take a chance and get me out of here?"

"What would that help?"

"Come on. Trevor isn't what you thought."

"Yeah, he's more. Supervisor in a company like *this*! Not to mention his businesses on the outside."

The Sticker looked down at his hand. It was shaking.

"What's wrong?" she asked.

"What's wrong?" he snapped. "Do you really have to ask that? Are you stupid or something?"

"Don't call me names."

"Are you kidding me? You don't give a shit about me."

"You know why you'd say that? Because you're selfish."

"*I'm selfish.*"

"Yes. You got yourself in trouble, screwed up in so many different ways imaginable, and now you want sympathy? Shit! You're going to get your arm and leg back."

"And then they'll be taken again and again and again and a-fucking-gain! Did you miss that part, Annette?"

"Stop saying I'm stupid. I said you were brave, remember?"

"Oh lord..."

She narrowed her eyes. "Just stop feeling so damned sorry for yourself. It's sad."

"Get out." He shook his head. "I... don't have anything else to say."

Annette left him there without another word. It was surprising she even had decided to talk with him, but then, she wasn't free of guilt completely.

He watched people walk by and wondered about their various stories, what had brought them to this company. Tasha never came back and he continued to sit there.

Trevor never got an official "yes," or a signed contract from him, but soon enough he spotted some orderlies pushing a gurney down the hall.

Pushing it, toward him.

* * *

The Sticker tested his new limbs, squeezing his fist and his toes together. Though he still had a sore throat from screaming and an intense migraine from the synthesis chamber, he found the simple exercise distracting in the best way possible. He didn't want to think about losing all four of his limbs tonight, waking up tomorrow to go into that chamber again. It didn't seem like his heart would be able to take something like that—but then again, perhaps they'd let him grow a new heart.

Absently he rubbed his tongue along his crooked teeth again, hoping for some residual sugar of this morning's breakfast—something was different though. His front teeth were straighter, in-line. He leaned closer to his hospital bed railing and opened his mouth. The reflection did not lie. His teeth were straight and bright white, completely unstained. It had to have happened while he was under. But why?

"Hi there, Slaughter Man," said a voice in the doorway.

"Do I know you?"

An older black man with snow white hair walked into the room. The Sticker studied his face for a moment, looked past the age lines and locked eyes. "Razz? Is that you? Holy shit, you're so old."

"Ha! Thanks." Razz pulled out a stool and sat before the bed, a big grin painted on his face.

"But they told me that nobody else came through the transport."

"Well, can't blame them for being wrong about that... I returned fifty years before you." Razz chuckled.

The Sticker opened his mouth but another voice said, "Time doesn't matter."

Tasha entered the room. "You could have told me, Dad."

"It had to happen the same way I knew it would. I'm not playing with what would occur if you'd altered the course of things. You knew that I started working contracts for this company as a young man. I told you that."

"You never told me it was on the Princess' slaughter ship. That might have been good information for the Slaughter Man here to take with him."

"I disagree."

"You..." said the Sticker. "You're Razz Willing then? How did I not know that?"

"Actually it's Arnold Willing. Harper and Timothy made up the name because I always razzed them."

The Sticker's gut twisted. "Do you know about what happened to Tim?"

"Yeah," said Razz sadly. "I've known for some time now. I think the tension of that last week really took him to a place he couldn't return from."

"I wish I could have..."

"Leave it alone for now. You've been through enough. I'm just glad to finally see you again. So yes, nobody except you three ever called me Razz. But what the hell, I never actually asked your real name either, Slaughter Man."

"So you became some Limbus big shot?"

" Well, maybe, but I still feel like I'm working on a slaughter ship some days," Razz explained with a wink.

"Your contingency plan worked, by the way. Whatever you did with the enzymes bought me enough time to get out of there."

"You don't know the half of it," said Razz. "Why don't you tell him, Milstead?"

The Sticker looked around Razz. In the doorway, Trevor stood with a file folder under his arm. He looked tired and frazzled. The Sticker couldn't help it but a pre-victory smile crept over his face. He sensed good news—the antithesis of Trevor's expression.

"Interesting report in about the Princess..." Trevor glanced around, uncomfortable with all the eyes on him. "She suffered massive *steel-shock* and slipped into a coma, shortly after sending her missive about you."

Razz turned to the Sticker. "All that scrap metal I found in the compactor—I tossed it in her enzymes. They broke down right away. If she ever recovers, she'll not be the monstrous eater of the past. Which is well for me. I'm tired of her getting everything she wants while other clients pay the price... not to mention, I haven't had a good game of backgammon in a long time."

The Sticker closed his mouth, which had fallen open. "So... I don't have to go into surgery tonight?"

"I hope not," said Razz, "you're being announced tonight at the company's annual dinner. All division executives have to attend. That's why we fixed your grill there. Hope you like the new pearly whites, makes you more diplomatic looking."

He looked at Tasha, who beamed. "I just found out this morning."

"It's been tough handling two divisions on my own," said Razz. "Now I can focus on Ganymede division and you can oversee here."

"Los Angeles?"

Razz laughed. "No, Earth, of course."

The Sticker choked on some spit that went down the wrong pipe. He looked at Trevor. "But what's he do? Besides be rich and an asshole?"

"Those businesses are fronts. I answer to the Earth Director here. My sole position is a supervisor of operations in the Los Angeles office," Trevor put mildly. "Are you going to fire me now?"

"Are you joking?" The Sticker swung out of bed. Both his feet touched the cold ground. It was a lovely, powerful feeling; he wasn't dreaming after all. He stood toe to toe with Trevor Milstead now. He'd never been afraid of the man, but he'd never felt like an equal either. "I'm never going to fire you, Milstead," said the Sticker. "Where the hell is the fun in *that*?"

Tasha sniffed out a laugh and looked away.

"Thanks, Director," answered Trevor. When nobody said anything, he hurried from the room.

Razz took the Sticker's hand. "And thank you, Director, for saving my life."

"I don't know how to do this job," the Sticker admitted.

"Nobody does at first. But with my help," he said, "you're going to do great."

"Phenomenal," added Tasha.

"But isn't this strange? Me... working directly for you guys."

"I told you before. This kind of thing happens all the time. Most of our recruiters were once clients, in fact. It's because our contracts are so blasted weak. I've been meaning to revise them."

"So you?" the Sticker asked Tasha.

The little girl smirked. "No, I've never worked outside the company. I was the first recruiter and I'll be the last."

"But how—"

"I'll send a courier later with your new clothes and invitation," Razz interrupted. "Sound good, Slaughter Man?" He lifted a hopeful eyebrow.

The Sticker threw up his hands. "Sounds good."

They left him there in the plush hospital room. He felt like hooting and crying and laughing all at once, but instead sat on the bed and closed his eyes.

When he opened them, Annette stood in the room.

"I don't expect you to forgive my actions or how brutal I've treated you lately. I just wanted to congratulate you. Trevor's not happy, but I know you'll be a good boss. I'm really stoked for you. I am."

The Sticker opened his arms and Annette moved into them. It felt so damningly good to hold her again, savor the moment, before he pushed her back and searched her pleading face. Annette studied his eyes for a moment. "You aren't still mad at me. Are you?"

He shook his head.

She smiled and went to embrace him again, but he put his hand up. "Of course I haven't stopped caring about you, Annette, but I do have a business to run now."

She frowned. "But..."

"So," said the Sticker, pointing to the hall, "if you please, kindly get the hell out of my building. *Now.*"

* * *

The last course was rainbow sherbet molded into a Limbus globe. The Sticker thought it almost too pretty to eat. Tasha and Razz argued a bit about something work-related into which he hadn't turned his attention.

"You're so sensitive," said Razz. "Must get it from your mother."

"You haven't even met my mother yet!" Tasha said.

"Uh, how, uh, does that work?" asked the Sticker, jumping into the conversation.

"Time doesn't matter, remember?"

"Yeah..."

"What's wrong?" asked Razz.

The Sticker sighed. The reality of what happened had finally connected. With everything he'd faced, this new world, a world of boundless responsibility, seemed even more terrifying. "It's just... I don't feel I've earned this." His voice betrayed him with a quiver.

Razz shook his head in respectful disbelief. "You have. More than anybody here."

The Sticker looked down under the table, at his loafers, so strange on his feet.

A representative stopped by the table with individual packets. "Hello, Mr. Willing. Hello Ms. Willing. Here are action items and annual budget breakdowns. Oh and hello, Mr. Fulsome, here is yours."

The Sticker took his packet and nodded thanks.

Tasha said, "Funny, I remember your name from our files, but it sounds strange to hear spoken. We all just called you the Slaughter Man."

"*Dean Fulsome...* not sure I ever knew the man," said the Sticker.

Razz raised his glass. "Happy Birthday, Dean."

Tasha lifted hers.

Dean lifted his.

"To time not mattering," he said.

Their three glasses met.

For Dean Fulsome, that was the moment everything began.

The Sacrifice

By

Brett J. Talley

He couldn't see anything, and all he could hear was a steady *drip, drip, drip* that thundered in his ears. *Drip, drip, drip* in regular beats, too loud to be real. And then it wasn't real anymore. It faded out and almost away—but not quite—as his consciousness expanded to encompass something more than just that sound. His eyes fluttered open, but all he saw was red. A pool of crimson that seemed to expand beneath him as he grew colder. The drip of blood from his forehead added to the flow, but it was a larger opening somewhere else on his body that served as the fountainhead.

He started to lose focus, and the black shroud of unconsciousness mixed with the crimson of the blood on the edges of his vision. As darkness took him, his eyes fell on a piece of white cardboard floating in the midst of the red ocean. It hung there like a ship on the verge of floundering, until a rivulet of red water poured over its side. He watched as the blood touched the thick, black letters. And then, in the instant before consciousness left him, he would have sworn those same letters ignited in a flash of red light, the name they formed glowing in the night.

* * *

"So what were you doing at *Cliff's Edge* last night?"

Katya. It all went back to Katya.

The detective waited, drumming his notebook with his pencil while Ryan thought about her.

"It's a simple question," he said finally, leaning forward in his chair and putting the sharpened end of the pencil to paper, ready to write.

Ryan looked at him. "No," he said, "nothing is ever simple."

Detective Fox frowned. Ryan wasn't trying to be mysterious, but he knew that's how he came off. The detective had been patient, giving Ryan time to recover after he was found that night, lying in a pool of his own blood outside of the *Cliff's Edge* nightclub. Ryan had almost gone over that edge. He was as near to death as a man could be and still come back from it.

"There's nothing much simpler than a bar fight, son. But I'll never find the guys that did this if you don't give me something to work with."

Ryan thought back to Katya. "I was there to meet a woman," he said.

"Ah," the detective mumbled in a knowing way that made Ryan cringe. It wasn't that simple, but he had chosen his words poorly. And now for Fox, it would always go back to the girl. A jilted lover, a guy who tried to flirt at the bar only to be rebuffed. A rival for her affection that saw Ryan as a threat, one that had to be eliminated. Yeah, for the detective, the answer was obvious. But he was right in one thing. The girl was the key.

But even that wasn't true. It went back further than her. It all started with the nightmares.

* * *

A few days before the incident at the bar, Ryan lay in his bed, fighting sleep. It was a losing battle.

When they first started, Ryan had told himself that the dreams would go away. That once he was home long enough, the familiar would kick in. He would be reminded of who he was. Not Lance Corporal Ryan Dixson. No. He was Ryan from Carbondale. Starting linebacker on his high school football team. Son of David and Joy. Regular guy with a regular life. But the dreams wouldn't let him forget. So he lay there, waiting. It hadn't gotten better. In fact, it had gotten worse.

At first, when he landed in the States, they had come once every couple weeks. But with every few days that passed, he saw them more. The last night he had slept through without having the dream was Saturday. Now it was Wednesday, and he didn't know if he could handle another one.

He wasn't sure that he should call them dreams. They were more like memories in dream form. Night terrors of an actual event. No embellishment needed, for it took no dark conjuring to turn Ryan's dreams into soul-rending flights of horror. No, the dirty work had been done in the real world. The only conjuring needed was the fumbling hands of a tribal rebel.

He was probably still alive, out there somewhere. That singular day was no doubt burned into his mind as well. Perhaps, on long nights in the Afghan waste, he and his fellows would sit round a low fire. In the sparking embers, as the others waited silently, ready to hang on his every word, he would weave the scene.

It was a convoy, seven Humvees deep. The Afghan raiders sat on a low hill a mile from the dusty, desert road on which the soldiers traveled. They were members of a local tribe. Not Taliban, but angry enough at the world and the invader to accept their generosity in the form of crude explosives.

Their methods were simple. Bury the device along the side of the road. Wait. When the target was over the area, trigger the bomb with a remote. Run.

The last part meant they were never really sure whether they succeeded. Sometimes the bomb went off too late or too early. Sometimes it just disabled the vehicle or caused minor damage. Most times it was more of a nuisance than anything else. But every now and then, it all fell into place. And that was the story the Pashtun man would tell his brothers in the dark watches of the night. Of the time that he killed an American.

Of course, Ryan never saw it that way, figuratively or literally. The dream was always the same. He was in the middle Humvee, the one that, by all rights, was the safest. He was sitting in the center of it, protected by the vehicle's most heavily armored section. His back was to the windshield, facing Philip O'Connor. Philip was grinning. It seemed like Philip always was.

That smile was the last happy memory Ryan ever had.

It happened in an instant, as these things always do. One moment Philip was smiling. Then, somewhere on that distant hill, a man Ryan didn't know and would never meet pressed a button. It took a split second for the signal to travel from the hill to the road. Long enough for a heartbeat. Long enough for the Humvee to roll the few extra feet it needed to for fate to have its due. But as thunder follows lightning, so too did the roar of the explosion follow the pressing of that button. On that roar rode death.

He only really heard it for a singular instant. After the pressure wave burst his eardrums, everything that followed was more of a low, echoing murmur, like he was sitting at the bottom of a well. Somehow that made everything all the worse.

He felt his stomach drop as the whole vehicle lifted into the air. But it wasn't the feeling of weightlessness or the bursting of his ears that filled his nights with horror. It was what he saw.

Philip was sitting across from him, smiling. Then he was ripped apart. Even as it happened, even as parts of his body were twisted and torn off, he still wore that smile.

They said he died instantly, and Ryan believed it. He often wondered what exactly it meant to die instantly, though. It was true—the smile never left his face. But that only meant that his brain didn't have enough time to register what was happening and send a signal to his muscles to better reflect it. Even if the control of every fiber was cut in that instant, even if that smile remained frozen in place, Ryan still wondered what the brain knew. If Philip's last thoughts were simply the echo of soundless screaming, confined within the walls of his own mind.

Then Ryan wasn't just thinking about it—he was living it. In that instant of reflected terror, he watched it happen again through his own eyes but with no power to stop it, a passenger in the flights of his own subconscious. As much a prisoner as one bound by chains.

He awoke from the dream as the sound of thunder ripped through the cabin of the vehicle and the body of his friend.

That night, the transition was a quiet one, his eyes simply fluttering open to the darkness that seemed eternal but in fact ended in the ceiling above. It had not always been that way. At first it was a shock. He would jerk himself from the dream, sitting bolt upright in his bed, drenched in sweat. At least, with time, he had overcome that part. Now that the dreams came more frequently, he had plenty of chances to practice self-control.

Not that it made it any easier to fall back asleep. No, in the hours that followed, he was as awake as he would ever be, even as he knew he would pay for it in the coming morning. There was no point in lying there and fighting it. If anything, that would probably make it worse, prolong the agony. He sighed as he pushed down the covers and pulled himself out of bed.

He wandered down the steps in the dark, not bothering with the lights. As if there was anyone else but him there, someone he might disturb, someone he might awaken. But he was alone, and he felt it.

He tripped on the final step, almost falling as he stumbled into his living room. He let himself collapse down into the recliner that sat in front of his television and turned it on. Then he reached over and opened the small refrigerator that he kept permanently stocked with beer. As he opened one, he couldn't help but think that he was drinking more of it these days.

Bottle in one hand and remote in the other, he pressed a button and the electronic firelight of the television outshone the meager glow of the moon that had, until that point, provided the room's only illumination. Ryan flipped through the channels, pausing briefly on an infomercial that made him smile for the first time in what seemed like ages. But it was a horror film that struck his fancy, one of those bad sci-fi flicks they only play at three o'clock in the morning. It wasn't long before his eyelids began to grow heavy. They had almost closed completely when the movie faded out and the commercial began.

If it hadn't been that particular commercial, Ryan wouldn't have remembered it. If it had been anything else, he simply would have slipped away into sleep, never recalling the televised message he'd seen before dreams took him. Maybe then things would have been different. Maybe then, everything would have changed.

But it wasn't just any commercial. It was something much different. Ryan watched through barely opened eyes, and later he would tell himself it had been a dream brought on by too much beer and not enough sleep. It started as a flash that filled the screen in blinding white before fading to an equally empty black. There was a pause then, the image emanating from the television now giving no light, and darkness held sway. But then from that black void, letters started to form, silhouetted in a dirty red. But it was the voice that broke through the dream-like haze that gripped Ryan.

"We are Limbus," it said, as the shadowed outlines cleared into letters that formed the word. "We stand on the edge. We stare into the abyss. We do not discriminate. We do not forget. We employ. Join us."

Then there was another flash of light, and in that flash Ryan saw a girl, no older than thirteen or fourteen. In that solitary moment, he watched her, wearing flannel pajamas covered in shooting stars and moons and unicorns. Rough hands grabbed her tightly around the arms and legs. And though she struggled, they did not relent. She screamed, and Ryan awoke, still in his bed.

* * *

The next evening he found himself in the bowels of Hendricksville Community College, standing in one of the basement hallways, staring down a corridor to a classroom that contained the support group for sufferers of post-traumatic stress disorder. HCC was housed in an ancient government building of post-War vintage. If it were one of the new lofts in the warehouse district, the exposed pipes and naked brick would no doubt have added hundreds of dollars to the cost of rent, and young couples and hip singles would call the place home. It just made Ryan feel dirty and worn down.

He had known for a while that someday, somehow, he would find himself in a place like this. It was hard enough holding down a job in the civilian world anyway, and bosses didn't like employees who at any moment might find themselves back in the middle of a firefight or a roadside bombing outside some dusty town in Iraq or Afghanistan.

The dream of the night before had been the final straw. Somehow, he'd grown accustomed to the other nightmares, as horrible as they were. But there was something about this one, something sinister and disturbing, that he could not shake. He needed to get help, even if that help was only the kind ear of someone who had suffered the same pain.

That had been the plan, but like all plans this one was laid waste by the unexpected. His started to unravel the moment he saw Katya.

He would always remember that moment, the one when he caught a glimpse of her for the first time. It had been a revelation. She had been walking from one open classroom to another, probably finishing one meeting before his own was set to begin. It was a passing glance, but in that instant she cast a singular look down the hallway, and Ryan froze.

Maybe it was her eyes, pale green flashes that grabbed him even from that distance. Or the hair, a bright, crashing red all the wilder above the tight cut of her black jacket, one that covered a matching skirt that somehow seemed incongruous with the rest of her. Whatever the answer, it lasted only a second before that locked gaze was broken as she passed into the next room.

The session had not gone as Ryan expected. Sure, there were the obligatory introductions, the stories, the heartbreak. In a way, everything about that hour had made Ryan feel worse. At least his problems didn't include lost limbs and shattered bodies. But he couldn't brood on it, because he barely noticed it. He had something to distract him. Those eyes and their flashes of green were always upon him.

She didn't make it obvious. She nodded at the right times during the others' stories. She said the right things, and some of it probably even helped the poor souls that surrounded him. But he was the only one she really saw.

* * *

"So," she said, leaning over the table, swirling with her straw the last remnants of cracked ice cubes around the bottom of an empty glass, "why did you come tonight?"

She had found him, after the meeting. He had pondered, as the last of the men's stories drew to a close, how he would approach her. For that had been the one conclusion he had reached during that interminable sixty minutes—that approach her, he would. But in the end, he didn't have to figure out an angle; she found him leaning against the refreshments table, pondering his next move, half-eaten stale cookie in one hand, watered-down Coke in the other.

What had followed had almost been too easy, one thing leading to another, tumblers falling into place in a lock. There was an Asian bistro down the road. Sushi place. He had never eaten there and he didn't care for raw fish. But the local scuttlebutt had been that it was good, and he judged, unfairly no doubt, that it was the kind of place someone like her would like. She just seemed the type.

Things were cautious at first. They made small talk over drinks and edamame. The alcohol helped to smooth the introductions. Asahi for him. Something more tropical, a Mai Tai to be exact, was her preference. When the drinks were drained and there was nothing left but the clinking of ice, she had finally broached the question.

"So, why did you come tonight?"

It had been one, in all honesty, that he had not expected. "You heard my story," he said, suddenly feeling uncomfortable.

"Oh, I heard your story. It's just, it's never the story, you know? Not the story by itself, at least. Everybody who comes to my meetings has a problem, but it's a problem they keep to themselves. Problems they don't deal with until something happens. Something bad. Guys like you, they come back damaged, but still unbroken. Usually it takes something that goes wrong here, in the States, to finally break them. PTSD is a lot like addiction. You can't even start to cure it until you admit that you have a problem, and most people can't admit that they have a problem until they hit rock bottom. What was rock bottom for you?"

Ryan leaned back in his chair until it creaked beneath him. Nervous laughter had never been his style, but it was the only thing he felt like doing in that moment. He rubbed his hand across his mouth and stared at the ceiling. Now he remembered why he never went to a shrink.

"I think it was the loneliness," he said finally. "Day after day, sitting in my apartment. No job, no family, no one to talk to. My parents died a few years ago. Car wreck. I always meant to settle down but I never quite made it. My buddies, such that they are, they're either still in or dealing with the same thing. Either way, I don't want to bother them with it."

"So you kept it in," she said, "simmering, just below the surface?"

"I guess you could say that."

"And what else?"

Ryan frowned and looked down at his empty plate. It didn't matter. Suddenly, he wasn't very hungry. "Well, the dreams. You know what I mean? I guess you hear that a lot," he said with a sigh. "It was fine, and then I started having them. I don't know. Dreams, nightmares, memories. Like I was there. Again. Like it was happening all over."

"And you had those every night?"

"Not every night. But more and more. And then . . ." Ryan trailed off. How to explain what he didn't quite understand himself? "I don't know. It's just . . ." He could feel the sweat beading around his forehead. He wished she would speak. He wished she would say anything that would let him off the hook. Instead, she just stared. "It's just, they seemed to reach a crescendo, I guess."

"They got worse?"

"No. It's hard to say. They got different."

At some point in the conversation, her friendly, almost flirty, demeanor had dropped away and the clinician had taken over. Now he was very much a patient with a doctor, and as she sat there, fixing him with her eyes, staring across that distance, he felt uneasy. Almost frightened for the first time in years, like she was peeling away the layers that he hid beneath, one by one. Uncovering something below the surface, and maybe even deeper, that he had tried to hide. But when she smiled, the magic was broken.

"I don't normally say this," she said, "'cause there are too many guys trying not to deal with it, trying to just cover up the problem. But you, I think your issue is a little different. I think maybe you focus on it too much. You don't bury it deep; you dwell on it. So what you might need," she said, "is a distraction. A diversion. Something to change things up."

He grinned. "And what exactly do you suggest, doctor?"

"Well," she said, blushing ever so slightly, "I was thinking maybe you should get a job."

"Ah, a job." He was disappointed, and he didn't do much to hide it.

"But," she added, "I can think of a few other things that might take the edge off."

This time when she smiled, it was with a touch of the forbidden.

* * *

That night was the first in many that he had slept till the morning, with neither the dreams nor the fear of them disturbing his rest. He awoke to the light of a risen sun shining through his uncurtained window, the soft feeling of her skin beneath his hands. Her breathing was deep, and it took all his concentration to remove himself from beneath her arm without waking her. He sat on the edge of the bed, smiling to himself about what had happened and what it might portend. He almost didn't notice the piece of white cardboard that was sitting on the side table, right next to his wallet and her cell phone. He saw it, and then looked away. But it took his brain only a second to process what the black lettering said. And when it did, he felt the sweat bead on his forehead, cold and foreboding. Beneath a globe sprinkled with sparkling flecks was the word, "Limbus" and then, "We Employ." He jumped when she put her hand on his shoulder.

"Whoa, there," she said, giggling. "I didn't mean to scare you."

"Where'd you get this?" he asked, letting it pass.

"Oh, that's this employment agency I heard about from one of the guys down at the college." She wrapped one arm around his chest and kissed his neck. "I thought you might want to look into it. Why?"

Suddenly, he felt very foolish. "It's nothing. I just thought I saw this before somewhere."

"So, you'll look into it?"

"Actually, I'm thinking of going back in." He felt her body tense.

"The Marines? But why would you do that?"

Ryan shrugged. "I've just been thinking about it for a while. I really belong there, you know? Maybe the best thing for me is to go back to what I'm good at."

He turned to her, and in the brightening morning he watched her smile weakly.

"Yeah," she said, "maybe that's a good idea."

Her heart wasn't in it though, and he could tell. But he didn't think long on it. If he'd had any doubts about his future, something about picking up that business card had removed them.

* * *

Ryan met Katya the next evening at *The Cliff's Edge*. He'd never been before; she clearly had. He'd heard of it, and he knew it was one of the trendiest places in New Orleans. The formidable rope line proved no obstacle, though. What must have been only a few words from Katya to the well-constructed man in the short-sleeve shirt resulted in a quick nod and a wave of his hand. Perhaps it was that she was wearing a slinky piece of black nothing that revealed almost as much as he'd seen the night before.

The music was thick and pulsating. He let it surround him as he walked in, and each step seemed to be a little more difficult than the last, as if the sound and the air formed a solid mass. Katya said something to him, but the noise ruled over all, and he couldn't make it out. She repeated it again, and this time he watched her lips. Does he want a drink. Yes, he does. He said so, but his voice was lost somewhere in the reverberations.

Katya left, and as she disappeared into the herd of people, Ryan turned to face the dance floor. It too was filled with bodies moving to the music that surrounded them. He supposed they were dancing, but it seemed more like a case of spiritual possession. Like the music was inside them. Like they were an instrument unto themselves. Or one of those crazy, psychedelic displays that changes based on the song played.

He felt Katya's arm slip around his waist, her other hand holding a drink to his lips. Then she smiled and pulled him into the mass. The beat took them. Ryan felt himself become one with the tribe, and with every hit of the thumping bass he heard words in the rumble. Katya lowered her eyes, and between the beat and her dress and the words and her stare Ryan lost himself. The song morphed into another and then another, but Katya's body always matched it, her knees bent and her hips swaying. Her hands traveled down Ryan's neck and his body. Her hair flowed and swirled around her face.

It was the third song, or the first depending on one's measure, before the feeling truly set in. A tingle in his hands and his toes, a fire in his stomach. Something unaccountable, as if he had ten drinks instead of half of one. A smile crept up Katya's face, and he thought he saw something sinister in it. Then the music seemed to grow quieter, but he felt it in his chest, more intense than ever.

Ryan fell backwards, the room starting to shift if not quite to spin. Katya stood at the edge, the crowd behind her and around her all at once. The music played on, and Katya swayed with her eyes ever on Ryan. Her hands moved up her body until they were at her head. Until they ran up her face and through her hair. And then they were higher. Climbing and climbing. And then it was the same with them all, each person that surrounded her. They swayed to the sound of the beat. Pagan penitents at prayer. For what did they pray? For what did they reach? What did they seek? Ryan never got the chance to find out.

There was a commotion behind the crowd. Shouting, pushing. Katya disappeared into the melee, while Ryan was caught up in it. The roiling mass carried him from one darkness to another. It was then he felt the sharp pain in his side, the one that opened a hole and spilled his blood upon the dirty asphalt, the one that nearly killed him. The stab wound that left him lying in a hospital bed, answering the questions of a police officer.

* * *

The detective flipped his notebook closed and looked up at Ryan. "So that's it then?"

"The next thing I remember, I was here."

The detective frowned. "That's not a whole lot to go on." Ryan didn't know what else to add, so he said nothing. "Oh well," the detective said, pushing himself up and straightening his coat, "I'll keep you informed, and I'll call you if we need anything else. Oh, and by the way," he said, turning as he reached the door and then walking back to where Ryan was lying. "I meant to give you this. Whoever stuck you took your wallet, and this was the only thing left in your pocket."

Ryan shivered as the detective removed the thin piece of white cardboard from his pocket and dropped it on the table beside the hospital bed. He could really only read one word, but that's all he needed: Limbus.

* * *

Ryan stood outside 453 South Rampart Street in New Orleans, only a couple blocks away from the Mississippi River. He removed the thin sliver of cardboard and studied it. This was the right address; the business card confirmed that much. But somehow Ryan had expected more than the non-descript and somewhat run down warehouse of which Limbus was one of the tenants. He checked the address one last time, and seeing that nothing had changed, stepped inside the front door.

There was no receptionist, only a callbox. It seemed as though at some time before there had been a number of tenants who called the warehouse home. But now the only name that remained was the one that he was looking for. He pushed a button, heard a beep, and waited only a couple seconds before a female voice answered.

"Yes?"

"Hi, this is Ryan Dixson, I have an appointment with Recruiter Hawthorne."

"Ah yes, Mr. Dixson. Please, come in."

The buzzing sound announced that he had been admitted, and Ryan opened the inner door of the warehouse, walking up the stairs that lead to a hallway. He had to pause half-way up, clutching his side where still-fresh sutures kept him from bleeding out of a wound that had cost him any shot at going back into the Marines.

"New beginnings," he whispered to himself. That's what Katya had told him when she encouraged him—almost made him, really—seek out Limbus. He started climbing again, and after only a few more steps, he found a sign that directed him down the right corridor. He hadn't gone far before he stood in front of the Limbus office.

The waiting room itself was relatively bare. The Limbus company logo hung on one wall, a large globe that seemed to sparkle, and Ryan assumed that each tiny point of light indicated an office of the agency. Beside the globe was the picture of a fresh-faced kid younger than Ryan. "Employee of the Month: Dallas Hamilton" was written beneath it. Otherwise, there were only some chairs and the receptionist desk to fill out the room. He didn't even see any magazines.

The brunette, who he assumed was the receptionist, was sitting behind an ancient looking computer screen, filing her nails and talking loudly on the phone. She winked at Ryan as he walked in, but didn't bother to interrupt her telephone call to give him any further instructions. Down he sat in one of the grubby chairs across from the logo and waited. He'd begun to wonder if this was all a mistake when the door opened and out stepped a man.

He seemed completely out of place here. Ryan was no expert, but he knew the suit the man was wearing was high-dollar. The lines were too crisp, the shirt too delicate and constantly on the verge of falling into a thousand wrinkles, the tie too bright and the cufflinks too shiny for this ensemble to be a Macy's special. Apparently, recruiter gigs at Limbus paid well.

"Ah, you must be Mr. Dixson," he said extending his hand. He smiled, and Ryan couldn't help but notice that his brilliantly white teeth lined up perfectly. "Of course, you are."

"Please, call me Ryan."

"Yes, Ryan. You may follow me."

The two men went through the door behind the receptionist. She still didn't say anything, but she did give Ryan a smile and another wink.

"So, Mr. Dixson," Hawthorne said as he led Ryan down a hallway of what seemed like row after row of empty offices, "we were most fortunate that you contacted us. It is quite difficult to find good help these days."

"Yeah, about that," Ryan said, wondering if they would ever reach Hawthorne's office, "what sort of positions are you looking to fill?"

"Oh," Hawthorne said, turning and smiling again at Ryan, "all kinds. You can't even begin to imagine the jobs I've doled out over the years. Everything from dog walking to other, more . . . how shall we say it . . . esoteric endeavors."

"Ah."

"But please, come in and sit down."

Hawthorne opened a door and made a sweeping gesture to the seat in front of his desk.

"So, Mr. Dixson, I believe we have the perfect job for you."

"Uh," Ryan stuttered, shifting in the chair he had only just sat down in, "how would you know that?"

"Oh Mr. Dixson, we do our research," Hawthorne said, reaching into a drawer beside him and pulling out a sheet of paper. "It's so easy these days to find out everything you want to know about a person. I mean, your entire life is on the Internet. Did you know that, with a simple search, I can find the address of every place you've ever lived? Every parking ticket you've ever had? It's amazing really. Of course," he continued, leaning back in his chair and putting his hands behind his head, "I've always preferred the more old-fashioned methods. I find the tried and the true to be more reliable, don't you think?"

Ryan looked at the strange man sitting across from him and a sense of unease settled uncomfortably on his shoulders. "I've never really thought about it."

"Ah, yes, of course not." Hawthorne put his elbows on the desk and picked up a rather attractive fountain pen. "Do forgive me. I tend to ramble on occasion. A bad habit, no doubt. But in any event," he said, uncapping the pen and placing it on the piece of paper, "we should get down to business."

He slid the document to Ryan, who leaned over in his chair and looked at it. "Employment Contract," it read in big, bold letters at the top.

"This is what we have available for you."

Ryan picked up the paper and began to read. "Not much to choose from, huh?"

"Well, you must understand. Our reputation is built upon our ability to provide the perfect candidate for every job."

"Wow, Boston? You couldn't find somebody closer?"

"As I said, our clients expect the perfect candidate. And in this case, that candidate is you. You will of course be compensated for the inconvenience. And, as you can see, the remuneration is quite significant."

"Yes, I see that. Though you are a little short on the details here."

In fact, the document Ryan held in his hands was completely devoid of details. The only concrete thing it provided was that the job was in Boston. Under the job description the document read only, "Perform instructions adequately, not failing to see the job through to the end."

"Yes, about that. I know this is unusual, but I must request that you sign the document before I tell you what the job entails."

Hawthorne saw the look on Ryan's face and held up his hand. "Let me explain. The details are quite sensitive. Once you have heard them, you can back out if you wish, but we need you to be bound by the confidentiality clause. If you decide the job is not for you, we will pay you a hundred dollars, no questions asked."

"But I didn't see a . . ." Ryan looked down at the contract, and sure enough, there was a confidentiality clause at the bottom. He would have sworn that it had not been there before, but there it was, nonetheless. "Well," he said after a moment, "it's not illegal, is it?"

Hawthorne responded as if that was the funniest thing he had ever heard, laughing to the point of cackling, before trailing off into a simple, "No."

"Alright," Ryan said uneasily, though swayed by the thought of what he could get for the easy hundred, "that seems reasonable, I suppose."

Recruiter Hawthorne watched as Ryan signed, the amiable smile never leaving his face. "Excellent. Now it is time to discuss your assignment. A week ago, a fourteen-year-old girl named Angela Endicott was kidnapped from her home in the Beacon Hill area of Boston."

"Whoa, whoa, whoa," Ryan said, throwing up a hand as if to defend himself from some assault. "What is this, man? Shouldn't that be something for the police to handle?"

Hawthorne frowned, obviously irked at being interrupted. "The police have been notified, I assure you. Her parents are cooperating with them fully. As of yet, they have no leads, nor do we believe they will find any. The culprits are professionals of the highest order."

"Was there a note? A ransom or whatever?"

"Nothing. There has been no communication between the kidnappers and the authorities whatsoever. It is as if she simply disappeared into thin air. If there is evidence to be had on her whereabouts or her ultimate fate, the police have not found any."

"Wow. And so now the parents have contacted you for help?"

"Not the parents, Mr. Dixson, the uncle. The parents are wealthy, yes, but the girl's uncle is extravagantly so. Only he could afford our considerable fee."

Ryan couldn't help but glance around the barren white walls of the office, decorated only with the stains of previous tenants. Hawthorne took note.

"We spend our money wisely, Mr. Dixson. And we long ago found that office space and the baubles and trinkets that often fill it are not a high priority. We put value in our talent, and we pay them accordingly."

Ryan nodded. "Understood. I meant no offense."

"None taken," Hawthorne said, the smile returning to his face.

"But I have to ask, why me and why you? Why not go with a detective agency?"

"Because the uncle, a man named Bernard Samuelson, understands that no detective agency will find the girl. It will take a man with a special skill set, one with which a person is born, not taught. A person such as yourself."

The two men stared at one another across the short gulf between them for a few moments before Ryan said, "With all due respect, I'm beginning to think you're a little crazy."

Hawthorne's grin never wavered, though Ryan wondered if he saw a touch of frustration work into the corner of it. "The payment is guaranteed, Mr. Dixon. You need only make a good faith effort and I assure you, succeed or not, you will be paid."

"But I still don't get it. Why me?"

Hawthorne's smile grew wider. "Sometimes it takes a hero to perform such a duty. Besides, can you really turn your back on a face like this?"

Hawthorne slipped a picture from inside a desk drawer and slid it in front of Ryan. Whether he expected Ryan to gasp or not, he didn't show it. For his part, Ryan could not hide his reaction. He had seen the girl before, a child no older than thirteen or fourteen. One with flannel pajamas covered in shooting stars and moons and unicorns.

"Good," Hawthorne said. "You leave for Boston in the morning."

* * *

Ryan pulled his jacket tight around his chest, fastening the second to last button in a stubborn if futile effort against the cold. It was a late April evening, and he had expected warmer weather, but the notoriously fickle Massachusetts climate had been his undoing. So he stood there shivering on the corner of Dartmouth and Newbury Street, in the shadow of an ancient Episcopalian church, watching as the girls in their too small—and too cold—outfits walked past, clinging to each other's arms, off to some night of excitement and excess in the depths of Boston's more enticing neighborhoods. For a moment, he thought of joining them. Of leaving the job and his life behind, starting afresh in a new place where the sun rose bright and clear each day. He thought of it, but only for a moment.

Ryan didn't notice the Mercedes until it pulled beneath a streetlight and stopped. Ryan stepped forward and stooped down as a window lowered and the face of a man appeared, framed by the upturned collar of an expensive coat.

"Mr. Dixson, I presume."

"And you must be Mr. Bernard Samuelson," Ryan said, reaching through the window to take the man's hand. "It's a pleasure to meet you."

"I'm sure. Please, Mr. Dixson, get in."

The man opened the door, and Ryan slid inside. Before he could put on his seatbelt, the driver had already jerked away from the curb, into Boston traffic and a sudden, gently falling rain. It seemed that Samuelson had arrived just in time to prevent Ryan from having a very uncomfortable night, indeed.

"Would you like a drink, Mr. Dixson?"

Ryan hesitated, glancing over at the bottle of scotch that rested in a panel obviously custom-made for the man who now sat looking him over. "Is that allowed?" he asked. Ryan had always been a straight arrow, no matter how much he tried to avoid it.

Samuelson smiled. "While you are with me, all things are permitted."

The man removed a stopper from the bottle and poured liberally, handing it to Ryan and filling his own glass.

"So Mr. Dixson," Samuelson said as the car maneuvered through Boston at speeds that could not be legal, "I understand you were a soldier in a past life."

Ryan watched as the car pulled off the city streets and on to the interstate. "I was," he answered, "what seems like a long time ago now." Without thinking, Ryan's hand went down to his side, rubbing across his stomach where the newly healed wound still ached.

"It's fortunate. I've found that men such as yourself possess an uncommon bravery. You'll need it if you are to find my niece and save her life."

"So you do think Angela's in danger then?"

Samuelson didn't immediately answer, but rather stared straight ahead. He clenched his jaw before nodding. "She is. Of that there can be no doubt."

"I'm sorry, Mr. Samuelson, but I don't think I understand."

The man laughed mirthlessly.

"No, my friend, there's no way you could. I am a very wealthy man, Mr. Dixson. And a man in my position learns things that others do not know. They see things that others do not see. Not all of those things are pleasant. I have been told you are a reliable man, and I believe that you are exactly what we need. But I must warn you now, once you commit to this road, you cannot leave it. You won't find our Angela without walking down paths that are better left untrod. If you wish to abandon this mission, now is the time for you to decide. But one way or another, I need your answer."

Ryan looked out the window of the Mercedes as it sped along through the rain. In the distance was the sea, and in the lightning that rippled through the clouds he could see the breakers as they pounded upon the shore. He couldn't know what he was getting himself into, but for a very long time he had felt as though his life was without direction. At least now he had a compass.

"No, Mr. Samuelson, I intend to see this through to the end."

Ryan wasn't certain, but it seemed that the compartment grew darker then, and if he were asked, he would have sworn that a flicker of a smile passed over the old man's face in that instant.

"Very good, Mr. Dixson. I expect you have some questions. Ask them now, please."

"The police . . ." Samuelson waived him off before the words could leave his mouth.

"You must understand now, the police are worthless in this. They will provide you no assistance, no leads. My sister is a sweet girl, but she has always been a fool. And the foolish never learn. Pay them no mind. The men who took my niece, they do not seek money, and no ransom will win her release. That task falls to you."

"You seem to know quite a bit about all this, sir. Is there something you want to tell me? Did you do something? Offend someone? Did they take her because of you?"

The old man sighed and drank deep from his glass of amber liquid. Ryan hoped it would loosen his tongue and clear up the riddles. But the riddles were only just beginning.

"Do you know, young man, where we are going tonight?"

Ryan glanced out the window, noticing for the first time that they had left the interstate and were speeding down what could best be described as a country road. Ryan had never been to the northeast, and everything about his background had told him not to expect this.

In his mind, New England was simply one great city, stretching from somewhere in Maine down through New York and Philadelphia and in to Washington, D.C. But as he gazed out into the black darkness of a rainy Massachusetts night, he realized he had been wrong. If anything, there was something ancient about this place, old and decayed.

"No sir, I can't say that I do."

"I don't suppose you would. We are headed to a place of legend, my friend. To one of the oldest townships in the Commonwealth, a place made famous for awful things that happened here long ago—Salem."

Ryan chuckled. "Witches? I don't understand."

Samuelson removed a cigar from his inside pocket and held it up to Ryan. "Care for one?" he asked.

"No," Ryan said, "but you go ahead." He watched as the old man pulled a gold-plated cutter from his pocket, snipping off the end before lighting the other with a match. The rich, thick smoke filled the cabin, reminding Ryan of a trip his friends had made to a local strip joint the night before he deployed.

"People are given to superstition, Mr. Dixson. No matter how rational they may claim to be. It's in our nature. And it has, at certain times, served us well. But so too has it cost us dearly. You speak of witches, and that is no surprise. Salem is famous for that incident and the lives that were lost because of it. But it is not purely without cause that something dark seems to stalk that village. No doubt you have heard speculation about what happened there. Superstition, mass hysteria, even poisoning. All or none of that may have substance. But what if I told you there was more to it than that?"

Ryan grinned, and though he wondered what all this had to do with the missing girl, he couldn't help but play along. "Mr. Samuelson, I hope you're not trying to tell me you believe in witches."

The man rubbed his chin and pursed his lips. "No, not quite, though I have seen enough to discount nothing. You see, my friend, the land you come from is mysterious in its own right. And those who have not seen it would say that the southern parts of this country are the darkest, the most mysterious, the wildest, and the most filled with the unknown. But they would be wrong." As Samuelson spoke, Ryan looked out the window of the car as it passed through dark forests of low hanging branches, across broken-down bridges and rock fences built with stones pulled from fields by the first men to ever break the land for farming. "This is an old place. Everyone knows, of course, that the first white settlers of this land did not find it abandoned. But what many do not know is that neither did the Indians who once roamed its vales and great, domed hills. There are ruined stone monuments, monoliths of an ancient culture far older than the Wampanoag or the Makitan. Who can say what purpose they served? Who can say what rites were howled upon them in the dark watches of some eldritch night?"

Samuelson shifted in his seat and took a long drag from his cigar, blowing a cloud of smoke that swirled and rippled through the air. "The settlers called these places the shunned lands, and, as the name implies, they avoided them. At least at first. Man's spirit is weak and given to laziness and sloth. The great stone monoliths served well as foundations for houses and stores and even churches. The infamous trials of Salem were held in structures built upon the altar of some old religion's stone of sacrifice. Ironic, don't you think? Ah, I see you've gone dry."

Again Samuelson uncorked the green bottle now half-filled with amber liquid, pouring another glass for Ryan, even as he tried to refuse. But his heart wasn't in it. He had other, more pressing, interests.

"All that's very interesting," he said, "but I'm afraid none of it will help me find Angela."

Bernard looked down toward his glass and sighed. In his frown, Ryan read disappointment. "Did you know," he said, "that every year, hundreds of people simply vanish? Just disappear? That one day, they wake up and they go to work or to school or to church. They wave to their neighbors, they say good morning to their co-workers, perhaps they even say goodbye to them as they head home. But somewhere along the way, something happens. And in that moment of ultimate mystery, they simply are no more. No ransom letter. No sign of struggle. No overdue mortgage or embezzlement scandal to give rationality to an explanation, whatever it may be. A life with all its complexity, the story of a soul, comes to an end with nothing more than a fade to black. Tell me, Mr. Dixson, how do you feel about that?"

Ryan shrugged. "I guess I would disagree with the premise. No one just disappears, Mr. Samuelson. There's an explanation, a story if you will, even if we don't know it."

"Ah yes," the old man said, raising his glass, "you are right. There always is a story. And there is a story here, Mr. Dixson. But you must discover it. If you are to do that, you must see what I have to show you. You must understand the world better than you know it now."

It was only a second later when the Mercedes pulled off the main thoroughfare onto another. Ryan had thought that the road through the forest was less than ideal, but it was nothing compared to the rocky path they now found themselves on, little more than a gash cut through a field. Ryan peered through the darkness, but although the trees had opened up to reveal a wide expanse of pasture, he could make out nothing in the cloud-obscured moonlight. But they hadn't gone far when a stone edifice seemed to rise from the black sea of undulating grass. Ryan's first thought was that it looked like a church.

"Long ago," Samuelson said, "this was a place of worship. It has since lost any ecclesiastical association. This ground is no longer holy, though it is hallowed, in its own way."

The Mercedes pulled in next to a long line of vehicles, many of which possessed luxury that put the German car to shame. As Ryan slammed the rear door, he looked up at the rotting steeple and wondered how many parishioners had spent countless Sundays called to worship by its bell. But that was long ago. The broken stained glass, the crumbling masonry. People had not come within those walls—at least to worship—for a very long time indeed.

"We enter through the back," Samuelson said. "The main entrance collapsed years prior. It's just as well. It would be unseemly, I think."

The chill from earlier had turned to ice, the cold rain that had fallen stealing what little warmth the air had held. But the clouds had broken, and the sky was clear. In the light of the moon, Ryan had no trouble marking his way.

The two men—what had happened to the driver, Ryan couldn't say—proceeded up the gentle sloping hill to a stone-walled fence that sat behind the church. The gate was open, rusted that way by Ryan's estimation. Beyond was a graveyard of the oldest variety, a great ancient oak in its center. The stones were marked well with the heavy chisel of some undertaker from long ago, the winged death's-head crowning most. Even in the wan moonlight, Ryan could make some of them out. The dead interred there went back to the Revolutionary War and beyond. Below their names were written their stories. Tales of men and women who travelled across the seas to settle the wilds and their sons and daughters who fought the battles to win them.

"These lands hold many tales. They were settled here long ago, during the first wave of immigrants from the old country. They found in this place something they did not expect, something that was far beyond the skills of the Wampanoag that made this their home. Something more akin to the old world than the new. A monolith of stone, one that went down into the earth. They could not destroy it, so instead upon it they built this church."

They passed through the last of the graves and reached an alcove with a low overhang that Ryan had to bend down to avoid. A man stood in front of a sturdy wooden door—a door that, unlike the rest of the church, did not seem old or run down. He was sporting a suit that, to Ryan's eye at least, was quite expensive. Either he knew Samuelson or information was conveyed to him through the plastic earpiece that he wore, because he nodded once before opening the door.

"The oldest and most honored tombs are within," Samuelson said. "It is there that we go."

"When was the church abandoned?"

"In the 1890s," answered Samuelson. "The pastor was a rather excitable man by the name of William Hickman. He was an eccentric, even in an age of eccentricity. He preached to his flock of the end times, speaking to them of his apocalyptic vision of a coming collapse of all things. But for him it was more than just mere speculation. He believed it, and believed its coming was imminent. And he told them so."

The chamber beyond was darkened, a black corridor. Samuelson removed two flashlights, handing Ryan one.

"There was an attempt once to light the church, but as you saw there is no electricity, and the noise of the generator was most unpleasant."

The feeble beams pierced the darkness but slightly, and for a moment, Ryan felt as though he were an explorer of old, cast into the darkened tomb of the Pharaoh with nothing but the pale glow of a torch to lead the way.

"So what became of the Reverend?" Ryan asked.

"Ah yes, the Reverend. Well, it has been said by many that the great and abiding human frailty of the preachers of our day is that they do not live what they teach. That could not be said of the old Reverend. He lived it, to the ultimate fault."

The passageway opened up, and Ryan realized that they were standing in what remained of the worship hall. The front had all but caved in, the pews moldered and rotted where they were left behind. An ancient baptistery sat at the front near where Ryan stood. It was bone dry, a scattering of dead leaves within, and Ryan thought it remarkable that such a thing ever contained water.

"When Sally Jenkins went missing," Samuelson continued, "the last place the authorities thought to look was here. But one can only search the woods and fields for so long before the truth becomes evident. They found the Reverend, bathed in her blood, in the heart of the stone edifice that is the foundation of this church. Her body lay upon the ancient alter, her insides spilled across the floor. He had cut off her arms and legs, leaving one in each of the cardinal directions of the circular room, as if forming a bloody compass.

"It is said that the old man had gone crazy. Mad, as any man who does such a thing must be. When they found him, he would speak not a word in answer to their questions, muttering only to himself that he had made a mistake. That he had been wrong. That more was required than her blood. When they found him, he held a needle and thread in his hands. One of her eyes, he had already sewed open. He was in the midst of doing the same with the other. It was said that, in his madness, he thought that if only her eyes remained open, life would return to her body as well. A foolish thing, though I suppose no more foolish than some other such beliefs."

"What happened to him?" whispered Ryan. "Was he tried for his crimes?"

Samuelson chuckled. "No, no, no trial. No, those were the days when justice for such incidents was often swift and devoid of mercy. When they found him, they did not waste their time with lawyers, judges, evidence, or courtrooms. The tree, the one that stands in the midst of the graveyard, the old oak with deep roots that burrow into the earth, the one that looks as though it has stood here since the beginning of time? It was there then as well, and its branches were strong enough to hold a man. It was from it that they hung him.

"He did not protest. Rather, he accepted his fate. Accepted it gladly even, some said. He thanked his captors, thanked his executioners. He told them that they were doing what must be done. It enraged them further, to hear him speak so. That he had killed the girl was bad enough. That he had butchered her as he had, sadistic. But the thought of this man welcoming the end? Praying for death? That was simply too much. Too much for any good man of Salem to bear. Thus they not only killed him, they left him there, hanging from that tree. Till the birds and the beasts and the insects of this land devoured the whole of him."

Samuelson looked at Ryan and smiled. "As you can imagine, such a thing had a negative impact on church attendance. With its flock gone, this edifice fell into disrepair. That is, until my associates found it and restored it to its former glory and purpose."

Ryan cast a glance around the empty worship hall, allowing his beam of light to guide his eyes. "No disrespect, Mr. Samuelson, but it doesn't seem like much restoration has been done."

Samuelson smiled. "Ah, let not your eyes deceive you, Mr. Dixson. All this is but an illusion. Follow me, and we shall see what goes on beneath."

Ryan did as he was told, following behind Samuelson as the man climbed the steps behind the broken down altar and empty baptistery. There was a tomb in the rearmost room, a stone sarcophagus. Samuelson's lamplight fell upon it. He looked to Ryan.

"You seem to be a perceptive young man, Mr. Dixson. This is the oldest of the sarcophagi in this church. Notice anything about it?"

Ryan looked, but he did not see. Before him was nothing but a great stone slab, the familiar winged death's-head at its crest. But it was only a moment before it became obvious.

"There's no name," he said. "There's no name on the tomb."

"That is correct, Mr. Dixson. There is no name, but there are words. Do you know your Latin, sir?"

Ryan grinned in the darkness. Where he came from, Latin was not high on the list of required courses. "Two years of Spanish," he said, "and I don't remember much of that."

"Well, then allow me to translate. It says, *'sepulchrum omnes'* which means, 'The Grave of All Men.'"

"I don't understand."

"Death, my friend, is everywhere. All men will die, whether they truly live or not. And when they do, they will return to the earth. But there are some places where death is more present than others."

Samuelson placed his hand upon the skull and pressed. To Ryan's amazement, the stone slab seemed to give away at the simplest of efforts, opening a great black maw, like the mouth of some unholy beast. But it was not so long before Ryan became aware of a preternatural glow emanating from the cavern beyond.

"Let us go, Mr. Dixson. What I want you to see is beyond here. What you need to see if you are to find our Angela."

Samuelson stooped low, slipping beneath the marble overhang, sliding into the shadowy mist, passing into what was both an unnatural light and a frightful darkness.

Ryan rose to find that the cavern opened up after he passed beyond the mouth. It was tall enough, in fact, that he could stand upright with no trouble. There were stairs that led further down. Without speaking, Samuelson began to descend. And so, without speaking, Ryan followed.

Down they went on that spiraling stone staircase, curving around itself into the depths of the earth, until the air that had been frigid seemed warm by comparison, the cool constant of an underground cave. How long did they descend? Ryan couldn't say. But when they reached the bottom, Samuelson turned and said, "Follow close. The corridors are many and winding. As in life, they are full of twists and turns. We must follow the right path, lest you find yourself lost."

The old man had not exaggerated. While the descent had been long, the walk through the curving tunnels was interminable. It was only when Ryan wondered just how far they had gone that they turned the final corner.

They came to a great archway. Two men, suited and stoic, were standing on either side of the rounded opening. Beyond them, Ryan could see the flickering light of great candles or torches. And he could hear the murmur of the gathered crowd. When the men saw Samuelson, they nodded. One turned, and from somewhere beyond the archway he produced two goblets, handing both to Samuelson. He in turn gave one to Ryan.

"The drinking of wine," Samuelson said, "is a holy rite in all the world's great religions. It is, in some, the only truth they bear. For as man bleeds, and in bleeding dies, so too does the grape give up its life to produce that which in lies truth. And just as the blood maintains its vitality even when it leaves the body, so too does wine give life even when it has been pressed from the grape. Don't you think?"

Ryan had questioned his presence here several times, but it wasn't until then that he began to consider that perhaps Samuelson might truly be mad. It was an unfortunate time for such a revelation, here in the depths of this place, where he was at the man's mercy. So he did all that he could to appear as if he believed fully in the person who stood before him. He nodded once, and took the cup that was offered him.

"Excellent," Samuelson said. "To the gods!"

He raised his glass, and without waiting for Ryan to do the same, drank down the wine in one furious gulp. Ryan followed suit. But just as the liquid had barely touched his tongue before he swallowed it, it was but only an instant before he regretted the decision.

Samuelson smirked, and there was something sinister there. "Exquisite, isn't it? The effects are almost immediate."

Ryan barely heard him. It was as if he had swallowed fire. The flame coursed down his throat and into his stomach, and then it was flowing through his arteries and his veins. Every inch of him burned, and even the sweat that drenched his clothes could not smother the conflagration that engulfed him.

"Come," he said, "I have much to show you."

If his legs hadn't begun to move of their own volition, Ryan would have sworn that he was unable to follow the old man's command. And yet, move they did. It was a bizarre sensation, a passenger in his own body, watching as his feet carried him into the great, vaulted chamber. His movements were swift, if unsteady. He passed through the archway into what could almost be called an amphitheater. There were four different entrances to the circular hall, cut into the rock at diagonals. In the center was a massive, raised stone slab. And surrounding it were men standing in ascending rows five deep. In another circumstance, Ryan would have felt underdressed, for all of them wore their finest outfits. The noise of their chatter had been deafening, but when Ryan entered, their roar fell steadily down to silence. They turned their faces upon him, and in their eyes, Ryan saw recognition.

"Yes," Samuelson said, "the guest of honor has arrived."

The old man led him to an empty spot a few feet from the stone slab, positioning him so that he faced it. And then it wasn't just Ryan's physical body that was affected, but his mind as well. The world seemed to shutter and then crack. The flames that leapt from the torches that flickered around the hall seemed to dance before him, as if they had a mind of their own, as if some hand guided them. The faces of those who surrounded him melted and reformed, and in the shadows that played upon the walls of that accursed place danced creatures that no mortal man has ever gazed upon and lived.

"The wine is powerful, yes? Tis the blood of the gods, or so the Greeks would have told you. The Christians too, if the rites are said properly over the fruit of the vine. And I can assure you, the rouge to which you were privy is most sacred indeed."

For a moment, the storm within Ryan's mind seemed to ebb, and he thought the room grew dimmer. But this was not his mind playing tricks on him, but rather the image of the truth as the men who stood guard extinguished all but one of the torches that had lit the chamber before. It was as if the sun set in that place, and in the coming dark Ryan's eyesight grew sharper, and although he should have been able to see little, his mind perceived all.

From the portal immediately across from him emerged a figure. He wore a cloak, long and black, and the hood obscured his face. The room grew still except for his movements—the exquisite, graceful flow of his body as it moved. And it was from those delicate sliding footfalls that Ryan realized—this was no man.

Her body flowed around the stone slab and came to rest in front of Ryan. His eyes grew wide as she removed the hood that had obscured her face. He had the same feeling of lightheadedness as he had experienced the first time he'd looked upon her. But the bright, crashing red of her hair had an unholy shimmer that night, and her eyes, those pale green flashes, glowed with a light of their own. But there was yet one more thing that was different from that first night in Hendricksville Community College. As the robe slipped off her shoulders into a black puddle around her feet, she was completely nude. And then she began to dance.

At first she moved to nothing, her hips swaying to the sound of silence. But then there was a change in the air, an almost imperceptible drumming sound, the beat growing louder with every second, but never so much that Ryan could say from where it came or that it was anywhere other than his own mind. And the piping, the demonic flutes that called from some swirling chaos.

"Why does she dance?" asked Samuelson. "She dances not for us, but for the gods to come. For dancing is like singing, don't you think? An expression of pure, human emotion. This one through action, rather than sound. It is a beautiful thing."

He removed a silver case from the pocket of his jacket, pulling a cigarette from inside. With a flick of his wrist he struck a match. The flame glowed brightly in the darkened chamber, and the smoke, more pungent than any Ryan remembered, stung his eyes.

"It's the dance of the seven veils, you know?" the old man said, gesturing towards Katya with the lit end of his cigarette. "'Tis an ancient dance, the one that cost John the Baptist his head in the long ago. Of course, in this instance at least, the veils are left to the imagination."

He took a deep drag from his cigarette, and as he flicked ash to the stone ground below, he blew the smoke in Katya's direction. But it did not dissipate as Ryan would have expected. Rather, it seemed to surround her, to cloak her in a translucent shroud. She moved within that mantle, her hands traveling over her body, starting with her hair and moving down her neck, farther, to her breasts. And then farther still, while her lips parted in the ecstasy of her fingers.

"Yes," Samuelson said, throwing the dying end of his cigarette down on the ground and crushing it beneath his heel, "she dances for they who are, for they who were, and for they who will be. For those who rumble in the darkness, who walk in endless night through the vast infinity of the cosmos. And for they who seek their return. She calls to them with her body, just as those nameless cults that built this temple—supplicants who never died and never will—shout and gibber their names into the howling winds in the lonely and forbidden places of the earth. And they hear them too, Ryan.

"They hear them, just as surely as you hear me. They seek a return, when the stars are right. As they shall be one night hence, when the Beltane moon rises above this place, and the night of Walpurgis begins. They who were can be again. But of course, their entrance into this world is no easy one. For there can be no birth without pain, no forgiveness of sin without the shedding of blood."

Ryan's eyes grew wide as it happened. As he saw. From behind where she stood, where she swayed to the deep drumming of the earth. And the piping, those insane, discordant melodies. The black figure rising, hooded and cloaked. Ryan sought to cry out, but he was only a mute witness, as much a prisoner as if chains bound him. On she danced, oblivious to her fate. As all are.

The hulking beast behind her—for Ryan could not be sure if it was a man or something else—produced a long, curved blade from somewhere within the folds of his cloak. He pressed the sharp metal edge to her throat. And yet still, she danced. Then, in one movement, he severed skin and tendons and arteries and veins. Her head hung in space, still attached to her body only by a thin flap of skin and the merest of pale, white bones.

As the bright, crimson fountain sprung from her throat, showering Ryan in her thick, sweet, viscous blood, she still danced. Until Ryan, the sound of distant laughter dying in his ears, collapsed into the black oblivion of throbbing drums and maniacal piping.

* * *

Ryan awoke to sunlight as it poured through his open window on to the bed on which he lay. His hand went immediately to his chest, and he fully expected it to come away covered in crimson ichor. But there was nothing, even if he could still taste the metallic tang of the unspeakable in his mouth. He threw the sheets away, and only then did he realize he was naked. He flung himself out of bed, nearly stumbling over his open suitcase. The clothes that he remembered wearing were draped over a chair, just as he had left them when he had showered the night previous. For a moment he paused, wondered if it had all been some sick dream. The darkest, most vivid nightmare he'd ever had. More real than even the visions of war-torn lands that had invaded his consciousness, memories of that awful day in the deserts of Afghanistan. Dreams of things that had been real.

"No," he whispered, even to himself. "That was no dream."

He picked up the phone, still standing naked in the dawning light of a Boston day. He rang the front desk first. "What day is it?" he asked.

"Saturday," the girl answered.

"No! The date! The date!"

The girl on the other end of the line hesitated, and he realized he must sound mad.

"April 30th," she stuttered, her voice shaking.

He swallowed hard. "Thanks," he mumbled as he re-cradled the phone. A whole day. He had lost a whole day.

Or maybe he had lived it.

He knew one thing though. Today was the day of which Samuelson had spoken in his dream or his vision or his memory. The 30th of April, the May-Eve, Walpurgis. He knew little of the date. Only what he had heard, read in certain forbidden books that he had enjoyed as a child. But what he did know frightened him. It was on Walpurgis, or so they said, when the veils between the worlds were sundered; when the ancients believed that those dark beings from beyond the borders of our world, could, if so invited, pass into our own. For centuries, they had built bonfires on that eve, great flaming beacons of light meant to chase away the night.

He considered his options. He was sure now, certain, that whatever had befallen him the night before, there was one thing that was beyond doubting. Samuelson was no innocent. Whatever had come to the house of Angela Endicott was his doing. And if she was in danger, it was he who had put her there. What had happened to Katya was but a prelude, a glimpse of what was to come. For if it was blood that was required, it would be Angela's that would be spilled, sacrificed to whatever dark gods, whatever fallen idols, that Samuelson and his associates worshiped.

Ryan picked up the phone again, intent, despite his previous instructions, on calling the police. That seemed to be the one course of action that made sense. But he had not pressed a single digit before he abandoned his plan. He remembered who Samuelson was and, more importantly, who were his compatriots that previous night. They had been of wealth and power and privilege. No, the police could not be trusted. It was as Recruiter Hawthorne had said. They would be of no help to him.

Hawthorne.

He fumbled for his wallet on the bedside table, removing the still pristine business card contained within its folds. The tiny specks of diamond on the dappled globe shimmered. He dialed the number. It rang once, twice, three times before a machine answered. Ryan almost hung up then. But something told him, if he did nothing else, he should at least leave a message. And so he waited. A voice came on the line, one he did not recognize and did not expect.

It said, in tones quiet and soft—yet steady—that were neither male nor female, "We are Limbus. We stand on the edge. We stare into the abyss. We do not discriminate. We do not forget. We employ. The job is the seeker's. The duty his, and his alone. To fail or to succeed, lies only on his shoulders. That is the contract. That is the promise. That is the bargain. There is only one."

Ryan waited for the beep, but it did not come. Instead a soft click announced the line was dead. He cursed under his breath and dialed the number again, but this time, something even more unexpected met his ear—the recorded voice of an operator telling him that the number had been disconnected. Ryan sat there, on his bed, still naked, cradling the dead phone to his ear, wondering what had happened, how he had come to this, how he had found himself here.

The light still streamed through his window, a blue shade dimmer. And then he realized—it was not the rising sun that he looked upon, but one that was setting. It was this realization that sprung him to action.

Thirty minutes later, he was speeding up Route 1 in a rented car. The night had fallen quickly over the Massachusetts countryside, faster than he expected, faster than seemed possible even. He wondered at it, though not for long. His mind was filled with other thoughts.

The night was not so black after all. A gibbous moon had risen, holding sway over the sky and the earth in its fullness. Yet somehow it was not comforting. No, it was hate-filled, angry. And in its glow, Ryan saw nothing but death. It was as if that great orb cast down darkness over the land, not light.

He drove by feel. He had only barely noticed the path they had taken the night before, and by all rights, he should have been unable to retrace it. And yet, his hands knew the way, and the car seemed to drive itself to its destination. The terrain grew darker and wilder, the road more worn, the path less trod. He wasn't surprised when he found himself on the narrow, winding gravel trail that led to the ancient church, though he marveled at how quickly he arrived. Nor was he surprised when he found no parked cars around it, as they had been the night before. But *they* were there, waiting for him. Of that, he had no doubt.

He left his car behind, but not before removing the 9 mm he had put in the glove compartment, his sidearm from what now seemed a lifetime ago. When he slammed the door behind him, the echo thundered across the hillside, rebounding through the cemetery and off into the forest. It was the only sound he heard. The normal life of the wilds was silent, and even the wind did not stir.

Ryan moved through the gravestones, training his gun on the rear entrance to the church. But there were no guards, and the door sat open, as if it had been locked in that position for all time. Ryan made his way inside, fishing the flashlight he'd bought at a Route 1 gas station out of his pocket. Somehow, the beam seemed even feebler than the last time he had come within this long dead house of worship, as if the air had grown thicker over the course of the day.

When he reached the false tomb, it was open, beckoning him, just as the door had been. He stopped for a moment and listened. And yet the silence held sway, though the eerie glow still floated up from below. Into that ethereal light he went, ducking low as he descended the spiral stair. When he reached the caverns, he paused. For the first time, from somewhere deep within the earth, Ryan heard something. It was a drumming, a throbbing, a pulsating beat, as if deep bass drums were pounding in regular rhythm. Somehow he knew it was nothing of the sort.

He stood before the entrance to the caverns, to the corridors that endlessly intertwined, that ran, as far as he knew, until the ends of the world. He could be lost forever in their depths, were it not for the preternatural sense that he knew precisely how he should proceed. For only a moment, he paused to consider what he was doing. Where this was leading him. Something was horribly wrong, something even worse than the young girl that had gone missing. She was only the beginning. But he couldn't stop now. He held the dimming beam of the flashlight before him and raised his gun. Then he ran.

He plunged forward, running hard through corridor after corridor. Turning here, going straight there, passing from one low hanging stone archway to another. He ran as hard as he could, letting his legs carry him wherever they might. To anyone watching, he would have seemed as a man mad, rushing mindlessly to an untimely end. But Ryan knew the way. And still, he was shocked when he turned a corner and stumbled headlong into a scene out of a nightmare.

The room was lit by great torches, smoke billowing up into the seemingly endless vaulted ceiling above. The room was filled with people, though because of their hooded cloaks Ryan could not say if they were male or female. But it wasn't to them that his eyes were drawn; it was to the naked girl tied to the ancient stone altar and the man who stood at her head, curved blade raised above her heart.

The assembled masses chanted and swayed to the thunderous beating drum that Ryan could not see but felt deep in his bones. So in thrall were they to whatever dark god they served that no one even saw Ryan. Not until he raised his gun above his head and fired a shot.

The booming roar died away much quicker than Ryan would have expected, swallowed up in the vast nothingness above. But it was more than enough to do the job. As the sound of the shot went silent, so too did the maniacal chanting. The congregation turned as one to face Ryan, and as the robed leader lowered his knife and looked up at him, Ryan recognized the face of Samuelson.

"Ah," he said, "we were expecting you."

"I can't say I'm all that surprised to see you either," Ryan answered as he pulled off his jacket, careful never to take his gun off the grinning madman. He stepped forward gingerly, making a mental note that no one tried to stop him. Even Samuelson stood quietly as he approached the quivering girl on the altar. He gestured to the old man with his open hand. "The knife," he said. "Come on." Samuelson flipped the knife around, holding it blade to hilt in both hands. He bowed as he offered it to Ryan.

"And so it begins," he said. Ryan ignored him. He was far more interested in freeing the girl. The blade sliced through her bonds without any significant resistance; it was sharp, and would have cut deep into her heart with ease. As the last rope fell away, the teenager jumped up, wrapping her arms around Ryan.

"It's OK, it's OK," he repeated, though he wondered if it would ever be OK for her again. His hand tightened around the pistol, and for a good five second he considered ending Samuelson then and there. But he was no killer. Not up close, at least. He wrapped Angela up in his coat and slid the knife into his belt.

As he took her hand and backed towards the exit, Samuelson laughed.

"You can't escape, Mr. Dixson. Of that, there can be no doubt. We will find you. You have chosen your fate, and now it is sealed."

With that, Ryan and Angela started to run.

He heard the roar from behind him as the assembled mass followed, hot on their heels. But that was only part of his worry. His sixth sense, the one that had guided him so unfailingly through these caverns before, now failed him. He and Angela stumbled through the twisting corridors with nothing to guide them, lost and hunted.

As they spun into one of those endless hallways, Angela tripped and fell. Ryan stopped to help her, but the girl had already dissolved into tears. "Come on, sweetheart," he said, kneeling down. Even as he spoke, the sounds of their pursuers seemed to close in on them, though Ryan could not say from what direction they came.

"I don't want to," Angela sputtered. "I don't want to do it. I want it to stop."

"You have to, darling. You have to. It's the only way."

At that, the girl's sobs suddenly halted. She looked up into Ryan's eyes, and in that instant, he saw something click. Then there was a steely resolve that had been absent until that point. "You're right," she whispered. "Of course. You're right."

"Yeah," Ryan said. "Now come on." He lifted her to her feet, but he also hesitated. He knew he should find some comfort in what he heard from her, that he should be pleased that she had seemed to regain her footing. But something was off. Something was wrong. He worried that if he couldn't put his finger on it, that something could be fatal. But the booming sounds of chase were too close, and there was no time to consider alternatives.

In another instant, they were running again, dashing down corridor after corridor, and Ryan took comfort in the thought that the sounds of pursuit seemed to be dying away. But that comfort only lasted for a moment. As he and Angela rounded another corner, Ryan felt his heart sink—they had come full circle, returning to the vaulted chamber with its altar and its endless darkness.

"It's OK," Ryan said, but the words had barely left his lips when he knew that was wrong. From every entrance, robed figures appeared. Ryan spun on his heel, only to find Samuelson standing behind him. Ryan pushed Angela back towards the raised, stone slab, leveling his gun at Samuelson as he did.

"You cannot escape, Mr. Dixson. It's time you accepted that."

Ryan looked down at the girl beside him, and then back to Samuelson. He knelt low next to her, keeping his gun pointed at the deranged man's heart. "Listen," he said. "I'm not going to let anything happen to you, OK? Whatever happens, trust that. If they get to me, you run as fast as you can and don't stop running till you find the staircase out of here. You got that?"

She nodded, and Ryan saw the same resolve as before. If she was scared, she wasn't showing it.

From all sides, the robed figures started closing in.

"Climb up there," Ryan said to the girl, gesturing to the altar. "We need to get to high ground." He pulled the curved blade from his belt, handing it to her. She took it, and he didn't need to tell her what to do with it. As the others surrounded them, they climbed onto the stone slab, and Ryan once again pointed his pistol at Samuelson.

"What are you going to do, Mr. Dixson? Shoot me? Do you think that will work? Do you think you can kill us all? Are you so delusional to believe you can play the hero?"

"I don't have to kill you all," Ryan roared. "But by God, I'll kill you. I may not make it out of here tonight, but you damn sure won't either."

Samuelson paused, as if thinking on Ryan's words.

"So you would die for the girl, then? You would lay down your life to save hers?"

Ryan didn't answer, not with words, but the truth was written in his eyes. Samuelson nodded.

"I knew it was so. I knew it from the moment I met you."

If what followed had not come to pass, Ryan might have pondered those words. He might have wondered what exactly Samuelson meant. But then he felt the fire, the explosion of pain in his back, starting between his shoulder blades, and then streaking like lightening down his spine. As the hot blood splattered on the altar, Ryan's legs gave way and he collapsed to the stone slab below. His head hit hard on solid rock, but not so hard that he couldn't see the girl standing above him, her hands covered in his blood, the knife slipping from them and clattering on the ground. In her eyes, there was inestimable pity, and Ryan, even through the pain, felt confusion.

There was a rush and rustling of cloth, and two figures came up to the girl and grabbed her shoulders. As they did, one of their hoods fell away, and in that moment, even though he had never seen her, Ryan knew that he was looking at Angela's mother. And as they pulled her back, something else dawned upon him.

It was never Angela that was the sacrifice.

A terrible thought occurred to him then, as his life left him, that he had done more than fail himself this night. His death was meant to bring about something horrible, and even now, the world might be ending, and all of it would be his fault.

"No, Mr. Dixson," Samuelson said as if reading his mind, all the malice and hate having melted away, replaced with what could only be called sadness, "it's not that at all. Not at all."

There was more movement, and then another face appeared above him, one he had never thought he would see again. But this time, the pale green eyes lacked their stormy fury. Tears had dimmed them.

"Oh Ryan," Katya said, taking his hand, "you wonderful, beautiful man. I'm so sorry."

As she spoke, the robed figures began to pull down their hoods, and in all their faces, Ryan saw the deepest sorrow. But as they closed in around him, none seemed more saddened than Samuelson.

"We live in a hard world, my friend," Samuelson said as he knelt low so that he could look into Ryan's eyes. Katya sobbed beside him, holding Ryan's hand and stroking his forehead. "A world that calls for the worst kinds of sacrifice. Even now, in places far darker than this, evil men are gathered. They call to worlds unknown and unseen, and through endless darkness float their words. They gibber the names of black gods, and they sacrifice the innocent in an effort to bring them back to rule over all. The stars are right tonight, as they are only once in a century, if that. And if we were to stop them, we knew it would take the most powerful magic, the kind only blood can call forward. The blood not of innocents," he said, looking up at Angela as she hugged her mother tight, soaking her robe with tears, "but blood shed *by* innocents instead. The blood of a hero. Only that can hold back the darkness. Many will never know your name, Ryan

Dixson, but we shall never forget it. And the world will sleep safe tonight because of your sacrifice."

Ryan couldn't speak, but tears now flowed down his cheeks. He felt at peace, somehow. He looked up and into Katya's eyes, and he even managed to smile. But he also knew that there was no coming back from this. Even if it wasn't his place to die, he'd lost too much blood, and he felt himself slipping away.

Samuelson put his hand on Ryan's shoulder and stood. He called out in a tongue that Ryan did not know, and yet understood. The congregation answered in one voice. Ryan stared up into the swirling blackness above, and as his life left him, suddenly, it was not so dark.

Matthew

The sun had long since dipped below the horizon when Matthew closed the book, and the thin fingers of light that had flooded through his windows had receded into shadow. He'd meant only to browse its pages, but he'd found himself consumed by the words, compelled to continue. He'd read two of the bizarre stories, and he'd found himself transported to a world of shadowy organizations with power and scope beyond his imagination.

He considered reading more, but the hour was late, and he'd promised to meet a friend at a bar on Hanover. At the entrance to his shop, he stopped to pull on a coat, casting one last glance back at the leather-bound tome that seemed to glow softly in the evening moonlight.

The door closed behind him, the jingle from the bell he'd placed above it tinkling into the darkness. He stepped out into a mist-filled night. The rain did not so much fall as it swirled about, dancing like snowflakes in the street light. But whereas snow might be comforting or romantic even, the tiny pinpricks of water in his face were only annoying. He pulled the jacket tight, zipping it to his throat.

Benefit Street was abandoned, and his footfalls seemed to echo like thunder down the slopping pavement. But with Hanover the silence was broken by evening revelers who made their way up and down the streets.

He met Jacob at a bar, the Florentine. It was a restaurant by day, but at night when the lights turned down and the music turned up, it was the kind of place the young Brahmins of Boston might be found, even if the bar had seen better days.

Jacob ordered two beers and paid the waitress before Matthew could even reach for his wallet. "I've been to the bookstore, Matt. I know things aren't going great. This one's on me." It was true, even if it made Matthew feel like he should have just stayed at work. The two men sat in silence, both contemplating the bottom of their glasses, before Jacob finally spoke again.

"So what are you going to do about it? The store?"

Matthew didn't have any siblings, and so Jacob had served as a sort of fill-in—the best friend who became more like an older brother.

"No idea."

"Fucking internet."

"Cheers to that."

The two men laughed, and for a moment Matthew forgot about the store, and he even forgot about the book. But then something happened that made everything much, much worse.

"It's funny, I was thinking about you yesterday and how you needed some extra cash. And I came upon this business card for an employment agency. Let me see if I can find it."

Matthew felt the blood rush from his face. The world started to spin, and Jacob, who was now cursing and fumbling with his wallet seemed to fade into the background.

"I can't remember what it's called. Had a funny name," he said, finally giving up the search with a "well shit." Matthew wanted to just run away. "Nimble, Nimbus, something like that. I'll let you know if I find it. Oh, and by the way. I saw the strangest thing today. I was walking through the park and I saw this little black girl, maybe ten or eleven, dressed in a business pantsuit, and she stared at me with eyes that were so bright green they could have been emeralds . . . hey, hey where are you going?"

Matthew stumbled out of the bar and into the street, nearly colliding with a man in what looked like a white butcher's apron. Or it had been white, before red stains covered it. "Hey, watch where you're going!" the butcher yelled, pushing him away.

Matthew couldn't think. All he could do was get back to the store. He had to read. He had to read more.

When he reached his door, he had the sudden sinking feeling that the book would be gone, spirited away or simply vanished into thin air. But there it sat on his desk, a mangled mess of arcane writings. He pulled out his chair and sat down. Then he opened the book, and once again began to read.

One Job Too Many

By

Joseph Nassise

Recruiter 46795 stood in front of the window of his plush corner office on the seventy-eighth floor of the Hamilton Building, staring out at the rain that was trying to pound the city into submission. Where others might have seen it as a wet, dismal day, the kind of day where you stayed indoors with a blanket wrapped comfortably around your shoulders and a cup of something hot to drink in your hands doing your best to ignore the world outside your window, he saw it as a day full of opportunity, a day where just the slightest nudge might be enough to set the course of reality spinning off in a different direction. The *right* direction.

That was his job after all; to keep the wheel of fate spinning, to act as the hand of destiny in the lives of those down on the street below him, scurrying like ants to escape the crushing sense of futility and unworthiness that haunted them. They would not rise out of their squalor, out of the limited view in which they perceived the world around them. No, that kind of perspective was reserved for those who had climbed to the lofty heights that he had, those privileged few who were entrusted with tending the gears that drove the machinery of the world, those that kept this great glassy orb spinning in its place in the universe.

He watched and felt a surge of satisfaction that he was not one of the nameless, faceless many below him. Never would be one of them, thank the heavens.

Turning away from the window at last, 46795 crossed the room and took a seat at his desk. It was an expensive desk, the teak surface positively gleamed in the light. He allowed himself a moment's satisfaction that his rise through the company was proceeding just as planned. A few more difficult cases and he should be primed to move up to the Executive Level on floor 88.

A few more difficult cases—like the one waiting for him now.

He opened the drawer in the center of his desk and drew forth a slim, red folder. He placed it on the desktop in front of him, opened it, and, taking a fine-tipped black marker from the inside pocket of his suit coat, wrote a single word on the tab at the top of the folder. He studied the word a moment, decided he'd performed the job to his satisfaction, and returned the pen to his pocket. The folder was then closed and returned to the desk drawer.

46795 sat back in his chair, feeling a real sense of accomplishment. The field had been plowed, the seed had been cast; now all that remained was to see if it bore fruit.

*   *   *

"Nate Benson to the Shift Manager's office. Nate Benson, please report immediately to the Shift Manager's office. That will be all."

Nate stared up at the loudspeaker mounted on the wall above his head and felt the sudden urge to rip the thing from its moorings and hurl it across the room as far as it would go.

He'd been expecting the call all morning, was not, in fact, surprised that it had come, only that it had taken this long. He had no doubt what that call meant for him and his future here at General Electronics. Rumors of layoffs had been floating around for weeks and it seemed that the day had finally come; not a single one of those who'd been called throughout the morning had come back to the assembly line floor.

Nate remained still until he was certain that he had a lock on his anger, then he shut down his drill press. He took off his work gloves, shoved them in the back pocket of his coveralls, and began making his way across the floor to the steel staircase that led to the boss' office on a platform high above the workroom floor. Most of his fellow workers studiously kept their eyes focused downward on the task in front of them, as if looking at Nate might cause them to share in his fate. But a few, George, Harris, and Daniels, for instance, caught his gaze and nodded in commiseration.

They were survivors, just as he was, veterans of the conflict that had consumed nearly an entire generation and left a third of the Earth as nothing more than a barren, decimated wasteland. What had started as a regional turf war over possession of natural resources had blossomed when the fanatics came to power, sending the religious and political ideologies of the east crashing headfirst into those of the west. Within weeks the conflict had spun out of control like a metastasizing cancer that consumed everything in its wake. For the third time in less than a century the major nations of the world found themselves embroiled in a war to end all wars. Twenty-three years later they were still feeling the fallout, both physically and figuratively. Millions had died. Entire nations were turned into twisted plains of blasted radioactive glass. Men like Nate came home to a country that saw them as nothing so much as living reminders of humanity's capacity for murder on a grand scale, and shunned them as a result.

The Faith War left the world's economy in shambles, with unemployment rates over twenty-five percent in even the most developed nations and inflation at an all-time high. The job market, already overburdened with too many qualified applicants for far too few jobs, was swamped by the return of thousands of trained soldiers. Nate was one of the lucky ones, landing this assembly line job after only ten months of searching. He knew guys who had been looking for two years and still hadn't found a job.

Looks like you're going to join them soon, he thought.

Nate knocked on the door to the boss man's office and then waited for the muffled "Come in" to reach him before palming the lock and stepping inside.

Southwick was seated behind his desk, his fat body oozing over the sides of the suspensor chair that strained to do its job of keeping him off the floor. Flanking Southwick were two corporate security guards. Nate glanced at them as he came through the door, then dismissed them as no threat. They stood with their backs ramrod straight and their arms crossed over their chests, reducing their ability to move quickly if the situation necessitated. They scowled at him, trying to be intimidating, and Nate had to squelch the urge to laugh. After what he'd seen and done in the Arabian Desert, a couple of thugs like these two barely registered.

As usual, Southwick didn't waste any time with pleasantries. Nate was hardly in the door before the shift boss tossed an envelope on the desk in front of him and said, "Two weeks' pay, which is more than I would have given you. The contents of your locker will be forwarded to your last listed address."

Nate didn't ask why nor did he bother protesting. It wouldn't have done any good. Southwick wasn't the one pulling the operational strings; he just did as he was told, like all the other management hacks this far down the food chain. For Nate to keep his job he would have to talk to one of the execs back at the home office and he didn't even know where that was, never mind who he'd need to speak to.

Besides which, they'd never listen to a guy like him.

Southwick's next comment made that abundantly clear.

"It's about time I got to fire your sorry ass. You go anywhere but straight through the back door and I'll have you arrested for trespassing and thrown into a hole so dark you won't remember what the light of day even looks like," Southwick sneered. "You hearing me, Cutter?"

Nate was in the process of turning away when the insult stopped him cold.

The end of the war had dumped thousands of troops onto an already overburdened job market. Someone higher up the food chain had recognized that leaving hardened men who'd just been through hell and back without anything to do was a sure recipe for disaster, so the government fast tracked applications from veterans over those from civilians, even those with more experience or training in the job. This, of course, generated a wave of resentment among the civilians and lines were drawn in the sand.

Violence broke out on more than one occasion, usually started by hot-headed civilians and normally ended by grim-faced ex-soldiers who were more than happy to take out some of their frustrations on those who didn't know well enough to leave things alone. Insults were tossed back and forth from both sides of the conflict, "Cutter" being one of them, a term meant to describe anyone who "cut the line," so to speak and received benefits for which they weren't actually entitled. It wasn't the strongest of insults—there were far worse ones being bandied about— but it was an insult nonetheless.

Normally Nate's desire to keep his job would have kept him from reacting, but Southwick himself just relieved the ex-soldier of that particular burden. Nate turned around to face his former employer, a grin spreading across his face as he realized he was no longer constrained by the need to behave.

"What did you say?" he asked.

Southwick either thought he was safe with his guards beside him or he'd forgotten the basic rule of the jungle—always know who the predator is and who is the prey—for he grinned up at Nate.

"I said get the fuck out of my office, Cutter scum!"

Nate wasn't the type to let an insult go by without answering it. All the crap he'd taken from Southwick during his time here welled up in the back of his mind and he decided it was time to teach the fat fuck a lesson about respecting his betters. Nate was still smiling politely when he threw himself across the top of the desk and slammed into Southwick, driving the man and his ridiculous floating chair into the tiled floor beneath their feet before the bodyguards realized what was happening. By the time their brains had caught up with the action going on in front of them, Nate had already landed several good blows to Southwick's face with his thick fist, smashing the man's nose and fracturing at least the left cheekbone, possibly the right as well. By the time the guards managed to drag Nate off of his former boss, the other man was lying bloody and unconscious on the floor.

There won't be any more layoffs today, Nate thought, just before the guard on his left drew his stun baton, jammed it in Nate's ribs, and pulled the trigger. Even the stun charge that shot through his frame and froze him into immobility couldn't wipe the smile of satisfaction off his face.

* * *

Lisa refused to come down and bail him out, so Nate was forced to use the services of one of the bondsman that set up shop across the street from the lock-up. The interest the sonofabitch was charging was outrageous, but what choice did he have? If he didn't make bail he'd sit inside the cell and rot for a few weeks before they brought his case before a judge. Nate knew he'd end up getting in trouble if he stayed on the inside. There were plenty of gangs who would shank a veteran just for the hell of it and Nate would have no choice but to kill anyone who came after him. That would add years to whatever sentence the judge would give him for assault against Southwick. So he paid the fee, ignoring the bondsman's vulpine grin as he did, then waited the requisite twenty-four hours for the paperwork to be processed. He kept to himself and made it through the evening without incident. Late the next day he went home, only to receive the second surprise in what was turning out to be a pretty shitty week.

The apartment was empty.

Not just empty as in "Lisa wasn't home," but more like "Lisa had cleared out and taken all their shit with her" empty.

He stood in the doorway, staring across the living room, now stripped of its furniture, and into the kitchen where only the built-in appliances still remained. She'd taken everything that wasn't bolted down, including the refrigerator.

He walked into the apartment and over to the tiny bedroom they'd shared as a couple. What little clothing he owned was still on the shelves in the closet, along with the box containing a few mementos from his time in the service, but that was about it.

She hadn't even left a note saying goodbye.

First his job. Then his girl. Could it get any worse?

A vision of the Waste flashed before his eyes, stretches of desert sand broken every few yards by the burning hulks of assault vehicles and the broken bodies of the dead.

Yes, he supposed it could, indeed, get worse. The thought helped prompt his decision to get out of there before things actually did. He had better things to do than to wait around for bad luck to find him.

Like getting drunk and forgetting it all.

He turned on his heel and walked out of the apartment, pulling the door shut behind as he went. He didn't bother locking it, as there wasn't anything to steal. If anybody was desperate enough to swipe his dirty laundry, they were welcome to it.

Nate took the lift down to street level, crossed the cracked plasticrete floor of the lobby, and stepped out into the night. Turning left, he headed down the block and slipped into the first bar he could find.

Two hours later Nate was just knocking back his fifth—or was it sixth?—synthetic whiskey of the night when someone slid into the booth across from him uninvited. He looked up, angry at the intrusion, and was just a hairsbreadth shy of telling the newcomer to fuck off and leave him alone when he realized he knew the squat, dark-haired man now seated across from him.

Charlie "Two-Fingers" Vantolini.

They'd served together in A Company shortly after the fall of Syria, when Charlie had been transferred into Nate's platoon after a rocket attack had blown their communications sergeant into a thousand little pieces. Charlie's nickname had been well-established by then, a result of the body parts he'd lost when an enemy bullet tore through his hand during the Battle of Al-Gahad, and he'd been received by the rest of the team with, if not enthusiasm, then at least acceptance. He wasn't fresh meat and for that they were thankful; at least someone else wouldn't go home in a quick-grown casket because Two Fingers had fucked up without knowing any better, as typically happened when the squad got a newbie.

Nate hadn't seen Charlie in close to two years and blinked up at him now, his alcohol-fuzzed mind trying to reconcile the sudden intersection of his old life with this one but failing miserably. Two Fingers Vantolini was probably the last person Nate would have expected to run into in a place like this. Not because he didn't like to drink; no, ole Two Fingers could knock it back with the best of them just fine. It was simply because Nate thought Charlie was dead. That was, in fact, the thought that tumbled out of his mouth thirty seconds later when his lips finally decided to follow the commands his mind was shouting down to them.

"Thought you were dead."

Charlie cocked his head to one side and stared at him unblinkingly. A sudden memory flashed across Nate's mind; a view of Charlie looking down at a wounded enemy soldier with exactly the same expression just before he causally lifted his gun and shot the man through the head. "Do I look dead to you?"

No, not dead, Nate thought. *Scared. You look scared.* Charlie was putting on his usual tough-talking wise guy exterior, but with a flash of clarity Nate saw beneath it all, saw the truth of the matter staring him right in the face. A thin sheen of sweat covered Charlie's forehead and the hand resting on the table before him trembled just enough to be noticeable if you were looking for it. For all his bravado, in that moment Charlie looked like nothing more than a little kid who was stuck staring at his half-opened closet door in the middle of the night, convinced that he'd just seen it move of its own accord.

For an instant Nate wanted to get up and run away, just get the hell out of there as fast as he could, before Charlie had a chance to say anything.

Then his old squad mate smiled his old devil-may-care grin and whatever crazy thoughts Nate had been having vanished as quickly as they had come.

He grinned back at his one-time squad mate. "Two-Fingers Vantolini, live and in living color. What the hell are you doing in this shithole?"

Charlie's gaze lost some of its intensity and he signaled the waitress for another round of drinks. He looked back at Nate.

"I hear you're looking for work."

Nate frowned as the warning bells in the back of his head went off, telling him something wasn't right here. Something was *off.* How the hell had word that he was out of a job gotten out so fast? He'd only been unemployed since yesterday. Or was that the day before? Given the number of drinks he'd had he couldn't be sure . . .

"I could be," he answered, the question making him uncomfortable for some reason he couldn't quite put his finger on. "You got something?"

Charlie glanced around, as if making sure they weren't being observed, and then slid something small and white across the table to Nate.

It was a business card, white with black lettering.

Limbus, Inc.
Are you laid off, downsized, undersized?
Call us. We employ. 1-800-555-0606
Jobs for your specific talents!

Nate stared at it. *Limbus? What the hell kind of name was that?*

He looked up to ask Charlie that very same question, only to discover the seat opposite him was now empty.

Where the hell did he go?

Looking around he caught a glimpse of his old squad mate pushing his way through the crowd near the door, clearly in a hurry to leave. For a moment Nate considered going after him, even got so far as pushing himself up and out of his booth, but when the room started spinning with just that little bit of physical effort, he decided the best course of action was to put his ass back in his seat and finish his drink.

He shoved the card in the pocket of his pants and raised his hand to signal the waitress for another round.

* * *

Nate was lying in a puddle of his own vomit when he awoke after his four-day bender. The stench drove him up off the living room floor and sent him stumbling to the bathroom where he fell to his knees just in time to retch miserably into the toilet bowl. The bile burned his throat; his stomach had already emptied itself hours before. Now there was nothing left to come up but his own sense of shame and that seemed to have firmly wrapped itself around his spine with no intention of letting go.

He had only the vaguest recollection of the last several days. He remembered going for a drink after finally getting out on bail, but everything after that was pretty much a blur. Apparently, he'd managed to achieve his goal of drinking enough to briefly forget his problems, and then some.

He spat several times to clear this mouth, then pulled himself to his feet through sheer force of will and leaned over the sink. He turned the faucet on, waited for the rusty tinge to clear itself from the running water, then bent down to drink from the tap, the cool water a welcome balm to his ravaged esophagus.

He straightened up, being careful to avoid glancing in the mirror as he did so; he didn't much like what he saw in it these days. His physical decline had started long before he'd lost his job. The lean, mean, fighting machine was gone and in its place was some sorry fuck that Nate didn't even recognize, never mind like. Looking into that pathetic loser's eyes after waking up in a puddle of vomit was not the way he'd intended to start his day, thank you very much.

He didn't have a towel handy—*when was the last time he'd done laundry anyway?*—so he just wiped his face with the back of his hand and headed for the kitchen.

He grabbed a mug out of the cabinet, one of the few Lisa hadn't taken when she'd split, and punched the power button on the coffee maker. He glanced idly about while waiting for his coffee to finish brewing, his thoughts already working to try and figure out how he was going to find the money to get a drink, and that's when he saw it.

A business card, propped up against the salt shaker in the middle of the cramped little counter he used as a kitchen table. The crisp, clean whiteness of the card stood out against the sweat-and-food-stained surface of the counter top.

What the hell?

He stalked over and picked it up.

Limbus, it said.

It was followed by what he took to be the company slogan—"We Employ"—and a telephone number. But it was the last and final line of the card that really caught his eye.

"You are running out of time," it said.

Nate scowled down at it. *Running out of time? What the hell did that mean?*

He flipped it over, hoping he might have scrawled something on the back to remind him of where he'd gotten it or what the company actually did, but there was nothing there. The back of the card was blank.

He racked his brains for a minute, a not insignificant task given how hung-over he was, and was just about to give up when a face floated out of the recesses of his memory.

Charlie.

Just like that the floodgates opened.

He remembered he'd gone to Julio's hoping to find something with legs and a pair of tits to shack up with for the night, and had run into

Charlie instead. It had been Charlie who'd given him the card; Charlie who'd told him that there was work available, if he wanted it.

Work.

The word was like a beacon in the night, jarring him from his apathy and setting his heart to beating again. He glanced around the hovel he was living in and mentally winced at the depths to which he'd sunk. He'd lost his edge, lost his drive, and this was where it had gotten him. It was time to turn things around, to get moving again. No more of this self-pitying bullshit. It was time to start living again.

Work.

That's what Charlie had said. There was work available if he wanted it.

Damn right he did.

He turned the card over again, looking for an address, but didn't find one. He noted with a start that he had read the last line incorrectly the first time around; he must be more hung over than he thought. Instead of telling him his time was running out, the line below the telephone number actually read "You won't regret your decision to join us!"

Yeah, we'll see about that, he thought.

He turned to the comm unit and punched in the number. It rang only once before a cheerful female voice answered it. "Limbus—We Employ. Will you be joining us, Mr. Benson?"

The connection was voice only, no video. Nate wondered if he was talking to a real person or just a computer simulacrum.

"How do you know my name?" he asked.

"Your comm unit identified you when you called in to our offices, Mr. Benson."

"Oh, right." Nate felt stupid for even asking. Of course the unit had identified him; all comm units used broadcast identification as a default setting.

A little paranoid, Nate?

He didn't bother answering himself.

"Are you still with us, Mr. Benson?"

Nate cleared his throat. "Yes, yes I am. I'm calling about a job opening."

"Of course you are, Mr. Benson. It would be my pleasure to serve you."

As it turned out, they were doing interviews all day in one of the corporate buildings downtown. Nate booked an appointment, wrote down the address, and then, after disconnecting the call, went to look for something to help his hangover.

* * *

Two hours later he stepped off the slidetrain and slipped through the crowds lining the platform, headed for the nearest exit to the street beyond.

He'd made himself look as presentable as he could. He wore a clean pair of jeans and a reasonably new button-down shirt under a light jacket to fend off the light drizzle that was falling.

This section of New Manhattan was all corporate high-rises and company-owned businesses. Everyone he passed on the street was wearing the latest fashions and he drew more than a few curious stares as he moved through the crowds in his far more humble attire, but he didn't care. He was here about a job and the rest of them could go take a flyin' hike for all he cared.

The address he was looking for turned out to be a one hundred and twelve story building several blocks from the train station. He checked with the robodirectory when he arrived and the squat humanoid-looking construct told him the offices he was looking for were located on the seventy-eighth floor. Gravlift eighteen was the easiest way of reaching that destination, he was told, so he sauntered off in that direction.

Once on the correct floor, it only took him a moment to find their offices at the end of the hall; the titanium plaque on the front door displayed the company name in letters a foot tall.

As he reached for the door handle a feeling of unease unfurled in his gut, a sense that if he went through that door things would be irrevocably changed, and that brought him up short, his hand hanging there in mid-air as if he'd forgotten what to do with it. For a moment it seemed he wasn't going to go through with it, that he was just going to stand there indefinitely, but then he shook himself all over, like a dog shedding water from its coat, and the feeling passed. He grabbed the door, pulled it open, and stepped inside.

He found himself in a large reception area. A row of leather chairs lined the wall to his left while a desk stood to his right. Both were empty. Beyond the desk was an open door, which Nate assumed led to an inner office.

He took a seat, assuming the receptionist was in the back office area and would no doubt return momentarily. He had only been there a few minutes when he felt someone's gaze upon him. Looking up, he started with surprise to see a bald-headed man in a dark suit staring at him from the open door behind the receptionist's desk.

"Hi," Nate said, his heart thumping at the man's sudden appearance. "I'm Nate Benson. I have a two o'clock appointment."

He guessed the man in the suit was somewhere in his late forties, which would make him about a decade older than Nate. He was tall and rather thin, with long fingers that reminded Nate of a piano player he'd once seen at an after-hours club in the Holy City, but unlike that piano player this man's suit was impeccably cut and probably cost more than Nate made in a month.

On second thought, make that two.

The man didn't say anything, just nodded once and waved for him to follow before disappearing back through the open door.

What the hell?

Nate got to his feet and did as he was told. The doorway led to a short corridor that ended in a large, corner office, an office almost as large as the reception area itself. A desk that looked as big as the Titanic stood in one corner and behind it sat the man in the suit. In front of the desk was a single, empty chair.

While Nate took it all in, the man said, "What can I do for you?"

"I'm here about a job? You know, for an interview?" Nate said.

The man nodded. "Of course, you are. Please, have a seat."

Nate pulled out the chair and did as he was asked.

The man looked him over, nodding to himself as he did so. He opened the top right drawer of the desk, removed a slim file, and then closed the drawer before placing the file carefully on the desk in front of him. The recruiter—that was how Nate was beginning to think of him— opened the file and began reading.

Nate opened his mouth to say something, but the man cut him off, holding up a finger in a "wait-a-minute" gesture without looking up from his paperwork. Nate's mouth closed with a snap.

The man continued reading for another moment, before looking up at Nate.

"You spent six years in the military?"

"Seven, actually," Nate replied. "Is that a problem?"

The man smiled. "Not at all. Just trying to get a better understanding of your background, that's all."

Another quiet moment as the recruiter continued to study Nate's file. Or, at least, that's what Nate thought it was. He was impressed that they'd managed to assemble a file on him so quickly when he'd only just called for the appointment a few hours ago; that was efficiency, that's for sure!

"Extremely high marks in small unit tactics, hand-to-hand combat. And an Expert Marksman with a rifle," the man said. "Were you a sniper?"

Nate shook his head. "Long Range Recon."

The man nodded, made a note in the file, then set it aside. "Did your friend Charlie tell you what it is we do here?" he asked.

Nate shook his head. "Just said there was work to be had, if I was interested."

"And are you?"

"Am I what?"

"Interested?"

"Of course I am! I'm sitting here, ain't I?"

Nate winced, instantly regretting his tone. His anger and impatience was going to cost him a shot at a legitimate job and he had no one to blame but himself.

Damn your mouth, fool!

But, to his amazement, the recruiter didn't seem to hear. He simply smiled in Nate's direction and said, "You seem to be particularly well-suited to our program, Mr. Benson."

"And what program is that, if you don't mind my asking."

The recruiter shrugged. "We . . . solve problems."

"What kind of problems?"

Another shrug. "Whatever kind need fixing."

Nate leaned back in his chair, frowning slightly. He'd come in looking for a job. He'd asked a straightforward question about that job and instead of being given a straightforward answer, what he was getting was the kind of double-talk he hadn't heard since the time he and his team had run cover for that pair of Defense Intelligence Agency spooks during the fall of Jerusalem. If they couldn't tell him what the job entailed, how did they expect . . .

Wait a minute!

He ran through what he'd seen so far, mentally comparing each element against a checklist he'd developed after years of working in clandestine ops. From the office address in a high-class business district to provide an atmosphere of success and privilege to the unremarkable front man with a face you'd forget five seconds after seeing it, it all pointed to one thing.

Limbus was a front!

It had to be. Nate would bet his left nut it was nothing more than a shell company set up to give them a public face, a sense of legitimacy, while the real work went on behind the scenes, hidden from prying eyes.

The recruiter had said it himself, hadn't he? *You seem particularly well suited to our program.* Nate had a certain specific range of skills, skills that weren't all that useful in your typical corporate setting, and it was for that very reason he'd been having trouble finding work since being discharged. He could defuse a bomb with a paperclip and a pair of salad forks in less than ten seconds or sneak into an enemy encampment, cut the leader's head off his shoulders, and get out again before anyone even noticed something was amiss, but he didn't remember seeing a spot for those particular skills on the last few dozen job applications he'd filled out.

If he was well suited to their needs, that meant . . .

Nate let out a slow, lazy smile of his own. "Ah, I see."

The recruiter cocked his head to one side. "Do you now?"

"I do. I really do." Nate wondered just which agency was running the show here. It didn't feel like the DIA, but then again, that was exactly the modus operandi that those boys used all the time. They were specialists in making it look like some other agency was responsible throughout the entire op. That way, if things went sour, they had plausible deniability and could let the other agency take the heat while their people slipped quietly away into the night.

It really could be anybody, though; the World Federated Government had far more clandestine agencies than the average citizen suspected or even imagined. From the Unified Police Agency (UPA) to the Federated Transportation and Safety Administration (FTSA), the possibilities were practically endless.

Not that it really mattered. One branch of the government was as good as any other.

"So then, are you requesting employment with us here at Limbus?"

Requesting employment? It seemed an odd way of putting it to Nate, but yes, that was essentially what he was doing, he guessed.

He nodded.

The recruiter shook his head. "I'm sorry. I need a verbal answer."

Nate frowned. Guy was a bit of a stickler it seemed. Fine. "Yes, I am requesting employment."

A sheaf of papers appeared and was placed on the desk in front of him.

"This is our standard contract and corporate non-disclosure agreement. Details all the usual benefits. I need you to sign here, here, and here." The recruiter placed a pen on the desk next to the contract.

Nate glanced at it. Twenty-something pages of typical bureaucratic legalese; made him dizzy just looking at it, never mind trying to understand. No way was he reading all that crap. He was only interested in one item and he found it under subsection 21-F Compensation. He took a look at the number listed there and then picked up the pen and signed where he'd been asked.

The recruiter positively beamed. "Excellent! Welcome aboard, Mr. Benson. If you would follow me, please, we'll get you started."

Nate was surprised. "Now?"

"Yes, now," the recruiter responded, his mouth twisted into a slight frown. "Or did you have somewhere else you needed to be?"

Nate heard the threat, loud and clear.

"No, no. Now is fine. Nothing like getting started right away to learn the ropes."

The recruiter seemed to ponder that for a moment. "Quite right," he said at last.

Nate followed him out of the office and down a hall to what turned out to be a cutting-edge medical suite. An examination table stood in the center of the room with a medibot suspended over it. Consoles lined the walls, the computer screens on them currently dark.

After the recruiter moved to one of the consoles and input a series of commands, the medibot surged into life, reminding Nate of a giant mechanical spider. It sent a chill up his spine at the sight.

He didn't like spiders.

Positively hated hospitals.

This was not, he decided, going to be fun.

"Please disrobe down to your undershorts and climb up on the examination table," the recruiter said, his attention on the command console before him.

Nate looked doubtfully up at the mechanical arachnid above the table and then back over to the recruiter. "Do you know how to operate one of these things?"

The recruiter slowly turned and stared at him.

Didn't say a word; just glared.

Nate took the hint, disrobed, and climbed up onto the table.

In ten minutes he'd had his blood taken, his brain waves recorded, and been scanned all the way down to the molecular level. As he dressed he considered the fact that his new employer now knew everything there was to know about him physically; had the technology existed they could have created a physically identical body double.

Nate wasn't sure how he felt about that.

"This way, please."

The recruiter led him out of the office and down the hallway to the same elevator he'd arrived in. Nate knew better than to say anything while out in public, where it might be overheard by any number of listening devices planted by competing organizations, so the short trip up to the ninety-seventh floor passed in silence.

They emerged from the elevator and moved down the hall to a door near the far end. A silver scanner was embedded into the wall next to the door. The recruiter fussed with the keypad for a moment and then stepped to the side, out of the way of the device. "If you don't mind . . ." he said, looking at Nate expectantly and indicating the scanner.

"Of course."

Nate stepped forward and placed his hand in the center of the scanner.

There was a sudden, sharp buzzing sound and a pale blue light flared briefly under his hand before the door beside him opened with the sharp click of a releasing lock.

With a wave of his hand, the recruiter—*what the hell was his name anyway?*—ushered Nate inside.

He found himself in a long hallway with doors on either side. The recruiter led him to the fifth door on the left where they repeated the business with the palm lock. The office suite just beyond contained a slim storage locker, a restroom, and a personal farcaster unit.

Farcasters had been developed ten years ago by the scientists in the Defense Research Agency and had yet to see even limited use among the civilian population. Owning one was a capital crime, punishable by forty years of hard labor.

The government gets all the cool toys, Nate thought with a smile.

The recruiter walked over to the locker and opened it. Inside was a change of clothing—a dark-colored suit, a shirt, tie, and dress shoes— hanging from the locker's only hook. On the shelf above were a hypoinjector unit and a personal beeper.

"Listen carefully, please, as I'd prefer not to repeat myself," the recruiter said, as he handed the beeper to Nate.

"Notification of a new assignment will come via this personal computing device, or PCD. You are to report to this room at the time indicated on the page. The farcaster will already be programmed with the proper coordinates and you will use it to travel to and from your destination."

He reached for the hypo, handed that to Nate.

"Inject yourself with the hypo, then change into the . . ."

Nate interrupted. "What's in the hypo?"

The recruiter seemed taken aback that he'd been interrupted. "Excuuuse me?"

"What's in the hypo?" Nate asked again. If he was going to inject himself with something, then he wanted to know what the hell was in it. Seemed a fair question to him.

The recruiter's nostrils flared in irritation but he answered the question nonetheless.

"Farcaster travel is . . . difficult. Traveling through the network without taking the proper precautions can leave an operator mentally disoriented, even physically ill. Reaction times and cognitive functions are slowed, sometimes drastically. All of which renders an operative unable to carry out their duties."

The recruiter pointed to the hypo unit Nate was holding. "The injector delivers a semi-aqueous solution containing a potent mix of microbial nanoselectors and morphotic radioisotopes that counteract the adverse reactions associated with farcaster travel, allowing you to make the transit with your mental and physical abilities intact."

"I . . . see," Nate said, though he really had no idea what the hell the guy was talking about.

"Please note that the counter agent has been designed specifically for you and you alone based on the results of the medical exam you just underwent. Taking a hypo injection meant for another operative could result in severe injury, possibly death. The same holds true for the farcaster you will be using. It has been keyed to your personal DNA signature. Use by another individual could be deadly."

Nate thought about the other rooms they'd passed in the hallway on their way to this one. Did each of those rooms contain a farcaster portal like this one? How many other hallways like that were in other buildings in this city? In other cities? Just how big was this agency?

He didn't bother to ask. He knew the recruiter wouldn't answer; that kind of information was well above Nate's pay grade.

"Does that satisfy your curiosity, Mr. Benson? May I continue with my briefing now?"

Nate nodded his head in acquiescence.

"As I was saying, inject yourself with the hypo and then change into the clothes that have been provided for you. As with the hypo, they have been specifically tailored to suit you and help you look the part at your destination."

The recruiter turned and walked over to the farcaster unit, a round metal dome with a door in the center and a maze of pipes and wiring coming out of the top. A small control panel was inset to the left of the door.

"When you arrive, your destination will already be programmed into your farcaster unit. All you need do is hit this button here . . ."—he pointed to a bright green button on the bottom right of the control panel—"and then step inside the unit. When you close the door, a countdown will begin. If, for some reason, you find you must abort the mission, you have exactly six seconds to do so."

Six seconds? He stared at the complex locking mechanism on the inside of the door and shook his head. *Better hope you don't have to abort or things are gonna get ugly . . .*

"Your PCD will deliver a set of coordinates to you once you exit the farcaster and can be used as a GPS device to locate those coordinates thereafter. At those coordinates will be instructions on what you are to do to complete the mission, as well as whatever specialized gear you might need to carry said mission out. You have exactly seventy-two hours in which to complete your assignment, not a minute more. When you have finished, you are to return to the same farcaster and use that to come home. Any questions?"

"No. I'm good."

It was simple and straightforward, which Nate liked. He wasn't thrilled with traveling by farcaster, but if that's what the job required, he could live with it for what they were paying him.

And they were paying him a lot.

*   *   *

Nate's PCD went off for the first time three days later at precisely 6:30 a.m. Nate glanced at the display, noted the report time of 10:45, and dragged himself out of bed. Fifteen minutes later he was stepping aboard a slidetrain, headed for the Limbus offices as he'd been instructed.

He used the employee identification card he'd been given to access the elevators and rode one straight to the ninety-seventh floor. Both the palm lock to the office suite and the one to the farcaster room opened at his touch.

Nate changed into the casual clothes that were hanging in the locker, leaving his own in their place. Unsurprisingly there were no tags or other identifying marks in the clothing and the clothes themselves were average, everyday wear that wouldn't stand out in a crowd. Whoever was running this operation seemed to know what they were doing, which he certainly appreciated. After all, it was his ass that was on the line should something go wrong.

He picked up the hypo, hesitated a moment, then said "fuck it" aloud into the empty room and pressed the device against the inside of his wrist. There was the quick hiss of the injection followed by a moment of lightheadedness and then he was ready to go.

Nate hit the green button, stepped into the farcaster unit, and pulled the door shut.

He counted down from six to steady his nerves.

"Six . . ."

"Five . . ."

"Four . . ."

"Three . . ."

"Two . . ."

The world faded around him and the last thought he had on this side of the cast was to curse the sonofabitch who shorted him two seconds.

* * *

Nate stepped out of the utility closet into which he'd arrived and scanned the immediate vicinity, making sure no one had seen his exit.

He appeared to be in a train station somewhere; travelers were hustling to and fro with bags in their hands and a voice over the PA system was announcing that the 10:51 express was ready to depart on track 118.

The PCD in his pocket beeped. He took it out and glanced at the display, noting that it was showing a drop location less than fifty feet from where he was now standing. He followed the coordinates to their source, which, as he'd already guessed, turned out to be a self-storage locker.

He spent a moment or two pondering what the combination might be, then shrugged and punched in the street address of the Limbus building.

The lock popped open with a flat clang.

An information disk for his PCD sat on the shelf inside, next to a small stack of currency. He popped the chip into his PCD and absently stuffed the cash into his pockets while watching the information that came up on his screen.

The mission looked to be a relatively simple. He was supposed to wait outside a certain restaurant—address included—and photograph a meeting between two men. Photos of each of them had been provided for identification purposes. Nate studied them for a moment, committing their features to memory. He was certain he'd never seen either one of them before; not that it mattered in the long run. He would have done the job even if he'd known them for the last twenty years. A job was a job.

It went without saying that there was to be no contact with either individual. Once he had obtained the necessary photographs, he was to leave the vicinity as soon as possible and make his way back to the equipment drop. There he would receive the coordinates for the return trip.

The equipment drop contained a nylon backpack complete with a camera, telephoto lens, and press credentials from some rag called *The Global Inquirer*.

He slipped the credentials into the pocket of his jacket and slung the backpack over his shoulder, then made his way out of the station to the street beyond. A glance at his PCD told him he had less than twenty minutes to get into position, so he hustled to the front of the cab line and climbed into the first vehicle, slamming the door in the face of the woman he'd just cut in front of. He handed some cash to the driver to get him to ignore the angry shouts of the woman standing outside and told him he'd pay double the fare if the driver could get him to their destination in less than fifteen minutes.

Tires squealed and Nate was pushed back into his seat as the driver rose to the challenge.

The driver was too busy concentrating on navigating to be chatting, which Nate was thankful for. The car he was in was an older model, without any modern conveniences it seemed. Even the ads seemed ten years out of date, for heaven's sake. But the cabbie knew the city and that's all Nate really cared about. Exactly thirteen minutes and twenty-two seconds later, Nate was getting out of the cab a block from his final destination, having told the driver to pull over to reduce the chance of being seen. Not that he expected to be recognized by his targets, but why take the chance if it wasn't necessary?

He walked the rest of the way to the restaurant and found a place to sit on a bench in a small park across the way. His position gave him a clear view of both the front entrance and the outdoor eating area on the side of the building. If his targets chose the former, he'd wander inside and get a table. If they chose the latter, he'd be in a perfect position to watch them while they ate.

In the end, it was all rather anticlimactic. The two men he was waiting for arrived a few minutes after he did. To his relief, they chose to eat outside, absolving him of the need to go inside and find a table. Instead, he didn't have to do anything more than point the camera in their general direction; the telephoto lens got everything he needed with the touch of a button. It was so simple a child could have done it.

When he was satisfied that he'd gotten what he needed, Nate put the camera back into the pack and went to find another cab, which would take him back to the station. Once there, he put the backpack containing the camera back into the locker and hit the lock button.

Already thinking about the paycheck that came with the successful completion of the job, Nate went to find his farcaster home.

* * *

Over the course of the next three weeks Nate handled two more assignments. The first required him to pick up a package from the equipment locker, cross town to a hotel, and leave it for an incoming guest. The second involved breaking into an office building on the outskirts of the business district and removing several files from the company president's office on the fifth floor. Both times he'd arrived with very little time to spare and had to hustle to get in position by the time indicated on his orders, but that was the only hiccup he encountered. Even the B&E didn't bother him; they were paying him, and paying him well, to take risks on their behalf and the petty crime barely registered on his personal morality meter. He'd done far worse during his time in the service.

About a week after his third assignment, Nate was having breakfast in an upscale joint on 84th Avenue, the kind of place that was so high above his previous standard of living that three months ago he wouldn't have even looked at it. A news clip on the screen behind the receptionist's station caught his eye.

He tapped the controls next to his right hand and the screen embedded into his table top came to life.

". . . for good behavior after serving ten years on espionage charges. Owens was caught on camera in a now famous photograph showing him exchanging documentation on the Raptor III drone-launched missile system with this man, Lee Fong, a member of a so-called Chinese trade delegation. Fong's diplomatic credentials were revoked and he was expelled from this country immediately following the incident. At the time, Owens claimed that . . ."

Nate stared at the photograph on the screen—*one of the photographs that he'd taken as his first job for Limbus!*

A ten-year sentence? How in hell was that even possible?

A trial like that would take months just to get scheduled in front of a judge, never mind the additional months it would take to try the case. There was just no way. The newscaster must have misspoken.

But as Nate changed stations and listened to several other broadcasts, he realized that they were all saying the same thing. Owens was being released after serving a ten-year sentence for espionage. A sentence that was the result of a guilty verdict that had been obtained using the photographs that Nate himself had taken!

Something was very, very wrong.

Nate paid his bill and then left the restaurant, his thoughts awhirl. He wanted to learn more about the Owens case, but wasn't about to make any inquiries from his PCD where it could be traced back to him. He needed a cyber café.

The first one he came to looked a bit too upscale to have what he wanted, so he passed it by and kept looking. After another fifteen minutes he found another place, sandwiched between an auto mechanic and a shoe repair shop in an alley off of 69th that would do the trick. He paid for an hour of time at a private terminal and the proprietor led him to a closet-sized space in the back of the room that contained a triD terminal with a built-in keyboard. The gear was at least fifteen years out of date but it fired up without difficulty when Nate sat down in front of it and that was good enough for him. The age of the terminal would make what he had to do next easier, actually.

He flexed his fingers and then punched in a coding sequence he'd learned from an electronics specialist first class while overseas. The commands rerouted the console's connection to the cybernet through twenty different pirate data havens, one after another, each one scrubbing the identifiers out of the data and hiding the originating signal in a blizzard of false streams that would take a decent hacker at least a week, maybe more, to unravel. By the time they did that, he'd be long gone.

Once he knew his efforts couldn't be traced back to him, Nate began digging into the background of the Owens case, trying to make sense of it all. According to the documents he was able to access, the government had been chasing a leak within their classified weapons program for more than a year before investigators began to focus their attention on Owens. The break had come when an anonymous source sent in half-a-dozen photographs showing Owens passing a packet of information to Fong while they were dining together at an outdoor restaurant. There was no way for the photographs to be used in court, as the investigators couldn't prove they were authentic given their anonymous source, but that didn't stop investigators from using them to confront Owens, who, upon seeing the evidence, broke down and confessed. Owens had then pled guilty, saving the government years of effort and no doubt millions of dollars that would have been needed to convict him.

Nate double-checked the dates. Owens had been sentenced just over ten years ago, according to the information.

Has to be a different photograph, he thought.

He called up the image and expanded it on the screen.

It *wasn't* a different photograph; he knew that immediately. While Nate had never actually held the images he'd taken that day, he had been looking through the camera's viewfinder when he'd taken them and the image he called up on the screen was identical to the one he had in his memory.

It *was* his photograph.

There was no mistaking it.

He thought for a moment and then hunched over the keys once more, tapping furiously.

The console obediently put the information he asked for on the screen in front of him.

Seeing it, Nate sat back in his chair. His stomach did a slow roll and he had to take several deep breaths in order to keep from throwing up.

On the screen was an article about the hotel he'd delivered the package to during his second assignment. According to the press, a terrorist bomb had gone off on the hotel's eighteenth floor, killing three people and starting a fire that rapidly burned out of control and ended up destroying the entire building.

The date of the fire was five years ago.

Nate's hands shook.

"Holy shit!" he breathed.

No sooner were the words out of his mouth than a loud beeping sound filled the cubicle, Nate jumped out of his seat, glancing wildly about, convinced in those first few seconds that the corporate bigwigs at Limbus had discovered what he was up to and had sent in the riot police to drag him downtown . . .

There was no one there.

The beeping sound was the pager on his PCD.

Telling himself to calm down, he fumbled it off his belt, slipped the switch to silence the alarm, and looked down at the readout.

1:15, it read.

Nate didn't know whether to laugh or cry. Not only did he have an immediate assignment, but he had twenty-five minutes to make it there.

He wiped all traces of what he'd been doing from the terminal, then exited the cyber café. Using his PCD he called for a limousine, knowing it would be faster than the slidetrain and might just mean the difference between success and failure. He had no idea what would happen if he missed the deadline and frankly he had no intention of finding out. The chauffeured vehicle had slid out of the sky seconds later and got him to the Limbus offices with three minutes to go before the deadline.

He rushed to the prep room, swapped his clothes for the ones waiting there for him, and jumped into the farcaster, his thoughts a million miles away.

As the countdown neared its final seconds, Nate glanced out through the porthole in the middle of the farcaster door and saw that he'd left the door to his locker open.

That was the least of his worries.

There, on the top shelf, was the hypo he'd forgotten to take.

In the next second reality dropped away from him and Nate felt like he was falling . . . falling . . . falling . . .

*   *   *

Recruiter 46795 entered Nate Benson's mission prep room ten minutes after the other man had left. Despite having six operators under his direct supervision, management had yet to see fit to provide him with an assistant, so he was forced to handle even the trivial tasks like refilling the hypos and resetting the farcaster units himself.

He considered that aspect of the job to be far beneath him and constantly railed to himself against the short-sightedness of those above him. When he was promoted to executive, he'd be sure to let the others know just how demeaning he'd considered the whole . . .

His thoughts trailed off as he caught sight of the hypo sitting on the locker's top shelf.

Unused.

Questions swarmed his thoughts.

How much did Benson know? Was it a simple accident that he hadn't taken the hypo or had he avoided the injection purposely? Was he an enemy plant? Or, God forbid, working for another agency? Could he still be trusted? What about . . .

Recruiter 46795 cursed aloud, once, and then got control of himself. It wouldn't do to let something like this cause the rest of his plans to spin out of control. Benson could be contained, if necessary.

He'd wait and see what the operative did when he returned from his current assignment and then make some decisions about how to handle the situation.

Patience, he reminded himself, *patience.*

*   *   *

Nate stumbled out of the farcaster and promptly vomited all over the floor. He straightened, wiped his mouth, and was overcome a second time by the sensation of falling from an immeasurable height, a fall that just went on and on and on . . .

He leaned against the nearby wall and vomited a second time.

With his stomach now empty, the feeling receded. He stayed where he was, waiting for the nausea to pass. Then, and only then, did he dare to straighten up.

He wondered just how totally fucked he was.

He'd gone through the farcaster without his injection and he had no idea what kind of effects that would have on his body. He felt all right aside from the previous bout of nausea, but he knew that meant nothing. He might be sprouting massive tumors deep inside his body this very minute and wouldn't even know it.

Fuck it. Can't do anything about it now so might as well put it aside and concentrate on the job at hand.

He found himself in a garage, empty save for a sedan parked nearby. It was a couple of years old, no more than that. The driver's door was open and when he slid in behind the wheel he found the keys and a note above the dash.

The note gave him a set of coordinates and instructions to bury what was in the trunk at that location.

It had been awhile since he'd driven anything other than military vehicles and he slid the key in the ignition with a sense of anticipation. A smile came to his face as the car's twin engines came to life, growling in unison like two caged beasts ready to break free. He steered around the empty garage for a few minutes, to get a feel for the vehicle, then took her out the front gate. As soon as he was clear, he hit the antigrav units and took the car up over the city.

The Detroit-Windsor megaplex shone off to his left, hugging both banks of the Detroit River. He turned the car to the right and headed south along the river, searching for the coordinates.

Twenty minutes later he set down on the north bank, in the midst of a clearing. He killed the engines and waited for them to shut down completely before getting out.

Nate glanced around, but didn't see anyone. He walked back to the trunk and opened it up.

A large black body bag and one long-handled shovel stared back at him.

"Color me surprised," he said with a certain amount of fatalism and reached in for the shovel. It took him another half an hour to dig a hole deep enough that he thought the bag wouldn't get dug up again by the local wildlife. He stabbed the shovel into the pile of dirt he'd created and went to get the body.

Except it wasn't a body at all. He knew that the moment he tried to pick it up. It was much too heavy and far too angular to be anything human. His curiosity getting the better of him, Nate reached for the zipper and pulled it down a few inches.

The bag was full of cash. Bundles and bundles of it, all neatly stacked and wrapped with rubber bands.

Nate stared at the money a moment, then, being careful not to touch any of it, zipped the bag back up again. Seeing all that money in one place was tempting, but messing with that kind of stuff was sure to put a price on his head. He intended to do what he was told and that was that.

He dragged the bag out of the trunk and over to the hole he'd dug, and heaved it over the edge. It dropped the half-dozen feet and hit the bottom with a flat thunk. Nate gave it one last look and then began shoveling the dirt over it.

There was about an hour left on the assignment clock when he finished the job, which left him plenty of time for the little outing he planned. He returned the car to the garage where he'd found it, leaving the keys inside and locking it up after him for safe keeping, figuring whoever had left it there would have a spare set of their own. If they didn't . . . hey, not his problem.

Instead of getting into the farcaster, Nate walked out of the garage and headed down the street to the convenience store he'd spotted from the air. The doors were locked and the lights off when he arrived, but that really didn't matter to him. He made a beeline for the vending machines outside the front door and peered through the glass at the day's newssheet.

Even though he was expecting it, the date still left him a bit stunned.

It was November, 15th, the same as when he had left but this November 15th was two years in the past.

"I knew it!" he exclaimed.

The final proof was staring him in the face.

His thoughts were skipping in a thousand different directions by the time he made it back to the garage where the farcaster was located. He reached for the hypo and then stopped.

Do I really want to take that? he asked himself. *What if the first dose was tied to the second somehow? Would taking one without the other be dangerous?*

He didn't know.

Had no way of knowing at this point, not really.

His gut was telling him not to, that the two were inexplicably linked and only bad things could come of taking the dose separate from the first. He'd learned to trust his gut.

He took one last look at the angular injector and then hurled it away into the darkness of the garage. He heard glass shatter and for some reason the sound made him feel better.

Time to go home, he thought.

*   *   *

Nate stepped out of the farcaster and rushed immediately for the rest room, determined not to vomit all over the floor. He leaned over the sink and waited for the nausea to strike.

Surprisingly, it didn't.

He gave it another moment, just to be safe, but his stomach remained strangely acquiescent.

Given what he had learned on the other side, it was clear now that his initial suspicions were correct. He was travelling not just in distance but in time as well via the farcaster, going back and fixing errors, adjusting outcomes, eliminating targets, so that the present, his present, would unfold in a certain way.

The implications were staggering.

It raised all sorts of interesting questions about his employer, Limbus Inc. Who were they really? He'd known from the start that they were a front, but a front for who? Or what? The answers to those questions seemed far more important now than they had when he'd first walked in the door.

Trouble was, he didn't know how he was going to find them.

As he finished getting dressed, his gaze fell upon the hypo he'd failed to use before leaving earlier that morning. It was still sitting there on the locker shelf, untouched, which meant the clean-up crew hadn't been around yet.

He took the hypo, walked into the bathroom, and dumped it contents down the sink. He ran the water, washing any trace of the stuff down the drain, then returned the empty hypo to the locker.

Satisfied that he'd covered his tracks, Nate left the prep room and closed the door firmly behind him. He planned on learning as much about Limbus as he could, but not before he got a decent night's rest.

As he walked down the hallway toward the elevator, he noticed that one of the other doors was slightly open.

The sight brought him up short.

All the time he'd been coming here, he'd never run into another employee. The only interaction he'd had was with his recruiter and even those meetings were few and far between. Nate was suddenly, intensely curious about his co-workers. Who were they? What were they like? How many of them were there?

Maybe he'd find some of the answers he was looking for inside that room.

The open door seemed to beckon.

What can it hurt?

Casting caution to the wind, Nate stepped forward and gently pushed it open.

The room beyond looked identical to the one he'd just left. The same lack of general furnishings. The same bare walls. The same locker and farcaster unit.

The stretcher was new, however.

It stood in the middle of the room, as if someone had been getting ready to wheel it out and had stepped away for a moment to deal with something else. There was an odd, lumpy shape resting atop the stretcher, covered by a sheet now stained with blood and other fluids.

That shape drew Nate like a magnet.

He stepped forward, watching as his hand reached out almost of its own accord and grasped the edge of the sheet. He'd seen more than his fair share of the dead and dying while on active duty and wouldn't be put off by the sight of a corpse, yet still he hesitated.

Something felt . . . wrong.

Off.

Something told him that he didn't want to see what was under that sheet, that he wouldn't be able to just forget about it and get on with his life, that once he saw it things would be forever changed . . .

He pulled the sheet back anyway.

And immediately wished he hadn't.

The thing under the sheet had once been human, but it was hard to tell that now. It was as if some higher force had taken a human form, twisted it inside out and then added hundreds of runaway growths between the glistening wet organs and miles of ropy blood vessels; it was horrifying and strangely, eerily fascinating at the same time.

Nate was staring at it intently, trying to understand just what the hell it was that he was looking at, when a pair of eyes popped opened in what had once been the thing's face and he nearly leapt out of his shoes.

It was still alive!

The two of them stared at each other and then the thing erupted with a mewling cry of such pain and despair that Nate cringed at the sound. He was frozen in place, unable to move as the thing on the stretcher continued to wail in misery, and so he didn't notice anyone else was in the room with him until a hand snapped forward and yanked the sheet back up where it belonged.

The awful, hideous cry stopped immediately.

"What do you think you are doing? This area is off-limits!"

Nate shook himself, trying to banish the memory of that awful thing, and turned to find his recruiter staring at him with murder in his eyes.

"Get out!" the man said, pointing behind them at the door.

"What was that . . ."

"I said GET OUT! Or I will terminate you immediately!"

The threat to his livelihood—*or was that to his life?*—was enough to get him moving. He scrambled backward until he found the door and then slipped out into the hall. He knew better than to leave; something in his recruiter's tone had made that clear, so he began to pace back and forth within the narrow confines instead.

When his recruiter emerged from the room moments later, Nate couldn't hold his questions in any longer.

"What the fuck was *that*?" he asked, jabbing his finger past the other man's head to point at the room he'd just left. "What happened to that guy?"

Nate was expecting his recruiter to give him the typical runaround and so he was surprised when the other man answered calmly.

"What happened?" he repeated, a superior little smile on his face. "He fucked up; that's what happened. Thought he could pull a fast one and claim that he'd done the job when he really hadn't. I don't take kindly to being lied to."

Nate stared at him, horrified. "What did you do?"

The recruiter laughed. "I flipped his switch, of course! Did you think we'd send you idiots roaming around out there without some means of controlling you? Do you really think we're that stupid? He tried to fuck with me so I flipped his switch and activated all those little bastards in his bloodstream. Turned him inside out before he even knew what hit him!"

A chill washed over Nate as he realized the implications of what he was hearing. Whatever had been done to that guy had more than likely been done to him as well . . .

He had to force himself to keep from grabbing the front of the recruiter's shirt and slamming him up against the wall.

"What did you do to me?" he asked, the anger clear in his voice.

The recruiter laughed, seemingly not afraid of Nate at all.

"I didn't do anything to you. You did it to yourself. *You* asked for employment. *You* signed the waivers. *You* submitted to the medical 'tests.' You'll just have to live with the consequences."

Nate stared furiously at the man, stunned to realize that what the recruiter had just said was true. He'd been so eager to get off the street and back to something useful that he hadn't even stopped to read the paperwork that had been placed in front of him.

But his recruiter wasn't finished yet.

"Don't even think about running, Nate," he said with a sneer. "Limbus owns you now and we take our investments very seriously. If you run, we'll use the subcutaneous tracking device we've implanted in your skin to find where you've gone and bring you back again, at which point you'll be punished for the trouble you've caused."

The recruiter looked back at the door of the room they'd just exited and Nate got the message, loud and clear.

Suddenly Nate understood why Charlie had looked the way he had in the bar that night. It hadn't been fear that had caused his hands to tremble and his face to drain of color. No, not fear at all. It had been guilt.

Guilt that he'd been getting Nate involved with this mess in the first place.

Nate glanced down the hall to the elevator doors. *He could run,* he thought. *Get out of here, find a doc who could take the transponder out of his system, lay low until the storm passes. He'd survived the Faith War, he could survive this.*

The other man caught the look, realized what he was no doubt thinking.

"Don't be stupid," his recruiter said. "You've got a good thing going here, why make a mess of it all? If you carry out the assignments as requested, you've got nothing to worry about."

Nate wanted nothing more at that moment than to knock the man on his ass, but he restrained himself. *You've got to keep cool if you want to get out of here,* he told himself.

"Yeah, you're right," he said aloud, forcing himself to smile. "No sense screwing up a good thing. You've got to protect your assets; every corporation has to do that. Just good business sense, right?"

The recruiter grinned at him. "That's right. Stick with the program and who knows? A few years from now I might even recommend you for the junior level management program. Get you off the streets for good. You'd like that, wouldn't you?"

Nate made himself nod. "Of course I would. Last thing I want to do is end up like that guy in there," he said, pointing over the other man's shoulder at the door behind him.

The recruiter watched him closely for a moment and then nodded, as if to himself. "Good. Glad to hear it. Go home. Get some rest. When you've had a chance to think everything over you'll feel much better. I'm sure of it."

Permission granted, Nate got out of there as fast as he could.

* * *

Two hours later Recruiter 46795 stood staring out the window of his office, trying to figure out how he was going to clean up the mess he currently found himself in.

It had not been a good day.

First he'd had to terminate Wojowitski's employment and then there had been that business with Benson. Two disasters in one day, both with the potential of screwing with his chances of getting the promotion he'd been angling for since he'd been relocated to this office from his former post in New Los Angeles.

One rogue operative he could deal with. The long-term effects of farcaster travel were still unknown and Wojowitski had been at it longer than most. Claiming the operative had simply cracked under the strain would keep the focus off of himself and on Wojowitski, where it belonged. Besides, Wojowitski had been recruited by his predecessor, so claiming it was a poor recruit in the first place was still an option he could fall back on to avoid any blame.

But Benson . . . Benson was a different story. He was one of his own personal recruits and had only managed a handful of assignments in the last few months. There was no way to claim Benson was someone else's responsibility nor that the farcaster travel had begun to mess with the operator's neocortex; everyone knew that only happened after more than fifty jumps.

Recruiter 46795 stepped over to the wet bar in the corner of his office and poured himself a stiff drink. He downed the first one in a single gulp in an effort to calm his nerves and then poured a second of equal size. That one he took back to his desk with him and slowly nursed it as he gave the problem more thought.

It seemed clear to him that he'd compounded the problem with Benson when he'd confronted him earlier that evening. Discovering the unused hypo in Benson's locker had put him on edge, a situation that hadn't been helped much when he'd found Benson inside Wojowitski's prep room hours later. That's where things had really gone wrong.

I never should have run my mouth off like that, he thought. *Benson wasn't an idiot; if he was looking for information, he'd been given a boatload of it when I did that.*

He shook his head. It was too late to do anything about that now; what was done was done. He needed to focus on the future. To contain this thing before it got more out of hand.

That, of course, brought the problem around full circle. Without knowing Benson's true motives it was hard to say what he would do next and not knowing what he would do next made it extremely difficult to decide how to handle the problem itself. It was a Catch-22.

Unless . . .

The idea was a bit out of the box, but that was why Limbus had put him in this position in the first place, wasn't it? To come up with out-of-the-box solutions to the problems at hand.

Of course it was.

Suddenly energized, Recruiter 46795 sat up and began making plans to handle Benson in a way that was certain to keep him and the potential mess he represented from ever posing a problem in the future.

* * *

The page came in just after one a.m., startling Nate into wakefulness. He grabbed the PCD off his nightstand and squinted at the readout.

2:30, it read.

Shit! Now what?

He didn't know. He'd spent the rest of the afternoon and the evening thinking about the things he'd seen and heard earlier that day, but hadn't been able to come to a decision about what to do. As far as he could tell, Limbus had his nuts in a vise and he was pretty much screwed no matter what he did.

If he ran, they would catch him; he was pretty sure of it. That didn't mean running was out of the question, just that he had to be ready to deal with them when they came. And come they would; he was certain of that. The question was with how much force? One, maybe two operatives he could handle. More than that would be a problem.

Of course that was only if they sent someone in his current timeline.

If Limbus was smart, they'd send someone back to an earlier point in his life and wipe him out before he even had a chance to become who he was today. That was the safest and most logical bet. It was what he would do, if he were in charge.

Given that possibility, running didn't make much sense. They wouldn't have to figure out where he was going, just find some place he'd already been. There were more than enough points in time where his presence had been public knowledge, like the time he'd been arrested for petty larceny when he was eleven or the date of his discharge from the armed forces, and either one of those would do.

He could drop off the face of the planet tomorrow and they'd still find him.

So running was out.

Nate didn't mind that so much, truth to tell. He hadn't run from anything in his life and hadn't liked the idea of starting now.

Fine, then. He'd stick around. Work from the inside and see what he could learn.

Starting with this very assignment.

He dressed quickly, left his spacious new apartment behind, and headed downtown for the second time in twenty-four hours.

His recruiter was waiting for him in the prep room.

"Right on time, as usual," the man said, smiling at Nate.

Nate didn't find the expression, nor the man's presence, reassuring in the least.

"No need to change today," his recruiter told him. "It's a quick in and out job. Shouldn't take you more than an hour."

Nate nodded. Tried to look at ease. Just do the job, he told himself.

He turned toward the farcaster, intending to get inside, when he heard his recruiter clear his throat. Looking back he found the other man watching him closely.

"Forgetting something?"

For a moment Nate didn't know what he was talking about, but then his gaze fell on his open locker and the hypo sitting on the top shelf.

"Oh, damn! Thanks for reminding me," he said, trying to appear earnest. "Guess I'm not quite awake yet."

His recruiter smiled. "I understand. I'm not much of a morning person myself. That's why I thought I'd be here to see you off this morning. Here, let me help."

He picked up the hypo and walked over to Nate. "Give me your arm."

Nate had no choice. He rolled up his sleeve and presented the underside of his left arm to the other man. The hypo was pressed against his flesh and there was a quick hiss and the mild sensation of something passing into his system—then it was done.

For a moment, he almost panicked. If they wanted to get rid of him, the injection would be the perfect opportunity. One quick shot and it was all over.

"There," said the other man, "all set." He glanced at the clock, saw that there were only a few minutes left to the deadline. "You'd better get going."

Not trusting himself to speak, Nate simply nodded. He walked over to the farcaster, rolling his sleeve back down as he went, then he stepped inside the device and tried to get comfortable.

Outside, his recruiter pushed the door shut and waited for the locks to engage. Nate could see the man through the porthole, watched as he lifted a hand and waved.

"Good hunting," his recruiter said, smiling.

Nate nodded—*what the hell was that all about?*—and then hit the green button.

He arrived in an empty apartment in a run-down tenement building, the farcaster set up in a back bedroom with peeling wallpaper and the smell of mold. A hard black case stood on the floor nearby.

Nate recognized the weapons case the minute he saw it. He set it flat on the floor and then used one hand on either side to trigger the latches. Inside was a disassembled Mark 56 sniper rifle, the exact weapon he'd carried while point man for his recon unit. It was capable of both single and burst fire, with a maximum range of just over one thousand meters. It had been designed for one thing and one thing only—killing people at a distance.

He should know; he'd killed more than his fair share with a weapon just like it.

A white card had been slipped into the case alongside the rifle. Nate pulled it out, read it.

The card listed a set of coordinates and below that, four simple words.

Terminate with extreme prejudice.

"You have got to be shitting me," he said to the empty room around him.

It seemed that his journeyman days were over and he'd just graduated to the big time. First surveillance photographs, then breaking and entering, and now assassination. He wondered how much of that had to do with what he'd seen the day before. *Did they trust him with the bigger jobs now that he had a sense of what was going on or were they just setting him up for a fall? Getting ready to hang him out to dry after he pulled the trigger?*

He didn't know.

To his surprise, he realized he didn't care either. All he wanted to do was get the job over with and get home again.

He pulled out his PCD and checked his current location against the coordinates he'd been given, only to discover that the target was practically next door. He should be able to get a decent look at the place from the roof of the building he was in.

He picked up the case, exited the apartment, and made his way up onto the roof of the building via the rear stairwell. The tenement building was three stories high and built on the edge of a residential area. His target was in a ramshackle two-story house about a block down the street. It looked familiar and for a moment he hesitated, but then he swept his hesitation aside by telling himself that all slums looked familiar. From where he stood, he could see through several of the windows and into the rooms beyond.

He couldn't have picked a better firing position himself.

A low wall ran around the edge of the rooftop, just high enough to act as support for his weapon. It was as good a spot as any and Nate settled down, prepared to do the job and be done with it. Assassination wasn't anything new for him; he had fifteen confirmed kills on his military record. It was the first time he'd ever taken out a civilian, he had to admit, but that wouldn't matter. Killing was killing in his view.

Do the job, go home, and figure out how you're going to get out of this mess, he told himself.

He opened up the case and swiftly assembled the rifle, barely having to look at it as he did so. He kept his eye on the house down the block, watching for movement in any of the rooms. It was still early, just before dawn, so he might be sitting here awhile, but he didn't want to take the chance of missing his target. Maybe the guy was an early riser, like he was. If he could get him before the street around him began to wake up, so much the better.

A thought occurred to him. *What if it's a woman?* The note hadn't given any indication one way or the other just who his target was, never mind whether it was a male or a female. He thought about it for a moment and then realized it didn't make much difference to him. He'd killed female fighters during the Faith War; was this any different? Given what he'd seen yesterday in regard to what happened to an operative who failed an assignment, he was as much fighting for his life now as he had been back on the battlefield. If he didn't do the job, his recruiter would "flip his switch," as he'd said, and turn him, quite literally, inside out.

Rifle assembled, he settled into position, kneeling in front of the low wall at the edge of the roof with his rifle braced over the top. He brought the scope to his eye and began scanning the windows for movement.

A few of the lights were on, indicating someone was likely up and about, so he concentrated his attention on those rooms. He could see what looked to be a kitchen and a living room on the lower floor and possibly a bedroom, though it might be a bathroom, on the upper.

There!

A man's upper body came into view, framed in the window, and Nate's body acted almost without conscious thought. He had the sight picture settled on a point just to the right of the target's nose and was pulling the trigger when the man turned his face into the light and Nate recognized him.

Too late! His mind screamed, but he jerked his hands to the left as the gun went off, hoping it was enough.

The bullet left the muzzle of his weapon, shot across the space between them in the blink of an eye, and slammed into the wood along the windowsill instead of striking his target as planned.

Nate breathed a sigh of relief and slumped down against the wall he'd been kneeling against. His heart was pounding and sweat was pooling in the small of his back as the adrenaline dump washed through his system. He didn't want to think about how close he'd just come to wiping himself out of existence.

The man he'd been sent here to kill was . . . himself.

Fuck!

He sat there, his back against the wall, rifle in hand, and wanted to hit himself for being so stupid. *How could he have missed this?*

Clearly he'd seen something yesterday that he shouldn't have. That had made someone back at Limbus nervous enough to order not just his death, but the complete elimination of everything he'd done in the last several years, judging from the age of his other self. They weren't just trying to kill him; they were trying to wipe the last several years of his life completely!

That pissed him off.

The question was what he was going to do about it.

He couldn't just go back and claim that he'd done the job; the very act of doing so would make it obvious that he hadn't. Going back would also put him in range of whatever it was the recruiter had used to turn the other agent inside out and Nate had no desire to see what that felt like up close and personal.

There was just as much risk in staying here, however. *What was it that sonofabitch had said? Something about the little bastards in his bloodstream?* Nate glanced down at the spot on his arm where he'd received the hypo shot less than an hour ago. *What if the trigger for his punishment was already inside him, just waiting to be activated? Or worse, would turn itself on when the seventy-two hour mission deadline passed?*

The second injection was designed to neutralize the effects of the first, he realized, in a moment of stunning clarity. Without it, the operative would essentially self-destruct. It was a fail-safe mechanism; it kept the operative from remaining in the past and fucking things up in the future.

Nor could he simply hire someone to go and waste his recruiter. If the bit about the farcaster being keyed to his personal DNA signature was correct, he was the only person who could use it.

Unless . . .

He glanced over the edge of the roof and back toward his target. He could see the other him moving around in the kitchen, oblivious to the twist of fate that had very nearly ended both their lives only seconds before. Aside from himself, he was the only other person he could think of that might have an interest in how all this turned out.

You're nuts, he told himself, but given the situation, that was hardly a reason not to do what he had in mind.

Five minutes later he was standing on the front steps of the target house, gun case in hand, knocking loudly on the front door.

After a few minutes the overhead light went on and he heard the sounds of someone fumbling with the locks on the other side. Then the door was thrown open and the figure of a man filled the doorway.

"Do you have any idea . . ."

That was as far as he got. There was a pause as the man standing in the doorway finally got a good look at him and tried to come to grips with what he was seeing. After a moment there was a whispered, "What the fuck?"

Nate knew exactly how he felt.

He felt a smile stretch across his face as he said, "Hello, Nate. I'm Nate. We have a few things to talk about. Do you mind if I come in?"

Another pause, longer this time, and then the other man held the door open and beckoned him inside.

Just as Nate knew he would.

* * *

Recruiter 46795 sat behind his desk, alternating between watching the mission clock on the wall and the red folder sitting atop his desk, next to a handheld device that contained a single switch. Personally he was betting on the folder disappearing before the clock ran out. Operator Benson didn't appear to be the smartest apple in the bunch. Clever, and curious as well, too curious actually, but smart? Not so much.

More than likely he'd carry out the mission assigned to him, never even realizing until it was too late that he'd just gunned down his younger self, thereby erasing every future event from that point in his timeline, wiping out both versions of himself, the past and the future, with the simple act of pulling the trigger.

It was an elegant solution and one Recruiter 46795 was particularly pleased to have crafted. Eliminating all traces of Benson would also eliminate the failure to control Benson from the recruiter's record, thereby solving that problem as well.

An hour passed.

Then two.

With each passing moment his frown deepened and his anxiety rose. He was confident the nanobites would do the trick when the mission deadline passed, but he hated to be forced to rely on them. It was such an incomplete . . .

"Did you really think you'd get rid of me that easily?" Nate Benson's voice asked from the darkness just beyond the doorway.

Recruiter 46795 didn't hesitate. His hand shot out and slammed palm down on the device, triggering the switch, suddenly thrilled that he was going to personally be able to resolve the problem and avoid any lingering doubts.

His triumphed shout died stillborn in his throat, however, as the younger Nate Benson stepped, unharmed, out of the darkness and into the light.

The gun in his hand loomed very large.

"You can stop that now," Nate said, nodding toward the desktop, where Recruiter 46795's hand was repeatedly slamming itself down on the switch.

He jerked his hand back and put it in his lap, unable to believe what was happening.

"How?" was all he managed to get out.

Benson smiled.

"Syncing the farcaster to the operator's DNA is a pretty neat trick; keeps the average citizen from stumbling on it and mucking things all up, I'd guess. But when the shooter and the victim happen to have the same DNA, as well as the same desire for self-preservation, well, there you've got a problem."

The gun in Benson's hand rose slightly to point directly at Recruiter 46795's face and then he knew no more.

* * *

The farcaster whined, shook, and then seemed to shimmer before his very eyes before going still. Nate Benson walked over and looked inside the porthole. Frowning, he punched the buttons on the keypad to open up the door and looked inside. On the floor of the farcaster was a padded envelope, the kind you might mail things in.

Nate reached inside and picked it up. Opening it, he found a single sheet of paper and a full hypo spray.

He glanced at the note as he readied the hypo.

Dear Nate,

Sorry I had to do this, but you really didn't expect me to come back there, did you? Not after all that crap you told me about the war and life afterwards? Thanks but you can keep that shit. Oh, and don't try to use this farcaster again; I've reprogrammed it to send whoever uses it to the bottom of the Arctic Ocean.

Nate

Nate laughed. He couldn't help it. It was just like him to take advantage of a situation. Hell, he'd been doing it for years.

Still smiling, he picked up the hypo and injected himself with it, imagining he could feel the nanobites in his bloodstreams dying off as the antidote washed through his system.

Let the kid have his fun, he thought. In about another six months the farcaster he'd used on his second mission was going to show up in a warehouse outside of Philadelphia and he could always use that one to go home if he chose to do so.

For now though, he'd hang around here. With all the information in his head about what was coming over the next several years, he was in position to make a good deal of money.

That wouldn't be so bad, now would it?

Whistling to himself, Nate left the apartment behind and headed out to live this day over for the second time.

Matthew

The streets were silent by the time Matthew turned the final page on the astonishing life of Nate Benson. Evening revelers had long since gone to whatever destination would hold them for the night, and the streets were empty of all but shadows. In the silence, Matthew sat wishing he had a fire so that he might consign the manuscript to the flames. But somehow he knew that even if he had the opportunity, he could never follow through. No, he had to know more. Picking up the phone, he dialed his friend Charlie. He just hoped he was working the night shift.

The phone rang three times before Charlie answered.

"Fifth precinct."

"Charlie," Matthew said, and he shuddered as he heard the tremor in his own voice, "it's Matthew." There was silence on the other end.

"Matthew? Man, it's four o'clock in the morning. Are you OK?"

"Yeah, yeah, I'm fine. Look, Charlie, I've got a question I need to ask you. Do you know anything about a girl named Angela Endicott?"

There was laughing on the other end of the line. "Angela Endicott? Of course I know her. Her uncle's one of the biggest players in the city. Why do you ask? Matthew? You there? Hello?"

Matthew had thought that the call would make things better. Charlie was a detective, one of Boston's finest. And if he had never heard of Angela Endicott, then she simply did not exist. And not existing would make the book that sat before him nothing more than fiction, and fiction can't hurt you. Not normally, at least.

But Angela did exist. And a girl like Angela Endicott simply could not be, not in Matthew's world. Not in a world of order. A girl like Angela Endicott was chaos personified.

"Matthew!"

It was the concern in his friend's voice—and oh, if only he knew—that finally shook Matthew from his stupor. "Do you know if she's ever been kidnapped?" he blurted out.

"Kidnapped?" Charlie said, laughing. "Of course not."

Matthew should have taken comfort there, but there was something off in Charlie's voice. A hitch. A pause. A singular moment of shock.

"Charlie," Matthew began, trying to stay as calm and even as possible, "have you ever heard of a company called Limbus?"

For a long moment, Charlie said nothing. Then, in a voice that Matthew had never before heard from his old friend, he spoke.

"Matthew, I don't know what the hell you've gotten yourself into, but you've got to get out of it. Get out of it right now."

Before Matthew could say a word, the line went silent. He put the phone on his desk next to the book. For a moment, he couldn't bring himself to look at it, but then he couldn't bring himself not to. Before he knew what he was doing, the book was open, and the next story began.

We Employ

By

Anne C. Petty

Dallas squeezed himself into the stall behind the guy from the bar. Trust his luck to pick the grubbiest shitter in the row. At least there wasn't anything floating in the bowl.

The guy went right for his fly, no messing around.

"Wait!" Dallas pushed his hand away. "Payment up front, we agreed."

"Yeah, but maybe I wanna sample the goods before I pay," said the man, Jim Beam leaking from his pores. He grabbed Dallas by the crotch.

Dallas' knee came up, but there was barely any room to defend himself. His foot slipped, and the guy pushed him toward the wall.

He landed on his butt between the toilet bowl and the stall divider. His head cracked against the tiled back of the stall and stars blossomed behind his eyeballs. The door banged shut. Heavy footsteps squelched away and soon were gone.

Dallas lay on the damp floor, the tang of urine infesting his sinuses. Well, that could have gone better. Granted, he was beyond desperate to resort to a stunt like this for money, but the alternative was sleeping on a piece of cardboard under the bridge.

Shaky, he emerged from the stall and was relieved to have the men's bathroom of the seedy South Beach night club to himself. He caught a glimpse of the nondescript street person in the mirror over the sink. Disheveled brown hair, skinny frame wrapped in a threadbare T-shirt, grubby jeans at half-mast. Not to mention he needed a shave and definitely a shower, things a reasonably civilized person took for granted until the means to make them happen were beyond reach. He regarded the reflection with distaste. You've sunk to a new low, Hamilton.

To complete the picture, there was toilet paper stuck to the bottom of his shoe. It figured, the way things were going. But on closer look, he saw it was a card. He bent down, head throbbing, and picked it up. Plain white. Dallas turned it over. He saw red print on a white field with some kind of holographic logo that looked like a globe of the world.

Limbus, Inc.
Are you laid off, downsized, undersized?
Call us. We employ. 1-800-555-0606
How lucky do you feel?

Dallas made a rude noise. That was about the lamest employment come-on he'd seen yet...and he'd seen plenty in the months he'd been out of school and out of work. He started to chuck it in the trashcan but stopped in mid-toss. The slogan had changed.

Live your life on the edge.

What the fuck? He looked again. It said nothing about feeling lucky. Where had he gotten that? Maybe banged his head a little too hard. He did feel kind of dicey, probably mildly concussed. He held the card up to the light. No address, just the phone number, which was a bitch because he didn't have a phone. At least it was a 1-800 number. He rubbed his finger over the globe logo and instantly the little image began to rotate, with tiny pinpricks of light exploding and disappearing over all the continents. Dallas stared. Was there a chip embedded in the card? An animation app? He blinked. An address had appeared just below the company name. Dallas stifled the urge to flush the card and get the hell out. But hallucination or not, his curiosity was hooked.

The address was an office tower near Bayfront Park, off the Macarthur Causeway and a couple of blocks down Biscayne—about a six-mile walk from where he was. The park, a thirty-two acre urban extravaganza of fountains, outdoor amphitheatre, rows of boxwoods, and tightly grouped ornamental trees, had been his nighttime refuge more than once. Dallas went outside and started walking toward the causeway. His circumstances were dire, but he was resourceful, even for a college dropout. If only his parents had given him a little cushion money before they'd disowned him for flunking out it would've made things a lot easier.

A cop car cruised by and slowed. He put his head down and kept walking. Stay unobtrusive, unremarkable. It glided on past. Once it was out of sight, he thumbed a ride as far as Watson Island, and headed up onto the high causeway bridge, walking fast, trying not to think about the dark, deep water underneath him. He hated bridges. The weather was warm and he didn't mind the hike, just as long as nobody fucked with him. He'd only been in one serious fight since leaving college and ending up on the street. He'd come out of it robbed and bloodied, but mostly intact—no broken bones or cuts that needed stitches. Since that encounter, he'd been more careful and much less trusting. Except for that stupidity back in the bathroom. He must have been losing his grip. If he could somehow find a job, even something as degrading as scooping dog poop from the sidewalks, he'd be willing to take it. He wondered if that Limbus agency had jobs like that. Maybe they were so high-level he'd need to be a laid-off AIG exec to even get an interview. That was unlikely, given where he'd found the card. He felt around in his back pocket and pulled it out by the corner, as if it might bite. To his relief, it hadn't changed since he'd last checked it in the South Beach restroom. He rubbed his thumb over the logo—nothing happened, which confirmed his suspicion that all the weirdness he thought he'd seen under the flickering bathroom lights had been a concussion headcase illusion.

He got to the office tower around noon of the next day. Standing on the sidewalk looking at himself in its mirrored windows, he knew there was no way in hell he could waltz into this glass and steel monolith and ask for a job. He was lucky its security guards didn't swarm out of their air-conditioned safety zone and lock him up for impersonating a human. He hauled his jeans up over his hipbones—had he lost that much weight?—and thumbed a ride to Miami Shores where his parents lived.

* * *

Dallas stood on the doorstep of the modestly comfortable house he'd grown up in, feeling like a complete stranger. The last time he'd been here, his father had slammed the door in his face and left him standing on this exact spot with no belongings and no money. Sink or swim, the man had said, or something to that effect.

Dallas pushed the doorbell. He knew his mother was home because her Camry was in the driveway. If she was on the phone or lunching by the pool it might take her a minute to answer. He waited, and then rang again. After a few seconds the door opened and his mother, a petit hair-salon blonde, looked up at him. "I'm sorry, this neighborhood doesn't allow panhandlers—" She stopped in mid-breath, took a closer look at Dallas, screamed, and slammed the door.

He sat down on the front steps. Pretty much the reception he'd expected, but what to do now? He needed to get cleaned up before he could go to the Limbus office. He heard the door open behind him.

"Good lord, it really is you, isn't it?"

Dallas got up and faced her. "I...I have a job interview and I just need to get some clean clothes."

His mother looked him up and down, frowning. "What kind of job?"

"Um, whatever they need. It's a new agency, so . . . they need a lot of recruits."

His mother's shoulders softened a smidge, by which he knew he'd won. "Stay right there, you smell like a landfill." She shut the door, more gently this time.

Dallas let his breath out. For once he'd made the right choice. He waited some more as she took her sweet time. Probably calling his father, which would be majorly awkward what with the potential for a parental meltdown but he hoped to be long gone before that unpleasant scenario could play out. His mother opened the door and handed out a stack of folded jeans, polo shirt, socks, and briefs. A towel and bath and shaving stuff rested on top.

"I can't let you in smelling like that. Go around to the back and use the cabana shower. And for God's sake shave your face." Her expression was grim.

He took the clothes. "Right. And could you . . . I'm really starving." No joke there—he felt and looked it. He could feel her disapproval like a force field that kept her from coming any closer. "Just go clean up." She pulled the door shut.

Dallas sighed and went around the side of the house where mango and grapefruit trees and a tall hibiscus hid the pool fence from the street. He went to the patio shower and stripped off all his clothes in front of God and everybody just for spite, giving any curious neighbors an eyeful. Soaping and rinsing in the cool water, he began to feel better, and after he'd toweled dry and pulled on the clean clothes, he thought he might live. He stepped into the cabana and shaved his ratty beard away. His face in the mirror looked like the old Dallas Hamilton, only not so naïve. Wary, less trusting. Nothing he could do about the hair for now. It wasn't quite long enough for a ponytail, but clean and pushed back behind his ears it wasn't too bad.

He retrieved the Limbus card before tossing his torn T-shirt and beyond-redemption jeans in the City of Miami waste disposal canister near the fence and was about to slide it into the breast pocket of his clean polo shirt when he saw it. Not possible—the slogan had changed again.

Gate expires May 31. Hurry up please, it's time!

Dallas' fingers shook as he held the card—something was definitely hinky and it wasn't the bump on his head. So, the mysterious card was quoting Eliot now? It was almost enough to make him laugh if he weren't so spooked.

His mother came out of the back door carrying his old high school book bag. She set it down on the patio table. "I put some extra clothes and a few supplies in it. That's the best I can do."

"Mom, I'm really sorry—"

She put up her hand. "Don't. Just don't. Sixty thousand dollars of your father's hard-earned money to finance your education and you manage to flunk out your last year with no degree." She crossed her arms over her narrow chest.

"I know how it looks, but—"

"I'm not going to tell your father you were here. His blood pressure and all."

Dallas gathered up the book bag. "It was good seeing you, Mom."

She nodded and went back inside without another word. He wasn't sure that bridge was burned, but he decided not to push it. He checked the book bag. A change of clothes, some fruit and a sandwich, and an envelope with $40 in small bills. He felt rich beyond expectations. Dallas inhaled the food, hoisted the bag strap over his shoulder, and headed down the sidewalk to the bus stop, feeling weirdly expectant. The first thing he intended to ask those Limbus people was how they did that thing with the card.

* * *

Dallas found the Limbus office without much trouble. It was on the second floor, down a very long hallway.

The company name was on a small plaque beside the door. He turned the knob and found himself in a waiting room that looked more like his dentist's office than an employment agency. Institutional green paint, uncomfortable vinyl sofa along one wall, matching side chairs on opposite walls, an old-fashioned umbrella stand and coat rack beside the door. To his right, the built-in reception window allowed a glimpse of file cabinets, fax machines, and printers crowded into a small workroom. He went to the window, but saw no one. No business cards or company brochures on the narrow ledge under the window. No bell to ring to call anyone. An open hallway directly across from the door he'd come through revealed gray carpeting and rows of cubicles on either side, filled, he supposed, with workers hiring people like himself into jobs they could live on. The only flaw in this assumption was the utter stillness of the office—no voices, no phones ringing, no keyboard clatter.

He walked over to the sofa and took a quick look at the dozen or so books and magazines scatted over a low table. *Brane Theory for Dummies. The Zoltron Dynasty Then and Now. Body Templates Catalog. Offworld Travel Tips.* The hairs along the back of his neck prickled. He should walk away now and forget he'd ever heard of Limbus Employment Agency.

Turning, Dallas stared at the company sign affixed to the wall over the reception window. There was the turning globe, with its little pinpoints of light pulsing on every continent. The slogan below it read simply, *We employ.* Without a doubt, this company had the dumbest motivational slogans of anything he'd ever seen. They needed to fire their copywriter.

This was looking less and less like anything he wanted in on. He turned to leave when a short, squat man stepped out of the first cube in the row. With bald head and bulbous features and practically no neck, he looked to Dallas like a toad in an ill-fitting suit.

"Hello, I am Recruiter Rigel." He beckoned to Dallas. "Please come have a seat." He motioned toward two folding chairs in front of his desk.

Dallas entered the cube, still fighting the urge to bolt for the door. "Is there some company literature I could have a look at?"

Rigel sat down. "Literature?"

"Don't you have any brochures? Every employment agency has brochures."

"Did you want a job or not?"

"Well, yeah, why else would I be here?"

"We have one. Tailored for you." Recruiter Rigel opened the central drawer of his desk and extracted a sheet of paper, an official looking document with very fine print, and pushed it toward him.

"Don't you want me to fill out some kind of application? How can you tell if I'm suited to a job if you don't even know anything about me?"

"This one was pre-selected for you. Please read it over carefully."

Exasperated, Dallas snatched up the page. It looked like an ordinary job description, with sections labeled Tasks, Qualifications, Duration of Work, and Compensation. He started reading the bullets under the headers. It was at that point all similarity between any previous job description he'd ever seen and this one took a sharp detour.

The job title was Dog Walker. He scanned the Qualifications column:

- Must like dogs
- Must be nondescript and not stand out in a crowd
- Must have a good sense of direction
- Must be dependable and resourceful in life-threatening situations

Dallas snorted. Who were they kidding? And what kind of effing dog were they talking about here? He imagined a bloody-fanged junkyard mastiff with red glowing eyes.

"It's a temp job, but the pay's high. They've had trouble keeping someone," Rigel was saying.

Dallas looked at the really fine print at the bottom of the page. "What's this about a bonus?"

"If you complete the job successfully by the deadline, which you'll notice is not far off, you will have earned a bonus."

Dallas mulled this over. "How much?"

"That's for you and the recruiter to decide."

Dallas glared at Rigel. "I don't see how you can run a business this way."

"I don't run the business. I am merely a recruiter." Rigel tapped his badge. It said RECRUITER in bright red letters.

Dallas ground his teeth. "I can see that." He consulted the Job Description again. That was a lot of money just to walk somebody's dog around the block for ten days. He checked the end date of the contract. Just like the card had said, May 31st. "I'll do it."

Rigel took a pen from the desk drawer and handed it to Dallas. "Sign your name, there at the bottom. Today's date is May 21."

Dallas wrote his name and dated it. He handed the page back to Rigel. "Don't I get a copy of it, for my files?" As if he had any such thing, but one should ask, shouldn't one?

"Why would you need a copy?"

"Well, in case I had questions, you know, about the job. Like how to find the freaking place with the dog." He'd given up being polite. This was clearly a fly-by-night operation and as soon as he got an actual payment from the owner of the dog, he was hitting the road.

"The address of the contractor is on the card," Rigel said with a trace of contempt, as if Dallas truly deserved his status of college dropout.

Dallas pulled the Limbus card out of his pocket and indeed, the contractor's name and address appeared in the spot where the spurious slogan had been entertaining itself. Her name was Marilyn Fairbanks and she lived at an address in Coconut Grove.

"I still want a copy."

The recruiter got to his feet, took the signed contract, and walked around his desk and out into the hall, presumably heading for the tiny workroom Dallas had glimpsed from the reception window. He heard a copier warming up and, eventually, its gears grinding.

Rigel returned and took his seat at the desk. He put the original contract in the middle drawer and handed the copy to Dallas with a look that telegraphed every ounce of how much trouble it had cost him to make that unnecessary copy. Rigel straightened his too-tight jacket across his shoulders. "This is a new client, so try not to embarrass us." He looked doubtful.

Infuriated, Dallas pushed back his chair and stood up. "I may be a failed academic, but you have no idea of the excellence with which I will be able to walk this dog." He assumed irony was lost on this toad, but he couldn't stop it from slipping out the side of his mouth.

Rigel's expression revealed nothing. "Just try to complete the task before the expiration date."

Dallas caught the Metro line to The Grove and walked to Marilyn's address. He'd seen trendy places like this smallish but cool apartment complex where upwardly mobile singles gravitated. That gave him hope that Ms. Fairbanks was at least good for the promised compensation. People who lived in places like this were hip, mostly in their twenties and thirties, stylish. educated. Dallas banished the bile that threatened his meager lunch and focused instead on the contract fee. Two thousand dollars for ten days' work came out to what . . . two hundred dollars a day for simple dog walking? There had to be a catch, but he intended to get his hands on the money before whatever it was kicked in.

Bounded on three sides by crepe myrtles and tamarinds interspersed among tall palms knee-deep in ferns, the property of Jacaranda Apartments gave the illusion of being surrounded by tropical jungle. Four tan stucco buildings rose three levels, each with a Spanish style red tile roof. A high wall of the same stucco buffered the apartments from the street. Spilling out of weathered planters on both sides of a head-high iron-grille gate, a profusion of multicolored crotons led into a small courtyard. Dallas could imagine the marketing copy: *"Providing that little touch of the Alhambra right here in the heart of The Grove."* A pool-sized terracotta fountain anchored the central patio with brick walkways leading to four pods that comprised the complex. He found building C, which appeared to have two apartments per level, and climbed the wide staircase with its black filigree railing to the third level. Ms. Fairbanks' apartment, number C-6, was on the left. He looked down on the lovely courtyard dozing in the sun and tried to imagine living in a place like this. He couldn't see it. Sad to say, he couldn't see himself living anywhere.

He reached the appointed door, painted black like the ironwork along the staircase. Putting his book bag down, he positioned himself directly in front of the peephole and pressed the buzzer. More waiting. It seemed most of his day had been spent waiting on someone—it was getting tedious. Impatient, he knocked a few times. At that moment, someone came up the staircase and unlocked the door to C-5. A nice-looking young man a little older than Dallas. Perfect haircut, perfectly matched navy shirt and khaki shorts, new deck shoes. Perfect smile, like a GQ model.

"I don't think anybody's home," he said to Dallas.

"What? But I was supposed to meet . . ." His thoughts went into freefall.

"Maybe they moved out. Apartment's been dark for a couple of days."

"Moved?" No other words came into his brain.

"Pretty sure. Sorry, man, looks like you got jilted."

"What? No, that's not—"

GQ guy smiled again. "Not what?"

Dallas stared at him blankly. He could feel the stupid settling in, the armadillo-in-the-headlights fog of incomprehension leaking out of his ears.

"Do you know her name, the person who moved out?"

The guy screwed his mouth up, thinking. "Marilyn? Like the actress. I think she had a dog, terrier maybe?" He grinned and Dallas' stomach flipped. There was something there . . .

"Say, you look a little unsteady. It's really hot. Want to come in for a drink? Something with ice in it?"

Dallas was sweating. Was the guy hitting on him? Not that he minded, but that was absolutely not on today's agenda. "No, sorry. I'm late for an appointment. Just thought I'd stop by before . . ." Before he lost his mind?

Marilyn Fairbanks' neighbor shrugged. "Suit yourself." He flashed another smile and went inside, closing the door quietly behind him. Dallas waited, then tried the buzzer to C-6 again. Knocked, tried the door handle. Nobody home. He consulted the card.

"Shit!" The address had changed. "Will you cretins make up your mind already?!" He was so tempted to tear up the cursed card and throw the pieces in the fountain, but he'd signed a contract and somebody was going to pay him to do the work. Where was it this time? "For fuck's sake!" The address was just about as far away from Coconut Grove as you could get, way out in Hallandale, at least half an hour's drive north. He considered his funds. Of the $40 his mother had given him, he'd spent a good chunk of it to get here. He'd have to thumb a ride to this new address if he wanted to have money to eat on for the next couple of days. If he managed to see this job to its conclusion with a yappy dog flapping at the end of a leash, he would damn well make sure that bonus paid for all his trouble.

It took three separate rides to get out to Hallandale, but Dallas was beyond determined at this point in the game. And that's what it was, a huge honking game of gotcha orchestrated by whoever was pulling the strings of his fate these days. He walked down 9th Street, a long narrow residential strip of asphalt with sporadic sidewalks, looking for the house number on the card. Where had he gone wrong? He'd done alright in high school, had friends, made decent grades, aced his English classes. What had been the turning point into his current downward slide? It was hard to pinpoint . . . a subtle shift in attitude where he'd realized that all the blather he listened to in class was just that, and the knowledge that nobody, not even his most favorite professors, had a lock on the truth. It had all seemed so pointless.

Dogs barked at him from behind chainlink fences and big-wheel pickup trucks rolled past, sound systems thumping. Broken sections of sidewalk with weeds pushing through the cracks dotted long stretches where he had to walk along the shoulder of the road, careful not to get run over. He passed rows of concrete block houses baking in the sun, interspersed by a few partially wooded lots with slightly better houses set off from the road. Not the best part of town, for sure. Quite a come down, in fact, for Ms. Fairbanks. Had she lost her job and been forced to move? Why this far away? Sweating, he checked the house numbers on the mailboxes. Another block to go.

The little frame house under the live oaks was so well camouflaged by a dense privet hedge he'd walked right past it before he realized X marked the spot. He backtracked and went up the overgrown walk, stopped at the front steps, and checked the card once more, daring it to do what it did. The address was still correct, but the contractor's name was different: Charlotte Birch. Dallas refused to be fazed. Fine. Marilyn Fairbanks had been abducted by aliens and her dog now belonged to someone named Birch. Whatever.

He knocked on the door with a little more force than normal. By now he was in a completely no-nonsense mood—get in there and get the job done. When there was no response within twenty seconds he banged again. The front door opened a crack and a tall slender woman with dark hair cut in a stylish bob peeked out at him.

"I'm here about the dog," he said abruptly. "The dog walking job?" He tried to sound upbeat.

"Oh." The door opened a little wider. "Come in," said the woman who might be Marilyn, or Charlotte. She was barefoot and wore cutoff jeans and a tank top. Her attractive face had a haunted look, something hollow around the eyes and the tight, thin set of her mouth that telegraphed unease. Maybe she had an illness. Dallas followed her down a short hallway, wondering what her story was.

A very small dog, a terrier of some sort by the look of its pricked-up ears and sharp face, sat on its haunches in the middle of the living room. An ordinary looking dog, mostly white with caramel splotched ears, it stood up and wagged its docked tail. A Jack Russell, Dallas decided.

"This is Buster," said the woman, gesturing toward the terrier. "I'm . . .Charlotte."

Dallas nodded. "Dallas Hamilton. I was sent by the Limbus agency. To walk your dog for ten days," he added, just so there was no mistake about the job.

"That's a relief," she said and plopped down into the shapeless cushions of an old sofa. Buster jumped up beside her, his flank pressed against her thigh. Charlotte crossed one long shapely leg over the other. "Well, Mr. Hamilton, please have a seat."

Dallas perched on a weathered rocking chair that had probably been dragged in from the back deck, which he could see through glass doors that faced a small fenced back yard.

"Here's the situation," said Charlotte. "I work for an ad agency in downtown Miami, and often I'm not home until dark. That leaves Buster here by himself all day."

"Sure," Dallas offered, "he gets bored."

"While I'm at work, I want someone reliable to walk him every day, wherever he wants to go."

Dallas tried to look as dependable as humanly possible.

Charlotte continued. "There's a city ordinance that dogs must be on a leash if you want to walk them. Unleashed strays get picked up snap! We can't have that. I rescued him from the pound and he's not going back because of somebody's carelessness. Understood?"

"Yes, absolutely. I'll be the best dog walker you ever met." Dallas felt like an idiot, but he so needed the money. "When did you want me to start?" She didn't look like she was headed off to work at a Brickell Avenue office in that outfit.

"Today." Charlotte got up and retrieved a braided leash with a loop on one end and a clip on the other. "I want you to do a test run. If it works out and Buster likes you, then your first day on the clock is today. Sound fair?" Charlotte was pretty no-nonsense herself.

"No problem." Dallas wondered if she had a map of the neighborhood for him to follow. "Um, how long do you want me to be out with him?"

"Just around the block for today."

She clipped the leash to a ring on Buster's collar. "Do you have a cell phone, Mr. Hamilton?"

"Just Dallas, please, and no, I don't."

She looked at him with that "loser" expression he'd seen too many times recently. "Well, you can carry mine while I'm at work, in case you need to contact me. The neighborhood's old, not too dangerous. It's all mostly rentals like this one. Just watch for cars where there's no sidewalk and make sure Buster doesn't get too hot."

"Got it."

"There's one more thing," she said, standing up. Her hand shook as she gave him the leash. "I need to show you something."

Before Dallas could breathe "holy shit," Charlotte's body began to stretch taller and go slightly blurred. Within seconds, a creature about seven feet tall with a head that mostly resembled a moray eel stepped out of Charlotte's rigid body and stood over him. It had long thin arms, terminating in agile three-fingered appendages. Its skin was leathery looking and kept changing colors, first dull brown and now luminescent green. The figure was semi-transparent, as if it were not able to fully materialize—sort of wavery, like looking through water. The rows of needle-sharp teeth resolved themselves into the semblance of a human smile.

"Charlotte is not quite alone." The voice was husky, strained sounding, like someone getting over laryngitis.

Dallas dropped the leash and scrambled away. He'd never felt such terror in all his scant twenty-one years.

The not-human voice spoke again. "I regret somewhat having to use her this way, but there wasn't much of a choice when I came through the gate. She was the only body available."

Dallas bolted for the door.

"Don't run. I need your help." The horrible voice took on a wheedling tone. "I don't intend to eat you, if that's what you're thinking. There are worlds beyond worlds that you don't even have a clue about. *Your* world's pretty tame, far as it goes, which is why I'm hiding out here."

"Hiding out?" Dallas' voice broke and he tried again. "Why?" Images from *The War of the Worlds* flooded his numbed brain.

"Well, that's the thing. I need to get offworld, but I can't find the gate."

Dallas blanched. There was that word. *Gate. Gate expires* . . . "This job isn't about dog walking, is it?"

The alien shook its ugly head. "No, friend, it isn't."

"T-then what am I supposed to be doing?"

"You and Buster here have to help me search for the gate so I can get out of here, which will be impossible after May thirty-first. That's when the gate expires, goes offline for good. It was a quickie patch job, just meant to get a body in and out in a hurry. So, you know, timeline's a little tight."

Dallas swallowed. He hated to ask. "What . . . who's after you?"

"Not sure. Somebody hired through Limbus, I think. Assassin job most likely."

Dallas' knees went shaky. "But that doesn't make sense! Why would a company hire someone—me—and then turn around and contract a hit on the client I'm supposed to be working for?"

"You don't need to know."

Dallas was having none of it. "And now that we're talking about this so-called Limbo Ink or whatever it is, how come Charlotte set up this job through them? And by the way, who's Charlotte, or Marilyn, anyway? HUH?" Dallas realized he was shouting. At an alien.

The creature whispered in its raspy not-human voice. "She's a human friend, with money."

Dallas didn't think Charlotte had bought into the "friend" part too much. If anything, she seemed in a state of controlled terror. His hand firmly on the doorknob, he took in the scene: Charlotte and her dog still as statues with an alien being towering between them, talking to *him*, fixing *him* with its round yellow eyes.

"What, exactly, are you wanted for on your homeworld?"

"Little of this, little of that, whole lot of the other."

"You won't tell me, will you?"

"It's really better if you don't know."

"Do you have a name?"

"You couldn't pronounce it. Charlotte calls me Gurtz."

The creature said a word that sounded like a blender going off, somewhere between a gulp and a hiss. *Gultranz.* "That is my species. We're friendly toward humans, in a number of ways."

Dallas shuddered, wondering how Gurtz had revealed himself to Charlotte. "Did you ask Charlotte's permission, before you took over her body?"

"Unfortunately, there wasn't time. She took it pretty well, all things considered. She's maybe a tad more adventurous than you."

"What's her reward for helping you?"

Gurtz was coy. "Adventurous, like I said. I might come visit her again, under better circumstances."

Dallas was sticky with sweat.

"So, you're like a shapeshifter. A body jumper. Could you take me over?" He gripped the doorknob.

"It's not that simple, and no, I can't jump from body to body. Took a clever bit of spellcrafting to get me into the human template. But it's been a good disguise, so far."

Dallas swallowed. "It said on the contract that I was hired to work for somebody named Marilyn Fairbanks but when I went to her address, she'd supposedly moved out, according to her neighbor at the apartments where Limbus *told* me she lived. Did I get any part of that right?"

Gurtz gave him a long silent look. "We had to make a quick change of plans. Once we found out about the assassin, it became necessary for Marilyn to go into hiding, just to be sure of my safety. Hence the name and address change."

"What did you mean by human template?"

"Once I take on a basic body template, *homo sapiens* in this case, I can slip into an available package, like Charlotte. Simple, for a spellcaster of my experience."

Dallas kept his mouth shut. His brain was in overdrive.

Actually, he was trying to work out what qualified him for such a dangerous job. He was about the least likely person one would want on their side in this kind of situation. He remembered the "life-threatening" part of the Qualifications list and knew with a certainty he should have turned down Rigel's contract and gotten the hell out. One of his not-so-good choices.

"How come her dog hasn't gone apeshit? He should be reacting to you but he's not."

"I had to tamper a little with its canine instincts, I'm afraid. Buster is highly protective of Charlotte, so it was necessary to imprint myself on his mind as well, in order to keep him from attacking me. I also imprinted the smell of the gate, so he could help me search."

"I see." Dallas didn't see at all, but it seemed like a safe thing to say.

"Well? Are you in or not?" Gurtz cocked his massive head.

It was only for ten days, nine if you didn't count today. Two thousand dollars and a bonus could go a long way toward redemption of this mess he'd landed in. And the sooner he could get the nasty creature back where it came from, the sooner Charlotte would be freed. "In."

"Excellent. I think my host needs a drink." The figure went transparent and slid back into the young woman beside it. Charlotte ran her fingers through her hair. "Just sit there for a minute, and then we'll talk." She headed for the kitchen.

Dallas hoped Charlotte had something alcoholic, with a good bite. His fingers trembled, his mind in denial. It was unthinkable, but he'd seen what he'd seen.

"So you really are Marilyn Fairbanks."

She returned with two glasses. "I was until last week. But don't call me that, forget you heard that name. So you've decided to stay?"

Dallas sank into the rocker and gulped the gin and tonic Charlotte had given him. "Yeah, I have, but I'd like to hear this thing from your side . . . if you can tell it." He wondered how much the alien presence controlled her thoughts and speech.

Charlotte settled into the couch cushions, pulling her feet up under her. "Gurtz came here through a portal of some sort, an interplanetary travel gate. He was on the run and made the gate somehow to escape from people who wanted to kill him." She closed her eyes, as if to make sure she got the facts straight. "But the gate's drifted. It opened in

Coconut Grove, but it's not there now. It was scent marked, but Buster couldn't smell it anywhere around the original site. So last weekend, we drove all over town with the windows down so Buster could get a whiff of it."

Charlotte shut her eyes again.

"Gurtz says to tell you he didn't have time to anchor its coordinates before it spewed him out. After driving around all over creation, we came back to my apartment and that's when Buster smelled him." Charlotte's wide dark eyes pinned Dallas.

"Him?" Dallas sipped at his ice-filled glass. He felt like rolling it across his forehead.

"The assassin. Another Gultranz. The whole place stank with his scent according to Gurtz." Buster sneezed, as if he'd sensed what she was describing.

"Buster wouldn't go past the gate, so I left him hiding in the ferns while I ran inside, threw some clothes in my gym bag, and locked the apartment up tight. Then we got in the car and I just started driving north, to get as far away as possible."

"And you landed here." Dallas hoped he sounded helpful, but he was well beyond any ability to reason.

"Well, I would have kept driving, but Buster alerted us on the gate somewhere around Aventura, in the mall parking lot. But it just turned out to be a trace of where it had been—it wasn't actually there."

Dallas nodded. "Pity."

"So we headed into Hallandale, still following the trace, and decided we needed a base of operations. I saw the "for rent" sign in the yard here and called the number. The owner, a very sweet Latina, drove in from Sunny Isles to meet us. I told her I couldn't rent under my real name because I was running from an abusive husband. She hugged me and said she knew exactly what I was going through." Charlotte beamed a cheeky smile at Dallas. "You have no idea how far a sob story and cash up front will get you. I have the house, no questions asked, as long as the money's paid."

Dallas kept nodding. "Okay, now what?"

"Well, you need to stay here with us, till the job's done. That way you and Buster can spend as much time looking as possible. There's only one bedroom, but you can have the couch. It's big and comfy."

"Okay, I don't mind." It was light years better than sleeping in the park.

"I can drive you back to your current address so you can get necessities and stuff, then we'll all be safe here. I think."

Dallas took a breath. "I don't currently have an address, and this is all I need." He pushed the book bag with his toe.

"So," said Charlotte. "You're a homeless person."

Dallas scowled. "It's just temporary."

Charlotte brightened. "That's good, though. Less likely you can be tracked through a landlord or neighbors."

Dallas had so many questions he hardly knew where to start, but there was one sticking up above the others. "If Buster can smell this hired killer just from his scent trail, can the assassin smell you, too?"

"No. He'll be wearing a human body, so he can't differentiate smells any better than you can." Buster hopped up beside her and leaned against her shoulder. Cozy. Dallas thought his head might explode.

Instead he asked, "Why does what's-his-name have to wear a borrowed body? Oxygen disagree with him?"

Charlotte gripped the cushions and shut her eyes. "He says it's not pleasant, but he can process it. The problem's with the density of the atmosphere. It's too thin—prevents the Gultranz from fully materializing into the earth plane. They need to take on the shell of an earthbound creature to fully function. There are a lot of body templates. He could have taken on Buster as his template, but that would have been too limiting. "

Dallas sucked in his breath, suddenly remembering a certain catalog he'd seen on the table in the Limbus reception room. "What happens if the alien's 'occupied' earthsuit gets killed?"

"The Gultranz wearing it gets sucked through the nearest official gate and spewed back, hopefully intact, onto the homeworld." Charlotte made an unpleasant face that Dallas was certain didn't reflect just her own reaction.

"Won't they catch you if you go back through the portal you made?"

Charlotte emitted a guttural noise that Dallas had never heard a human make. "Gurtz asks if you think he's some novice who doesn't know how to hide his own patch gate."

"Well, you let it drift all over the greater Miami area like the Hindenburg . . "

Charlotte quivered and Buster growled in the back of his throat. She scratched him behind the ears, defusing the moment. Maybe Buster still had a desire to sink his teeth into that luminous greenish hide. Dallas winced. In spite of his terror, he was starting to empathize with them.

"How many miles do you think we have to walk before this gate thing drifts across our path?" He'd been mildly confident when he'd set out this morning, but now the task seemed enormously hopeless.

Charlotte was massaging Buster's shoulders. "Do you have a driver's license? I could let you drop me off at work and borrow my car."

"I do, but I don't have it on me." Dallas' cheeks flamed.

"Well, can you get it?"

Dallas imagined standing on the front steps of his parents' house and asking his father to give his license back. "Doubtful," he said.

"Well, then, we'll just have to improvise."

Dallas found himself warming to Charlotte. Here she was, possessed by an entity that was anyone's worst nightmare, yet gamely making plans to move forward with an impossible task. He could learn a thing or two from her.

"We could catch the bus, or maybe a taxi," he offered. "I'm good at thumbing rides. I could wear dark glasses and pretend he's my seeing-eye dog."

Charlotte/Gurtz eyed him. "You catch on fast. No wonder you've survived on the street with basically nothing. I like you." She smiled and it was Dallas' turn to shiver, remembering the rows of needle-sharp teeth.

Dallas drained his glass and rose to go place it in the sink of the tiny kitchen. He turned to Charlotte. "Why'd you place your dog walker ad with Limbus?"

She shrugged, looking at Buster. "It was the biggest display ad in the yellow pages for employment agencies. You can look it up if you want."

"No, that's okay." He didn't need to consult the yellow pages—he knew there wouldn't be any such ad. Charlotte—Marilyn—had seen what was meant only for her. Like she said, he caught on fast.

*　*　*

Dallas took Buster out on the leash and spent the next several days trying to follow the very faint trace of the drifting gate, wandering through neighborhoods in Miramar, Miami Gardens, and Opa-Locka. By Tuesday, Dallas tried skirting the Miami River along a jogging/skating path that gave him a good view of Miami Beach across the water. They'd been out walking for nearly an hour, with Buster catching occasional whiffs of spots where the gate had lingered and moved on.

Suddenly Buster took off at a run, dragging Dallas after him. The leash was wrenched with a slap out of his fingers. "Hey!"

Buster disappeared down a residential street, across a back yard, and into a copse of willow. Dallas caught up with him in seconds. "What the hell—" The dog cowered between his feet, teeth bared and snarling.

Dallas swallowed hard. Buster must have smelled something dangerous, something deadly. Dallas grabbed the leash. "C'mon, I know the neighborhood." Of course he did. His parents lived in it.

He ran across yards, between houses, and ended up in a small wooded park, its circular boundary marked by chest-high holly hedges. In the center of the park grew half a dozen centennial oaks with branches so wide you could stand on them. In the tallest tree, a weathered clubhouse hid among its upper forks, a few climbing slats still nailed to its gnarled trunk.

Dallas huffed, grabbing the dog around the middle and wedging it up under his arm. He jumped and caught the highest slat, scrabbling with his feet onto the lowest fork, and worked his way up into the canopy of dark green leaves. The tree house had no door, and Dallas flung himself and Buster through the entrance and onto the rough plywood flooring. He lay gasping, listening for pursuit but heard nothing. Finally Dallas sat up and took stock of their refuge. It looked remarkably the way it had when he'd played in it as a kid.

Buster was peering down through the doorway at the ground below, snarling.

Dallas pulled up his T-shirt and wiped sweat out of his eyes. He chanced a look out the door just in time to spot a jogger coming into the park. In tank top and shorts, he looked harmless enough. Buster was shaking all over, pressed against Dallas' leg. The dog emitted a low growl but Dallas grabbed his snout. "Shhh!" He flattened himself against the floorboards and took another furtive look.

The jogger had stopped on the sidewalk leading into the park and stood wiping his face. Perfectly normal behavior for a runner. Nothing to see. Until he walked slowly to the center of the small grassy area near the oaks and stood perfectly still, head raised slightly, as if listening. He faced east, then west, with a questing behavior much like a bird dog seeking its prey after the fowl has plunged out of sight into the reeds of a marsh. Dallas crouched against the wall of the tree house, hardly daring to breathe. Against him, Buster shivered in silent terror. Dallas had no doubt the jogger was someone, or something, to be feared.

The stranger below took his own sweet time, but eventually moved on across the park and back out to the street. Dallas let his breath out and then called Charlotte.

"I think we narrowly missed your friend," he said in a whisper. "If Buster hadn't taken off like a streak I don't know what would have happened."

"Be very careful coming home," she warned. "We can't have you leading anyone to the house."

"Roger that." Dallas disconnected the call.

He sat in silence for awhile, just listening to the breeze off the river rustling the tops of the oaks and palms. Occasionally Buster sniffed the breeze, but he seemed to no longer find any threat hiding there.

Buster walked to the door, his dog nails clicking on the boards of the tree house. Dallas picked him up. "If you don't smell the guy anymore let's get out of here." The first thing he wanted to do when they got home was get some better details about the assassin, something he'd failed to do when Gurtz's situation was first explained to him.

Charlotte called around five-thirty to say she was on her way and would bring Cuban take-out home with her.

A brief thunderstorm broke overhead and rained just enough to make everything steamy. Dallas and Buster sat on the back deck, listening to rain drip off the trees and shrubbery, while legions of frogs sang their rain-conjuring songs. The sound of Charlotte's Grand Cherokee pulling up under the carport some time later brought him back to the fact that his stomach was chewing on itself. He went inside and found Charlotte unloading Cuban sandwiches onto the kitchen table. "Help yourself," she said.

Dallas took a wrapped sandwich from the bag and sat down across the room, as far away from her as he could get. They ate in silence until Charlotte got up and poured herself a glass of burgundy.

"You're awfully quiet."

"Just thinking."

Charlotte put down her glass. "That was a close call you had today."

"No shit."

More silence. Finally Charlotte got up and stretched. She headed out into the living room and Dallas followed.

"Can I...talk to Gurtz? I mean, physically?" He could feel the blood beating a tattoo against his temples.

Charlotte cocked her head. "All right, but you have to promise you won't run out the door."

"I won't run." Since that first terrifying day, the alien hadn't showed itself outside its host, in the interest of keeping him employed, Dallas assumed. Now that he felt reasonably sure Gurtz wasn't about to abduct him for medical experiments on some distant planet, he wanted to see, as clearly as possible, the creature he was contracted to help and ask those nagging questions.

Gurtz slowly lifted out of Charlotte's body. Dallas was shaking but kept his eyes riveted to the ungainly form partially coalescing in front of him. Seven feet tall, for sure, maybe more. Dallas was holding his breath. There was the moray eel head, which he now saw had two slightly protruding perfectly round eyes with a tiny red pupil in the center. The eyes seemed to move independently of each other, one giving Dallas the once over and the other angled toward the doorway, like a chameleon he'd once kept in a terrarium back in his college days. But Gurtz wasn't a chameleon, or an eel. What had he called himself? *Gultranz.*

The Gultranz sorcerer stepped away from his host, who remained frozen in mid-step, and Dallas took a good look. Although partially transparent, it was still a terrifying sight. The alien was bipedal but also had a long thick tail that it leaned back on for balance. Dallas licked his dry lips. He'd seen a kangaroo do that once at the Miami Zoo. The creature's skin was luminescing greens and blues and ochres. From the front of the mouth, a cluster of prominent upper and lower serrated teeth jutted at a bucktoothed angle. As the hinged jaw moved, Dallas saw double rows of triangular shredding teeth. Sharp as razors, he was willing to bet. A flesh eater.

"You don't look much like a Little Grey," Dallas croaked out.

"What's that?" Gurtz's voice was raspier than he remembered.

"You know, Little Greys, alien abductions... medical experiments?"

"Is that a DC comic? I might like it." The Gultranz stood to his full height and stretched his long thin arms out from his sides, flexing his three-fingered hands as if unwinding the kinks. Dallas noted uneasily the suckerlike pads on each digit. The creature took a step forward.

"Don't!" Dallas skipped backwards.

"Seen enough? I can't hold this form too long outside the host."

"Yes! Please go back in." He was hyperventilating.

Charlotte shuddered and settled stiffly onto the couch. "Gurtz wants to know your story."

"Me? I don't have a story. I'm your basic loser, a nobody."

Charlotte's dark eyes went wide, looking at him with such fixation it felt like a trowel scraping at his brains.

"I see a lot going on in there, but I don't see stupid," Charlotte/Gurtz said. "How's a smarter than average guy like you end up homeless?"

"Long unpleasant story involving a lot of money spent on an education I failed to get."

"Studying what?"

"I was an English major."

"Mm. Sympathies."

"Noted." Dallas sighed deeply. "I'm what's known in this world as a slacker."

"Looks like we have something in common, then."

"How's that?"

"We're both in trouble with somebody over money. Isn't that always the way it goes . . ."

"What happens if you miss your gate?"

"I'll be stuck here."

"And if your host dies?" Dallas had every intention of keeping Charlotte alive, but he had to ask.

"My essence gets sucked into the nearest official gate. If I survive the transfer in one piece, I'll probably be executed."

But Dallas' mind was on another track. "What happens if the assassin catches us?"

"It won't be nice. Body parts, yours and ours."

"What's he armed with?"

"A splitter, most likely—a stealth weapon, highly portable and deadly. You think a Japanese katana's sharp? Phhht. A splitter's particle beam cuts through anything with substance, boulders, steel, meteorites, you name it. Small neat handle, fits in the palm of your hand, beam opens up as wide or as narrow as you want, depending on what you need to cut."

Dallas shivered. "I still don't get it. That recruiter guy said this job was tailor made for me. But you need somebody from the Avengers or the Justice League, not a college dropout."

"You're doing okay so far. Charlotte likes you. Buster likes you. "

He had to admit that had been the nicest part of the job—besides the money, which he received in cash at the end of each day. It felt good, being praised by someone smart and successful, which Charlotte obviously was.

Dallas cleared his throat. "How come you're so familiar with the way things work here on Earth? You seem pretty savvy to me for a non-native."

Charlotte closed her eyes and hugged her chest, her voice husky. "It's on my regular route. I've been coming here for a long time."

Dallas felt a chill creeping over his skin despite the ninety-plus heat. "For what?"

"I thought we weren't going to talk about that."

"I want to talk about it now."

"I told you—I'm a Masterclass Spellcaster."

Dallas was persistent. "Casting spells on what?"

"Body templates. I figure out the design and make the prototypes with all their thousands of variations. I have to use originals to work from, to get the details right."

Dallas wasn't liking where this was headed. He felt his guts tighten. "How do you get those originals?"

Charlotte had pulled herself into a near-fetal position. "Slaves. I work with the Slave Traders Guild to get body types . . . and do a little refurbishing for them on the side. There. Happy you asked?"

Dallas scrambled toward the door. "I knew it! You lied to me."

"How do you figure that? You were yammering about little grey guys and medical experiments. This is about commerce."

"But a slave means abduction! And 'refurbishing' means torture, I assume." Dallas was freaking, heart pounding against his ribs.

"Offworld slaves have to be refurbished before they can be used. I take away their breathing apparatus and embed a little methane converter at the base of the throat. Eliminates their ability to talk, but they can't speak our language anyway, so no loss. I'm good at what I do. Better than most of my competitors, which doesn't make them happy," Gurtz conceded.

"But that's inhumane, it's horrible! You're despicable!" He suddenly realized he had Charlotte by the throat, squeezing tighter with each shout. The Gultranz lifted partway out of the woman's body and unfurled one of its long skinny digits. It touched Dallas on the forehead and he fell back as if he'd been tazed. A mild electric shock ran through his body, just like the time he'd stuck a fork in a toaster as a kid to get at a piece of trapped toast.

"I don't want to harm you, but I will defend myself. You were trying to attack my host and I can't allow that. Be assured that if I could fully manifest, you'd be dead now." The husky voice had changed in pitch. Dallas had sort of gotten used to the timbre of that unnatural voice filtered through human vocal cords, but right now the voice had an edge that frightened him to his core. The Gultranz settled back into its host and glared at Dallas with an expression that could have meant anything from *fuck you, earthling,* to *you poor stupid sod with the brain of a flea.*

Dallas sat with his forehead on his knees and tried to rearrange his scrambled brains. Part of him just wanted things to go back to the way they were before he'd ever heard of Limbus Inc., but that was helpless loser thinking. He was sick of being a loser.

He pushed his hair out of his eyes and gave her eye contact, not confrontational, but not backing down either. "Understood. I signed a contract. So, I agree to put my personal problems with your occupation aside for now, and I *will* see this job through to the end." *So you can leave and get the hell off my world.* Gurtz probably understood that part, too.

Charlotte leaned back against the cushions. "Alright. Just so we understand each other." She shivered visibly and gave Dallas that haunted look. "Sorry about that." Her normal voice was back.

Dallas let his breath out. He didn't know if he'd won or lost, but he understood he'd had a narrow escape, his second of the day. He continued to sit on the floor, watching the light fade and listening to sounds of traffic along the street outside. The naked reality that "aliens are among us" had come crashing down with a vengeance. To be honest, the whole job experience had felt like some surreal prolonged cosplay event until tonight. This was no pop culture dress-up-like-monsters weekend, and his rational mind had ground to a halt.

Dallas felt the anger leak out of him, like an oversized gasbag punctured and wilting. He closed his eyes, too wrung out to think.

He felt her hand on his shoulder, a barely-there squeeze.

"Sleep on it. We'll talk more tomorrow. I just want you to know, Dallas, that I think you're a fine person." With that, she entered the bedroom and shut the door.

Dallas curled up on the couch and willed himself not to think about the kinds of dreams she must have been having.

* * *

When Dallas woke, Charlotte had already gone to work. He rubbed his eyes and sat up, feeling fogged over. Buster was stretched out near the glass doors, watching him. He wasn't sure how he felt this morning, but the thought that he'd lain asleep under the same roof as a creature whose race harvested humans for slaves and worse gave him goosebumps.

"Today's the twenty-ninth," he said to Buster. "What's the game plan?" Dallas ran his hands through his hair. "You know what? I think we're going at this all wrong. Chasing the gate but never quite catching it isn't working." It was like a game of quantum tag. All these little contiguous events looked random when you stared at them head on, but under the surface they felt deliberate, controlled, planned. What he really wanted was to see the bigger flowchart. And then the light went on in his head. He called Charlotte at work.

"I think we need to go back to the place where the gate came in and," he wasn't sure how to describe what his brain saw as a strategy, "cut it off at the pass, so to speak."

"Not bad," she said. "I could see that."

"It's fractal. My strategy."

"Excuse me?"

Dallas tried to explain. "When you're down in a little eddy current of a fractal arm, you can't see the larger pattern it belongs to. You may not even be aware there is a larger pattern. All you get are those little separate details of the hook-curve you're meandering around in. So, Gurtz's gate is oscillating on some pattern of its own. We just need to see it. We know the farthest out it went was Hallandale, and then it started heading back south."

"Gurtz says he thinks you're onto something." Charlotte's voice sounded hopeful.

* * *

Dallas and Buster spent the morning combing neighborhoods near the airport with no results, eventually working their way south toward downtown Miami. By mid-afternoon, footsore and overheated, they met Charlotte for food at a Calle Ocho sidewalk café in Little Havana that Dallas liked to frequent when he was a student at FIU and had spending money. Charlotte treated them to pork-stuffed tostones rellenos and tres leches cake. With good food in his stomach and a sea breeze drying his sweaty face, Dallas felt better. He poured ice water from his glass into the empty salsa bowl and put it down for Buster, who noisily lapped it up, ice and all.

"I dunno, maybe I was wrong about the gate coming back. It made perfect sense to me this morning." He watched a couple of old-timers playing chess at a table nearby. Beyond them, a young black girl with very green eyes stared at Dallas. It was a pain in the ass to have to be suspicious of everybody around them, but if the assassin was in a human body, he could be stalking them right now and they wouldn't even know it.

"What do you think, keep heading south toward Coconut Grove?"

Charlotte drove them back to the financial district around Brickell Avenue and parked in the company lot. They wandered among the glass and steel towers for a block or two when Buster suddenly yelped in surprise. He took off trotting, Dallas and Charlotte running to catch up. "After him! Down that street!"

They ran flat out, Buster catching the scent and then losing it.

"It's here, I know it!" Charlotte gasped, as Dallas leaned against the side of an office building, trying to catch his breath. "It's circling southward, like you guessed."

They chased the trail of the drifting gate down to Bicentennial Park. It occurred to Dallas that if the damned thing sailed out over open water, they were SOL. Besides which, the sun would be setting before long—a few street lights were starting to come on, and the Art Deco magenta pylon lights along the split lanes of the MacArthur Causeway cast rippling ribbons of color across the bay all the way to Watson Island.

Dallas was about to give Gurtz some grief for being such a half-assed sorcerer when he heard Charlotte mutter under her breath. "Oh shit."

In Dallas's current experience, he knew exactly what that meant.

"Where?"

"Can't course the direction exactly, but Gurtz says his scent is strong near the causeway." Buster was trembling and growling, his nostrils blown wide.

Behind them, a lone figure came up the cracked sidewalk. Dallas retreated onto the causeway's pedestrian corridor. The stranger advanced, walking steadily. Dallas quickened his pace. "Hoof it. I don't like his looks."

They headed over the causeway at a trot. The incline wasn't overly steep, just enough to prevent them from seeing beyond the top of the bridge. Dallas took a quick look over his shoulder. The guy behind them was still there, but not gaining on them. They'd nearly crested the bridge when another figure came into view, walking toward them from the other direction. A nice looking guy, hands in his khakis, he came quickly along the walkway. As they passed he nodded and smiled, a familiar face. Instantly a thin whine like a dentist's drill erupted as the man stooped and slashed at Charlotte, the splitter shearing across ribs and belly. Without hesitating, Dallas grabbed her and did the unthinkable. He jumped.

It took longer to hit the water than he would've thought, but maybe time dilated when you were in shock. Clutching Charlotte's body tightly to his chest, they hit the water hard and sank for terrifying seconds as everything went cold and black. Silently giving thanks to all those high school swim meets that had pushed his aquatic skills to the limit, Dallas crested the surface quietly, trying to spread as few ripples as possible. He was drifting under the causeway, close to one of the gigantic pylons and some yards nearer land than the point from which he'd jumped. He was a strong swimmer and under normal circumstances wouldn't have given a second thought about swimming the distance to the shoreline ramp where the causeway met land, but holding a mortally wounded friend made it a wholly different game. He had no problem swimming laps in the clear, chlorinated pool at his high school, but navigating the dark turbulent waters of Biscayne Bay at dusk ranked right up there with his most favorite nightmares. Buster's snout broke the surface not far from them.

Like a light switch flipped on, he suddenly remembered where he'd see the assassin—Charlotte's, Marilyn's, apartment—the friendly next door neighbor. He should've known. But he hadn't quite got the hang of being on the run back then, so he hadn't been suspicious enough. He shuddered to think that he might have actually gone into the guy's apartment for drinks . . . and body parts? He shoved those thoughts aside and concentrated on staying alive.

A powerboat bore down on them, so close he could see the pilot's face in the glare of the pylon display lights, his head tilted back chugging a beer and oblivious to anything in the water he might run over. Dallas had always considered the nighttime show that defined the MacArthur decorative lighting project as uselessly garish as the rest of Miami Beach, but tonight it kept him from floundering around in complete darkness. The wake from the cigar boat washed him up against the horizontal concrete span between two pylons. Spluttering, he held Charlotte's head above the waterline and bit down on the pain as barnacles encrusting the pylon raked his back and shoulder. Buster whimpered and treaded water beside them.

"Hold on," he whispered. "I won't let them kill us."

The distant drone of the Miami Coast Guard's small search and rescue vessel got louder and filled the space near the bridge as a searchlight played over the water. Within seconds, it caught him in the eyes.

A radio crackled. "Yeah, we found them. Pulling alongside now."

Dallas counted the seconds as the rescue boat idled closer. A crew member leaned over the side and tossed him an inflated ring like a giant peppermint lifesaver. "Are you all right? Can you grab on?" Dallas hooked his free arm over the ring and felt the tug as he was pulled in toward the boat.

"Got a couple of 911 calls from people who saw you go off the bridge. That's a sixty-foot drop or so. You fall or get pushed?"

Dallas was shaking so hard he could barely get the words out. "W-whack job up there slashed my friend. She's bleeding to death, n-need a doctor."

It didn't take seconds for the Coast Guard rescue crew to assess the situation. The guy at the helm made another call on his radio, while the crew helped Dallas, Charlotte, and Buster aboard. The man who seemed to be in charge turned to Dallas. "Closest 24/7 emergency service is a few miles upriver. I just put in a call—the ambulance'll be waiting for us at the dock."

He shook out a blanket and wrapped it around Charlotte. "People are crazy, you know?"

"D-did you spot anybody up on the bridge, near the top?" Dallas' teeth clacked together, mostly from the adrenaline shock of jumping and dropping such a long way down. Who would've thought the water would be so cold this late in May?

"No, but we alerted the police. They'll catch him before he can get off the causeway. Who would want to hurt someone like that? It's inhuman, ain't it?"

Dallas kept his mouth shut and held Charlotte to his chest. His shirt was wet with blood, his and hers…the wound looked bad. He just hoped the Gultranz wouldn't pull out of his damaged host and show himself. There'd be no explaining that.

The ambulance was ready for them at the dock with lights flashing. Two cop cars parked beside it added to the light show. Charlotte was carefully loaded onto the gurney and whisked away as Dallas gave his statement to the officers. There was no way he could explain that his employer had just been slashed by the weapon of an offworld assassin, but he gave them as good a description of the guy as he could remember. Not that it would do them any good if they found him.

The police car trailed the ambulance to the hospital, and Dallas got out almost before it came to a stop at the emergency entrance.

"If you think of anything else useful, call me. I'll take your little buddy here to Mojo's. It's an animal boarding service nearby. You can collect him when you're done with the doctors." The officer wrote a phone number on the back of a card and pressed it into Dallas's hand.

"I really appreciate it. More than you can imagine." Dallas stuck the card in his pocket next to the dreaded Limbus card and ran up the steps of the hospital, his thoughts in freefall.

* * *

"Your girlfriend's one lucky lady." The doctor came into the waiting room where Dallas was hunkered down in his bloody clothes. "She lost a lot of blood, but we got her stabilized and put back together. She's lucky—the cut missed her heart and lungs."

Dallas had gotten over his shakes and now simply felt numb. "She's going to live, right?"

"I think she'll make it. We'll know more in the morning." Dallas nodded. He was prepared to spend the night in the waiting room, because as the doc said, there was nothing more to do now but wait. He was getting good at that. But those barnacle scrapes were starting to hurt like hell. He pulled the shirt away from his back and grimaced. The doc gave him a look and sent him off to a treatment room. After what seemed like hours, a young RN knocked at the door and came in, only mildly appalled at his blood-soaked appearance. As an emergency nurse, she'd probably seen worse. Efficiently peeling off his shirt, she swabbed his scrapes with a light touch, taping gauze over the worst ones. She also found his story fascinating, at least the part of it he was willing to share. "You *jumped* off the MacArthur Causeway? The section with all the party lights?"

He closed his eyes, trying to decompress. "Yep." The only act of heroism he'd ever performed was going to be fuel for many nightmares to come.

"Done. I hope that feels better." She patted him on the shoulder.

"Much. Funny, it didn't start hurting until I got in the police car." He wondered what his parents would have thought of the stunt he'd just pulled—an idle thought because it was a chapter in their son's life they weren't ever going to hear about. He considered his bloody shirt. "You wouldn't happen to have a spare T-shirt lying around, would you?"

The RN smiled and patted his shoulder again. "I think I can find you something."

Engulfed in an oversized Miami Hurricanes green and orange tee, Dallas caught what sleep he could in the waiting room, but by early morning he was prowling the maze of hospital corridors looking for the cafeteria. He couldn't help giving anyone who got too close to him a second look because who knew how many assassins had been sent to collect their bounty on the outlaw Gurtz. He wolfed eggs, sausage, and black coffee, and then went to the Central Registry to find where Charlotte was recovering. He found her in a tiny private room on the third floor. A transfusion blood bag suspended on a pole near the bedside dripped dark red slowly through the I-V line taped to her arm. He was shocked at how pale she was, lying still in the white sheets.

"Hey," he said softly, coming into the room and shutting the door.

Charlotte turned her head. "Dallas. You're safe. I was worried."

"I'm fine, it's you we need to be worried about. How do you feel?"

"Drugged up. The nurse told me I've had four units of blood." She cast her eyes up at the drip bag. "It must have been a mess. I don't remember much after the assassin showed up on the bridge. I recall falling and being in the water, but nothing after that until early this morning. How bad is it?"

"The doc says you'll make a full recovery. Police are looking for the slasher, but a lot of good that will do. It might be better if they don't find him."

"Where's Buster?"

"Boarding at a nearby vet. The cop assigned to your case took him there."

Charlotte looked relieved. "I knew you were the right one the day you showed up on our doorstep. Just a gut-level instinct. A smart guy who's basically good at heart."

Dallas felt his ears heating up. "How could you know that about me?"

Charlotte laughed and then flinched. "I work all day among people whose job it is to dress up the worst products in the best possible package. We make our living telling lies, big and small, for commerce. Sincerity is rare in my line of work, so when I meet someone who has it in spades, I can't help but notice."

"I almost chickened out, you know. A couple of times."

Charlotte smiled. "Doesn't matter. You're still here, and so am I, thanks to you. You saved my life without thinking."

"I'm not a hero. I was scared shitless . . . still am."

Charlotte frowned. "You sell yourself short and I don't know why. But you've proved yourself to me. I couldn't be more grateful."

Dallas swallowed and asked the question he dreaded. "Is Gurtz still there?"

Charlotte nodded. "He's not enjoying the sensation of human pain any more than I am."

"Good."

Charlotte closed her eyes. "We have one day left before the gate shuts down. Somehow I have to get out of here and go looking with you."

"No way. I'm not letting you risk your life for him."

"You'd rather have him stuck in my body for good?"

Dallas shuddered. "No! But I don't see how—"

"We'll figure something out. We have to." Charlotte hesitated, then added, "Gurtz needs to survive."

"Why? If he died you'd be free! He's an *alien*, for chrissakes." Dallas could feel his blood pressure spiking.

"I know, but it's not the whole story." Charlotte frowned, whether from pain or frustration he couldn't tell. "He corrects the horrible mistakes made by others not as skilled as him. The truth is he's on the run for being the instigator of a dissident group trying to create better treatment and conditions for offworld slaves."

"And you believe this?" Dallas didn't even try to conceal his incredulity.

"I want to."

"Why, exactly?"

Charlotte turned toward him. "There's a movement to change the way the Slave Guild operates, and Gurtz is at the heart of it. He knows he can't wipe out an institution that's been around for millennia, but he thinks he can at least change the way slaves are treated. He's trying to establish rights for them."

Dallas listened, his tenuous grip on The Truth evaporating, only this time it was cosmic truth that refused to cooperate, not some meaningless classroom debate about the significance of poetry. And even as he grappled with enough stuff to drive him mad into the next century, a new truth dawned on him. Charlotte wanted to believe because it was the only way to cope with the whole experience. If it ended up being for a good cause, it wasn't so horrible, right? Dallas tried to imagine lovely Charlotte being 'refurbished.' He just couldn't deal. "He abducts humans and animals for body templates!"

Charlotte's expression shifted, the rasping voice emerging. "Who do you think sent the assassin after me? It's a government hit, to stop me from upsetting the way the Gultranz have done things for eons."

Dallas stood beside the bed, trying to gather his thoughts. He didn't believe the alien's sob story for a bleeding second, but Charlotte was right about one thing. They had to find the gate.

* * *

Thursday morning, the thirty-first of May, dawned gray and storm-tossed. Rain whipped through the trees and pounded the roof of the house snug under the live oaks. Dallas fed Buster and found a change of clothes for Charlotte. Their plan was simple: focus on the area south of Brickell, moving toward Coconut Grove where the gate had opened.

"He said the gate expires today. Does that mean we have all day or just part of it?"

Charlotte had shrugged in her hospital bed. "Who knows? It could be expiring right now, for all we know."

"That should give the hospital staff a thrill." Dallas had to forcibly suppress the image of the Gultranz sorcerer being sucked out of its human shell before some astonished personal care assistant's bleary early-morning eyes.

"Then we need to get moving."

"This is a terrible idea." Dallas pushed the wheelchair through the automatic double doors and out onto the hospital parking deck. The SUV sat in a loading zone near the wheelchair ramp. Charlotte gripped the arms of the chair with white knuckles and said nothing. He knew she was in pain, but she'd been adamant. There was no choice.

He eased her up into the passenger seat and left the wheelchair on the walk beside the driveway. Trying to go over the speed bumps as carefully as possible, Dallas wound their way out of the parking garage and into morning traffic, heading south.

Dallas was just pulling into a South Miami Wal-Mart to gas up when the urge to go hit him. There was no ignoring it, and he couldn't expect to hold it for hours of driving if that's how long it took. Cursing his uncooperative plumbing that ran on its own timetable instead of the one he and Charlotte had devised, Dallas reluctantly parked out front.

"I won't be a minute, I promise." Charlotte nodded and closed her eyes, her arms wrapped around her midsection, as Dallas got out of the SUV. "You protect her, got it?" he said to Buster who sat alert on the back seat.

Inside, he quickly found the men's room and stepped past the freestanding signage—CUIDADO! PISO MOJADO—warning him the floor was freshly swabbed. Pushing the door open, he was met with an overpowering Lysol aroma that had scoured away any piss smell left by guys who couldn't aim their stream into the small porcelain urinal. There were two stalls with doors, both unoccupied. Dallas selected the nearest one, locked the stall door, pushed his jeans to his ankles, and sat down.

At that moment, he heard the restroom door open. Footsteps came slowly into the room, passed the first stall, and stopped outside the one where he sat. He stopped breathing. Unable to see the shoes of whoever was obviously standing outside his compartment, he sat still as a fawn hidden in the tall grass with hyenas on the prowl. Then he heard the shrill dentist's drill whine and the stall door sheared away. It fell sideways with a shocking clatter.

GQ model guy was as nattily dressed as ever. The handsome face winked at Dallas. "Nice view." Then the inhabiting Gultranz lifted partway out of the body, revealing its hideous toothed snout. It was similar to Gurtz, only this one's skin was shiny black like obsidian, no colors playing over its surface. The pinpoint pupils of its eyes flared yellow. It held the splitter, about the size and shape of an iPhone, loosely in its left hand.

"I'll ask once. Where have you hidden the traitor?" The voice rasped at Dallas's eardrums like an industrial file.

Aiming low, Dallas launched himself at the human host's ankles, toppling them both. The assassin crashed forward into the stall framework, unfurling its Gultranz fingers out toward him. The splitter went flying, hit the far wall, fired . . . and cut the Gultranz assassin in half just as he was getting up. Intestines and other body parts spilled over the restroom tiles in a wet squelch right over the drain hole in the middle of the floor. Blood dripped through, joining the sudsy slosh of urine and cleaning fluids. Dallas rolled away from the carnage and scrambled to his feet. Its host shell dead, the military Gultranz exited the body as if it were the object of a taffy pull, stretched, extruded, and thinned until with a howl it tore and shredded and finally disappeared. Dallas leaned over the sink and lost his breakfast as the human shell's head eyed him, its startled expression frozen on the generically handsome face.

Turning on the faucet, Dallas splashed cold water over his face, staving off the ringing in his ears that suggested he might be about to pass out. Straightening up, he saw the splatter-spray of red across his bare thighs and chest. It made the T-shirt look kind of tie-dyed. Dallas retched again, but there was nothing left to yark up. He peeled the shirt off and stuffed it in the trash receptacle beside the sink. Wetting a handful of paper towels, he washed off his arms and legs and pulled up his jeans. A red splotch painted the left side at the hip, but there was nothing he could do about that.

Dallas looked around for the splitter and found it against the wall under the urinal. With trembling fingers, he picked it up by its edges and went back to the doorless stall. Maneuvering around the lower half of the assassin's shell without stepping in the mess, he slid the weapon into the water of the toilet bowl and flushed, cowering in case it went off again. When nothing happened, he let his breath out and watched the water swirl and gurgle, sucking the splitter down but not all the way. He could still see the top of it in the neck of the toilet. He flushed again and pushed it with the tip of his finger. As the water drained, it slipped out of sight with a scrape and the toilet completed its flush as if nothing peculiar had been shoved down its throat.

Dallas got out of the restroom as fast as possible without drawing attention to himself, even in his shirtless condition. That was part of why he'd been hired, right? Mr. Invisible. He was beginning to sense a larger connectivity, leading from the Limbus agency to this moment playing out in grisly perfection in a South Miami shopping strip. Any rational person would've packed it in right there, but now he felt more determined than ever to see the game through to the end. He made his way back to the Cherokee and collapsed into the driver's seat.

Charlotte stared at him. "Dallas, what the hell…?"

"Met your ex-neighbor again." He saw the panic in her eyes. "He's dead, lucky accident. Got anything I can wear?" He felt like he was babbling.

"Look in my gym bag, back seat."

Dallas found the bag and extracted a Yoga shirt decorated with the slogan *When in Doubt, Just Breathe*. He sighed and pulled it on over his head—he was in no position to be picky. He fastened his seatbelt with shaking hands. Cranking the engine, he cut across the parking lot and headed for the highway.

As rain lashed the windshield, Dallas drove the speed limit along the South Dixie Highway toward Coconut Grove, aiming for the place where Gurtz had come out of the gate. The Gultranz hovered in semi-transparent form over Charlotte's body, looking like an ailing reptile pulled from a tank that'd never been cleaned.

When they reached Coconut Grove, Dallas drove to the grounds of the old Plymouth Congregational Church and stopped. Built in the 1800s and picturesquely ivy covered, it was a peaceful photo-op on any tourist's walking tour of the Grove. It was here, in front of this very landmark, that the portal from another world had opened in the middle of the night.

They waited in silence for a few minutes, and finally Dallas asked, "What'll you do if Gurtz manages to leave?"

Charlotte's breath was ragged. "I don't think I can go back to that apartment in the Grove. I still can't believe the assassin was right there next door." Dallas couldn't believe he'd almost had a tryst with the guy.

She sighed and leaned her head back. "I'll probably look for a place close by. Maybe Coral Gables, somewhere like that. If he ever comes back..." She'd be waiting for him, Dallas thought, especially if he came in a human shell.

An idea took root in Dallas's mind. "I want it, the house in Hallandale. I'll take it over when you move out."

Charlotte gave him a weak smile. "It's just the right size for a single guy. Secluded, functional, cheap. Landlady who doesn't ask too many questions."

Dallas grinned. "It's perfect." All he needed was an income.

They continued to sit. Charlotte opened the window, giving the terrier a chance to sniff the air outside. "Buster doesn't smell anything. Maybe we got here ahead of the gate."

Dallas was feeling antsy. "I don't want to just sit here and wait. We might run out of time. I'll cruise around the neighborhood and see if we get lucky."

Dallas didn't like the way the alien's skin had turned a dull muddy brown, its form hovering just above its host's body as if too traumatized to stay fully engaged. A yellowish second membrane seemed to have slid over its eyes, although it was hard to tell as the alien got more transparent by the minute.

"Dallas, open your hand." The sorcerer's voice was a rough whisper.

Dallas was shocked—Gurtz never addressed him by name. "What, like this?" He held out his hand, palm up. Gurtz slowly unfurled one long digit and pushed it toward Dallas.

"Hey," Dallas snatched his hand away. "I'm not falling for that electric eel trick of yours again."

"You mistake..." Gurtz wheezed. "I, , , want to show you something. . . won't hurt."

Heart thudding, Dallas opened his hand again. The sucker pod of the alien finger brushed lightly over the center of his palm, right across his lifeline. Primary colors exploded in his mind, painting a surreal landscape. Saturated hues and fluid shapes formed sky, jagged landmasses, and a sinuous river whose pearlized surface resembled an oil slick. There were no pastels to rest the retinas. The wide river wound its way around tall mounds and high peaks in bright sulphur yellow, dusky orange, and darker ochre—massive shapes folded, rounded and featureless, as if carved from foam or shaving cream. On the horizon two enormous moons of mottled cerulean dominated the sky, one so close half its spheroid shape was hidden below the mountain range while the other hung low and full in a poisonous lime green sky so bright it hurt Dallas's eyes from the inside out. Further beyond the two satellites, the sky darkened to cyan and then to cobalt and finally black where a sprinkling of stars dusted the heavens.

But most astonishing was the gate, or what Dallas assumed must be the portal that allowed travel from this strange world to places unknown. The track began as a pinpoint far out in the starfield and as it homed in on the alien landscape, it resolved into two distinct crimson tracks that paralleled each other much like the twin east/west bridges of the MacArthur Causeway. The trackways then spread into a wide red Chinese-fireworks flare when they reached what he guessed must be the gate itself. Straddling the river, it seemed a marvel of fractal engineering, with strands like dazzling gemstones arching up over the oilslick surface of the river, forming whorls and spirals on a deep purple field that held a center point of blinding white light.

It was terrifying, and beautiful.

"This is your homeworld?"

The Gultranz didn't answer, but he didn't have to.

Dallas drove in silence up one street and down another, passing Charlotte's old digs at Jacaranda Apartments at one point. The storm had mostly blown through, leaving the air damp and steamy. Finally, he stopped at a red light near the entrance to a gated community and looked over at Charlotte. "I give up, he's got to give us some direction." He touched her shoulder gently.

"Gurtz? Can you hear me? We're just going in circles. Can you slip back in for a few seconds, just to see if we're anywhere close?"

The Gultranz sorcerer shut his eyes and faded from sight. Charlotte shivered and opened one eye. The alien's voice was muted. "...so much pain."

Suddenly Buster barked sharply from the back seat and poked his nose out the window.

"It's close!" Gurtz's voice was barely audible.

"How far? Should I keep driving straight or what?"

"Turn left."

"That's a dead end. It doesn't go anywhere."

"Just do it!" Dallas knew Charlotte hadn't meant to yell at him, but clearly this was the life-threatening situation he'd signed on for. Failure was not an option.

The Cherokee lurched as Dallas pulled a hard left.

"Are you sure? I don't see anything weird looking." Dallas scanned the sides of the road, having no idea what he was looking for. Buster was yipping, his head out the window.

Charlotte gripped the seat. "Doesn't matter . . . smell's strong."

They cruised past hacienda-style homes deep in foliage, then a clutch of mango trees, then a few more houses. Charlotte shuddered. Blood seeped around her sutured side and belly. The alien inside tried to talk, his voice grinding like a shot transmission. "You know, Dallas. . . at first, I thought you were. . . the most. . . inept human I ever met."

Dallas squinted. Was that a shadow across the sidewalk? It stretched into the street ahead of them and turned the bright crimson Dallas had seen in Gurtz's vision of home.

Gurtz rasped, "I was wrong. You were my frien—" The Gultranz sorcerer suddenly lifted out of his host's body and dissolved with no fuss right in front of Dallas's nose. Charlotte's body went slack.

The SUV slowed and rolled to a stop.

"Hey, I think it worked! Is he gone?" Dallas touched her arm. But Charlotte was dead.

His mouth settled into a hard line.

How lucky do you feel? Dallas wanted nothing so much as to punch Recruiter Rigel in the middle of his ugly face.

* * *

"I want your fucking job."

"What?"

Dallas stood in the entrance to Rigel's cube. "Just what I said."

"That wasn't in your contract."

"That contract was crap and you know it. I did the job but it nearly got me killed, *twice*. But maybe you knew that too, huh? Maybe I wasn't supposed to come back. How big was *your* bonus if the assassin took out Gurtz and me before we could find the gate?"

"I don't know anyone named Gurtz." Rigel looked unperturbed, but Dallas plowed ahead.

"Of course you know who Gurtz is. An innocent woman is dead because of him!"

"I hired you to be a dog walker. Recruiters are not allowed to interfere with the execution of a job once the applicant is hired."

Dallas was hyperventilating in his fury. He took a deep breath and tried to connect the dots. "I see. So you hired someone you figured was incapable of performing the job to the end."

He glared at the toad man, who glared right back.

"Well, surprise, I survived. . . so I'm here to collect *my* bonus. And that's what I want." He dragged the wrinkled contract from his jeans pocket and spread it out on the desk. "See, right there." His finger stabbed the fine print at the bottom. "It says to tell the recruiter what you want if a bonus is earned, so I'm telling you."

Rigel looked at the contract and then back at Dallas. Without a word, he reached into his jacket and pulled out a cell phone, popped it open, and thumbed a number. He texted something and waited, then texted back. Waited. Finally he closed the phone with a snap and slipped it back into his jacket. Without a word he got up, removed his badge and laid it on the desk blotter. He gave Dallas a squint-eyed look, then turned and went out through the door in the wall behind him.

Dallas waited, angry but determined. They were not going to get away with this. He'd been set up and misled by shady employment offers before, but this was the worst. He waited some more, got up and went out to the reception room, which was empty. No surprise there. He went back to Rigel's cube.

"Hey, are you coming back?" he shouted. Apparently not.

Fed up with waiting, Dallas went around to Rigel's side of the desk. Under its Plexiglas cover he saw a map of a world which he assumed was Earth, with small pulsing red targets in hundreds, maybe thousands, of locations. Limbus offices? He pulled out the wide front drawer—empty. In the right-hand drawer he found, to his great surprise, a stash of Japanese Pocky in his two favorite flavors, strawberry and chocolate. He checked the date on the back of several boxes. They looked fresh. He couldn't imagine Rigel munching on sweet-coated biscuit sticks, but how could anyone at Limbus know it was his own guilty pleasure?

The left-hand drawer held an industrial-sized key on a metal ring and a flip-top phone. The tag on the ring gave him a start: STAFF ONLY, D. Hamilton. A key to the front door? Or maybe the one behind the desk? He turned the key over in his hand wondering when it would have been made and why Rigel hadn't given it to him. He flipped open the phone, which instantly lit up with a message: HELLO NEW RECRUITER.

Dallas checked the phone's contact list and saw two entries, his own name and just the one word, Limbs. He punched it and put the phone to his ear.

An androgynous voice of indeterminate age responded.

"Greetings, new recruiter. Thank you for joining Limbus, Incorporated. Always remember your primary mission: we employ." The call disconnected. Annoyed, Dallas hit redial but got a flashing message instead: SORRY, YOUR CALL CANNOT BE COMPLETED AS DIALED. He was about to try again when a small voice interrupted.

"Excuse me, are you the recruiter?"

Dallas looked up to see a teenaged girl in full Goth drag, her kohl-rimmed eyes and cropped black hair a perfect complement to the fat-bodied tarantula clinging to her shoulder.

Dallas hesitated a moment, then sat down in Rigel's chair. "Yes. I am." He put the phone back in the drawer.

"We answered an ad I saw on the Internet." She shrugged, as if that should be explanation enough.

Dallas smoothed his hair away from his face. An inexplicable calm seemed to have settled over him. "Certainly. Have a seat, won't you?"

She sat in one of the chairs fronting his desk. "It's for him, not me." She nodded to the arachnid, who leapt from her shoulder to the empty chair with a substantial thump.

"Of course." Dallas took the recruiter's badge and pinned it to his shirt front. "I'm Recruiter Hamilton. I'm sure we can find you something." Instinctively, he pulled out the main drawer again. There was a single sheet of paper inside.

He took it out and slid it toward his applicant. The tarantula climbed up onto the desk and the girl leaned forward, studying the job description carefully.

Dallas leaned back in the recruiter's chair and discovered it to be more comfortable than it looked, as if molding itself to his body. He watched the girl and the spider communing over the various points of the contract, and only idly wondered what deep shit they might be getting themselves into. Whatever it was, the pay would probably be more than enough to seal the deal, and in any case, it was not his problem. His intention had been to confront the Limbus agency, to pull the curtain aside a la Dorothy and reveal the evil piss-ant manipulators pulling the strings. But that didn't seem so important anymore, because clearly he *was* on the inside. . . and employed.

Dallas opened the right-hand drawer of the desk and extracted a box of strawberry Pocky, the cascade of Kanji on the packaging telling him it came in crunchy almond as well. He popped the top and tore along the perforation, pulling out two long crispy-sweet Pockysticks, the most sought-after snack treat in Japan. The aroma of sweet biscotti and fresh, otherwordly strawberries broke over his tongue. He couldn't remember why he'd been so angry a moment ago. Maybe this Limbus gig wasn't so bad. He might even grow to like it.

Strip Search

By

Jonathan Maberry

The card was on the floor. I kicked it when I opened the door.

Not the first time somebody slipped something under my office door. At least this time it wasn't a threat, a fuck-you letter from a girl, a summons, or an eviction notice. Been getting way too many of each of those lately. Economically speaking, this year sucks moose dick.

This was just a business card. It looked crisp and expensive. The kind lawyers sometimes use.

I have three ex-wives, so I left it there. I do not want to hear from another lawyer. Sure, maybe if there was an estate attorney trying to find me to tell me I'd just inherited a mansion and a vault filled with gold bars. But, since the odds on that were on a par with me getting laid this week, I didn't bother picking up the card.

Instead I went through the ritual. I closed my office door, flopped into the piece o' crap faux leather chair, sorted through the mail for job offers or checks from satisfied clients, found none of that shit, listened to my answering machine, didn't hear a thing worth listening to, opened my laptop and checked my agency email, didn't find anything except a Nigerian prince who wanted to transfer thirty million into my account and an ad for the latest dick pills. Same shit, different day.

I had a mildly masochistic urge to log into my bank account to see how much I had left, but I drank beers until I came to my senses.

Outside it was the kind of spring day that Philadelphia gets a lot of but doesn't deserve. Maxfield Parrish blue skies, a few sculpted white clouds, temperature in the mid-seventies, and low humidity.

The city was pretending to be San Diego, and it fooled a lot of tourists, but only those who weren't here in the summer, when the humidity and the temperature jump into the low nineties and refuse to fucking budge. For months. I sometimes think the real reason the Founding Fathers started the Revolution was because they were hot and cranky. When Philly summers really start to cook even a Buddhist monk would lock and load and go looking for someone to shoot.

But it was May tenth.

The day was beautiful. I had windows open and the breeze was perfect.

I sat there, sipping a Yuengling and looking at the door, trying to will it to open at the touch of a client with an expensive job.

Nothing.

I was four beers in and the door still remained closed.

I sighed.

I looked around. I run a one-man investigation office. Industrial, domestic, whatever. I'll look for Hoffa if there's a paycheck in it. I have a secretary who works on a per diem. Right now there was nothing to type or file, so she was at home with a dozen cats and her skewed perception of reality.

I saw the card on the floor. Yup, still there.

Another beer came and went.

The card was still there.

I would have knocked back a sixth but I didn't have one. The only thing left in my little cube fridge was a three week old yogurt that was evolving into a new life form.

That was the only reason I got up to get the card. Boredom and no beer.

Funny how things start.

I bent and picked it up.

Frowned at it.

On the front, printed in black on cream stock, raised lettering.

Limbus, Inc.
Are you laid off, downsized, undersized?
Call us. We employ. 1-800-555-0606
How lucky do you feel?

"Balls," I said. I've seen this sort of thing before. Sometimes it's an ad for low-end commission work-at-home crap. Cold calls to sell products people wouldn't want even if it was free. Follow-up calls for people dumb enough to put their email addresses down at a restaurant, hotel or resort. Or time-share pitches. Stuff like that.

If that was what it was.

I turned it over. There was a hand-written note on the back. That was different. Most of these kinds of cards are just the basics. A hook, no real information, and a contact number.

With the 'How lucky do you feel' thing I wondered if this was a new marketing scheme for second-string call girls.

I'm horny, but I haven't ever been so horny I wanted to pay for ass.

The note on the back said:

2:45, your office.

I looked at the wall clock.

2:43.

Shit.

There was still time to pull the shade, lock the door and turn off the office lights. I wanted a client, not some yuppie entrepreneur trying to see some college-girl tail.

But then I caught a whiff of something.

Literally a whiff. I put the card to my nose and sniffed it.

The odor was very faint, but it was there. Just a hint of it. Like freshly-sheared copper.

The smell of blood.

Human blood, too. And, yes, I can tell the difference. Some people can do that with wine or truffles or chocolate. Me, I can tell you anything you want to know about blood. Other things, too, but in my trade it really matters that I can tell a lot from a little noseful of blood-smell.

Thing is, there was no stain anywhere on the card. Not a drop, not a smudge. Nothing.

Smell was definitely there, though.

I put the card against my nose and took a longer, slower sniff.

There's so much you can tell if you have the knack. My whole family has the knack. My grandmother, Minnie, is best at it. She can tell blood type. I may not be in her league—and really, no one is, old broad or not—but I could tell a lot. If I ever sniffed that blood again

I'd know who owned it. Better than fingerprints for me. Back when I was a cop in the Twin Cities I closed a shitload of cases that way. Finding the right perp was the easy part for me. Finding evidence that tied him to the case was harder. Sometimes it was impossible, which frustrated the living shit out of me. Nothing worse than knowing someone did something bad and then having to watch him skate through the courts back onto the street with a free pass to hurt someone else.

Most of the time.

A few of those guys tripped and hurt themselves. Or, um, so I heard.

I tapped the card against my chin, thinking about it. What kind of marketing stunt was this? What kind of—?

Out in the hall I heard the elevator open.

The wall clock told me it was 2:44.

"Early," I said.

But as soon as the visitor knocked on the door the clock ticked over to 2:45. The exact second.

* * *

I went around and sat behind my desk before I said anything. I let the seconds tick all the way to 2:46. Just to be pissy.

The person outside didn't knock again. But I saw a figure through the frosted glass. Tall, dressed in some kind of suit, and definitely female. Her silhouette was rocking.

With my luck, though, she'd have the right curves but a face like Voldemort.

"Come in," I yelled.

The door opened.

She came in.

I actually said, "Holy shit."

* * *

She had the kind of face that you read about. The kind of face that if it looked down at you from a movie screen you'd absolutely believe you were on your knees in the Temple of Athena. The kind of face Hollywood women pay a lot of money for and never quite get.

You're either born with that face or you spend your life in therapy because it's just not going to happen.

That kind of face.

Pale skin with pores so small it looked like she was carved out of marble. Not white marble, though. She had some natural color that I'm pretty sure wasn't a tan. Couldn't peg her race or nationality. Maybe she was from the same island Wonder Woman came from. I don't know. I never visited that island. I knew right there that I couldn't have afforded the boat fare.

She was maybe thirty, about five-eight. Tall, with good bones and great posture, and enough curves to make my hair sweat, but not so many that it walked over the line into cartoonish. That's a very delicate line. Her hair was a foamy spill of black with some faint red highlights. Her lips were full and painted a discreet dark red. Make-up applied with skill and restraint. Pearl earrings, a drop-pearl necklace that rested half inch above the point where her cleavage stopped. Yes, I looked.

The only flaw—if you could call it that—was a small crescent-shaped scar on her cheek near the left corner of her mouth. If she was a different kind of woman I'd think that it was the kind of scar you can get when someone wearing a ring pops you one. But I couldn't sell that story to myself. This was a class act. But, I like scars. They're evidence that a person's lived.

She said, "Mr. Hunter?"

"Sam Hunter," I said, rising and offering my hand.

Her grip was cool and dry, but she withdrew her hand a half-second too quickly. Maybe she was afraid I hadn't washed. Not an unrealistic thought. I suddenly felt grubby.

I gave her an expectant smile, waiting for her name, but she didn't give it. Some clients are like that. Either they like being mysterious or they have to be careful. A lot of them hedge because they seem to think that if they withhold their names it somehow distances them from whatever problem brought them here. Nobody comes looking for a guy like me unless they've stepped in something. A bear trap, a pile of shit. Something.

"Have a seat," I said, gesturing to the better of my crappy visitor chairs. She sat and smoothed her skirt over her knees. She wore a charcoal jacket that had a pale blue chalk stripe that precisely matched the color of her silk blouse. Her skirt matched her jacket. Her shoes looked more expensive than my car, and probably were.

She sat there and studied me for a long time without speaking.

So, apparently the ball was in my court. Fine. I tossed the card onto the desk between us.

"Yours?"

"Ours," she corrected.

She waited for me to ask, but I didn't. I couldn't tell from the mouth she made if that was a good move on my part or not. She was clearly evaluating me, but I didn't know what kind of yardstick she was using. So I leaned back in my chair and waited.

After a while she gave a single, short nod and said, "We want to hire you."

She leaned on the 'we', so I guess I was supposed to ask.

"We being. . . ?"

"The Limbus Corporation."

"Who are they?"

"That's not really—."

"No," I said.

"Pardon?"

"You're going to tell me that it's not really important. It's a cheap answer to a question that actually *is* important. You left a card with the company name. You're here as a representative of that company. That puts the company into play. So. . . who or what is Limbus Inc?"

She gave me a few millimeters of a smile, but she didn't answer the question. Instead she opened her purse—an actual Louis Vuitton that would have paid off my mortgage—and removed two items. One was a standard-sized envelope with a thick bulge in it that was exactly the right size and shape to make me want to wag my tail. She placed that on the desk and held up the second item. A plain black flash drive.

"Will you agree to help us in this matter?" she asked.

I blinked a couple of times before I said, "Is that a serious question?"

"It is."

"You haven't told me anything yet."

"I know."

"And yet you want to know if I'll 'help'?"

"Yes."

"This isn't how it works."

"This is how it works with us."

"With Limbus?"

"Yes," she agreed.

I drummed my fingers on the desk top. "You have your own car or should I call you a cab?"

The smile widened. Just a little tiny bit. But she didn't answer. She wiggled the flash drive back and forth between her fingers.

I sucked my teeth. "What's on it?"

Instead of answering she handed it over.

I hesitated for a moment before accepting it, but figured what the hell. This would be the world's most absurd set-up for someone trying to infect my computer with a virus. Maybe the flash drive had photos of girls and this broad was a very charming pimp. Or maybe the Jehovah's Witnesses were going high-tech and this was the latest issue of the Watchtower in eBook format.

I took the drive.

Something really weird happened when I did, though. Flash drives are small so it's not unusual for fingers to touch when giving and receiving. When my fingertips brushed the edges of her painted nails, there was a shock as sharp and unexpected as an electric shock. Like the little snap of electricity you get on cold days when you touch a doorknob. I could even hear the crack in the air as the energy arced from her to me.

I snatched my hand back.

She didn't.

She withdrew it slowly, smiling that cat smile of hers. There was an opportunity to make some kind of joke about how shocking it all was, yada yada, but it would have been lame. She wasn't a chatty, laugh-a-minute kind of gal. She also wasn't the kind to waste a lot of her time in idle chitchat.

So, I plugged the flash drive into my laptop, located the device, accessed the menu and saw that there was one Word document and sixteen image files. Jpegs.

"Open the pictures," she suggested.

I selected all of them and hit the preview function.

My computer's preview function acts like a slideshow unless I hit a key to give me static images. By the time the first image popped up I forgot about the keys. I forgot about pretty much everything.

The picture was high-definition and tightly focused. No blur to soften any of the edges. No grain to reduce the impact.

It was a girl.

Or, at least it was girl-shaped.

She lay in the open mouth of a grungy alley, her body partially covered by dirty newspapers. Her mouth was wide open, the lips stretched as far as they could go, tongue lolling, teeth biting into the scream that must have been her last. The scream that was stamped now onto the muscles of her face.

Muscles, I said. Not skin.

She had no skin.

Not on her face.

Not on her body.

Not anywhere.

Not an inch of it.

The image vanished to be replaced by another girl.

Different girl, and I could tell that only by location—this one had been spilled out of a black plastic industrial trash bag—and by size. She was bigger, taller and bigger in the breasts and hips.

But that was the only way to tell the difference. All other individuality—skin tone and color, scars and tattoos, marks and moles—had been sliced away. All I saw was veined meat.

Another image. Another girl.

Another.

Another.

Another.

Sixteen.

The slideshow ground on mercilessly and I was absolutely unable to move a finger to stop it. The images flicked across my laptop screen. Sixteen young women. At least, I think they were young. Somehow I *knew* they were young.

All dead.

All stripped of more than flesh. Someone had torn away their lives, their individuality and their dignity along with their flesh.

When I raised my head to look over the laptop at her, there must have been something in my eyes because her smile vanished and she physically shrank back from me. Not a lot, but a bit.

"What the fuck is this?" I asked, and I barely recognized my own voice.

The woman cleared her throat, licked her lips, smoothed her skirt again. Rebuilding her calm façade.

"Beyond the obvious—the murder and mutilation of young women—we don't know what it is."

"A serial killer?"

"So it would appear. Sixteen dead girls over a period of roughly sixteen months."

"This isn't happening here in Philly," I said. "I'd have heard something."

"The first girl was found in Seattle. Felicia Skye, seventeen," she said. "Other bodies have been found in nine cities in five states. All girls ranging in age from sixteen to eighteen. They're all runaways, and all of them have worked as prostitutes. Eight have also worked as exotic dancers."

"Strip clubs don't hire kids."

"Anyone can get a false I.D., Mr. Hunter," she said coldly. "You know that."

I pointed at the screen. "Where's this shit happening?"

"The most recent—the sixteenth—was found in a storm drain in New York."

"When?"

"Twenty-six days ago."

"It wasn't in the papers."

"No."

"Why not?"

She took a moment on that. "We don't know. None of these have been in the media. Not one."

"That's impossible. Murders like this are front page."

She nodded. "They should be. This should be all over social media and Internet news, but it's not."

"That doesn't make any sense. If *you* know about it and you want something done, then why don't you take this to the press?"

Another pause. "We have."

"And—?"

"We've contacted six separate reporters in six cities. All six have died."

"Died?"

"Three heart attacks, one stroke, one fatal epileptic seizure, one burned to death after smoking in bed."

I stared at her. "You're shitting me."

"I'm not."

"What about the Feds? If this is happening across the country, then the FBI should—"

"They are investigating it. But they've had some problems of their own with the case. The lead agent fell down a flight of stairs and broke his neck. Freak accident. His replacement was killed in a car accident when an ambulance ran a red light. That sort of thing. The investigation is ongoing but agents have been shying away from it. They think it's jinxed."

That didn't surprise me. Even this deep into the 21st century there was a lot of superstition. Everyone has it—from people who knock wood to baseball players who have to wear their lucky socks. Cops have it in spades, just like soldiers, just like anyone whose day job involves real life and death stuff. When I was on the cops back in Minnesota I heard about several jinxed cases. No one wants to say it out loud because of how it sounds, but people still fear the boogeyman.

I got up and crossed to my file cabinet, opened the bottom drawer, and took out the only bottle of really good booze I owned— an unopened bottle of Pappy Van Winkle's 23-Year-Old bourbon. At two-hundred and fifty dollars a bottle it was way out of my price range, but a satisfied client had given it to me last Christmas. I brought it and two clean glasses back to my desk, and the woman watched while I opened the bottle and poured two fingers for each of us. I didn't ask if she drank. She didn't tell me to stop pouring.

I sat down and we each had some. We didn't toast. You don't toast for stuff like this.

The bourbon was legendary. I'd read all about it. It's aged in charred white oak barrels. Sweet, smooth, with a complex mix of honey and toffee flavors.

It might as well have been Gatorade for all I could tell. I drank it because my laptop was still fanning through the images. And because that, even if I didn't take this case, those dead women were going to live inside my head for the rest of my life. You can forget some things. Other things take up residence, building themselves into the stone and wood and plaster of the structure of your mind.

I suppose if I was capable of dismissing this, or forgetting it, then I wouldn't be who I am. Maybe I'd be happier, I don't know.

I closed the laptop, finished the bourbon and set my cup down.

"What do you want from me?" I asked.

The woman opened her purse again and removed another envelope. She placed it on the desk and slid it across to me. When I opened it I could see the glossy border of a photograph. I hesitated, not wanting to see another mutilated girl. But I was already in motion in this, so I sucked it up and slid the photo out of the envelope.

It was another girl.

This one had her skin.

She was a beautiful teenager, with bright blue eyes and a lot of curves that were evident in the skimpy costume she wore. A blue glitter g-string and high heels.

"Her name is Denise Sturbridge," said the woman. "She's only fifteen, which makes her the youngest of the women in question, but as you can see she looks quite a bit older. She's a runaway from Easton here in Pennsylvania. Abusive father, indifferent mother. Pretty common story, and very much in keeping with the backstories of the other girls. She took off four months ago, got picked up by the kind of predator who trolls bus stops and train stations. He got her high and turned her out to work conventions. She was scouted out of there to work in a gentleman's club near the Philadelphia airport. Fake I.D. that says she's nineteen. She dances under the name of Bambi."

I set the photo down.

"Tell me the rest," I said.

"She went missing two days ago. We believe that she will be number seventeen."

"That's a big leap. A lot of girls go missing."

She nodded. "She fits a type."

I glanced at the closed laptop and the black flash drive. "So the killer is targeting exotic dancers."

"Yes."

"And he's been on the move from Seattle, across the country. Now you think he's here."

"Yes. And there's not much time."

I cocked my head. "Now how the hell would you know that?"

"Because it's been four-hundred and seventy-five days since the first girl died. The coroner in Seattle was able to determine the day she died. We think Denise will be murdered in the next twenty-four hours."

"How do you figure that?"

"Do the math, Mr. Hunter."

I did.

Didn't need a calculator, either. It was simple arithmetic. Add a day to the span of the killings and divide by seventeen.

I could feel my blood turn to ice.

"Oh shit," I said.

She studied me with her dark eyes and I could see the moment when she knew that I knew that *she* knew. Chain of logic, none of it said aloud.

Seventeen murders. One every twenty-eight days.

A cycle.

Sure.

But a very specific *kind* of cycle. She gave me a small nod.

I didn't need to look at the calendar. Not for the next kill and not for any of the kills before that. The pattern screamed at me.

She slid the first envelope across the desk. "Fee and expenses," she said.

I didn't touch it, didn't look at it. I stared down into the smiling eyes of a girl pretending to be a woman who was a couple of days away from becoming a red horror someone would dump in an alley.

Maybe tomorrow.

"We want you to find this girl," she said.

I said nothing.

"There's a Word document on the drive that has a complete copy of the case file. Police and FBI reports. Coroner's report, lab reports. Everything."

I didn't ask her how she'd obtained all of that.

"What if I can't find her in time?"

The woman shook her head. "Then find who's doing this before there's a victim eighteen. This isn't going to stop, Mr. Hunter. Not unless someone stops it."

"The last kill was in New York. This is Philly. I wouldn't know where to start."

She reached across and picked up the business card I'd found on the floor and held it out to me. "This should help."

I didn't touch it. Didn't have to. I could still smell it. I could still smell the blood.

But now I understood.

The woman stood up.

This was the point where I should have asked 'Why me?' With all of the other cops and private investigators out there, why me?

We both knew that I wasn't going to ask that question. We both knew why me.

Twenty-eight days.

I didn't stand up, didn't shake her hand, didn't walk her to the door. Didn't tell her whether I was going to take the case.

We both knew the answer to that, too.

"I haven't said that I'm taking the case," I said.

She flicked a glance at the envelope, then shrugged. "You will if you want to, and you won't if you don't. Our policy is to encourage, not to compel."

"Your policy. You still haven't told me who you are. I mean, what's your interest? What's this Limbus thing and why do you people care?"

No answer to that.

"Okay," I said, "tell me this. The reporters who died. The heart attacks and strokes and stuff. You think any of that was legit?"

"Do you?"

"Was there any investigation?"

"Routine, in all cases. No one connected the cases because there was no evidence of foul play."

"Anyone do autopsies on the reporters who croaked?"

"On heart attacks? No. None of the victims were autopsied except for the man who burned to death, and that was ruled death by misadventure."

"And the stuff that happened to the feds looking into it?"

"As I said, this has become known as a bad luck case."

"Do you believe in bad luck?" I asked.

She gave me a smile that lifted the crescent scar beside her mouth. "We believe in quite a lot of things, Mr. Hunter."

With that she turned, walked out and pulled the door shut behind her.

* * *

I sat there and stared at the closed door for maybe ten minutes. I don't think I did anything except blink and breathe the whole time.

Twenty-eight days.

Bodies torn apart.

I picked up the card and sniffed the blood again. Deeply. Eyes closed. Letting the scent go all the way into my lungs, all the way into my senses. I took another breath, and another. Then I put the card down. I wouldn't need it anymore. That scent was locked into me now. I'd know it anywhere.

Interesting that this broad knew that about me.

We believe in quite a lot of things, Mr. Hunter.

"Shit," I told the empty room.

I glanced at the envelope. Even if it was filled with small bills, fives and tens, it had to be a couple of hundred. I guessed, though, that the denominations were higher. If it was twenties and fifties, then there were thousands in there. It was a fat envelope.

It sat there and I didn't pick it up. Didn't really want to touch it. Not yet.

I had this thing. If I took the money then I was definitely going to take the case.

Then I opened my laptop, accessed the Word document, and began reading. While I did that I tried not to look at the big calendar pinned to the wall by the filing cabinet. It was this year's Minnesota Vikings calendar. I liked the Vikings but I didn't give much of a warm shit as to who was featured on this month's page. Or any month. The calendar's only important feature was a set of small icons that showed the phases of the moon.

Twenty eight days.

One day to go.

One day for little Bambi.

A single day until the killer took her skin and her life and emptied her of her dreams and hopes and breath and smiles and life.

A day.

One day until the next full moon.

In my blood and under my skin I could already *feel* the moon pulling at me. Tearing, clawing.

Screaming at me.

Howling at me.

* * *

When you don't have a clue you start at the beginning and see if you can pick up the scent. For most guys in my line of work that's a metaphor. Guess I'm a little different.

The case file for Bambi—Denise Sturbridge—said that she worked four shifts a week at a strip club called *ViXXXens* in Northeast Philly. A quick Google search told me that the place was owned by Dante Entertainment and managed by one George Palakas.

I live in Old City near Front and South, so it was an easy trip up I-95. I got off at Grant Avenue, cut across to Bustleton Avenue and followed that to within half a block of the northeastern-most city limits. Couldn't miss the club. The sign was massive, with a neon silhouette of an improbably endowed woman winking on and off in blue and pink. Beneath the sign squatted an ugly three-story building that looked like it might have been built in Colonial times. Who knows, maybe Washington even slept there. But that was then. Now it crouched in embarrassment. Whitewashed plank siding, smoked windows blocked by beer signs, twenty or thirty cars in the parking lot, and bass notes shuddering along the ground from speakers that were way too powerful for the size of the building.

I parked near a pair of Harleys and got out.

I've been in a hundred places like this. As a cop, as a P.I. Once, when I was in high school, as a patron. Sure, I'm a healthy straight guy, but I'm not the demographic for joints like this. It's not an economic thing or a class thing or even an education thing. I think it comes down to personal awareness. It's hard to sit on a stool, drinking beer after beer, watching a woman you don't know and can't touch gyrate and take off her clothes to bad dance pop, when everyone else is doing the same thing. None of it's really for you. It's for your beer money and tip money. It's about you bringing your friends so they can spend their money. It's about you becoming a regular so you contribute to the profit of both dancer and club. But it lacks anything of true human connection. You aren't friends with the friendly bartenders and you won't have sex with the sexy dancers. You're an open wallet.

So who goes to places like these? Like I said, it's not a class of men. Even before I entered I knew that there would be guys in construction worker boots and denims, and guys in good business suits. There would be married guys and single guys. There would be college grads and high school dropouts. There would be white, black, Asian and Latino guys. What there wouldn't be would be very many guys who were genuinely happy in their lives. The ones who were, probably only came here with buddies. More for their friends than for the silicone tits and painted mouths up on stage. Or guys coming here for their first *legal* drinks, surrounded by fathers, uncles, friends; a big shit-eating grin stapled onto their faces to hide their actual embarrassment.

The rest?

You couldn't even call them lost and lonely. A lot of them aren't. But they're missing something. Some connection, or maybe some optimism. Whatever it is, they either came here looking for a thread of it, or because they gave up looking and the music here was too loud for introspection and self-evaluation.

I drew in a breath through my nostrils, held it, let it out, and went inside.

It was two o'clock in the afternoon and the place was already three-quarters full. Too early for a bouncer, so there was no cover and no hassle. The bar was a big oblong with seats all the way around it and two small square stages inside, intercut by a bank of cash registers and liquor shelves. A dozen beer taps, but none of them were for good beers. The two brands were Heineken, which was a short step up from dog piss, and Budweiser, which was a full step down. No Yuengling, no good local microbrews. You didn't come here to sample a good beer. You came here to drink a lot of beers quickly and cheaply so that you didn't feel weird tucking part of your paycheck into a girl's g-string for no god damn good reason at all.

There were two dancers working the afternoon shift. The one closest to the door was probably pushing forty but she'd had a lot of work done and kept her muscles toned. My guess was that she was a single mother with no college and shaking her ass earned her more cash—particularly unreportable cash—than asking drive-through customers if they wanted their Happy Meal giant-sized. Her eyes flicked around, looking for the kind of guy who would pony up a buck just to have her come closer, or the kind of guy who would toss her a buck to make her go away. There were plenty of both. When her eyes briefly met mine she got no signal that she could use and her gaze swept on. A rotating spot swept across her face and I could see some old acne scars that were nearly buried under lots of pancake. Not a pretty woman, but probably not a junkie or a hooker. Someone willing to do this to put food in her kids' mouths and make as good a life for them as she could.

I moved on and took a seat between the two stages.

The second dancer was half the age of the first. She'd be skinny if it wasn't for plastic boobs and a decent ass. Sticks for arms and legs that had shape only because of high heels and patterned stockings. She wore a red thong and flesh-colored pasties over her nipples. And although she had a pretty face, she was about as sexy as a root canal. At least to me, but like I said, I'm not the demographic.

The bartender drifted up and used a single uptic of his chin to ask what I wanted.

I ordered a vodka martini with three olives just to see what kind of expression it put on his face. His face turned to wood.

"Bud," I said, and he curled just enough of his lip to let me know that he appreciated the joke. He drew a Budweiser and slid a mug in front of me. I put a twenty on the bar and tapped it to let him know I was starting a tab on it. He nodded and moved away.

The song that was playing was so gratingly loud that it could sterilize an elk. The lyrics were meaningless pap. Something about 'high school charms', which gave it all a pedophile vibe.

The other patrons were staring at the dancers. The music was too loud for conversation. One guy was playing video poker and eating fistfuls of beer nuts without looking at them. Two guys in dark suits sat at the far end drinking dark mixed drinks that I'm pretty sure were actually Coke in highball glasses. I marked them in my mind. Strip clubs don't let you sit there and drink soda, which means that these guys were either part of the staff—off-shift bouncers, maybe; or they were friends of the house. I saw them watching me as I watched them. One of them gave me a nod and I nodded back. That's not a friendly exchange, not in places like this. It's one player letting the other player know that they're all in the game.

When the record changed, I left the beer and the twenty as placeholders, turned slowly on my stool until I spotted the entrance to the back rooms. I headed that way, and a short hall took me past employee restrooms, a store room, a fire door, all the way to a door marked OFFICE.

I knocked.

The man who opened the door was a burly forty-something, probably Greek face with a bald head, Popeye forearms, a thick mustache and wary eyes. He gave me a quick up and down and apparently decided I wasn't a cop or someone from L and I. I was dressed in jeans and a Vikings windbreaker over an Everlast tank top. Cops and license inspectors all dress better than me.

"George Palakas?" I asked.

"What if I am?" he demanded, unimpressed.

"Need to talk to you."

Palakas narrowed his eyes. "About what?"

"I'm looking for Denise Sturbridge."

The manager gave me a slow three-count of silent appraisal, then he said, "No." He turned away and started to close his door.

I got a foot out and blocked it. The edge of the door hit the outside sole of my Payless running shoes and rebounded.

Palakas wheeled on me. "Yo, asshole," he growled. "The fuck you think you're doing?"

"I told you," I said mildly, smiling.

"Get your ass out of here before I have you—"

I shoved him. Quick and light, but it caught him off guard and sent him running backward into his office. His ass hit the edge of the desk, the impact spun him and he fell onto the floor, dragging a desk-light and a coffee cup full of pencils with him. He landed on his knees hard enough to make me wince. The lamp and coffee cup shattered.

I closed the door and leaned my back against it.

Palakas looked up at me. His knees had to hurt and his face was turning from a fake tan to brick red.

"You stupid motherfucker," he whispered through teeth that ground together between curled lips. "I'm going to—"

"No," I said, "you're not. Stop trying to scare me to death."

He cursed some more.

I kept smiling.

When Palakas paused for a breath I said, "You hired a fifteen-year-old girl to strip in your club. We could start there and see how fast I could get you shut down."

"Bullshit," he said, but suddenly his voice lacked emphasis.

"Right now that's all that I know she did here. It's enough for me not to want to take any shit from you."

"Who's she to you?" he asked as he got heavily to his feet.

I shrugged. "Maybe I'm her father."

He actually laughed. "Her old man's a methed-out schizo up in Easton."

"Then maybe I'm her brother."

"She doesn't have a brother."

There was a pack of gum in my pocket. I took it out and popped a couple of pieces out of the aluminum blister pack, put them into my mouth, crunched through the candy coating and chewed the gum. Palakas watched me do all this.

I said, "Does it really matter who I am?"

"It's going to matter when I—"

"I already told you, stop trying to scare me. I want to have a conversation with you and I really don't want to have to wade through a bunch of lines cribbed from old Sopranos reruns. I'm going to ask you some questions. You're going to answer my questions. If I'm satisfied with the answers then I'm done and you can forget I was ever here."

"Why should I tell you a god damn thing?"

"Ah," I said, "this is the part where *I* threaten *you*. You see, if you don't tell me what I want, or if I don't like what you tell me, then I will kick a two-by-four so far up your ass you'll be spitting toothpicks."

"Think you could?"

"We can find out," I said mildly. "And afterward we can have this conversation while we're waiting for the paramedics."

Palakas tried a sneer on me. It was supposed to look fearless and defiant, but this wasn't a movie and he knew that if I was telling him

I could hurt him then that's how it would play out. Even if he had my legs broken later on, it wouldn't stop him from taking the full weight now and very few people want to play it that way. Besides, the door was closed and I think he was actually curious.

"The fuck you want to know?" he said, playing it out, though. That was okay. He could posture all he wanted as long as he talked. What he didn't know was that I could smell his fear. Beneath the deodorant, the residual smell of his soap—Ivory, I think—and his cologne—Axe—I could smell the fear stink.

"Denise Sturbridge," I reminded him.

"Bambi. Yeah, so what? What about her." He stepped over the debris on the floor and sat down behind his desk. I came and stood close to him and we both knew that it was because I wanted to make sure he didn't get cute and pull anything unfortunate from a desk drawer. Small office. Even with a loaded gun I could get to him before he could take a shot. We both knew that.

"I'm looking for her."

"She's not here."

"I know that, numb-nuts. That's what 'looking for her' means. If she was here I'd have already found her." I tapped him on the forehead with my index finger. "I want you to tell me where she is."

Palakas gave a half-hearted swipe at my hand. "How should I know?"

"She works for you?" I suggested.

"No, she don't. She missed three shifts in a row. That's her ass as far as I'm concerned."

"You're saying she's missing?"

"I'm saying she ain't here. I don't know where she is and I couldn't give a hairy rat's ass. She stiffs me on three shifts, am I supposed to give a wet shit about her? Am I supposed to keep her on the schedule? Fuck no."

"I need to find her."

"Then go to her damn apartment. What are you bothering me for?"

I shrugged. "Last known whereabouts."

"Look," he said, taking a breath, "who are you? I mean really."

"I'm nobody," I said.

"You're not a cop?"

"No."

"You're not with Vice?"

"I said I wasn't a cop."

"You look like a cop," Palakas said. From the sour shape his mouth made you'd think the word 'cop' was smeared with dog shit.

"Used to be a cop."

"What are you now?"

"Private."

He stared at me. "You serious?"

"As a heart attack."

"Bambi a bail skip or something?"

"No. She's a kid who should be in school, not showing her boobs to a bunch of degenerate jerkoffs."

Half a laugh burst from him before he could clamp it down. I edged closer.

"You want to tell me what's so funny? Maybe we can both get a good laugh out of it."

Fear flickered in Palakas's eyes. I am not a big guy—pretty ordinary, really. Five nine, one-seventy; but I've been told I have a quality. Even people who don't know what I have under the skin say that. A quality. When I wore the badge, it must have been there in my eyes. It made some pretty serious thugs back off and back down.

Palakas licked his lips for a moment.

"I don't know where she is," he said. "You want her home address? I can give you that."

"I have that. Give me some names. She have a boyfriend?"

"She has a—."

He almost said something smartass. Probably something like 'she has a million boyfriends'. He stopped himself in time. Two or three more syllables and I'd have belted him, we both knew it.

"Do I need to repeat the question?" I asked quietly.

"She don't have a boyfriend," he said. "Actually I don't think I ever heard of her going on a...um...on a real date."

He didn't have to explain what he meant.

"But...?" I prompted.

"But there was this kid she hung out with."

"A girl?"

"No. A boy. Works in the kitchens. Black kid. Queer."

"They hung out together?"

"Pretty much all the time. Name's Donny Falk."

"Is he working today?"

"No."

"Know where I can find him?"

"Same place as Bambi. Windsor Apartments on Red Lion Road. Same building and floor. His apartment's two doors down from hers."

"You have a phone number for him?"

Palakas licked his lips again. "Yeah," he said, and he very carefully opened the top drawer of his desk and removed a sheet of paper. I leaned over to look at it and saw that it was a list of employees—bar staff, bouncers, kitchen staff, cleaners, dancers— along with contact numbers and email addresses.

"You have a copy of that?" I asked.

"Yeah, but—."

I plucked it out of his hand.

"Hey!"

I turned to him.

"Hey. . . what?"

Palakas gave me a long, disgusted look. "Hey, I guess help your fucking self to whatever you want. You got a P.I. license, which isn't worth the toilet paper it's printed on, but sure, go ahead, knock around a guy who's got a heart condition. You kick dogs, too?"

I folded the paper and slipped it into my pocket.

"Gosh," I said, "I'm really embarrassed that you think I'm a bully. You think I'm being mean? I certainly don't want to convey that impression."

He glared at me, not falling for it.

So I put a button on it for him. "It's just that I'm pretty sure you knew that girl was underage. I'm actually showing a great degree of restraint here, 'cause my real instinct is to wail on you until I feel better. The only reason I'm not is because you're cooperating—after a fashion. And," I added before he could say anything, "because I don't know for a fact that you're her pimp. If I knew for sure that you were making a fifteen-year-old girl sell herself, then I think we'd have to explore how really mean I can get. Believe me. . . neither of us wants to let that dog off the leash. You reading me here?"

"Yeah," he said. He meant to say it tersely, but it came out like a wheeze.

I patted his cheek. "Good."

I could feel George Palakas's glare of hatred as I turned and left.

* * *

As I passed through into the bar toward the exit I saw the two men in dark suits watching me, and I saw their eyes flick from me to the hallway that led to the office. They stood up. The guy on the left was about six foot but had to go two-fifty, most of it in his chest and shoulders. The guy on the right was slimmer but also four inches taller. Big and Tall were not giving me friendly looks. Then Big crossed to the hall and disappeared in the direction of the office while Tall stood there and kept his eyes on me.

Not good.

There were too many people around in the bar, so I began walking toward the exit. Tall saw me and started heading in the same direction. My choices were these —I could wait for them to do something here in the bar, which meant risking injury to civilians. Nope. Or I could let them chase me outside, which opened this up to witnesses with cell phone cameras. Also not good.

Or...

The door to the men's room was closer than the exit door. I gave Tall a smile and ducked through the door.

It took Tall about four seconds to come bursting through. He had an old fashioned black-jack in his right hand. You don't see them much anymore. It's a big slug of lead sitting on a spring and wrapped with thick leather. You use it with a snap of the wrist. In skillful hands it can brush the skull and send a person into dreamy land and when they wake up they're sick, disoriented and tractable.

Used wrong it's a skull crusher.

Tall was already starting to raise his for a heavy overhand swing before he was all the way into the bathroom. He was going for the full impact.

I stood with my back to him and saw all this in a mirror.

The blackjack whipped up and was just starting the accelerating drop that would end me when I turned.

I don't just mean that I turned around. Sure, I did that, too. But when I say I 'turned', what I really mean is that I changed.

He swung the blackjack at a man.

It wasn't a man he hit.

His eyes flared wide and his mouth opened to scream in total, sudden horror when I crashed into him and dragged him down to the floor.

The music outside was so loud, nobody heard him scream.

Nobody heard me snarl.

* * *

I was thirteen the first time I changed.

The first time took almost half an hour. I thought I was being torn apart. Guess I kind of was. Torn apart and put back together beneath the skin. Muscles melting into jelly and reassembling; bones reshaping, hair jabbing like needles through my flesh, mouth reshaping, new teeth bursting through the gums. And all of it in a paroxysm of screaming, inarticulate agony. Maybe it feels like dying. Maybe it feels like being tortured. While it was happening I begged God or whoever else is at the help desk to kill me right there and then.

My grandmother was with me through it.

She'd been making that change for nearly seventy years, since she was eleven. Almost everyone on her side of the family had been through it. And, yeah, it actually killed some of them. Depends on your blood line, or maybe if you have the right genes. There are several families like ours and whenever possible we've interbred. Not enough to go all Arkansas back-country, we're not looking to turn out a bunch of moon-faced, slack-jawed brother-cousins. Just enough to strengthen the DNA.

What are we?

There's a lot of folklore out there. A lot of legends. Lots of stories about things like me.

Lot of names.

Lycanthrope.

Berserker.

Vargulf.

Loup-garou.

Werewolf.

We call ourselves the Benandanti. That's an old Italian name that means 'good-walker'. It can also be translated as 'those who go well'. Or even those who 'do good'.

Yeah. Werewolf. Good guy. Same package.

They don't make movies about my kind. You don't see them in too many books or comics. We're not like the Hollywood werewolves, but we've left claw marks all through history. One of us, an eighty-year-old guy named Thiess from Jurgenburg, Livonia, was even arrested by the Holy Inquisition in 1692 and put on trial. Not my direct bloodline, but we all know about him. He's kind of a hero to us. The Inquisitors used every kind of torture, every manner of 'enhanced interrogation' to try and force Thiess to say that he was a servant and agent of the Devil. Lot of people would have cracked and said anything to stop the pain. Lot of people *did*, which probably accounts for every single signed confession of Satan worship those fruitcakes ever obtained.

Not Thiess, though. That one was one tough, stubborn fucker. And he was eighty!

He *admitted* that he was a werewolf. But he also told them that the Benandanti fought evil on the side of heaven. It was what we always did. It was who we were.

That story didn't go over too well, so they really went to town on Thiess. Thumbscrews, hot irons, the rack. All of it, the works. He should have broken. He should have died.

He didn't.

And he never once wavered in his assertion that the Benandanti have been fighting the true 'good fight'. Against monsters.

Actual monsters.

The Inquisitors tried and tried and tried.

And failed.

Eventually they got to a point where they simply ran out of shit they could do to him. It was down to kill him or let him go.

And. . . they let him go.

The church court issued a letter saying, in effect, that no servant of the Devil could endure the 'tests' imposed on it by the Inquisition. Thiess, having survived, must have done so with the grace and protection of God Almighty.

Not only did they let him go, but they even gave him a nickname. A label of honor.

The Hound of God.

Not to say that the church was all kissy-face with us after that. The official result of the trial was exoneration for Thiess. The actual result is that they were embarrassed and probably scared of us. So, in secret and way off the record, they began hunting us down. Not for trial but for quick, quiet execution. There were never many of us, and there were a lot of killers working for the Inquisition. We were very nearly wiped out, and for a while the gene pool was so shallow that whole centuries passed before the wolf once more began screaming in the blood.

My grandmother is the strongest of all of us. Sweetest little old broad you ever wanted to meet. Most of the time. Frail-looking dame with blue hair and a bit of a dowager's hump. But . . . she can make the change faster than you can snap your fingers, and when the werewolf emerges from beneath the wrinkles of the human, anyone giving her problems—or bothering someone to whom she's offered her protection—is literally in a world of hurt.

For me, I can get pretty cranky, too. On both sides of the skin change, but I do everything I can to keep that change from happening. I don't trust my level of control when I'm a wolf. Bad things have happened, things have spun out of control more than once. It's why I'm not a cop anymore.

But there are times…

I'm telling you all of this so you'll understand what happened in the bathroom at ViXXXens. Tall expected to beat the shit out of some schmuck asking the wrong questions of the wrong person. He had every reason to expect to win that fight. He even scored his hit with the blackjack.

It just didn't do him any damn good.

* * *

The blackjack hit my shoulder as I turned. It hurt. I'm a monster but I still had nerve endings, I'm still meat and bone, and I could still feel pain.

It's just that as a werewolf it takes a lot of damage to slow me down. A whole hell of a lot. Decapitation will do it. Fire will do it. Maybe a machine gun, I don't know. It hasn't ever come to that.

A blackjack?

Oh, please.

And pain is like gasoline on a fire. It dials everything up.

I slashed at his arm and the tough double-stitched leather of the blackjack ripped apart. The lead slug bounced off the ceiling and dropped into a sink. The tips of my nails stroked his hand and wrist and blood splatted the metal toilet stall.

I could have taken the guy's head off.

Easily.

But here's the thing about werewolves. In the movies we're ravening, blood-mad, mindless monsters.

In real life, not so much.

Sure, there's rage.

Sure, there's a lot of animal urges. Lots of subliminal kill-kill-kill impulses.

And, sure, there's a big temptation to chow down because we're predators and humans are tasty prey. Yeah, that's gross, I'm well aware of that. And I've had a lot of next-day puke sessions after I've done some chomping. Less so these days because I have more control. At first, though, I went after the bad guys like they were blue plate specials. Live and learn.

It was Tall's good fortune that I had that control now. And that I'd eaten a couple of quarter pounders on the way here. Otherwise he might have been missing some juicy parts.

Instead, all I did was slam him against the wall over the sink. Kind of hard.

He crashed down onto a row of three filthy sinks, ripping two of them off the wall. He crashed to the floor in a quivering heap, covered with porcelain debris, bleeding from a lot of little cuts. Alive, but not enjoying it.

That's when Big pushed through the door.

The first thing he saw was his friend. I was off to one side. He didn't see me until I got up in his face and *made* him see me.

He started to scream.

I threw him into a toilet stall. He hit the back wall hard enough to turn his eyes blank and knock him all the way to the edge of la-la land. I got to him and caught him before he fell.

Even as I grabbed him I shifted back. I jerked the chain on the wolf and made him go away before he did something we'd all regret.

Takes a lot of effort to do that, though. The wolf does not like to go back into the kennel. Not one bit.

It was with human hands that I shoved him onto his knees and stuck his face in the unflushed toilet.

I held him there until my personal disgust told me to stop. Maybe three, four seconds. Then I pulled his dripping head out, spun him around and stuffed him down into the corner between the toilet and the wall.

I squatted in front of him, watching a piece of toilet paper slide down his cheek. He coughed and sputtered and stared at me in total confusion. This wasn't the face he'd seen a second ago. His eyes shifted to find the big bad wolf, but he couldn't know that the monster had already left the building.

Oh, yeah . . . that whole cycle of the moon thing? That's mostly fiction. During the three days of the full moon we're a little more aggressive, our rages are harder to control, but that's all. We can make the change anytime we want. Into the wolf and back to our own skin. Just like that. On a dime.

A few seconds ago there was a snarling monster with black hair and lots of fangs. Now there was a skinny guy in a baggy Viking's windbreaker. If you don't come from a home life like mine, that's pretty hard to process, and Big was blowing a lot of mental circuits trying to make sense of it.

I crossed to the door and locked it, then squatted down again in front of Big. He was borderline catatonic with fear.

"What's your name?" I asked.

He started shaking his head. Either refusing to answer or in denial of what was happening.

"Your name." I said it slower, but got nothing.

A slap across the chops would probably have helped unscramble his grits, but, y'know, he was just bobbing for turds, so . . . no thanks.

For his part, he started flapping his arms around. At first I thought he was trying to fight me or fend me off. But that wasn't it.

He made a half-fist, extending his index and little finger so he could fork the sign of the evil eye at me.

Fair enough. Even though he looked more German than Italian, I figured what the hell. He had just seen a monster. Besides, I've met wiseguys and wiseguy wannabes who did that sort of thing. They were every bit as superstitious as cops and ball players.

Then he began mumbling something. It first I thought it was Italian, but it wasn't.

It was Latin.

" . . . *defende nos in proelio; contra nequitiam et insidias diaboli esto praesidium. Imperat illi Deus; supplices deprecamur: tuque, Princeps militiae coelestis, Satanam aliosque spiritus malignos, qui ad perditionem animarum pervagantur in mundo, divina virtute in infernum detrude...*"

Unfortunately I don't speak Latin. I mean, who needs to? Even priests don't use it much anymore. But you can *tell* when something is Latin. It doesn't really sound like anything else. Sounded like church stuff. Sounded like stuff you hear in movies.

"Hey," I snapped. "Hey, asshole."

He kept rattling on with the Latin. I yelled at him again. No change.

If I hadn't destroyed the sinks I might have belted some sense into him and then washed my hand. Instead I reached around and under him and took his wallet. He didn't try to stop me. He was totally freaked out, kept pointing the horns of his fingers at me, kept muttering church stuff at me.

The driver's license in the wallet told me that Big's real name was Kurt Gunther. German, like I thought. Or German heritage. All his I.D. was American. There was about four hundred in mixed bills in the wallet, a bunch of credit cards, membership cards from everything from Sam's Club to the library in Doylestown. I smiled. Am I prejudiced because I don't expect thugs to have library cards? Not sure.

There was a glassine flap that had something that really caught my eye. There were two items in it. One was a card the size of a credit card, but it was blood red and had no markings on it except a magnetic strip on the back. But as I turned it over I caught a flash of something. I held it close to my eye and turned it over more slowly, and this time I could see a symbol hidden on the front. It was very subtle, a hologram, like they put on driver's licenses. Only this one was red upon red, with but the slightest 3D effect. It was too small to see clearly, but I could tell that it was circular, with a symbol in the center and lots of radiating spokes. There were other symbols between the spokes, but I couldn't make them out. It reminded me of one of those astrological wheels, but there were more than twelve spokes. Although it was difficult to count, I think there were eighteen symbols around the edge.

The other item was a business card. It had the name, business address, email and contact phone number of a broker at one of the big-ticket national chains. Dunwoody-Kraus-Vitalli. The broker's name was Daniel Meyers.

That's not the thing that made me go 'hmmmm'; it was what was written in blue ballpoint on the back.

A single word.

A name.

Bambi.

I leaned toward Mr. Gunther and showed him the card.

"Bambi," I said. "Where?"

" . . . *hostium nostrorum, quaesumus, Domine, elide superbiam: et eorum contumaciam dexterae tuae virtute prosterne . . .*"

"Stop that," I said, "or you'll get to meet your lord and savior sooner than later, capiche?"

He stopped the chanting.

I wiggled the card and repeated, "Where?"

He looked from the card to me and back again. His eyes, which were already pretty well bugged out, bulged nearly out of their sockets. The steady stream of Latin dribbled to a stop.

He said, "N—no . . ."

Behind me Tall was starting to groan and move sluggishly among the rubble.

Outside the music was still pounding, but who knew what Palakas was doing. Calling the cops. Calling more thugs. Loading a gun. I could hear a big clock ticking in my brain.

"Talk," I said. "Or should I let the dog out to play?"

* * *

Turns out, he didn't want to see the dog again.

Didn't really want to talk, either, but we crossed that speed bump without anyone losing a wheel.

Kurt Gunther and his partner, Salvatore Tucci—Mr. Tall—were bouncers. Not a major surprise there. But they didn't work here at ViXXXens. They worked at a place called Club Dante. I'd heard of it but had never been there. It was one of those so-called 'gentlemen's clubs'. Lots of girls with almost nothing on and lots of booze, but they don't consider themselves a titty bar. The girls are prettier—or have more expensive cosmetic surgery—the booze is all top shelf and over-priced, and lap dances cost more than most of the customers here at ViXXXens make in a week. Places like that are usually fronts for the sex trade, but proving it is a bitch. You have to be a member, and anything hinky happens behind closed doors. The clientele are the local rich and powerful, which means the place has a lot of money and a lot of juice. Places like that don't get raided, or if they do, word has already come down and when Vice breaks in everything is a-jay squared away.

"Is Bambi out there?" I asked him.

Gunther started to tell me that she wasn't, that he didn't know who she was, but I reminded him that if I had to show him the wolf again, then the beast was going to take home a trophy. Gunther clearly didn't want to sing in a high squeaky voice for the rest of his life.

He told me that Bambi was hired to work a special party out at Dante's. They had lots of small rooms for parties.

"Who hired her?" I asked.

"Meyers," he told me. "Daniel Meyers."

The stockbroker.

"Where is she now? Where's Bambi?"

Gunther said he didn't know. He and his partner picked her up at ViXXXens and dropped her at Dante's two nights ago, but the manager over there said that she split. They'd come back here looking for her but had so far come up dry. They were hanging around the place hoping she walked in.

I can usually tell when people are lying to me—it's a smell thing—but Gunther was telling the truth. Or, at least as much of the truth as he knew.

I left him there and got out of the bar pretty quick. I caught a quick glimpse of Palakas across the bar talking on the phone. Didn't wait to find out what kind of heat he was calling.

Bambi's apartment building was close, so I headed over there and parked outside of the Windsor South Apartments. It was a six-story block built like a slab, with balconied apartments front and back. Cheap but not squalid. Lawn out front needed mowing but it wasn't full of crab grass or weeds.

There was no doorman. The lobby had an intercom, but no one answered at either Bambi's apartment or that of her friend, Donny Falk. So I loitered around until someone came in. When they used their key to open the inner security door, I went through with them. I gave a grunt and a nod like I knew them, and busied myself by pretending to look at something interesting on my BlackBerry. We got in the elevator. He got off at four; I went up to six, then found the fire stairs and went down to three. The apartments on the right-hand side were odd numbers, left side were even. Bambi's apartment was 309. Falk's was 307.

I knocked on 309 and heard nothing but echoes.

The hall was empty, the door was locked. I sniffed the door and smelled only those things I expected to smell. Wood, old cooking smells, a little mildew, and dust.

The place even felt empty. It had that kind of vibe. Like a dead battery.

The other doors along the hall stayed shut, so I bent to study the lock. Every P.I. worth his license can bypass a lock without much trouble. The really good ones require a set of lock-picks and maybe three minutes work. This one was a cheap-ass lock, and I opened it with a flexible six-inch plastic ruler I carry for exactly this kind of thing. It pushed the tapered bolt back on its spring and the lock clicked open. I glanced up and down the hall and then stepped inside.

Denise Sturbridge's apartment was neat and small and clean. And empty. I ghosted my way through it. There were dishes in the dishwasher, leftovers in the fridge, some trash in the cans that told me nothing, the usual stuff in the bathroom, and exactly what you'd expect in the bedroom. Drawers filled with cheap but attractive clothes. Dance stuff. Shoes, but not too many and most of them inexpensive. A hamper with soiled items in it. Twin bed, pink sheets, a stuffed turtle.

I touched very little, but I sniffed it all. And, although that sounds intensely creepy, think of it more like a dog and less like a thirty-something adult man.

I catalogued the scents of Denise Sturbridge as a living person. I added that to the already-logged scent of her blood.

There was nothing of note anywhere. A work schedule was posted on the side of the fridge, held in place by a magnet from a pizza shop. There was a TV and DVD player, and most of the disks she had were romantic comedies or Disney stuff.

Girl stuff.

Kid stuff. Like the stuffed turtle.

My heart hurt looking at it.

"Where are you, kid?" I asked the empty apartment. "Give me a little help here."

But there wasn't even a whisper of anything useful.

I wiped off everything I touched and left her apartment. I drifted down to Donny Falk's door and froze in my tracks.

There were splinters on the carpet and when I peered at the frame around the lock I could see where the wood had been cracked. Someone had forced the door and then pushed the splinters and twisted metal back into place as far as it would go. You had to look close to see it. I was looking close.

Which is when I caught the smell.

Faint.

But there.

Sickly sweet and gassy.

Only one thing smells like that.

I put my ear against the wood and listened for any sound of movement. Anything at all.

Nothing.

Shit.

I leaned my shoulder against the door and pushed it open. There wasn't much resistance beyond the friction of the broken lock and torn frame. I stepped inside and immediately pushed the door shut.

Donny Falk was kitchen help in a strip club, and he clearly lived small. Mismatched Salvation Army furniture, plastic milk crates and boards for shelving, posters thumbtacked to the walls, a threadbare rug over worn linoleum.

Maybe that had been enough for him. Maybe he kept the place clean and filled it with music and friends and his own hopes and dreams. Some people cruise along that way. If they don't have much then at least they have some measure of freedom. They make genuine friendships, and they're loving and loyal to anyone who shows them respect and kindness.

Now, though, the place was a wreck.

It looked like a storm had blown through it.

The couch and chair were overturned, cushions slashed, stuffing pulled out, posters torn down, CD players smashed, CD's crushed underfoot, baseball bat rammed through the TV screen, flowers torn out of pots, cereal boxes torn open and spilled, toaster-oven crashed onto the floor, refrigerator door open and everything pulled out and smeared onto the cheap linoleum and carpet. I moved carefully through the debris, careful not to leave footprints in anything sticky or powdery. There was a short hallway leading off from the living room, with a bathroom door on one side and a bedroom at the end. I peered into the bathroom to see the same kind of destruction. Everything that could be smashed had been, everything that could be cracked or spilled or torn was in ruins. I caught a glimpse of fifty different angry versions of my face in the fragments of the shattered mirror. None of those faces looked happy. This wasn't wolf face, but it was every bit as dangerous.

The bedroom door was closed, but the smell was coming from there.

For a moment I felt so old and depressed that I wondered if I should leave the door closed, turn around and go home. I wasn't a homicide cop anymore—not since they asked me to turn in my badge back in the Cities. I was a P.I. with no legal reason to be here, and I couldn't prove that I hadn't been the one to kick in the door and trash the place.

If I walked into that room then I would be tampering with a crime scene.

They could and probably would put me in jail for something like this.

Best thing in the world for me to do was get the hell out of there. I had other leads to follow—the stockbroker and Club Dante. It was a better, smarter choice to walk away.

But then if I was a better or smarter guy I wouldn't be working this job.

I opened the door.

And stood there.

I didn't enter.

Everything I needed to see I could see from where I was.

Donny Falk was about twenty, maybe five-six, one-thirty. I could tell that much.

George Palakas had said that Donny was black and gay. The posters on the wall were all of good looking men in skimpy outfits, so I could make the case for him being gay. As for black?

You'd need to look at his skin to make that call.

And he didn't have any.

The whole room was painted in his blood. Not artistically, but from arterial sprays. He seemed to float in the midst of it, but that was an illusion. His arms and legs were spread wide. Someone had driven big iron nails through his wrists and shins. I would like to think they'd done that after the kid was dead, but I don't think mercy was really any part of this scenario.

I could see why his screams didn't alert the neighbors. You need a tongue for that. His was nailed to his forehead.

And...the killer had torn open Donny's chest and removed his heart.

I forced myself to look around the room, but there was no sign of the stolen organ. The killer had taken it with him.

But the killer had left something behind. Something I recognized.

On the wall, drawn with care in Donny's blood, was a large circle. There was a small symbol in the center, and eighteen spokes radiating out to connect with the big outer circle. Between each circle was another symbol. Each symbol was unique. Each was entirely unknown to me. I removed the Club Dante card from my jacket and held it up at an angle where I could see the hologram.

Same symbol.

If it was astrological, then it was from some philosophy other than the normal one I knew about. Eighteen symbols.

The pattern was strange, alien to me.

Looking at it made my heart hammer and my skin crawl.

Was this killer hunting according to some crazy religious thing? Was this part of some ritual he was acting out? While on the cops I ran into religious maniacs before. Some of them had this view in their heads that they were on the verge of *becoming* something greater than what they were; that they were about to ascend, and that it only required blood sacrifices and an adherence to specific rituals to open that door.

Is that what I had here? Was Bambi waiting to become a victim to the grand designs of someone who wanted to become God?

"Bambi,' I murmured. "Denise...Donny..."

I stood there for a long time as a series of weird emotions crawled through my shocked brain.

Donny Falk was not my client. I hadn't known him, and differences in age and location and profession would probably have prevented us from ever crossing paths, or if we had, we probably wouldn't have anything to say to one another.

And yet...

He was the friend, perhaps the *only* friend of Denise Sturbridge. Bambi. She was a lost little girl pretending to be a jaded woman of the stage and streets. Donny was probably the only 'safe' man in her world. The only one who didn't want to plunder her silky loins or sexualize her beyond her years. And maybe she was an equally safe zone for him. Nonjudgmental, a kindred innocent in a corrupt world.

Bambi wasn't my client any more than Donny was. The unnamed woman from Limbus had hired me to find her. Donny was a side-effect of that search.

And yet...

My brain is wired in a certain way. I know that some of it has to do with my Benandanti heritage—we're pack animals, and you always protect the pack. But I'd like to think that I would have some approximation of that sensibility even if I was a normal man. The desire to protect the pack, to protect anyone who can't protect themselves. When I take on a client it's like they become part of my family, part of my pack. I will do absolutely anything, go to extreme lengths to protect what's mine.

But Bambi and Donny weren't mine. They weren't part of my pack.

Were they? Did the protection I afforded clients extend to people like them? Or was what I was feeling merely the normal outrage a moral person feels in the face of a demonstration of so clearly an immoral act?

Inside my head the wolf howled.

Aloud I said, "No."

I removed my cell phone and used it to take several photos of the symbol, and immediately forwarded them to a woman I knew at the University of Pennsylvania. An anthropologist who'd helped me on another case involving ritual symbols.

Then I backed out of the room, turned in the hall and leaned my forehead against the wall.

Shit.

Who was this maniac?

I looked down at the Club Dante card in my hand. I removed the business card for the stockbroker, Daniel Meyers.

That place and that man were tied to Bambi.

Somebody was going to give me some answers.

I only hoped those answers led me to the monster who tore the skin from these young people. sixteen girls, one boy. I knew that the girls were all prostitutes, but in my heart they were all children. Innocents. The damaged and discarded ones. A lot of them were victims of abuse at home, or from shattered homes. Drugs was one way out, a way to blunt the jagged edges of the pain and self-loathing. Hooking bought more drugs and it completed the cycle of destruction that often began at home and ended on the streets. When I thought of them as 'innocent' I didn't mean pure. Some of them were willing participants in their own destruction, but I've found that few people are truly self-destructive. Usually self-immolation of the moral kind is an end result, a skill learned from others.

For seventeen of those lost souls there was absolutely nothing I could do. Even revenge or managing to get the killer arrested wouldn't cloth them in their lost skin or breathe life into their empty lungs. Nothing I did would make their hearts beat again or coax a smile onto their dead mouths.

However, Bambi might still be alive.

Out there.

Somewhere.

At Club Dante?

I was going to have to find out.

Donny Falk hung on the wall and I couldn't take him down. Maybe the cops could find some evidence in all that gore. I couldn't risk disturbing that process. But there was something I could do.

I closed my eyes and drew in all of the scents of this place. Identifying Donny's, filing it away. Separating out Bambi's. Discarding all of the neutral smells—food, clothing, all of that. Then picking through the commingled animal smells.

Donny didn't have any pets.

The only animal smells had been left by people.

There were two smells that were stronger than the others. Fresh and pungent. Male smells. Not Big and Tall. Other male scents.

I catalogued them the way my grandmother taught me. If I smelled them again, even months from now, I'd know them.

Not one scent, but two.

Two killers?

Those smells were both in the killing room.

Two killers.

There was nothing else to learn here, so I wiped off the wall where I'd leaned my head, smudged any footprints I'd left on the floor, pulled the door shut as I left, and wiped the doorknob.

I walked down the fire stairs with every outward appearance of calm.

Appearances are so incredibly deceptive.

* * *

The offices of Dunwoody-Kraus-Vitalli were in Center City, but by the time I got down there it was after five. I stood at the receptionist's desk and tried to look affable, upscale and charming. In the parking garage I'd changed out of my oversized Vikings jacket and put on a three-button Polo shirt. Like most working P.I.'s, I have all sorts of clothes in my trunk. I combed my hair and tucked a pair of Wayfarers into the vee of the shirt.

The receptionist was a snooty brunette with too much eye-makeup and too little warmth.

"Mr. Meyers has left for the day," she said.

"Ah, damn," I said mildly and started to turn away, then paused, snapping my fingers. "Hey, did Mike say he was going to the club tonight?"

The receptionist lifted one eyebrow about a quarter of an inch. My attitude and apparent familiarity with Meyers, along with the reference to a club, was at war with the fact that she didn't know me from a can of paint.

"I...think he said something," she said evasively.

It was enough.

"Cool," I said. "I'll catch him there."

"He may call in. I'll tell him you stopped by, Mister . . . ? "

I grinned. "Wolf," I said.

"Very well, Mr. Wolf."

I gave her a smile and a wink and headed for the elevators. Wolf.

Sometimes I crack myself up.

* * *

Two calls came in while I was on my way south to Club Dante.

The first was Jonatha Corbiel-Newton, the anthropologist at University of Pennsylvania.

"Hey, doc," I said. "Thanks for getting back to me so fast."

"No problem. You caught me in my office grading papers."

"You get the images?"

"I did. Where did you take them?"

"They're attached to a case. Something I'm working on right now."

"Are these from a crime scene?"

I was careful to make sure that Donny wasn't in the shots I'd forwarded. "What makes you ask?"

"Well...it rather looks like the medium used to paint the symbol is blood."

"Pretty sure it's paint," I lied.

"It's very dark and viscous-looking."

"Red poster paint. That tempura stuff."

"Uh huh." She clearly didn't believe me, but then again I hadn't contacted her because she was an idiot.

Even so, I sidestepped the topic. "Is that an astrological symbol?"

She took a moment before answering. "Not precisely. It has cosmological connections, but it isn't a chart for any of the common astrologies. It's not the zodiac or the Chinese astrological grouping. It doesn't represent planets, animals or aspects of the natural world."

"Okay, but—."

"However I *do* recognize it."

"Ah."

"It's a symbol used by a group who call themselves the Order of Melchom."

"The who of who?"

"Order of Melchom. There are several versions of the group, some new and some very old. The new groups vary between covens of modern neo-pagans and RPG-ers."

"Who?'

"Role playing gamers. Like Dungeons and Dragons. Those groups have adopted thousands of names and symbols from various arcane sources and used them as backstory for their games. It's all over the Net."

"I'm pretty sure this wasn't posted by geeks playing games," I said. "You said the others were neo-pagans? Do you mean witches?"

"Well, wiccan, of one kind or another. Not the white-energy wiccans, though. This symbol is tied to dark energy."

"You mean evil?"

"Evil is relative. Most modern pagans view the universal forces as white and black, light and dark, or positive and negative."

It wasn't quite the way I saw things, but I kept that to myself.

"You said there was another reference," I said. "Something older? What's that?"

"In Biblical terms, Melchom is often cited as a variation of a god worshipped by the Ammonites, Phoenicians and Canaanites. The more common name is Moloch, which is itself another name for 'king', The worship of Moloch was brutal."

"In what way?"

"In sacrificial ways," said Jonatha. "Devotees practiced a particular kind of propitiatory child sacrifice in which parents gave up their children."

I had to clear my throat before I asked, "What *kind* of sacrifice?"

"The biblical and historical records vary. Most likely the children were burned alive. There's a reference to that in the Book of Leviticus, but other texts include plenty of references to various kinds of mutilation that include a 'sacrifice of the flesh'."

"Which is what?" I asked, though I thought I already knew.

"The sacrificed children were very carefully skinned so that they would be 'unclothed to the soul' and still alive when given up to Moloch."

The day outside was bright and there were puffy white clouds in the gorgeous blue sky. All of that didn't belong in a world, in any world, in which this conversation was a part. I told myself that, but the bright clouds and the flawless sky mocked me for my naiveté. Lovely skies have looked down upon every despicable thing we humans have done. What's truly naïve is to think that horrors are always hidden away in shadows.

"This Moloch sounds like a charmer," I said.

"He is. He's nasty and he's fierce. The ancients considered him one of the greatest warriors of the fallen angels." I heard her rustling book pages. "John Milton wrote this about him in *Paradise Lost…*

"…MOLOCH, horrid King besmear'd with blood

Of human sacrifice, and parents tears,

Though, for the noise of Drums and Timbrels loud,

Their children's cries unheard that passed through fire

To his grim Idol."

"Nice."

"There's more," she said. "Milton listed him among the chief of Satan's angels, and he gives a speech at the Parliament of Hell to argue for war against God."

"He's an angel?"

"Depending on which source you read," she said, "he's either a fallen angel, a god, or a demon. In his aspect as Melchom, he's the accountant for hell. He holds the purse strings to all of the Devil's gold, and he inspires men to strive for wealth, often by any means necessary. He's a monster in all of his aspects, really."

And that fast something went skittering across my brain. A demon worshipped by men striving for money.

"Sam—?" asked Jonatha Corbiel-Newton. "You still there?"

"Yeah."

"Is any of this useful to you?"

"Christ," I said, "I hope not."

Seventeen skinned teenagers. 'Hope' was a pretty vain luxury.

"What have you gotten yourself into?"

"I'm not sure, doc. I'm still blundering my way through it." I paused. "Tell me something, though…are there any *modern* cults of Moloch? Does anyone still believe this sort of thing?"

She was a long time answering. "Back when I first began studying anthropology I would have said no unreservedly."

"But now?"

"Now I'm not so sure. The more I get out of the office and into the field so I can see what people are actually out there doing, and practicing...I'm not so sure. Especially lately."

"Why lately?"

"It's the world, Sam. There's no peace anywhere. Wars everywhere, the economy falling apart, such extreme political divisiveness, even the return of class wars. People are scared, they're angry and they're desperate." She paused again. "These days people are looking for something to change the way things are going. They're looking for an edge to help them get through all of this upheaval and carnage."

"Geez," I said with a small laugh, "so much for the detached scientist."

She laughed, too, but it was thin and false. "Objectivity is taking as serious a beating as idealism these days."

I saw my exit coming up and drifted off of I-95.

"Sam...what *are* you into?"

"As of right now, Jonatha," I said, "it beats the shit out of me. I've got too much of the wrong information and not nearly enough of the right kind."

"Sam...," she said hesitantly, "that wasn't tempura paint in that picture, was it?"

I drummed my fingers on the knobbed arc of the steering wheel as I waited for the light at the end of the exit ramp to turn from red to green.

"Thanks for the info, doc," I said. "I owe you a steak dinner."

Before she could reply to that I hung up.

The light turned green and I drove on.

Moloch. Melchom.

An ancient cult that involves sacrifices of flesh to an ancient god. Or demon. Or fallen angel. Or whatever the fuck he was.

A sacrifice of the flesh.

How in the big yellow fuck did that make any kind of sense? This wasn't ancient Israel. This wasn't medieval Europe. This was Phila-damn-delphia.

Then I thought about the stockbroker. Daniel Meyers. He was almost certainly a college graduate. I wondered how old he was, and if he used to belong to a fraternity. I worked some frat hazing cases before. Some of those clowns went way over the line. Branding each other, lots of ritual behavior, beatings. Even rape.

Could a group of frat brothers have crossed a harder line? Was this some kind of brotherhood thing? A Skull and Bones thing, or something worse?

That felt both wrong and right at the same time.

Either way, I was still shooting in the dark.

* * *

Club Dante was a big block nothing of a building from the outside. Tall, stuccoed walls, a pitched roof covered in faux terra cotta tiles, and massive wooden doors that would have looked better on the front of a medieval castle. Twelve feet high, wrapped in bands of black wrought-iron, and lined with chunky studded bolt-heads. The parking lot was behind a fence and a pair of armed guards worked the entrance. I parked across the street and studied them through the telephoto lens of a digital camera. The guards had that thin-lipped, lantern-jawed, unsmiling look of ex-military and possibly ex-special forces. Tough men, and from the way they moved and worked it was pretty clear that they were too good for the job they were doing. You don't hire guys like that to check cars into a strip club parking lot, not even a very expensive strip club parking lot.

Hmm.

The cars were interesting, though. Nothing that looked more than two years old, and nothing that had a sticker price under fifty g's. Some of them were way above that mark, too. Lots of sports cars. That made a certain kind of statement. The kind of guys who over-paid to come to a place like this were the kind who wanted everyone to know—or think—they had a big dick. Expensive clothes, ten-thousand-dollar wristwatches, hand-sewn shoes, nothing that was ever off the rack, and cars that cost more than my education were all ways of saying look at me and bow to my dick. It was the equivalent of attaching a fire hose to a tank of testosterone and hosing down everyone around them.

And because they made so damn much money, and money really is power in almost every way that matters in this world, everyone with less money dropped down and kissed their privileged asses.

For a whole lot of reasons I am less inclined to kowtow to assholes like that.

Maybe that's why I'm always broke. I won't play those kinds of games and I've never felt any urge to stand in a crowd of moneyed jackasses and pass around a golden ruler while we all measured our johnsons.

I drove slowly around the building, studying the fence from all sides. It was a tall chain-link affair with coils of stainless-steel razor wire along the top. Very inviting. There was no back gate and, as far as I could tell, only a single locked and alarmed red fire door. Odd for a building that size. Couldn't possibly have passed code, which suggested that the owners were greasing the right palms.

There was movement among the parked cars and I saw another armed guard on foot patrol, walking a brute of a Doberman on a leash. Ninety pounds of sinew, muscle and attitude. Black and brown, with a bobbed tail and devil ears. As my car drifted past, the Doberman came suddenly to point and focused all of its senses on me. He couldn't see me through the smoked windows of my car, but he *knew* that I was there, just as he knew that I wasn't right.

Dogs always react to me. The ones who aren't alphas tuck their tails between their legs and want to lick my hand. People always smile and tell me that I'm a real dog person.

Yeah, in a way.

The alphas are always instantly wary of me. The ones who are alphas but haven't been trained for combat or patrol will keep their distance and watch me with wary eyes. If I push it I can get them to roll to me, but I seldom want to do that because some of them don't reclaim their mojo afterward. I like dogs, so breaking their will isn't high on my to-do list.

Alphas with guard dog training are a different matter. We've had some issues in the past. Their training is sometimes so intense that they will make choices they wouldn't make in the wild. I'm one-seventy, which means that when I do the change, the wolf is one-seventy, too. That's a lot of wolf. Even the biggest gray wolf is only about a hundred pounds. I'm closer to a dire wolf, the old prehistoric species. Their top range was one seventy. My grandmother thinks that we have dire wolf genes. I don't know. Maybe I'll get that checked one day, if I can figure out how to get a DNA lab to do it without freaking them too much, or outing myself.

When I'm face to face with a trained attack dog, there's usually trouble. I hate to kill a dog. I'll play slice and dice with a person before I'll open up a dog. Yeah, I know, a psychologist could really have fun with that, but there it is.

That Doberman had the kind of focused, barely suppressed aggression that let me know that it wouldn't turn belly-up for me. If I wolfed out, then he'd make a run at me. And I'd have to kill him for it.

Club Dante wasn't filling me with feelings of joy and puppies. Way too much security, the presence of a certain kind of money, and a definite connection to the missing girl. None of that added up to comforting math.

On the other hand it didn't necessarily add up to involvement in seventeen brutal murders. It was, however, the only lead I had.

And in a way that was only semi-rational it *smelled* right.

When I stopped at the light I fished in my pocket for the red membership card. I sniffed it, but all I smelled was that guy Gunther. It was possible that by now he'd called to say that I'd taken the card from him. Was that the reason for the heavy security?

No, I decided. The patrols here had a lived in look. I was pretty sure this was their regular security.

Hoping that things wouldn't play out that way, I drove four blocks away, parked, hailed a cab and had the taxi drop me at the club. I couldn't risk that the guards would have a list of all of the tag numbers of regular members.

With my Wayfarers on and just enough indolent slouch in my walk, I strolled past the gate and entered through the massive front doors. They had a doorman in a tuxedo right inside. He was roughly the size of Godzilla and I had to lean back to look up at him. He gave me a quick up-and-down appraisal and shifted to stand between me and the door.

"May I help you, sir?"

I pulled the card out and held it up between two fingers. "Been a long day," I said casually, "and I hear a martini calling to me."

He was well-trained. His scowl became an agreeable smile and he stepped aside to allow me access to a key-swipe station mounted to one side of a second set of doors. I kept a bland smile on my face but held my breath as I fitted the card into the slot and swiped it.

The little red light on the station blinked from red to green. There was a faint *click* behind the door, and the doorman's smile became less artificial and more genuine. He pushed the door open for me.

"Have a glorious evening, sir," he said.

"Count on it," I assured him as I stepped through the doors and entered the belly of the beast.

* * *

The club was pretty much as you'd expect. It was shadowy as a closet, an effect insured by low-wattage indirect lights and lots of dark wood. The motif was, apparently, early dungeon. Wrought iron fixtures, low couches, rough stone walls, rich draperies hung from brass rods. As I passed one of these I glanced at it and then gave it a double-take. What I first thought was a hunting scene of mounted riders, a dog pack and a bunch of frightened deer was actually something a lot less enchanting. The riders all wore burgundy-colored robes, the dogs looked half-starved and ravenous, and the 'prey' were men and women scurrying on all fours. Naked, some with antlers tied to their heads. The tapestry was old and woven from thick, rich threads, so it was hard to tell much about the people on all fours...except that the more I stared at them the younger they all looked.

I said, very softly, "Uh oh."

I made myself turn away from the tapestry to study the room.

There were probably forty men in there. Most of them were dressed in expensive suits. A few had loosened their ties; a few others wore Polo shirts like mine. None of the customers were women. This was clearly a men's club. Not sure I'd go as far as 'gentlemen', though.

The wait-staff were women of a type. Busty, leggy, barely dressed and very young. If any of them was older than nineteen then I was the Tsar of Russia.

I wondered how many of them were even eighteen.

For a few seconds I debated short-cutting this whole thing by making a call to the cops and Child Protection Services. Maybe the press, too. Blow it open. Pedophilia is not a popular crime, not for the common guy on the street. People will sometimes look the other way if politicians or white collar criminals run money scams, or take kick-backs, but when it comes to sex with kids, my fellow citizens have a very admirable tendency toward pitchforks and torches. Look what happened with Penn State. Look what's happening with all those priests.

But what could I prove?

I mean, right here, right now, what could I prove? That there are *possibly* underage girls showing their breasts and serving drinks? The news might like that, but I doubted I could get a warrant happening.

And if Bambi was here, then it might encourage the bad guys to dispose of any evidence. That girl was evidence.

So I drifted through the place and pretended to be a part of the debauch. I obtained a drink as protective coloration. I exchanged a few words with other 'members'. We talked sports, we talked politics. We talked stocks and investments.

Nobody mentioned Moloch. Nobody mentioned dead girls.

I noticed that nobody used names. They didn't offer or ask names.

There was a small stage at the far end of the cavernous main room. When I'd come in, a redhead was beginning a veil dance. She discarded about a dozen of them until she was stark naked. There was some mild applause and she gathered up the gossamer scraps and trotted lightly off. Then the lights changed and I saw a lot of the men shift their attention more seriously to the stage. Two women came out. Twins with masses of blond hair. They wore stylized bullfighter costumes. Then a pair of very large Latinos came out, both of them wearing bull horns. A small band began playing dramatic bullfight music, and the foursome launched into a variation of the *paso doble*. But instead of the man acting as bullfighter and the woman, with her swirling skirts, acting as his cape, the men were the bulls and the women the toreadors. They were all pretty good dancers and for a moment I thought that this was a surprising bit of real art in this place. But then the horns of the bulls caught on pieces of the women's costumes. With each lunge and twist the clothing was torn away, gradually revealing a lot of flesh and turning the women from bullfighters to helpless victims. The bullish men began stripping away sections of their costumes, particularly their pants. I saw where this was going and turned away. I like sex as much as the next four guys, but the theme of this had rolled down hill into a presentation of female defeat and use. I wanted no part of that.

There was a wooden apron that ran around the outside of the main room, with several hallways and doors leading off from there. As the action onstage grew more heated and the club's members became more focused upon it, I faded to the back and began looking for a door I could open.

Movement to my left made me pause and I saw one of the men get up and walk toward the back of the big room. He threw a few glances over his shoulder at the increasingly X-rated action on stage, but I got the impression he was leaving. He didn't head for the door, though. Instead he made for a hallway that cut off out of sight on the far corner. A few seconds later another man followed. And another.

It wasn't an exodus. Only a small percentage of the customers vanished down that hallway. The rest were staring with total attention at the sweaty spectacle on the stage. The timing of it all seemed odd to me. That many guys couldn't need to use the bathroom at the same time; an assumption supported by the fact that the men didn't return. As I moseyed nonchalantly in that direction I could see that there was another guard just inside the mouth of the hallway, and beyond him was a door with the same key-swipe station as outside.

If I had spider sense it would have been tingling.

I watched a couple of guys to see what the routine was. They approached the hall, flashed something to the guard, then swiped their keycard and passed through the locked door. It took me three or four times before I realized that all they were showing was their red cards. Nice.

I waited for a moment when no one else was heading that way and I stepped into the hallway, flashed my red card, got a terse nod from the guard, swiped my card, and stepped through the doorway.

That easy.

As soon as I was inside I met a second security guard. He was even bigger than the Godzilla at the front door. Where do they get these guys? Thugs'R'Us?

He smiled at me. "Good evening, brother."

Since I didn't know what else to say, I returned his smile as I walked over to him. "Am I late? Have they started yet?"

He frowned and looked at his watch. "Uh . . . no, brother, it doesn't start for another—."

He stopped talking when I screwed the barrel of my Glock into his ear.

People tend to do that.

"Be smart," I told him.

He froze into a statue, eyes wide, sweat bursting from the pores on his face.

"Where's the girl?" I asked. I kept my voice low and level, letting the gun do all of my shouting for me.

I had no idea if he knew anything about anything, but sometimes you go on balls and instinct and a flip of a coin. Most of the times you waste your time. Once in a while though...

"She's still upstairs," he said.

I pressed the barrel harder against him. "Is she alive?"

"Who are you?" he asked.

"Her fairy godfather. Answer the fucking question."

He hedged. "Yes," he said. But there was too much uncertainty in his voice. "They're getting her ready."

It was a simple statement that in any other circumstances might have meant something relatively innocent. But it filled my mind with terrible images and awful potential.

"How many are up there?"

His eyes shifted away and I knew he was about to lie to me. Before he could push us both out onto a ledge, I leaned close and whispered. "I don't mind blowing your head off, slick. You have one chance to walk out of this, but you're on a short fuse here."

"I don't know," he said. "God's honest truth. I only came on shift twenty minutes ago and some of them were already up there. Only about a dozen members have checked in."

A dozen was the number of men I'd seen leaving the action outside.

I moved in front of him and put the barrel under his chin. I wanted to see his eyes better when I asked the next question.

"Do you know what they're going to do to her?"

His mouth opened but it made a lot of shapes before he finally spoke, trying on different answers, seeing if any of them fit well enough.

"I'm just a grunt, man," he said at last. "I just work the door."

Jonathan Maberry

I leaned close to him and took his scent, sniffing at his face and chest the way a dog would. The gun stayed in place as I sniffed and I could see the total confusion on his face. He must have thought I was some nutcase. Sniffing like a dog.

I smelled fear on him. I smelled booze and tobacco and hashish. I smelled sweat and sex and blood.

And I smelled Bambi.

Not her blood scent.

Her *living* scent. The subtle perfume of hormones and skin oils and glands. The scent I'd picked up at her apartment.

He'd been close enough to her to get that scent on his clothes.

No blood, though.

No blood.

It was the only reason I didn't kill him right there and then.

But it was a damn close decision.

Instead I kneed him in the nuts as hard as I could. His eyes bulged, his mouth puckered into a tiny Oh and he caved forward, cupping his balls. As he bent down over the pain, I clubbed him on the back of the neck, right where the spine enters the skull. It jerks the brain stem and short-circuits the nerve conduction. In the movies James Bond chops a guy there and the man goes out and wakes up ten minutes later with a headache. I'm not James Bond and this wasn't the movies. He dropped like he'd been pole-axed, and when he woke up—maybe half an hour from now—he'd puke, he'd be dizzy and dazed, and he'd probably have neck problems for years.

Fuck it.

Behind me the door clicked as someone else used their keycard. I lunged toward a set of light switches and slapped them down just as the door opened. A man-shape filled the doorway, pausing in confusion at the unexpected darkness. I grabbed a fistful of his tie and jerked him into the hall, then kicked the door shut. The guy was a businessman in a nice wool suit. About my age, a little bigger, a whole lot richer.

I punched him in the throat.

He dropped, gagging and coughing, clawing at his neck.

The security guard said, "Hey!"

That was all I allowed him to say. I grabbed him by the tie and jerked that as tight as a noose while putting my foot as far through his nutsack as I could manage.

He said, "Oooooof," in a high, squeaky voice. I used the necktie to pull him into the hallway. I took a one-second look to see if anyone in the main hall noticed any of this, but both couples onstage were going at it loud and weird, and the band's speakers were cranked all the way up to eleven. No one saw shit.

I slammed the door, pivoted and kicked the key-swipe station off the wall.

The businessman was thrashing around on the floor trying to breathe. The security guy was on his knees, eyes popped nearly out of his head, face purple. I gave him a little bit of a shuffle side-thrust and he flopped back into bad dreams. Then I turned and kicked the businessman in the jewels and in the face. He groaned, rolled over and passed out.

It was suddenly very quiet in the hallway.

I was doing some real damage here and a small splinter of my mind was watching, aghast. The rest of me was remembering the faceless faces of the sixteen dead women, and the boy who'd been stripped of his life and nailed to a wall. And remembering the smell of Bambi, still alive, on the one guard's clothes.

So, yeah, sure, compassion and all that. But not now and not for these guys. They were lucky I hadn't wolfed out and really gone to town on them, and believe me that was a very strong temptation.

I paused to listen. If anyone upstairs heard the commotion they weren't reacting. There was music drifting down the stairs. Drums and some kind of pipes. Very tribal. Voices, too. Some kind of chanting.

Ever since I spoke with Jonatha Corbiel-Newton my overactive brain had been conjuring a series of ugly pictures of what was going on here at Club Dante. I suppose the most dominant one was of frat boys going through some bullshit pseudo-ancient ritual before gang-banging Bambi and carving her skin off, all in some crazy belief that Moloch—fallen angel, demon or half-ass ancient god—was going to make them rich.

I shoved the businessman against the door and then dragged the unconscious guards over. That was more than a quarter ton of dead weight. If anyone tried to get the door open they could manage it, but not in the next five minutes.

Better for them if they didn't.

Then I spun around and ran up the stairs.

* * *

I took the stairs two at a time, fast but quiet, thinking to myself, *Hold on, kid. Hold on.*

There was one more door at the top and one more key-swipe. I chopped the card down through it and then made myself slow down. I eased the door open and slipped quietly inside. The chamber was big, as wide as downstairs though with fifteen-foot high ceilings. Lights in recessed alcoves provided minimal illumination, but overall the room was dark. Shadows lay draped across everything. I squeezed my eyes shut for a moment to goose along my night vision.

When I opened them I saw that there were at least twenty men in the room. Most of them were clustered around an open cabinet as one of the staff handed out robes of dark red silk. The men were stripping out of their expensive suits and then pulling the robes on over their naked skin. The expectation of what was about to happen must have been electric because some of the guys had hard-ons. I didn't need to see that.

Music blared from at least a dozen speakers mounted high on the walls. It was the tribal stuff I'd heard downstairs, and the chanting was actually part of it. The guys here weren't chanting. No idea what language the chant was in. Not Latin. Not anything I'd ever heard.

I faded into deep shadows thrown by a tall wooden carving. When I glanced up at it I was surprised to see that it was a bull. Kind of. The body was human, but the shoulders were massively overdeveloped and the head was that of a massive bull with long horns. I glanced around to see that there were other statues like this one. Not exactly like it, and some made out of stone or metal, but all of a gigantic bull-headed man. A minotaur? I wasn't sure. My knowledge of mythology was pretty thin.

Another of the bull statures dominated the center of the chamber. At first I thought it was made of polished brass, but the more I stared at it the more I realized that it was gold. Maybe it was gold paint or gold plate, but somehow I got the impression that there was a serious amount of actual gold there.

And in a strange way it fit with the whole Moloch vibe. A demon who was the treasurer of hell. A creature who the ancient

Ammonites and Phoenicians believed would guide certain men toward wealth. Would men like these—the financial kings of this city—have a false idol, one painted with sham gold?

No, I didn't think so.

Somehow that made me a little more afraid.

This was looking a lot less like a frat stunt that got too serious and more like an actual cult. Or, I guess . . . a religion.

Did people really believe in something like this? *Could* they?

I mean . . . a cult that required human sacrifices wasn't something you simply joined. Every man here risked life imprisonment or death row. At the very least this was felony murder, kidnapping, conspiracy, and a laundry list of capital crimes. I don't care what kind of big-ticket lawyer they trotted out, everyone even remotely attached to this would go down for the hardest of hard falls.

And yet here they were, putting on robes, waving their chubbys around as they got ready to commit *another* murder.

What was the payoff that made this kind of risk worth it?

I mean . . . how could one member of the club ever sell this kind of thing to a friend?

Shit.

The thing that really chilled my blood, though, was the art on the walls. Spaced at regular intervals around the room were two-by-three foot posters in wooden frames. Women's faces. All very young, all very pretty. Each of them looked absolutely terrified, some looked like they were in terrible agony when the photos were taken.

I counted them.

There were sixteen pictures. And empty frames for another ten.

I could only see a couple of the faces—and they were strangers, but I'm pretty sure I'd seen them before, but in pictures I'd seen none of them had their skin. Were these trophy shots, taken during rape or torture? Or at the moment of their deaths?

The wolf began to growl, low and with dark intent, deep inside my brain.

One man, a very tall, thin guy with prematurely white hair, kept glancing toward the door through which I'd entered and then down at his watch. He was probably wondering where the rest of his fellow worshippers were.

My time was running out. Bambi's, too.

So where was . . . ?

Suddenly a curtain in the back of the chamber opened and two burly guards came out, supporting Bambi between them. She was dressed in a little tunic that was made from the sheerest of fabrics and belted by a gold sash. The girl was able to walk, but even from across the room I could see that she was totally whacked out. Drugged on something. She seemed to float along with the men, her mouth slack, eyes glazed.

The gathered men all turned and began applauding. Some of them were still naked. They beamed smiles at her and gave her a thunderous great ovation, pounding their hands together with enthusiasm that was clearly genuine. One of them started a chant and within seconds the others joined in. Someone cut the tribal music and chants to allow this new mantra to dominate the room.

No real surprise what they chanted.

"Moloch . . . Moloch . . . Moloch . . ."

Balls.

But they were chanting like frat boys. "Moe-*lock* . . . Moe-*lock* . . ."

Made it sound a little silly, but for all that it was still scary as shit.

The man with the white hair nodded to the guards and they half-led, half-pushed Bambi up a short flight of steps in front of the golden statue. Then they used red silk scarves to tie her wrists and ankles to small rings set into the statue.

The gathered men applauded this, too. They were a happy bunch. They laughed and elbowed each other and hurried to pull on their robes.

White-hair looked at his watch again and spoke to one of the guards, nodding toward the door as he did so. The guard immediately began heading toward the door.

My time was up. If the guard went downstairs he'd see the three guys I'd trashed.

What choice did I have?

I stepped out of the shadows and pointed the gun at the center of the crowd. As I did so I yelled to the whole crowd, very loud and very clearly.

"Shut the fuck up."

They did.

They actually froze in place, their chant snapped off like someone had hit a switch, leaving their mouths hanging open. White-hair pointed a finger at me.

"Who the fuck are you?"

It was a reasonable question.

Wasn't one I wanted to answer, though.

"Cut the girl down," I said.

They didn't. They also didn't move or speak. The whole bunch of them simply stood there and stared at me. So I swung my gun toward White-hair, aiming it at his face.

"Cut her down," I repeated. "Right now."

He didn't even bother looking at the gun. Instead he looked at me and a slow smile formed on his face.

Smiles are not what you want to see when you have someone in your sights. You want to see fear and a cooperation born from a desire for self-preservation.

"Who are you?" he asked.

"The fuck does that matter to you?"

"You come in here, waving a gun, disrupting our religious services—we should at least know who you are and why you're here."

"I'm just here for the girl," I told him. "I'm taking her out of here and I'll blow a hole in anyone who so much as blinks."

The rude son of a bitch actually blinked. Deliberately and repeatedly. Smiling all the time.

"You're not a policeman," he said.

"I could be."

He shook his head. "We own the police."

Ah.

"And you're not FBI."

"You own them, too?"

Another shake. "No...but they're too smart to show up alone."

"Now that's just mean," I said.

He chuckled. So did I. The other guys didn't laugh, though there were a few tentative smiles. Most of them were still trying to figure out what was going on. Me, too. Only White-hair seemed to be comfortable with the way things were falling out. I didn't find that comforting.

I cut a look at Bambi. She was still on her feet, but the glazed look in her eyes was intensifying. I wondered if they shot her up with something just before bringing her out. It looked like the drug was still hitting her system. She tugged at her bonds but instead of being alarmed at being restrained she seemed only mildly surprised.

"Look, chief," I said to White-hair, "let's cut the shit. Cut the girl down now."

"Or—?"

"I thought we covered that. I shoot you and take her anyway."

He nodded at my gun. "That's a Glock 17 with an optional floor plate, which gives you nineteen rounds instead of the standard seventeen. That's nineteen shots max and there are more than twenty of us, not counting the guards. Even if you dropped one man with each bullet—and I think we can both agree that's unlikely—the rest of us will drag you down."

"Maybe."

"Definitely," he said.

"You won't live to see it happen."

"I don't care."

He looked like he genuinely didn't.

"Bet you'll feel different when your brains are on the wall."

He shook his head. "If I die then I ascend to the golden halls of Lord Moloch where I will sit on a jeweled throne and have a thousand slaves bowing at my feet."

"Or, you'd be worm meat in a box."

One of the security guards chose that moment to go for his gun. He was to my right and probably thought he had a reach chance.

I pivoted and shot him in the chest. I don't care how big your pecs are or how much Dianabol you take, a nine millimeter slug is going to punch your ticket. The round went in beside his sternum and punched its way out through a shoulder bone, taking pieces of his heart with it. Blood sprayed some of the gathered men.

The guard dropped right there and then.

The crowd looked down at the blood on their clothes and skin, and immediately began rubbing at it. I thought they were freaking out and trying to rub it off. But that wasn't it. They were smearing it into their skin, smiling as they did so, laughing as if they were in ecstasy.

The rest of the crowd...*cheered.*

The second guard was also cheering as he pulled his gun. He was standing five feet from Bambi, and I swung around and put one into his chest and a second through the bridge of his nose. The back of his head exploded, splattering the girl and the golden statue with brain tissue and blood.

The crowd began yelling, laughing, applauding.

I turned back to White-hair, who was clapping his hands together with slow irony.

Around us the cheers were turning into a new chant of *Moloch...Moloch*.

White-hair said, "Do you have any idea what's happening here? Do you have any idea what you've stepped into? What you've interrupted?"

"Some," I said. "Bunch of dickheads making human sacrifices to an ancient god in the hopes of getting some divine assistance with your stock portfolios."

He beamed at me. "That's wonderful. Oversimplified and a little naïve, but wonderful."

"So, fill in the blanks," I suggested.

"Why? Are you hoping to join us?"

"I don't know. Let me hear the recruitment speech."

He spread his arms and turned toward the golden statue. "You said it, friend. We're praying to the god Moloch. We sacrifice to him as man was instructed to do—a sacrifice of the children, made in blood and flesh and flame. In return he guides us and protects us and fills our pockets with gold."

"Uh huh. Tell me, sport," I said, "how many of those sacrifices are your *own* kids?"

He snorted. "Our own? Do we look crazy?"

"Pretty much."

He glanced around. "Okay, sure, in the moment, but you came in at the wrong part of the show. If you'd been a little patient you'd have seen the main attraction."

"Which is what, you going all Hannibal Lecter on a teenager girl who can't defend herself? Excuse me but that's hardly a—"

"No," he said. "The life or death of that worthless slut is nothing. You're a man, you should understand that. She's a cow, a piece of meat. If you're here looking for her then you must know her history. A whore and a junkie whose life would never have mattered. If we hadn't given her the chance to *matter*, then she'd have wound up in a crack house giving two dollar blow jobs while marking time until disease and a cirrhotic liver took her down to the hell that is surely waiting for her."

"Oh, right, and you guys are the Salvation Army. Skinning her alive is the best way to save her soul."

"*Her* soul doesn't matter," he said, his smile flickering a bit. "She is a means to an end. Our god is appeased only through the offering of living flesh, and the only flesh that matters is that of the young. That is the pathway to glory. It is through such offerings that every man here—every devout believer in the majesty of Moloch—has become wealthy beyond his dreams." He scowled at me for a moment and shook his head. "You probably can't grasp this. You put on an expensive shirt and think that's going to make you look rich? You stink of poverty, of cheapness, of weakness, so this might all be beyond you."

"Maybe not."

He gave another shrug. "But we were all born to money. We deserve the good things we have. It's in our blood, in our breeding. We are the elite of this world."

The men all applauded this. Some of them gave each other high-fives.

"It is our right to take what we want," White-hair continued.

"Even if it means killing the innocent?"

He spat on the floor between us. "Innocent? That's a bullshit word and it doesn't mean a fucking thing. That girl and everyone like her is a parasite. It's because of people like her that our whole country is on the edge of economic collapse. She's a leech on the system, and who pays for her free food and medical care? Us! The very ones who actually make the money and whose skill and genius made America great in the first place. It's people like her—and you— who want to take it from us."

"Seriously," I said, "you want to turn this into a political rant? Now? With a gun in your face and your guards' brains on your shoes? That's where you're going with this?"

He stopped and cocked his head as if listening to a replay of his own words. Then he sighed.

"Sorry," he said. "I got caught up in the moment."

"Sure," I said.

"Where were we?"

"The girl. You were about to come to your fucking senses and let her go."

"Ah," he said, gesturing to a small table near the golden statue on which were various knives and scalpels. "No. I think I was going to invite you to watch our god accept the sacrifice of flesh and blood."

"I'm pretty sure we weren't going there."

Behind me fists began pounding on the door. They must have broken through into the hall downstairs. My time was up. His eyes flicked to the door and back to me, and his smile returned, brighter and broader than ever.

"Playtime's over," he said.

I shifted around to stand between Bambi and the crowd. White-hair turned with me, so I edged closer to him so he could get a better look at the barrel of my gun.

"You're right," I said. "We're done fucking around. I want you and all of your asshole buddies down on the floor, hands behind your heads, fingers laced. Last man done gets a bullet in the head."

Nobody moved. All the chanting died away and the room fell into silence except for the fists pounding on the door.

Bambi stirred and moaned.

White-hair smiled.

Behind me, Bambi suddenly screamed.

I whirled, bringing the gun up, expecting to see a guard or one of the men trying something fancy, maybe sneaking up behind me.

I wish that's what it was.

But it wasn't.

When I'd shot the second guard his blood had splattered all over the statue. As I turned I saw that almost all of it was gone.

It hadn't dripped or rolled off.

As I watched in absolutely stunned horror I saw the blood vanish as if it were being absorbed, pulled *into* the skin of the golden statue. Bambi screamed and screamed. Not because the blood was vanishing...but because the statue was moving.

Moving.

Moloch, the bull-headed god.

Moving.

Flexing its massive limbs, muscles rippling beneath a skin that glistened like polished gold but which was becoming real, tangible flesh. Still golden, but pulsing with life. Wherever the blood had touched it, the statue's surface became *alive*.

Behind me I heard White-hair say, "Behold the glory of Moloch. Behold the demon-god made flesh through a sacrifice of blood. Behold your death."

* * *

Bambi screamed and screamed.

And I screamed, too.

My mind reeled just as my feet staggered backward. This was impossible. This wasn't some fucked up frat stunt...these men had actually conjured a monster, a demon, from the darkness of the ancient world. It was real.

It was real.

The giant bull head was still immobile, but the blood-spattered chest expanded and the muscles of its abdomen rippled. Then from the open mouth of the statue an impossibly long tongue lolled out, uncoiling like a pale serpent until the tip of it touched Bambi's shoulder. Her whole body was speckled with blood, and the obscene tongue licked it up, drop by drop, hooking gobbets of meat and curling them back into that golden mouth.

The face—the solid metal mask of its face—*moved*. Jaws opened and eyes blinked once and again, losing the blank stare of a statue and flashing with hideous life. Its lips curled into a sneer that was part sensual delight in the taste of human blood and part in cruel expectation of a greater feast to come.

The gathered men once more began their chant.

"*Moloch...Moloch...Moloch...*"

White-hair laughed like a madman as the demon-god drew in a massive lungful of air and then let loose with a roar that was unlike anything I could ever imagine. It was so loud that it knocked me backward. I lost the gun and clapped my hands to my ears. Blood burst from my nose. I landed hard on the floor as the sound smashed me like a fist.

Then it stopped.

I gagged and rolled over onto hands and knees, vomiting onto the hardwood.

"*Moloch...Moloch...Moloch...*"

My ears were so badly damaged that the chant sounded like it came from the bottom of a deep well.

"*Moloch...Moloch...Moloch...*"

Out of the corner of my eye I saw White-face bend down to pick up my pistol. Beyond him the men in robes were crowding the table on which the knives were displayed. Bright steel seemed to sprout from every hand. There was a weird sound like bending metal as the demon-god Moloch began to move its massive limbs.

Bambi's screams were rising to the ultrasonic as the full horror of what was happening pushed through the protective haze of the drugs. Somewhere deep within that scream I could hear the lost sea-gull cry of a little girl. The desperate and utterly hopeless shriek of a child who is being used and used and who knows that no one will ever, could ever come to save her. It was the most horrible sound I'd ever heard. It was the sound of innocence being destroyed.

I think that's what did it.

Not the threat of the gun.

Not the men with their knives or the pounding of guards' fists on the door.

Not even the first earth-shaking footfall of the demon-god.

It was the sound of the lost child within the woman's scream.

It was primal.

Feral.

And in my mind, the wolf heard the scream and he—it—howled back in unbridled fury. The young of the pack were in danger, and the strongest of the pack had to answer. Had to respond.

Had to fight.

I transformed without knowing I was going to do it.

No...that's wrong. I transformed without resistance. All of me—man and wolf—*wanted* this. All of me needed this.

On one side of a broken second I was a man, smashed to the ground, broken and lost; and on the other side of that second I was the werewolf.

I rose from the floor just as White-hair raised the gun.

I saw the surprise in his eyes. The shock.

The fear.

The doubt.

Even with all of that he pulled the trigger.

Again and again. Each bullet found its target. In my chest. In my heart.

And it did him no damn good at all.

I leaped into the air, closing the fifteen foot distance between us in the space between his third and fourth shot. I took him with my front paws, claws extended. He exploded around me. Arms and legs and head.

His blood was a cloud of red mist that I flew through as I rushed toward the other men.

They had their knives.

They tried.

They tried.

But they might as well have turned their knives on themselves.

I filled the room with screams. Theirs. Bambi's. Mine.

They died around me. Beneath me. In me.

The room shook and I wheeled amid red carnage as the demon-god came toward me. Bambi was still tethered to him, tied wrist and ankle with red scarves. As he reached for me with one massive hand he reached for her with the other.

Most of him was flesh.

Some of him was still metal.

Whatever process of transformation was necessary for him to come from whatever hell he lived into the world of flesh and blood, it was not completed. Maybe there hadn't been enough of the guards' blood. Or maybe adult male blood was not enough. Maybe Moloch really needed the blood of a child sacrifice to gain his full power. Maybe that's why he reached for her, to feed his need, to create the bridge between his world and ours.

Maybe.

Maybe.

But who gives a fuck?

Bambi was still alive. And I was never more alive than I was in that moment. Fully the wolf. Without hesitation or resistance on my part. A monster, and reveling in that.

On the walls all around me were framed posters of women who had died. I could feel their eyes watching me. I looked at their faces. Recorded every image with the clarity of mind that is a gift of the wolf. Every face, every line, every curve, every scar and blemish. Sixteen beautiful girls, each of whom had been torn apart and had their blood and flesh fed to a monster.

An actual monster.

My ancestors, the Benandanti, fought evil. They fought monsters and demons. Until now I thought evil was a human thing. Entirely human. I thought the whole 'fighting monsters' thing was some kind of metaphor, a grandiose way of describing struggles with human corruption.

Moloch, by his fact, by his presence, by his reality, changed all of that. It made the unreal real.

It also made the stuff of nightmares real.

Demon-gods.

Fallen angels.

Blood sacrifices to conjure something impossible.

Gold made flesh.

Maybe being flesh was the only way Moloch could exist in this world. I don't know, I'm not a mystic, I don't do metaphysical questions. All I know is that if Moloch was flesh—or even partly flesh—then it meant that he belonged to this world. And this world has rules.

One of which is that all flesh is vulnerable.

With a howl as loud as the roar of the demon-god, I threw myself at Moloch, slashing at him with my claws.

The golden flesh was tough.

Damn tough.

But flesh is flesh.

I had claws as sharp as razors. I had all of the muscle given to me by whatever power or gene or curse created my family's bloodline.

I had the rage of a werewolf. A Benandanti.

A hound of God.

And I laid into that evil son of a bitch with everything I had.

Golden flesh opened as I raked him back and forth.

Red-gold blood splashed out, striking Bambi, who screamed and screamed. Hitting me in the face, in the mouth. I snarled and drank the blood down as I slashed.

Moloch roared in sudden pain and his surprise was awesome to see.

Maybe in all of his thousands of years of existence he'd never felt pain. Maybe he thought that pain was beyond him, that he was immune to it.

But he chose to be flesh. That's what he wanted from his worshippers. They killed so many girls to give him that gift.

And I used it against him.

I tore at him. I bit into his stomach and pulled out organs and meat. I covered the floor and the walls with the blood of a fallen angel.

It burned my mouth and throat.

I drank it anyway.

When the guards knocked down the door they found shattered pieces of a statue standing in a lake of molten gold. Bambi crouched on a table that had once been covered with knives. She hunkered down, arms wrapped around her head, unwilling and unable to witness this.

I stood in the center, in the hollow of what had been the chest of the bull-god, a golden lump of heart-shaped meat in my hands, muzzle buried in it, feasting.

The guards saw this. They pointed guns at me.

I raised my head and growled at them.

They dropped their guns and fled.

* * *

Later…

I'm not sure how much later.

I dropped Bambi at the E.R. of the closest hospital. I walked her in. She was catatonic. She had some minor burns from drops of molten gold. She couldn't speak, and the drugs were still in her system. I left her with nurses who tried to get me to tell them who she was, who I was, what had happened.

I walked away and found my car and drove back to my office.

That was six hours ago.

I showered in the tiny bathroom, then took the bottle of Pappy Van Winkle's 23-Year-Old bourbon back to my desk, poured a big glass, and drank it slowly. When it was gone I refilled it. And refilled it again.

Around midnight I fished for the card I'd found on my floor and laid it on my desk blotter.

Limbus, Inc.
Are you laid off, downsized, undersized?
Call us. We employ. 1-800-555-0606
How lucky do you feel?

How lucky did I feel?

Hard to say.

Hard to really know what to think.

I'd fought something that shouldn't exist. On the other hand, to most people I *was* something that shouldn't exist. Hang both of those on the wall and look at them.

Moloch.

Jesus.

But with all of that, there was something that hung burning in my mind.

After I'd let the wolf out, I'd looked at the faces of the sixteen murdered women. Those images were indelibly recorded in my mind. Every single detail. They were all strangers, women I'd only ever seen as skinned meat.

Except.

There was one face, one woman. A little more beautiful than all the others.

It was the kind of face that you read about. The kind of face that might have looked down at you from a movie screen if she'd been allowed to live, to grow up, to become what she'd wanted to be. Pale skin with pores so small it looked like she was carved out of marble; with good bones and full lips and only a single visible flaw. If you could call it a flaw. A small crescent-shaped scar on her cheek near the left corner of her mouth.

I thought about that face. It had been on a poster, screaming down at me, dying.

Maybe the cops would be able to match it against one of the sixteen bodies in morgues across the country. That scar, though, wouldn't be there. It had been stolen with her skin.

But I'd seen it.

Yeah, I'd seen that scar.

I reached out and touched the Limbus card. I traced each digit of the phone number.

If I called it, I wondered who would answer.

I wondered if anyone would answer.

I sipped some more of my bourbon and wondered about a lot of things.

My cell phone lay on the blotter next to the card. I looked at it.

I poured myself another drink.

And another.

Epilogue

It happened just as he had come to understand that it must. As Matthew turned the final page, as he left behind tales of sacrifices, of ancient gods, of unimaginable futures and beings that span time and space, it fell, fluttering almost, down to the table below, landing with the audible flop of thin, cream-colored card stock. Where had it hidden in the book he'd just read every page of? It didn't matter. All that mattered was what it said on the front. There, printed in thick black letters that were illuminated by the day's first rays of sunlight, was a name and a slogan that he didn't have to read to know.

Limbus, Inc.
Are you laid off, downsized, undersized?
We employ.
How lucky do you feel?

And that was it. No phone number. No email. No address. Nothing. He didn't need it. Matthew had only a moment to comprehend the words when the bell rang and the door to his shop opened.

The man stood in the doorway, outlined by the dawning glow of a Boston morning. He stood there on the threshold. He did not move forward. And he did not speak. It took a moment for Matthew to realize he was waiting on an invitation.

"Come in," he said, stuttering.

The man stepped out of the light, and somehow he was precisely what Matthew had expected. A proud face, marked by sharp features and an air of absolute authority. He wore a suit, nothing too fancy. Nothing that would stand out.

"Mr. Sellers," he said, "I am Recruiter Hawthorne. And I have a job for you."

As he crossed the short distance that separated the two men, Matthew shook his head.

"I don't understand."

Hawthorne smiled. "Ah, Mr. Sellers, let us not play games with one another. You know who I am, and you know for whom I work. I see you even have our business card."

Matthew glanced from the card to Hawthorne and shuddered.

"One of our other employees visited you yesterday. He left you that book." Hawthorne said, pointing down to the tattered manuscript that still sat on Matthew's desk.

"Templeton was an employee of yours?" Matthew said, truly not understanding. The frail man who had come into his store only a day before was terrified of something. Now Matthew knew what that something was.

"Of a sort, yes. We are all workmen in this world, don't you think? And if we do not always know exactly what the work entails—or even who pulls the strings behind the scenes—it is no great matter. I believe he presented you our offer, did he not?"

"Your offer? You mean you want this book published?"

Hawthorne reached down and rubbed his hand across the shabby cover of the manuscript. "It surprises you, does it? I suppose I can understand that. You think that we wish to hide our work from the world. Yes, it is true, I suppose—what we do, we tend to do in secret. But we do not wish to hide in the shadows. The whispers of our existence have grown too loud, and the curiosity of mankind is never satisfied. People will seek us out, and when they do there is no telling what trouble they may cause. No, Mr. Sellers, we hide best when we hide in the light. Make the story of Limbus one of fiction, one of myth, and one will no more look for us than they would the lands of Narnia or Middle-earth. But first, we need a publisher, Mr. Sellers. That is our offer of employment to you."

"And what makes you think I would agree to that?"

Hawthorne looked around the shop, sweeping with his hand as if to include it all in one great gesture. "This is your dream, is it not? You built this with your own hands? And now you are in danger of losing it. I offer you a goldmine, sir. A book that will sell millions of copies. A story that will make you rich and perhaps even famous. The job is made for the man, Mr. Sellers. You are the only person who we believe is right for this employment."

"Are the stories true?" Matthew asked.

The corner of Hawthorne's mouth crept up into the hint of a smile. "To a measure. They are visions, you see. Visions of things that have been, things that are, and things that are yet to be. They are truth, to the extent that truth exists in this world."

Hawthorne removed a single sheet of paper from his inside jacket pocket and placed it on the desk.

"Our offer is simple, Mr. Sellers. We pay you a retainer fee to put you back on your feet. That is yours to keep, as are all the profits from sales of the work. We ask only for your discretion and a promise never to reveal from whom you received the book. Do we have an agreement?"

With a flick of his wrist, Hawthorne produced a pen, placing it on the desk. Matthew stared hard into Hawthorne's unflinching eyes. He glanced from the pen to the manuscript to that single sheet of paper. And then he made his choice.

It isn't over yet.

About the Authors

Anne C. Petty is the author of three horror/dark-fantasy novels, a Florida Gothic suspense series co-written with P.V. LeForge, three books of literary criticism, and many essays on writing, mythology, and J.R.R. Tolkien. Recent short fiction includes her award-winning story "Blade," and the novella "The Veritas Experience," published in *The Best Horror, Fantasy & Science Fiction of 2009.* Anne is an active member of the Horror Writers Association, the International Thriller Writers, and the Science Fiction & Fantasy Writers of America. She is a founding member of the Tallahassee Writers Association and has been a presenter at writers' conferences and pop-culture conventions such as Dragon-Con in Atlanta. In 2006, she founded Kitsune Books, a small press specializing in literary fiction and book-length poetry collections. She has a Ph.D. in English from Florida State University, specializing in Mythology & Folklore. www.annepetty.com

Jonathan Maberry is a NY Times bestselling author, multiple Bram Stoker Award winner, and freelancer for Marvel Comics. His novels include *Assassin's Code, Flesh & Bone, Ghost Road Blues, Dust & Decay, Patient Zero, The Wolfman,* and many others. Nonfiction books include *Ultimate Jujutsu, The Cryptopedia, Zombie CSU, Wanted Undead or Alive,* and others. Jonathan's award-winning teen novel, *Rot & Ruin,* is now in development for film. He's the editor/co-author of *V-Wars,* a vampire-themed anthology; and was a featured expert on The History Channel special ZOMBIES: A LIVING HISTORY. Since 1978 he's sold more than 1200 magazine feature articles, 3000 columns, two plays, greeting cards, song lyrics, and poetry. His comics include CAPTAIN AMERICA: HAIL HYDRA, DOOMWAR, MARVEL ZOMBIES RETURN and MARVEL UNIVERSE VS THE AVENGERS. He teaches the Experimental

Writing for Teens class, is the founder of the Writers Coffeehouse, and co-founder of The Liars Club. www.jonathanmaberry.com/.

Benjamin Kane Ethridge is a Bram Stoker Award winner, author of the novel *Black & Orange* (Bad Moon Books 2010), *Bottled Abyss* (Redrum Horror 2012), and *Dungeon Brain* (Nightscape Press 2012). For his master's thesis he wrote, "CAUSES OF UNEASE: The Rhetoric of Horror Fiction and Film." Available in an ivory tower near you. Benjamin lives in Southern California with his wife and two creatures who possess stunning resemblances to human children. When he isn't writing, reading, or videogaming, Benjamin's defending California's waterways and sewers from pollution. facebook.com/Benjamin.kane.ethridge, twitter:@bkethridge, email: ben@bkethridge.com

JOSEPH NASSISE is the author of more than twenty novels, including the internationally bestselling *Templar Chronicles* series, the *Jeremiah Hunt* trilogy, and the *Great Undead War* series. He has also written several books in the popular Rogue Angel action-adventure series. His work has been nominated for both the Bram Stoker Award and the International Horror Guild Award and has been translated into half a dozen languages to date. He has written for both the comic and role-playing game industries and also served two terms as president of the Horror Writers Association, the world's largest organization of professional horror and dark fantasy writers. For more information about Joe's work, visit him on the web at www.josephnassise.com or on Facebook at www.facebook.com/joseph.nassise.

 Brett J. Talley is the Bram Stoker Award-nominated author of *That Which Should Not Be* and *The Void*, as well as numerous short stories and a haunted history of Tuscaloosa, Alabama. A native of the South, Brett received a philosophy and history degree from the University of Alabama before moving to witch-haunted Massachusetts to attend Harvard Law School. He seeks out the mysterious and the unknown and believes that the light can always triumph over the darkness, no matter how black the night may be. You can find him at www.brettjtalley.com.

Check out these titles from JournalStone:

That Which Should Not Be
Brett J. Talley

The Fall of Night
Joseph Nassise

Nightmare Ballad
Benjamin Kane Ethridge

Forever Man
Brian Matthews

Twice Shy
Patrick Freivald

Fade to Black
Jeffrey Wilson

The Devil of Echo Lake
Douglas Wynne

The Burning Time
JG Faherty

The Cornerstone
Anne C. Petty

Available through your local and online bookseller or at
www.journalstone.com

CPSIA informati
Printed in the US
LVOW11s15331

429949LV

936 564521